Praise for

THE
BRILL PILL

———

"*The Brill Pill* is a lively and thought-provoking novel from a highly promising young writer. In scientist anti-hero Will, Akemi Brodsky has created a Victor Frankenstein for our time—an ambitious academic who lets personal rivalries deflect his moral compass, making him push the boundaries of genetics too far."

—ANDREW CRUMEY,
author of *Beethoven's Assassins* and *Pfitz*

"Brodsky transports us into a strange new world of regenerative science that is uncomfortably close to our own. Dark, intense, and compelling, this fully immersive lab-based tale— told through the eyes of a flawed but all-too-human scientist— probes at deep questions of medical ethics, society, love, friendship, consciousness, and the all-consuming landscape of modern scientific research."

—JENNIFER L. ROHN,
author of *Cat Zero*, *The Honest Look*,
and *Experimental Heart* and editor of LabLit.com

THE
BRILL PILL

THE
BRILL
PILL

A Novel

AKEMI C. BRODSKY

SHE WRITES PRESS

Published 2023
Printed in the United States of America
Print ISBN: 978-1-64742-523-4
E-ISBN: 978-1-64742-524-1
Library of Congress Control Number: 2023903613

For information, address:
She Writes Press
1569 Solano Ave #546
Berkeley, CA 94707

Interior design by Stacey Aaronson

She Writes Press is a division of SparkPoint Studio, LLC.

To Christian, who makes everything better,
and to Lauren, who makes me better.

PART I

Chapter One

———

Viki *was* kind of a bitch, he conceded. More than kind of. He could tell by the way other girls looked at her, as if they had to swallow a tablespoon of honey before speaking to her. He didn't care. In fact, he admired her ability to fake such a disinterested expression over such sharp features. What he couldn't necessarily see was that she had drawn them in herself. It took about twenty different pots and pencils to orchestrate her face each morning. He would probably marry her. He *wanted* to marry her. But he wondered, in between these mental professions, if he could come up with even one really good reason why.

He could tell that she was smart enough for success, but at the same time he knew she would never bother to really support herself. It wasn't worth her time. Maybe it was her style that won him over. *Even he would admit he wasn't above that.* When she was all dressed up, she disappeared inside her #ootd, and he was attracted by the small, shiny objects that dangled from her ears and swept her thin neck. He still couldn't figure out why she'd ever agreed to date him. He used to be cool, he supposed. *He used to be fucking cool.* He wanted to know what their children would look like, what they would be when they grew up. But it had been that way with Eva too. And with Kate.

In any case, he wouldn't see Viki until the weekend. It was Tuesday, and the weekdays were for working. She lived in New York—that is, New York, New York—and he appreciated the separation. On weekdays he had to focus. He lifted the pipette for the hundredth time that morning, discarded the tip, and stretched his hand, extending his cramped fingers. He hated lab work; it was tedious, and it left too much room in his mind for daydreams. He didn't believe in daydreaming, but he couldn't help himself. It was his only vice, apart from vanity, an excess of assiduity, what some would call a drinking problem, and what anyone would call a quick temper. It was his only vice, in his eyes.

———

"*Guten morgen*, Wilhelm! Just kidding—hey, William."

It's just Will, he said to himself. "Yeah, J?" he said out loud.

"Can I just borrow that, one quick sec?" Joe smiled and scooped a bottle of reagent off of the counter in front of Will before he could give an answer.

"Sure. Borrow whatever you like." He nodded at the back of Joe's head.

The three other postdocs, the three other people with whom Will spent virtually all of his time, were Joe, Jenny, and Jon. He referred to each of them simply as "J" so as not to get confused. But he knew the difference. Jenny was the worst. Of course, he could never admit that out loud. There still weren't a lot of women in his field. Will was a forward thinker, though, always had been. He knew it; *he prided himself on it*. But *God*, how Jenny sucked. She ordered expensive enzymes she didn't need, she left her food in the fridge for months, she booked lab equipment and was then perpetually late getting her samples ready, so the time would go to waste. Worst of all, she was dumb as a brick. Just plain stupid. And she wasn't even hot. Sometimes Will worried that the reason her food was left in the fridge for so long was that she had gotten it confused with a sample somehow and either eaten the sample or was planning to throw the food into a centrifuge. He was pretty sure that was the only piece of equipment she knew how to use properly.

Joe was okay. At least he knew what he was doing. And he was friendly besides, even if the small jokes and obvious cultural references were sometimes lost on, and more often ignored by, Will. He often borrowed things off of Will's bench, but he always returned them. And Will was pretty sure if he ever found himself short of something, he could rely on Joe for it. But he was never short. And if he was short, he would go to the supply room and take whatever he needed. *He didn't rely on anyone else.* Except for the technician that ordered all of the materials, kept them stocked and up to date, who also fixed anything that was broken, replaced parts, tinkered, tested, and tuned everything in the lab. *Of course— that was his job.* Joe had moved to America years ago to do his PhD, but he still seemed unseasoned. It was charming to most people. He was taller than Will, and sportier; he had a lot of energy, and he knew a lot of people. *One of those.*

Jon was his favorite, someone he could talk to, about science and girls and sports, occasionally politics—everything worth talking about. And they had published some good papers together. That was good. Jon was stout, like a scientist ought to be. He didn't spend time playing basketball on the weekends, just watching it. He was from one of the Carolinas;

Will could never remember which it was. And Jon had a family—a wife and a kid. The kid's name was Gloria, but Will called her Jon Junior—that is, in his head.

Will joked with his PI that they couldn't ever hire anyone whose name didn't start with "J". He suggested George be on the lookout for Jeffs, for Janes, for Jaspers. Sometimes Will thought that he really would have a hard time if a Fred were to join the lab, or worse, a Wesley.

"Thanks, dude." Joe was back to return the reagent. The sound of his Chinese accent, forming American words rarely used by Americans anymore, woke Will from yet another reverie.

"Anytime, man." He replied in kind and looked down at his work, realizing now that he had already finished and had lost minutes spacing out when he could have already been running the PCR. *Fucking inefficient, Will.*

"Yo, want to grab some beers later?"

"Yeah, sure, sounds good." That was what was good about Joe—he didn't have a family to go home to, so he was always up for a drink.

While the PCR was running, Will went to the library. It was a straight shot down the hall from his lab, and he often dropped by while he was waiting for an experiment to run. He generally didn't get much exercise and, on average, it added another five hundred steps to his day. Besides, if nothing else, it would keep him from falling into his daydreams again. The only problem was coming up with a good excuse to visit. On this occasion, he had one ready.

"Hey, girl." He was leaning over the counter and speaking to the librarian, Margot. "Can you look this up for me? Pretty please." He handed over a piece of paper with the title of a book he had scribbled down just seconds earlier. He smiled wide but thankfully stopped himself just short of a wink.

Margot squinted at the paper as if she were being forced to decipher an ancient scroll but didn't remark on it. After all, if he had messaged her, he wouldn't have come to the library in person. "Sure, William. I read this book last month, and I have a recommendation for you." She scribbled a title down on the other side of the piece of paper he had given her and handed it back. "I know you *are* capable of loading it yourself." She looked back down at the text she had been reading across the screen that doubled as her desk, letting her dark hair fall like a curtain in front of her face, even before she finished the sentence.

Will knew he was capable of downloading a book from a library database. Of course he was capable, *more than capable*. He was even a little bit ashamed to show his face in the library itself; barely anyone went in person anymore. But flirting with Margot was just an excuse to use her. Every time he showed her something he was interested in, she returned with ten times more. He never left the library without a recommendation from her that was inevitably more clear and more thorough than what he had come in for. He figured she was marginally insane, because from what he could tell, and he had tested this theory, she had read every text in the entire medical library. Though he knew it wasn't possible, he believed it. He felt on some level that she must know more about his work than he did. Boy, was she clever. But she didn't have a PhD. He wanted to rub it in.

"Thanks, *Ms.* Margot."

"You're very welcome, Will."

"*Dr.* Will." He said it under his breath, but he could see that she had raised her eyebrows, though her head was still facing downward, resolutely, into her reading. "Want to grab a drink later? I mean, Joe is going, and he asked me, so I'm just extending." He raised a hand, palm up, in her direction.

Margot hesitated before briefly looking up at him. "Thank you, but I have some reading to catch up on." And she was suddenly fully refocused on the journal she still had open on her desk, the horizontal screen casting light under her chin and reflecting off of the glasses that Will noted were new. He would mention that next time he needed her help.

The rest of the afternoon was a wash. Will downloaded both books onto his tablet and brought them up on his desk. He only had to read a small portion of each to predictably find Margot's recommendation to be far superior. He wasn't even sure why he had bothered with downloading the first book, but he enjoyed the satisfaction of proving her right, or rather proving that he had been right to ask her about it. Will closed the original text, then deliberately deleted the file. It felt good to free up the space. He often got annoyed sitting at his desk. The screen was so cluttered with unread papers and hastily jotted-down notes of varying importance. He couldn't understand how it always became so messy when everything he actually used was on his tablet, which folded up neatly into his pocket. Still, at least he sat by the window. Will looked out onto the rows of labs in the building across the street—a mirror image. It wasn't a great view, but it was something.

———

In the Genner Lab, every member from undergraduate intern to postdoctoral fellow had their own desk situated at the end of a long countertop, with shelves above and cabinets below for storage. Keeping desk work and experimental work adjacent meant higher productivity for everyone, and Will couldn't complain about the easy sidelong stride back and forth to confirm a data point or check on a forgotten sample. In the room where he worked, there were five such parallel constructs lined perpendicularly along the window wall where ten lab members could set up camp, one on either side. Jon was just one row south of Will, and Joe worked directly behind him. Jenny technically worked in her own bay at the very end of the room, but she was so often asking advice that she seemed to work anywhere and everywhere she could.

At the back of the lab were two hoods, one for working with tissue samples and one for more volatile chemicals, and at the front of the lab there were two refrigerators, one for storing samples and one for storing snacks. Though usually one or the other refrigerator was full, so often there was crossover. Will despised this negligent practice. *It was bad enough they kept snacks in there at all*, but he seemed to be the only one who gave a shit, so he never mentioned it. He wasn't going to be *that guy* in the lab.

Will was waiting for his time slot on a thermocycler for the next step in his experiment, and waiting frustrated him. As he sat staring at his samples, George walked by, down the length of the room, shooting finger guns and throwing away words that were strung together to sound like sayings but that were impossible to interpret: "Keep on lining them up,

Joe," and "Don't waste a bucket in the rain, Jen." Despite archetypal academic eccentricities, George Genner was at the top of his game, and he knew it. He wore an eyeglass chain and a pocket tee with confidence as he strode through the lab to his own tempo. "Ingenuity is one size fits all, Jon. Don't try to use a fork as a spoon, Will." It reminded Will that he hadn't done the dishes in a week and he had been stealing plastic utensils from the lunchroom to get by.

He finished up some reading and then went to get a drink with Joe at the bar called Bar. He ordered dinner as well, pizza topped with mashed potatoes and bacon. Will loved this pizza, not because it was better than any other pizza in town, but because it was particularly unwholesome and yet so widely popular he didn't have to feel embarrassed about ordering it. He excused the meal because he needed to go back into lab afterward to finish up the experiment he had started that morning, and he wouldn't have time to eat at home. But it didn't stop him from finishing three beers. Will secretly hoped that Jon would be staying late in lab too, even though Jon would want to be at home with his family.

After a few drinks, he was sloppy at his bench. He left used test tubes and paper towels around the hood and spilled more chemicals than he ought to. But his samples were fine; he always paid close attention to what mattered most. Of course, he forgot to call Viki as he promised himself he would do most days, but it was already past midnight and he hadn't finished his experiment yet. He would text her in the morning.

Chapter Two

———

William Dalal was raised on the outskirts of Boston, in a cramped two-bedroom apartment with both of his parents and his mother's father. He had very nearly been blessed with a younger brother, but Will's mother had miscarried late, and his parents had taken that as a sign that the bulk of their affection was meant for William. His father worked as a mechanic in a bread factory, and his mother worked at the local bank branch, nine-to-five jobs. At the end of the day, they left work at work and came home to spend time with Will, to teach him what they could and to give him the support and find him the resources to learn what they couldn't. They weren't proud people, but all of the pride they possessed, they splurged on him.

When he was just seven years old, his grandfather had died in a car crash. It wasn't a terrible crash, but he wasn't young, and a few unlikely and unfortunate coincidences had led to an unhappy end. It was hard for Will to remember now if he and his grandfather had been very close before this happened, but in any case, they were close now. Or Will felt a close connection to his grandfather, that is, and he was sure he had been the favorite grandson, even if it was only for lack of competition. What was more coincidental than his grandfather dying in a minor accident was the fact that his grandfather had been a researcher in a field in which, only a few short months later, there would be a breakthrough that could have saved him.

In the years following that incident, the years in which Will was growing up, starting school, learning to read, learning to bully some of his classmates and avoid others, learning to play soccer, and learning to drive, there were incredible advancements being made in regenerative medicine. And by the time he was taking the SATs, swiping a number of "V-cards"— *he used to be cool*—applying to college, graduating with honors, becoming much nerdier, and applying for a PhD, Will, latching on to his grandfather's memory, was following with interest.

By his sophomore year of college, it had already come to a point where most organs could be reproduced—grown from small tissue samples, relatively easily and with full functionality. Certainly not cheaply yet, but still. Hospitals were inundated with patients, previously untreatable, that now struggled to stay alive while missing components were propagated in test tubes and on petri dishes, in incubators, in tanks and in vats. Companies emerged that would take precautionary samples for a price and produce the necessary replacements as soon as they were needed or, for an exorbitant monthly fee, maintain a continuously available product in case of a sudden emergency. Business was booming. Immortality had never looked so achievable, so tangible, so close.

But as always, there was a catch. Though almost all human organs could be replicated with enough precision to replace the God-given ones, the brain often turned out just slightly awry. It wasn't possible to tell in early trials—mice were challenging to interview. But the more human trials there were, the more it had become obvious that lines were getting crossed, and in nearly every case, it seemed some areas came out lacking. Many patients experienced a loss of memory. Some lost motor functions. Some lost common sense, simple reasoning skills, or several IQ points. Many patients wound up plain sociopathic. Many simply did not make it past the first week. It wasn't all bad—a very few patients even gained IQ points—but one way or another, none of them were quite the same person they used to be.

The funny thing was that people still went for it. Loved ones, usually making the hard decisions, went for an uncertain chance over the certain alternative. It was true that a few patients, maybe a handful in a hundred, were perfectly fine, so perhaps the slim possibility that everything would return to normal outweighed any risks. But Will didn't think that was the reason—it just didn't occur to close relatives that having an altered version of someone was really the same as them being gone. Plus, you were left with an annoying and potentially dangerous stranger as a permanent houseguest. Worse yet, they wore the face of someone you loved. Most people Will had encountered years or even months after such a decision had been made carried a look of regret.

———

That is where one could find Will during his free time when he was an undergraduate student: in the hospital. He volunteered with these patients. He worked in physical therapy with the ones who had lost motor skills, and he worked with others to relearn basic mental math and reading skills. He observed with curiosity the patients who had lost the ability to emote and the ability to feel. He looked forward guiltily to their interactions with the friends and family who had chosen to save them and who they now saw only as a lifeline to hang onto out of necessity, without gratitude or satisfaction. He was a witness to hope, to doubt, to pain—to change.

And all the while, Will was taking notes, mental notes and physical notes in a notebook with real paper and real pens. It was a composition notebook, a relic. He had found it unused among his grandfather's things, and he felt prideful when the other volunteers and hospital staff looked askance at him. Besides, it seemed safer than a tablet; it didn't have a pass code or fingerprint entry, but it couldn't be hacked into, and no one could read his handwriting. Barely anyone could read anyone's handwriting anymore, and his was *particularly appalling*. Still, he kept it close to his chest.

Why Will considered his notes worth coveting was, at this point in his life, more to do with vanity than to do with genius, but arrogance and application functioned as perfectly good substitutes for the time being, and he surrendered to the scientific stereotype. He understood that he wasn't cool anymore. He could still pretend to be cool when it worked in his favor. He would pretend to be cool when he was visiting home. He would act cool around the boys he used to be buds with, so they would go drinking with him, and around the girls he used to flirt with, so they would sleep with him. But at school, he was often too busy. And besides, if he saw the same girl too often, she became a distraction, *though he loved distractions*.

By the time he had completed his sophomore year, he saw himself for what he was: average height, average weight, below average vision, above average intelligence. He would take what he could get, and when he wasn't visiting home, he let his dark hair grow two inches too long and his stubble reach a five-day shadow. He discarded the contact lenses that irritated his deep brown eyes. He wore horn-rimmed, rectangular glasses, which he would remove and replace at intervals, pressing his right thumb and forefinger around the bridge of his nose each time. He got dressed in the same outfit every day, a loose-fitting button-down over a pair of faintly wrinkled, brown trousers. It didn't matter whether or not the crumpled shirts were reworn or fresh duplicates; it saved time so he could focus on studying.

Chapter Three

———

He was daydreaming again. This time about Eva. She was the girlfriend in college. They had met in the library café back when he used to go up to random girls in cafés. He had said, "Pardon me." *No, he hadn't.* What he had actually said was, "What up?" He had jerked his chin up at her. "Can I ask what you are reading? You seem so wrapped up and well"—a thoughtful pause—"it's so strange these days that you can't glance at a cover." He indicated her tablet. "I went to a show at MoMA last week of old book jackets, and it was just incredible; it's really a lost art form, I think." *He really had lost his "cool" since then.*

The book she had been reading was too boring to recall. They dated for junior and senior year. In Will's daydream, they were still together; he went home to her after work. She was prettier in his daydream than she was in real life—in his fantasy, her face was perfectly symmetrical, her skin was unrealistically smooth—though she was pretty in real life too. They all were.

He wondered to himself which one was the prettiest, and settled on Viki. Viki had never once had a bad hair day. He messaged her before he would forget to again: "Hey, babe, how's work? I have to stay late in lab on Friday. I'll come down Saturday morning? Xox." Even he was annoyed that he would have to work late. He would have preferred to arrive Friday night. He would just have to convince her to go to bed with him Saturday morning when he arrived. Maybe after a quick shower.

Jon was sitting across from him, watching him type. "Keep your eye on the ball, Will. Don't shit where you eat." He imitated the boss.

"Those are actual sayings. I can't understand a fucking thing George says half the time."

"Try all of the time. Hey, did you get the results back from yesterday?"

"Yeah, I haven't had a chance to analyze them yet though. Look okay at a glance. I'll send them to you." Will extended his tablet and unfolded it on his lap.

"Nice. I'm feeling pretty good about this round. Feels like we're finally getting somewhere."

Will chuckled and shrugged his shoulders. He felt good about it too, but he didn't want to jinx it by saying it out loud, so he changed the subject. "How's Gloria doing? And Beth?" Beth was Jon's wife's name. It always took Will a minute to remember if she went by Beth or Elizabeth, but he could tell from Jon's relieved expression that he had gotten it right this time. He mentally congratulated himself.

"Really good. Gloria is turning six this weekend. We were planning to have a little get-together on Saturday, super last-minute. You should stop by."

"Ah, man, I wish I could. I promised Viki I would head down to New York for the weekend." Will forced a disappointed expression, but he really *was* disappointed. He didn't understand why, but he liked spending time with Jon's family. It marked one of the few times he felt connected to a community in New Haven, not counting the bureaucratic quirks and quandaries of the Department of Molecular, Cellular, and Developmental Biology. Beth was absolutely pleasant. She was caring and even funny. She and Jon made a perfect couple. And the girl was cute, clever too, for a nearly six-year-old. He would buy her a present—a doll or a computer game. *What was appropriate these days?* He could bring it over next Monday or Tuesday. And on the train down to New York, he would call his own parents; he hadn't spoken to them in over a week.

"How is Viki? You really have to get her to come up to New Haven more often. It's not so bad, really. Doesn't she like pizza?"

"She doesn't really eat . . ." Will paused to think about what it was that she didn't eat but decided against saying "anything" and went for "Italian food. She's into that . . ." He got confused again, and instead of coming up with a word, made an indication with his hand of the size of portion she would typically choose, in a half-inch space between his thumb and forefinger. "Cheese." It was all he could come up with. "Stuff like that. I don't know what the fuck it is."

Jon wasn't surprised. In fact, he thought, *No shit. I bet a girl like that counts the calories in cum,* but he was a polite guy and chose instead to say, "I guess you're the cook then?"

"You bet. Viki would burn the apartment to the ground if she tried to fry an egg." Will laughed heartily at the thought of Viki cooking, then stopped himself before it got awkward. He wondered if Margot could fry an egg with all of her book smarts. "Anyway"—he performed a mini drumroll over the countertop on his left, where he had been working and daydreaming before Jon had appeared, then he swiped at his tablet a few times—"there you go. I sent it to your Yalebox. Let me know how the data looks. I'll try to take a look at it tonight too."

The data was looking very promising.

Chapter Four

———

A fter spending three years volunteering at the hospital as an undergrad, Will made the decision to pursue a PhD researching drug development to help improve the lives of the victims of brain regeneration. By the end of those three years, Will had also begun to think of the patients, in a surprisingly fond way, as zombies. The majority of the zombies were old and harmless. They most commonly had suffered from Alzheimer's or other degenerative diseases that struck late in life and were being kept alive far past their expiration dates and often against their wills. *But who knew if they even had their own wills anymore.*

Will felt sorry for them, and the more time he spent caring for these elderly convalescents, the more irritated and eventually angry he became with their families. There were at least two separate occasions that nearly caused him to be fired from his volunteer position. He confronted family members, telling them boldly that they were making mistakes, selfishly terrorizing their own father or mother or grandfather or aunt by dragging out the sad, sorry years, spreading them thinner and thinner just to put off having to deal with their own sentimental or practical issues. *It doesn't take a genius to plan a fucking funeral; who gives a shit if you have to see your moronic brother for an hour?* They didn't get a lot of volunteers in that ward, though, so he knew any threats to his position were largely idle.

It was the young ones, the victims of accidents and illnesses that brought them to the hospital in their prime—those were the ones he worried about. He was careful around them. He recognized that they deserved pity, that it wasn't their fault they had been taken apart and put back together in a slightly different way, but he saw defects. The small problems that had occurred made them inhuman in his eyes. He didn't fear that they would roam the earth craving natural-born brains, eating the gray stuff and turning the remains, but he wondered what would happen if they reproduced. Every day, every year, there were more and more of these patients, and as soon as they were well enough—*whatever that meant*—they were released out into the world. They disappeared into the crowd. Will wondered to himself what would happen over time. Would the world get slower? Would the world get crueler? How long would it be before the planet was overrun? The global population was always increasing, as was life expectancy, but now that life could be artificially and perhaps indefinitely extended, it would skyrocket. *Weren't humans defective enough as it was?*

The lab that Will joined for his PhD was at Harvard. Will had been stunned to get into Harvard. He had been so proud, he had called his parents out of work early and taken them out to a $300-a-head dinner when he barely had a thousand dollars in the bank. Once he got in, he was determined to be top of his class. Of course, he soon found out that isn't really a thing in graduate school, but the aggressive drive to succeed remained with him. The project he was working on was geared toward understanding the areas of the brain that were affected by regeneration and targeting those areas with medication. He did want to make life better for the patients he had grown so wary of over the years, but he also wanted to make life better for the rest of the world who would be forced to deal with them soon enough. Drugs already existed that improved memory, helping the brain make connections while being able to distinguish between past, present, and future. Memory was an old problem—people had been losing that for as long as anyone could remember, and the research was comprehensive if not nearly complete. Similarly, reduced motor function was treatable. The illegal use of steroids in the world of professional sports had largely been replaced by a new wave of still-legal drugs that instead improved reflexes, coordination, and dexterity.

Will had wanted to participate in something cutting-edge, something new to him and new to the field. But more than that, though he didn't like to admit it, he had wanted to work on a drug that would treat the symptom he most feared: the dead eyes he had seen staring back at him while he took vitals and avoided small talk. He felt a chill every time one more was released from the hospital, free and clear. What his lab at Harvard had been focused on was the science behind emotions. They were developing a pill that would make you *feel*. Pills that simply made you happy had been around forever; they were available over the counter at any CVS. A simple chemical dump, as caused by Prozac or NRIs, was easy enough to understand, easy enough to re-create. In his lab at Harvard, they were working to treat the lack of empathy that was so often a side effect of brain regeneration. *The goal was a prescribed medication that would trick your brain into giving a shit.*

Harvard was also where Will had met Arthur Green. Arthur was a fellow PhD student. He worked in the same lab as Will, and his fluffy blond hair, pointed nose, and light blue eyes that seemed to be as freckled as his face was, were what drove Will to succeed. Similarly, Arthur found inspiration in outachieving Will. It might have been that Will never bothered to properly iron his shirt, even for conferences, or that his teeth were so close to white despite the fact that he drank coffee incessantly, that got to Arthur. Most likely it was the fact that deep down they were so similar in so many ways that made it intolerable to fall behind. Together they pushed themselves, spending more and more odd hours to try and get the jump on the other. In lab meeting each week, it was a struggle to keep secrets while also prodding one another, asking difficult questions, and appearing the more knowledgeable one in front of Carlos, the lab head. But really they were more concerned with the competition than how they looked in front of anyone else.

Arthur was still there. He had been offered a postdoctoral position in the same lab. Will had not. He had been pissed off; he had thrown a mouse against the wall. It had squealed as it fell to the floor. He would have had to kill it anyway, he reasoned later, and it was supposedly a psychopathic mouse, *so whatever*. Will liked his new lab, and he liked his new project. Arthur was a jerk. Will thought that he was probably dating Kate purely to spite him.

In fact, they were not dating, but Will had seen a picture of them together, so he just figured.

———

Will was daydreaming about Arthur. And also about Kate. He couldn't separate the two ever since he had seen that photo of them together. When he thought about Arthur, it usually turned into a daydream about himself. He was giving a speech— "Thank you, thank you"—an acceptance speech. "I couldn't have done it without the help of blah blah blah"—he had yet to fill that part in, because he hadn't won anything yet—"and the support of my wonderful parents," who he hadn't seen since Christmas, though they were sitting front and center in the imaginary audience. "Of course, our scientific process is nothing without the work of so many dedicated researchers out there, like my good friend Arthur Green, who don't always get the credit but who *really* put in the hours." He bowed.

But if Arthur got Kate, then maybe he had already won. Kate was Will's Harvard girlfriend. He thought she was the smartest one. They had met in class, and he had pretended to need a study buddy to get her number. *That was one he couldn't use anymore.* Kate had green eyes. That was the feature he remembered most. Often he found it hard to recall specific details, words, voices, but there was always one thing that stood out. With Kate, it was her eyes. With Eva, it was a thin roped silver ring she wore every day. With Arthur, he could unfortunately imagine his entire *stupid* face floating over each of the *stupid* ties he wore to do all of his *stupid* work. With Viki, he guessed he would find out one day, unless they did get married, then he would never have to know what it really was about her that drew him. He looked up from his work and Jenny was loitering.

"Do you need something?" It came out harsher than he intended; it always did.

"Just, um, I had a question, but hey, don't worry about it. I heard you and Jon got some good results the other day?"

"Yes. We did." Will smiled. She wasn't pissing him off as much as usual all of a sudden. "What can I help you with?"

"It's just the FACS machine; I'm having trouble calibrating it. It keeps like, I don't know, would the filter settings be very different for fourteen-color flow? I only set up twelve colors before . . . I guess I'm just doing it wrong." She looked sheepish.

"Uhhhhh." Will sighed. She clearly hadn't even tried to turn the thing on. It would be easier to just do it himself rather than trying to get her to explain what she was trying to do, let alone what she was supposed to be doing. He walked over with her to the machine.

"So, you going down to New York this weekend?"

"Yep."

"Would you mind picking me up something?"

"Yep."

"Great. It's just this shampoo I use. 'Cause my hair, in the summer . . . Anyway, I'll write down the name for you. And you can get it, like, almost anywhere. Except not, like, CVS or Walgreens or, like, just *anywhere*. Do you want me to give you some money?"

Will was in a trance. He had already fixed the settings on the FACS machine and was just staring at the monitor while she talked at him. The message from her, containing the name of the shampoo, appeared on his tablet. "What? Uh, you can just pay me back on Monday," he mumbled.

He went back to his desk to recover. He always needed a minute to recover after any interaction with Jenny. He unlocked his desk drawer with his fingerprint and opened it just about three inches. He glanced around him to make sure that no one was watching, and then he reached in and pulled out a tiny plastic bag full of a white powder. He reached in again to check on the rest. There were only three bags left, including the one in his hand. Will enjoyed the way that it looked like cocaine. If anyone found out, that is definitely what he would say it was. But he had never done cocaine, surprising as that was; he hadn't been an *undergraduate* at Harvard, after all. In reality, it was a sample of the latest drug they had been testing in his lab right before he had finished his PhD. It had already gone out for evaluation by the time he had swiped it, and it had since been approved for clinical trials. Will reasoned that pretty soon, or someday at least, it might be offered over the counter to practically anyone, so what was the harm?

The "e-potion," as he liked to call it, was designed for the emotionally challenged, but who was to judge whether his own brain, which had been born and not built, couldn't be improved upon? When he had used it before with Kate, it worked wonders. He had felt vulnerable, and she had loved it. Even *he* liked the feeling . . . and the sex was fantastic. He had nearly cried that one time. Besides, Viki was living in a different city now, *a big city*. She went the whole week without him. *He had to keep her from cheating on him.* He pocketed a bag to take with him to New York.

Chapter Five

———

W ill went to the library to see Margot first thing Monday morning. He didn't need to look up any papers or books. He just wanted to chat. He had found that talking to Margot often cleared his head. Perhaps it was because she didn't usually say much back, so he could talk out whatever was on his mind. *Perhaps it was the few things she did say that did the trick.* His head almost always needed clearing after the weekend if he had gone down to New York to see Viki. Will figured it was just the contrast between play and work, city and suburb, that muddled his senses, that the farther he physically was from the lab, the more he began to lose focus. Since starting his postdoc, he had left the country only once, to take Viki on a one-year anniversary trip to the Caribbean. Looking back, that guy seemed like a perfect stranger. *He was having a great time, though, whoever he was, beers on the beach and sex in a hammock.* Actually the hammock sex was terribly awkward, but it had sounded like a cool thing to do.

Margot was behind her desk as usual. There was never any stacking to do now that everything was digitalized, though they kept most of the shelves stocked for decorative purposes, a thick layer of dust growing over the bound antiques. Will was fond of the paper books. He liked the idea of standing by the window, flipping through each thin page with the afternoon sun streaming brass yellow, illuminating ivory against the raised ink. In the conjured scenario, he was wearing thin-rimmed spectacles and a loosely fitted tan blazer. In reality, he had barely picked up a book once, and when Margot had returned from wherever she had been, he had replaced it with just as little thought as he had removed it.

Margot was not fond of the paper books; she thought they were a waste of space.

A few people still went to the library to study, or more often to sleep. Digital desks and a few old wooden carrels were scattered throughout, along with couches and cots for all-nighters or afternoon snoozes. It was still one of the only places of quiet in a world that otherwise buzzed with an inescapable low hum that vibrated under the streets, crossed through walls, bounced between buildings, and rained down from the sky. Will had gotten so used to it that he couldn't fall asleep without the dull lullaby. When rain or wind covered the constant drone, he felt more alone than ever, more detached. He found the absolute silence of the library even worse. It gave him the creeps. So he broke it.

"What happened to your glasses?" He pointed to his left temple as he leaned on Margot's desk.

She looked up at him, biting her lip slightly but not in a provocative or even piqued way, just as if she felt like chewing on something. "I wear contacts most of the time. My eyes must have been irritated before."

"Can I ask you something?" Will pulled up a chair and sat down to the right side of her desk so he could see her profile. She didn't say no, nor did she turn away from him, so he continued. "Would you rather . . ." He paused to think of something. "Eat . . ." He paused again. "One of those nasty little French birds you take in one bite . . ." He had seen it once on TV. "Or would you rather . . ." His eyes searched the ceiling for ideas. "Survive a plane crash?"

"I'll go for the ortolan."

"The what?"

"The nasty bird."

"But you don't die in the crash."

"I know."

"Okay. Would you rather, hmm, pick your nose in public for five minutes, or . . . break your leg?"

"Pick my nose. What is wrong with you?"

"Okay, okay, okay. Last one—would you rather be filthy rich, or cure a serious disease?" This question came out quickly, as if it had occurred to him before.

"Does the disease get cured by someone else otherwise?"

"Doesn't matter."

"It *does* matter." She finally looked directly at him, entirely ignoring the work on her desk.

Will decided he didn't want to hear the answer after all, so he stalled for a few seconds, then substituted a different question. "Do you like what you do?" He pointed to the screen across her desk. "Being a librarian?" Now that he had her full attention, he asked her something he had been curious about since they first met.

"Yes." She hesitated. "It's a great job. Good hours, no boss really, *almost* no one bothers me." She raised her eyebrows slightly at him. "Mostly I just sit and read." She looked down out of habit but quickly lifted her gaze again.

"It's pretty quiet though." *It must be lonely*, he thought.

"True. It's nice to talk to someone. I might not always sound like I do, but I appreciate it."

Will could tell she had a hard time saying what was on

her mind; he did too. He wanted to say something kind, something that would cause her to smile, but he couldn't come up with anything off the bat, and he couldn't help filling in the silences. "If you could take a drug that would make you smarter, would you?"

"No." She said it as a matter of fact, without pausing to consider.

"Why not?"

"What if it fucked me up in some other way?"

Will was surprised by her language, but not by her answer. Of course she was already gifted with cerebral genius, quietly tucked away in that petite skull of hers, so *how would she know*? He wasn't surprised by her answer, but he was a little disappointed all the same. *Not that it mattered what she said.* He noticed she was waiting for him to reply, so he nodded and made a small sound of assent. That was his normal tack for dealing with awkward silences, that or pretending he couldn't hear properly, but that one wouldn't work in the dead-quiet library.

Margot just shrugged. "Anyway, I would cure the disease."

"Hm?"

"Earlier, you said, 'Would you rather . . . ?'"

"I know you would."

He would, too, but for some reason, he didn't want to admit it.

————

This time, speaking to Margot had not cleared his head. But at least he was no longer thinking about New York, what a great time he had had, how much lab time he had lost, and how there were only two more bags left of the white powder he kept locked up in his desk. *It had been one hell of a weekend*, he thought. He was always conflicted about pleasure. Maybe the release he had given himself over the weekend would help him to work harder during the week. *Maybe he was just kidding himself.* Will sat back down at his desk and mechanically started to look up Arthur Green on his tablet. He scrolled through publications, skimming for inconsistencies. He glanced through the ongoing research projects at his old lab at Harvard, where Arthur still worked. Will checked up on his archrival regularly, on average once a week, but this time he had the particular feeling that he was searching for something.

All academically funded projects had to be public these days. Even before publication, every lab group was required to post updates to a centralized website. LabHub was meant to encourage collaboration over competition and to prevent the same experiments from happening twice on two sides of the world, or just a two-hour train ride apart. Instead, it had made scientists more conniving than ever. There was a certain pride involved in providing just enough information so as not to be investigated for concealment but not enough that any other lab could catch on to the specific methods, or indeed learn anything that would further work in the same field. The organization that regulated LabHub and determined what was sufficient disclosure was not composed of practicing researchers. Enforcers were generally pulled from the mass of enthusiasts who had jumped on the STEM bandwagon eager and early and made it as far as the doctorate level before steadily dropping off due to lack of masochism or lack of positions. For the most part, these guidelines were carefully worked around, and for the most part, labs didn't call each other out. They were all in the same boat.

But Will was good at reading between the lines. Arthur had a new project. He could see it now. He had reused so many of the same keywords from former projects: "neuronal," "functionality," "astrocytes," "neurotransmitters," "synapses," *et cetera, et cetera*. But there were a few new ones that Arthur had snuck in, hoping that Will wouldn't notice: "fluid intelligence," "prefrontal cortex," "synaptic proliferation," "axon pruning." Will laughed darkly and then stood up fast. He threw his stylus across the room, then walked over to Joe to retrieve it. "Sorry, dude."

He walked back to his desk and hit it hard with one fist. Passing screensaver images of his parents, of Viki, and of himself in a cap and gown gave a digital tic as the desk shook, and then came back into focus. He picked up his tablet and called Arthur. The tone came in over his headphones, and he walked out into the hallway in case Arthur picked up and he would be forced to raise his voice.

It only rang twice before going to voice mail. "You have reached the inbox of Dr. Arthur Green, postdoc at Harvard and baseball enthusiast. Feel free to speak your mind, but please note that I am much more responsive when contacted by email or textual message."

"Motherfucker." It was all he could think of to say before he hung up.

Chapter Six

Now Will was part of a race. Sure, there had always been a race against time, but now there was a race against a *sniveling, toilet-dressing, milk-drinking, mouth-breathing douchebag.* He threw himself into his work and spent the morning injecting mice, more than double what he would normally do. This would force him to do more work later in the week. The mice he had injected last week were running through their challenges. He watched them on the monitor. He had already taken samples from them, looked for the new markers, and recorded all of their vitals. He had already noted their blood counts and checked for unusual mutations or metabolites that hadn't been present before. Every mouse had to be tested carefully before and after being injected. After that, they were no longer his problem. The techs would keep an eye on them as they ran through the trials, in case they fought with one another or just dropped dead partway through. When they were finished going through each of the tasks, most of them would be euthanized. A few would be kept alive in cages to see whether there were any long-term effects after the injections wore off. After all, the current formula was only a treatment, not a cure. Will would watch the footage later. He had a backlog to watch; it never seemed as productive as running samples and giving injections. There was data associated with the live-mouse challenges that he knew would give more weight to his paper, but it had to be interpreted, and interpretations were subjective. He preferred data to be spit out of a machine in simple numbers. Numbers could be correlated to present a strong case; interpretations were always flimsy.

In the meantime, he had to find out more about Arthur's research. He needed to know if Arthur was catching up, if he was truly close competition or if it was all just an elaborate tease. But he should have already known from experience. *Arthur and he had always been neck and neck.* He opened his tablet to start digging but stopped short—there was a new message waiting. Arthur must have received his pointed voice mail. The thought made Will smile slightly, though he was soon frowning again. All that the message said was, "Don't h8 the player, h8 the game," but it confirmed his every suspicion. Will very nearly threw his tablet in the trash. Instead he kicked the space under his desk where what used to be a small dent was turning into a fairly serious crack in the drywall. Soon there would be a legitimate hole, a couple of inches in diameter, about the width of the toe of Will's shoe. He went to find Jon.

"Jon, take a look at this." Will pulled up the page that he had found listing Arthur's new project. He waited while Jon read.

"Oh shit. Looks like we have some real competition." Jon exhaled audibly.

"I used to work with that son of a bitch." He pointed at the headshot of Arthur.

"Hey, man, I think we're pretty close to publishing. It would be great to just get a few more runs to be safe, increase the *n*. Otherwise, if we can reproduce our results from last week, we're good to go."

"I'm not usually one to hold a grudge"—this was manifestly untrue—"but we need to crush this guy. Also, we put in so much fucking work. We deserve this paper." He put his hand down on Jon's shoulder, rocking him forward.

"Okay. I'll start writing up the background and methods tonight. Then we just need another week or two to scrape together a bigger data set. Easy." Fist bump.

"I'll go through the challenges. It will make a stronger case, and I've been putting it off for too damn long anyway." Will volunteered himself for this time-consuming task. He knew it would be boring as shit, but it had to be done, and it just didn't make sense for Jon to waste time on it. Jon had a wife. *Jon had a life.*

———

Will spent the rest of the day and late into the night watching the footage. One mouse at a time would go through each trial over and over again—before being injected, one hour after being injected, two hours after, different challenges, different doses, different mice, and so on and so on. They were being timed. There was a total time to complete the entire trial, and then there were specific times taken for each cognitive task, such as choosing between left and right, turning back at a dead end, or removing an obstacle.

The first challenge was a simple maze with a tiny pellet of peanut butter at the end. They each went through at least a dozen times. The mice that had been injected got faster. They found the best path, and by the end, they remembered it.

Will had seen stuff like this before. The last mouse came to the realization that it was stuck on a plane, climbed out of the maze into the third dimension, and walked over the top, straight to the peanut butter.

The second task was a tiny room full of doors. First they learned to open the doors—each opened in a different way. Some pushed, some pulled, some opened by pressing a button at the other end of the miniature room. Then they learned which doors to choose; they ascertained and memorized what was behind each one. Some hid food, some hid a nonlethal poison, some hid nothing. The tasks got more complicated. There were trapdoors and trick stairs. It was hard to determine specific quantifiable measures, but it was clear that, overall, the injected mice were getting better, smarter. They succeeded in the challenges more completely and more rapidly than the control mice. Not only that, but the mice that were given higher dosages got through the challenges further and faster than the ones who had been injected with a low dose.

One of the things that had bothered Will most about the zombies was the possibility that you could wake up one day, still seemingly the same person, but average. The only thing that made Will special was his brain. He had long ago accepted the fact that he wasn't particularly attractive, athletic, or artistic, and aside from being astute, those were the only attributes he saw as having value. He could deal with the idea of having to relearn facts, but the thought of suddenly not being able to think as critically or as quickly, of not being able to understand concepts that used to come easily, gave him a crushing feeling in his chest. That is why he had joined George Genner's lab at Yale for his postdoc. It was the only way to save himself and everyone else from the epidemic. If they could give the zombies back their intelligence, their reasoning and common sense, then maybe the world would be safe.

There was still a long way to go; they had only tested wild-type mice. If the good results continued, they would soon experiment on mice that had undergone regeneration themselves. Will pictured an infinite row of tiny brains in tiny jars. He didn't know what would happen if a zombie with an artificial brain then had a child, whether the original, unmodified code would be inherited properly. Theoretically, it should. They weren't messing with mutagens, but you never could tell what would happen with these things. Eventually they would have to breed the mice to find out. It didn't really matter, Will supposed. *Their kids would certainly be fucked up either way.*

Soon he had fallen into daydreaming again, speculating about the future. The trials moved across the screen in front of his eyes, but he wasn't really watching them anymore. He could make mental notes in one part of his consciousness while the rest of his mind wandered. He was thinking beyond the zombies now. What would happen if he slipped a sample of the injection into Jenny's coffee in the morning—would she become suddenly competent? Would she stop asking him stupid questions and wasting his time every minute of every day? Could Viki ever become as smart as Kate? *Would she leave him if she were?*

Chapter Seven

―――――

Will was in Mory's with Joe. He liked Mory's because it was old. It had history. *Gravitas*. Will wasn't sure why he liked the idea of history. Maybe mismatched bricks and wrought iron were just tangible proof that things had lasted before. Yale liked the idea of history too. Even the oldest buildings on campus had been acid etched and water damaged to appear especially antique. Brand-new buildings were still built to look like castles. It was fascinating to see them under construction, modern cranes struggling to lift clumsy stones, engineers floundering with the delicate art of stained glass. Outside of campus, the rest of New Haven was fairly new, even if the city itself wasn't. There was always some generically hip restaurant, bar, or coffee shop opening on . . . *whatever corner that was*. Will had heard that New Haven used to be a bit of a dive, that if you went off campus, you would likely get mugged or stabbed or caught in a drive-by. He liked that Mory's had been around back then, and even before then.

It had the feeling of an old schoolhouse. There was wood paneling along the walls of the bar and faded black-and-white photos hung down the hallway that led to the "ladies" and the "gents." The sturdy tables and chairs were decades-old desks and benches that had been inscribed with the names of generations of Yalies who had carved themselves into tradition. Will had never owned a wooden desk before. He was running his fingers over the names that had been lacquered into their table, when Joe reappeared with beer. This was round four.

"So I hear you have got somebody on your tail with the Brill pill?"

Will couldn't help laughing. "'Brill pill'?"

"Do you like it? I have been trying to think of something catchy. Maybe 'Intellinject' is better. Or how about 'Sharp shot'?"

Will was giggling now. "Those are fantastic. I'll leave it up to you."

"I think I can do better. Anyway, good luck. You guys deserve to get this paper. I hope you do." He patted Will on the back.

"Thanks." Will was grateful for the sentiment. *Joe was a great guy.* But he didn't feel like talking about the paper right then. He felt like drinking beer and talking about things he would only talk about when he was drunk. "Hey, what would you do if you were offered the Brill pill?"

"Why, you offering?" Joe laughed into his beer.

"Nah, I mean, I'll look the other way if you want . . . but seriously." He took a swig. "It's not just going to be used for the zombies, let's be honest."

"I love that you call them fucking zombies." Joe shook his head in jest, but behind his smile, his expression was more serious than it had been all evening. "Look. What is done is done, right? There's going to be regulations, laws, all that bullshit. It's not like they just gonna start handing it out in SAT prep." Joe's hands were deftly dealing out imaginary pills like playing cards across the table. "And beside that, it has got to be years before it's even tested on humans. And . . . it's expensive as shit to produce."

"Still." Will was staring at the television over the bar, but he didn't register what was playing.

"You think too fucking far ahead, man." Joe waited for a reply, and he stared at the TV too, for something to do in the meantime.

It took Will a minute to respond. "It might not be a bad thing. Handing it out in SAT prep." Will let out a stunted laugh. "Kids would literally kill for that." He wondered to himself whether a smarter world would be a better world. *It would probably backfire somehow.*

"At the least, you should spike Jenny's coffee with one of the samples," Joe suggested, lightening the mood.

"I had that exact same thought the other day."

———

Will was back at his desk, still pretty buzzed from Mory's. Joe had gone home. That was the sensible thing to do, but Will didn't want to go home. If he went home straight after drinking, he usually fell asleep on the couch while watching some dreary documentary or true crime special that would then haunt him in his dreams while he slept and keep him looking over his shoulder for the rest of the week. That, or he would call Viki and say something sloppy. He did want to call her though. *He just wanted to sober up first.* In his stupor, he wouldn't go into the mouse room—even *he* recognized that wasn't a good idea.

But at his bench, he methodically, incompetently set up everything else he would need to run the samples first thing the following morning. He laid out several boxes of Eppendorf tubes and began to fill them with the necessary reagents. He couldn't maintain his focus. After a few minutes, he kept halting mid-pipette and wondering to himself if he had already added this or that to each small capsule. There was a specific recipe, and he was fucking up the proportions—in one batch he might have doubled the sugar; in the other batch he might have halved the baking soda. He knew he would throw the whole thing out and start again in the morning, but right then he needed something to do. If he wasn't doing anything, he wasn't moving forward, and Arthur would catch up and surpass him.

Will was frustrated with himself, and as he finished, he flicked the last pipette tip across the counter. The tip landed on one of Jenny's slide trays, and he left it there. He stared at his bungled work for a minute, holding completely still, before glancing around the lab to see if anyone else was working late. It was empty. He got up from his work space and walked, without thinking too much about it, over to the refrigerator where they kept the injections—the nice refrigerator, not the refrigerator where they kept Jenny's old lunches. He opened the door and the cold hit him in the face, bringing some feeling back into his beer-numbed cheeks. He closed it again. Then he went back to his desk to think about what he had done.

But he hadn't done anything. It was an overreaction to something that was never going to happen. But he had thought about it, in the back of his mind. If he had had one more beer maybe . . . *but he hadn't.* He was pretty sure it wouldn't kill him; the mice were all fine. Mostly. The effects wore off after a while; it would just be this once. Maybe if he helped himself out a little bit, he would be able to beat Arthur and leave something behind. If it went wrong in the future, he told himself he didn't care. The important thing was to have a legacy. Will wondered what kind of legacy it would be, something to be proud of, or something to be ashamed of. *Either way, it would be something to be remembered for.* And he would start with a small dose, and he would monitor himself carefully. But there was a big difference between sniffing a bit of e-potion every now and again and injecting himself with the Brill pill serum, and he knew it.

"I have to get out of here." He spoke out loud to the silent sorters and the stationary centrifuges, to the vials and the tube racks, to the flasks drying in the sink. He blinked hard two, three times, searching for an image to ground him, then abruptly stalked out of the lab. He turned mechanically to the right and walked straight down the hallway to the library to see if Margot was still at her desk.

———

"Excuse me." Will had accidentally let out a sizable burp just as he entered into the silence of the library. There were more people there, studying in the middle of the night, than there were during the daylight hours.

Margot nodded in his direction and then waved her hand theatrically in front of her nose and mouth. "Sure you shouldn't be at home, sleeping it off?"

"I'm sure I should be." He paused, recalling what impulse had brought him to the library, while his eyes scanned aimlessly across the room. They settled back on Margot. He didn't want to be alone right now. "Do you have to stay here all night? Want to go for a walk?"

"Sure." Her voice had an edge of curiosity to it, but she maintained her typical, even tone. "I'm not really working, just reading."

Will was immediately and utterly relieved. He grinned. "You got to get a life, girl."

"Likewise." Margot suppressed a smile.

She folded her tablet up into her bag, and they walked out of the library and down the long hallway in silence. Will wanted to break it, but he couldn't come up with anything normal sounding to say. Instead he fidgeted with his keys and pulled on his shirtsleeves. He wondered if she could sense his apprehension. He thought he had hidden it well enough, but as the clouds of intoxication and alarm began to part, he was suddenly unsure of the exact words he had employed or the tone in which he had used them. He pushed open the door at the end of the hall and let Margot out first into the night. It wasn't cold. There was still humidity hanging in the air, making it thick like a blanket, but an occasional breeze blew through as a reminder of the late hour. "Uh." Will panicked, looking back and forth down the street. He didn't have any idea where to walk to.

"Let's get you a coffee."

"Good idea."

Will bought her coffee. It was the least he could do, considering he had disturbed her this late at night. It was the least he could do, considering he had come to her, drunk, for support, when she barely knew him or owed him anything. *It was the least he could do*, considering he habitually relied on her as a discerning database every time he wanted to double-check or accelerate his research. *Constantly*. Really, *he owed her*. He decided he would do something nice for her soon. *When was her birthday?* he wondered. But he didn't ask.

They sat across from each other at one of the clean square laminate tables in the hospital café. The hospital was just down the street from the building they both worked in, and the café stayed open late. In general, Will liked visiting the hospital. Being near to the hustle and bustle typically made him feel peaceful, with purpose. It reminded him of the time he used to spend with the zombies, and it reminded him that he was still helping them, just from a different angle now. The white walls and antibacterial surfaces usually had a calming effect on him, but today the established oasis felt unfamiliar. For whatever reason, being there with Margot made him slightly uneasy.

"So what's up?" Margot looked straight at him as she said it, the steam from her coffee rising in front of her face.

He wasn't sure how to reply. As he started to sober up, the incident in the lab seemed far away, like it had happened to another person in another time. "You know, it's weird looking directly at you. I'm used to talking to the top of your head while you proclaim encyclopedic wisdom from behind your desk." Will sidestepped the question and shifted in his seat.

"Well, take advantage of my full attention. It doesn't last long."

He couldn't help smiling. "Are you kidding? You must have the longest attention span of anyone I've ever met. I swear you've read through the entire medical library." But at the same time, he got the distinct impression that she had more patience for written words than for spoken ones.

"I read other stuff too." She defended herself. "Not that it matters—you're the only one who asks for my advice."

"I guess I'm just cleverer than the rest of them . . ." Will fumbled to sound composed, then he added, not ever able to resist trying to piss her off, "I got you figured out."

"Sure." She paused, unaffected. "So what did you want to talk about? When you came into the library earlier, you looked like you'd just been stopped from jumping off a cliff."

"Nothing, it's not important. I just . . ." He searched for the words to describe almost destroying his life and career, but instead he found sanity in the ordering effect the caffeine was having on his sloshing mind. "Had a weak moment." He felt guilty for the omission. "Sorry, I know that's not what you came with me to hear. Maybe I'll explain it to you soon. In a couple of months when things—" He paused again and made a gesture with both hands, like he was pushing something away, then closed both hands into fists. "Anyway, it helps to talk to you. I find your lack of interest in me relaxing. Keeps me from getting too out of touch with reality. So thanks."

"No problem." She didn't press him. "By the way, are you allowed to work in the lab drunk?"

Was she joking? "What? I mean, of course." *No one's going to stop me.* "Besides, I'm completely capable. If I weren't, I would *know*, and I wouldn't go in." He shrugged.

"Obviously." Margot laughed at him. Will had never really heard her laugh. Her coffee was halfway gone and he was still sipping the top of his. It was too hot, but he tried to take a gulp anyway. It burned going down. He grimaced, and she laughed again.

Will didn't think she would tell anyone about the state in which he had been working. But he couldn't be absolutely sure with her. *He better say something charming.* "So . . . what do you do for fun?"

She looked bored by the question. "Oh, I have a few

friends still in town. I go to the movies sometimes. Went to see that new Shimozaki film the other night. There's only so much to do around here, I guess." She paused, thinking, her expression changed.

"There's a lovely wood, up in Guilford, big, beautiful out-crops." Margot lifted a hand slightly as if she were picturing a massive rock. "The whole place is brimming with trees, birches and maples—even in the winter it feels sheltered . . . a mass of leaves abandoned, littered across the footpaths." Her open hand pointed toward the slick hospital floor, but she didn't seem to see it. "Like walking on a soft carpet."

Will was moved. He had never seen Margot so candid—a rare combination, organic and genuine. He had probably never heard her speak more than five words together. He wanted to be there, in the woods with her. She had such an undeniably nostalgic timbre in her voice. Will flinched slightly. He *was supposed to be charming* her. At least she had moved on from the drunk thing. He took another swig of his coffee. It was almost gone now; he was almost free from this conversation. He struggled through. "I didn't picture you as the outdoors type." *Lame.*

"It gets stuffy over there." She gestured toward the library, but Will got the sense that she wasn't talking about the books or the ventilation. "I need the fresh air." Margot finished the last sip of her coffee and stood up to leave, but she hesitated before turning away. She spoke abruptly. "I've been reading a lot about your work lately . . . Be careful." She nodded once and then picked up her handbag, smiling wanly before turning to walk back toward the library.

Chapter Eight

———

Meanwhile, just about 120 miles away, Arthur was sitting in his office, looking out his window across Cambridge and thinking how easy it had been to catch up to Will's research. Of course, Will shared far too much. He made it so easy to read between the lines, to guess exactly what he was up to. His work was good, but he was simple in a way. Despite the ability to innovate, his reactions to his own brilliance were remarkably predictable. Admittedly, being able to remotely log into Will's tablet and read all of his notes, all of the background papers he had been reading, and all of the data he had collected didn't hurt either.

But more importantly, Will was lazy. He always had been. Arthur remembered when they used to work together. He remembered that time Will took two days off work to take Kate to Vermont, and he was stuck watching all of the cages like he did *every weekend*. The mice always needed babysitting. Left to their own devices, they just defecated, fornicated, and murdered each other in cold blood. Sometimes the mothers ate their own newborn babies when there was a pile of food sitting just inches away. When they were injected with the serum, they were supposed to develop feelings—empathy, the capacity to give a shit about one another. But Arthur could have sworn they got worse. Brothers killing brothers, sisters literally tearing each other apart. There were certainly more litters being conceived, but the proportion that made it past one week old had dropped overall. Arthur had watched them carefully. He cared more about them than Will did. *He wanted to save them.*

Arthur turned back to the paper that was open on his tablet. He had it screen shared onto his desk and enlarged across the full surface so that he could view all of it at once. It was very nearly complete. He was just working on the final image, making certain that every label had the correct font size and that the color contrast was no less than perfect. He would send it off for review in a few hours. He didn't feel bad about it. He believed that if Will hadn't been so lazy, he would have gotten it done first. But he remembered working with Will. He remembered the time he came into lab drunk. *Which time?* Arthur chuckled to himself. The time he spilled liquid nitrogen all over the floor, or the time he snuck into the lab next door to steal an enzyme he had forgotten to order himself? He would have been in *huge* trouble if Arthur had told anyone. It was better to have something to hold over his head, in any case. But it wasn't about Will. It wasn't even about Kate—Kate, who still wouldn't listen to him even now that Will had broken up with her and moved to another state. He could tell when he spoke to her that she wasn't listening. She didn't even try hard to fake it—she nodded at all the wrong times.

Arthur shifted in his chair. He had become sidetracked. His thoughts had taken him to Kate when he should have been focused on the work in front of him. Arthur was a day-dreamer too. He pushed her from his mind and followed his train of thought back again to the mice. During his PhD, he would watch over them in their cages, and when he couldn't be in the mouse room, he would worry about them. He would think about them before going to bed at night, and he would dream about them after he fell asleep. They were such sloppy creatures, no matter how many tags they wore, and he saw himself in their beady little eyes. If empathy couldn't save them, what could?

Arthur's eyes were drawn to his desk drawer. He used his fingerprint to unlock it and slowly pulled it open. Inside there was an unused stylus, a jar of hand lotion, and a deck of playing cards. He kept the cards not because he played but because they still made them out of paper just like they used to, and he thought it was funny, the idea that you could lose one card and the whole pack would be useless. He picked two off the top of the deck. He liked the feeling of sliding them against each other. He found the smooth drag of one card against the other inexplicably pleasing. Turning them over, the jokers smiled up at him. The deck had never been shuffled, and the two wild cards remained together at the top. *What was their purpose?* He put the cards back where they came from, facedown, and moved his hand toward the near right corner, where the only other item in the drawer resided. It was a syringe.

His plan had been to finish the paper and send it off first, just in case anything went wrong. But the temptation had been growing ever since he had decided to go through with it, and it had since become unbearable. Arthur tied a rubber tube around the top of his arm and sprayed the length below with the disinfectant he used to clean his desk. He picked up the syringe and muttered, "Call me crazy," his scientific prayer, before taking it to his arm and injecting it into his vein.

If you would have asked Will or Jon, or someone who knew about these things, they would have said it was a high dose, even for a human.

Chapter Nine

——————

A month later, when Arthur's paper was published in *Nature*, Margot could hear Will shouting, "FUuuuuCK!" from all the way down the hall. She had already seen the paper and had been avoiding her desk all morning on the off chance that he'd come in to see her. This was an awkward task, given that her main responsibility was to man the circulation desk, but she occupied herself by rearranging some hard-copy books on one of the shelves at the far end of the library and then taking them down again and putting them back where they had originally been. In the process, about twenty years' worth of dust was unsettled, and she nearly walked herself to the hospital in a coughing and sneezing fit.

But Will didn't go to the library to see Margot. Instead he went with Jon to the nearest liquor store. They bought a bottle of bourbon and a six-pack and sat on the roof doing shots out of fifty-milliliter beakers and chasing them with beer. Will was daydreaming about punching Arthur in the face. He would punch him right in his face right in his office. He would pull him across his desk by whatever hideous tie he was wearing and hold it steady while he swung. He would sneak up behind him while he took his stupid walk along the stupid Charles, tap him on the shoulder, and then *pow*! Will's hand ached with the thought of the damage it would cause, and it felt good to him. It was more than a daydream—it was an aspiration.

"Did you read the paper?" Jon asked.

"No." Will hadn't even considered it. "I wish we still had printers in the lab, so I could print it out and then burn it."

"Sounds cathartic. They might still have one in the history department. I bet they still use it too." Jon was amused at the idea of a printer still being used by those bearded hippies, but he was just distracting himself from the searing injustice still fresh in his heart. He came back to it quickly. "I read it. You should read it. It's almost unbelievable how similar their methods are to ours." He took another shot of bourbon and then spit onto the roof. "It *is* unbelievable."

"You think?"

"I do."

"But how could they?"

"I have no clue."

"That rat-fucking, fat, shoe-tying bastard."

———

After the bottle was empty and the six aluminum cans had been smashed underfoot, Will headed home. He hadn't been home in almost three days, aside from once to pick up his toothbrush. He had been napping in the lounge for a few spare hours now and again, and he had been in the lab or at his desk the rest of the time. He hadn't even gone to the trouble of picking up his toothbrush until just the day before, and he wouldn't have bothered if he had known there was only one day left to work.

He abandoned the pile of greasy cardboard boxes on the

table in the cramped kitchenette where he and Jon had been sharing family-sized meals of take-out pizza and Diet Coke for the last three nights. He couldn't bear to walk back by the lab today. Jon had gone home for a solid eight hours every night to sleep near his wife and daughter, but Will hadn't had a good reason to reset his brain. So, as he walked home, drunk, at eleven in the morning, he felt as if he was returning from a failed quest.

Will lived up north, past the take-out joints and the pizza bars. Past the restaurants that ran all year in anticipation of parents' weekend and the three red brick churches on the green. Past all of the Dunkin' Donuts, and the old cheese shop that had been there forever, and past the bronze triceratops that stood out in front of the Peabody Museum. Usually he jumped on the shuttle that took students and staff up and down from the residential area through campus, to the med school and back, but he was embarrassed by the idea of noticeably slipping on the stairs up into the bus or passing out in the back seat only to be brought full circle again.

He thought the walk home would be sobering, but as he came in the front door, he nearly lost his balance. He glanced up instinctively to make sure that no one had seen. It was a shared house. He lived with two other postdocs, one from Germany and one from France, but no one else was home at this hour. He sat down on the couch and called Viki because he missed her and he needed to hear someone else's voice. He had been listening to only his own in his head the whole way home, and he hadn't been in a good mood. Of course she didn't pick up, because she was at work too. *Shit. Stupid.* He fell back onto the worn, dimpled cushions and passed out for a few hours, hoping to wake up to a world less cruel and less fuzzy.

———

In the already infuriating state of having an evening hangover after a day of drinking and napping it off, Will read Arthur's paper. Jon was right. There was no way that Arthur hadn't somehow replicated their experimental plan. *Though the asshole could have at least covered it up better*, Will thought. By the time Will got down to the discussion section, he was fuming, but the conclusion took him by surprise. He read it over once, twice, maybe three times—he had lost focus. He was curious if the reviewer had even read the final section before publishing, or if they had just assumed it was a restatement of the earlier facts. Will felt cold welling up around his stomach and leaking into his chest, cutting off the expanding heat of his recovering liver. All he could think was, *What is that asshole doing? What* is *that* asshole *doing?*

Instead of allowing himself to fantasize, he emailed Carlos, his old PI at Harvard, told him he would be in Boston in the next few days, and asked if he could come by to say hello, to catch up. Then he called Viki again. She would be home from work by now, and he desperately wanted to hear about whatever she would pretend she had eaten for lunch or the necklace she was thinking of buying (he was sure he would love it), or her boss's bitchy assistant or the color of her manicure. *Anything.*

Chapter Ten

———

It was the middle of the week, but Will took a few days off work to go to Boston. He almost never took time off, but other people did. Jenny took about six weeks off a year, it felt like, and George never noticed, or more likely never cared. He was barely ever in anyway. Once you got to being the head of a lab, it seemed you never really did that much research anymore, not in a hands-on way at least. You had minions to do it for you. Will liked the sound of that. He knew if he had gofers to do all of his busy work and experiments for him, he could spend all of his time reading and thinking and developing all of those brilliant, genius, light-bulb ideas that he knew were floating just below the surface. And naturally he wouldn't spend so much time daydreaming about the future and the past and about direction-determining decisions and alternate paths and about Viki and Kate and Eva and Arthur. George spent about 80 percent of his time traveling. He was flown all over the world to give talks and appear at conferences. To Will it sounded glamorous, but if he was being entirely honest, he wasn't sure if it was something he would enjoy.

Will took the morning Amtrak to Boston. It was about a two-and-a-half-hour journey, so he had downloaded a set of papers to his tablet to read on the train. He wished he had asked Margot her opinion on what papers to read, but he had been too pissed off the morning before to do anything productive, and too drunk after that. Besides, he hadn't been sure he wanted her to see him in a temper, so he had avoided the library. It didn't matter—he wasn't reading the papers. He was staring out of the window, counting the seconds or the minutes between the swift swaths of water that would appear time and again, glittering in the sunlight. Each time the smudged window lit up in that quick shimmer, Will felt himself smiling slightly. He felt his chest rising, and he sat up a little bit straighter. He knew it was only a trick of the light, but he couldn't help his attraction to such shiny things. In between, as he counted the seconds, he let out his breath and sank back into his daydreams.

The train to Boston was also the first leg he would take to get to his parents' home. Counting backward, he hadn't been in . . . one, two . . . six months. *Crap.* The guilt sank rapidly into his chest. When he had been living in Cambridge, he had gone home for dinner at least every other week. He was a good son, *or he used to be.* His parents were still working, still keeping busy, but they had cut back hours here and there, he knew from phone conversations. And he also knew, listening between the lines, that they would appreciate the company. Time moved so quickly lately. There was always one more experiment, one more meeting, one more excuse. And then Viki lived in the opposite direction. He had always assumed his parents would move in with him when they were too old to care for themselves, as his grandfather had moved in with them. He wondered if Viki would allow it. *Would he still be with Viki that long from now?* He shook his head sharply. *This was not the fucking time.* Will tried to clear his mind and returned his focus to staring out the window. But it didn't last long.

He thought of Kate and whether he should text her, to see if she wanted to meet up for a coffee. To see if she really was dating Arthur, and to find out if she *really* knew him. Then he thought about Arthur. In Will's mind, he would confront Arthur in his office. He would be sitting with his back to Will, facing the window, looking out over Cambridge and across the Charles, over Boston, and farther still. When Arthur looked out of his window, he saw the whole world below him, humans just being human. He looked at them the way he looked at the mice in their cages, as if they simply couldn't help themselves. The moment he heard Will come through the door, he would turn around in his swivel chair. He would probably have to pump it up to look Will in the eyes, and he would probably be stroking some sort of hairless cat or pit bull. But Will knew Arthur wasn't badass enough to own a pit bull. More likely, he would be stroking a vial or a rabbit's foot. He prayed it was the latter. As the train pulled into South Station, Will texted Kate. She was free for coffee in less than an hour.

———

Will took the T straight to Harvard and met Kate in the ABP just outside of the station. He thought he had been running about ten minutes early when he arrived, but she was already sitting down, *eager as usual*. She looked up as he approached, her familiar green eyes peering through the window, and it was magical to see the rest of her materialize around them with the evocative feeling of coming across a once-intimate image. Her features were pleasing as ever, but she lacked the sheen that had drawn him in when they had first met, that had still lingered in his memory of her eyes. *What was I thinking?* Will said to himself, before charging through the front door and up to her table. "Wow, how long has it been? You look great!"

Kate blushed. "Thanks, it's . . . Thanks, it's good to see you." She giggled and pulled a strand of hair in front of her face, and then she laughed again as she moved it back behind her ear. *Why* had *she been so eager to meet him?* Will suddenly felt sorry for her.

"Can I get you something?" he offered.

"Oh no, sure." She smiled an awkwardly large smile and breathed out loudly through her nose.

"What?" Will said aloud. To himself, he added, *The fuck is up with her?*

"Just a coffee, thanks." She looked down at the table for a few seconds before looking straight back up at him.

"Decaf?" He said it hopefully.

"Nah, you know decaf is for people who have given up on life."

He returned with a latte for himself and a decaf coffee for her. He hoped she wouldn't notice.

"What the hell, man?" Kate made a face. "This is totally decaf. What, you don't think I can handle it?" She rolled her eyes. "You know, we're not dating anymore. You can't make decisions for my 'own good' anymore." Using air quotes for emphasis, she made it obvious how annoying he could be, but just as quickly she dropped the exasperation. She paused briefly in contemplation, then made an entirely different and unreadable face. "And I can't make decisions for your own good either, but you know what? I'm going to make a suggestion to you. Go home. Go back to Yale. Get the pants out of Dodge. Got it?"

"God, you're even weirder than I remember. I thought you were a little *too* eager to see me just a few minutes ago. What was *all that* about?"

"God, you're even more narcissistic than I remember," she mocked, then sighed. "Look, it is good to see you, but you're not here to see me. I'm not stupid. I know there's some shit going on with Arthur and that paper and . . ." She waved her hands in the air. "When you texted me, I half expected you'd knocked him over the head with an Erlenmeyer flask and needed help disposing of the body."

"I haven't even seen him yet. I came straight here from South Station." Will took on a defensive tone out of habit but still only managed to appear slightly ashamed, and even that much was mostly for show. In the back of his mind, he weighed the value of a flask as a murder weapon. Poetic justice and then into the autoclave.

"Good. . . . I really do think you should leave it. Though I really don't believe that you will." She raised her eyebrows questioningly. "It's just, I saw him the other day—I don't see him often," she added quickly, and Will relaxed slightly. "He was acting *so* weird. I can't describe it. For one, he asked me out. I know he's wanted to for years, but I never thought he'd actually do it." She mimed putting a gun to her temple and rolled her eyes some more. "I made an excuse. I should have said flat out *no*, but I don't think it would have made a difference. He was just like, 'Sure. Next time.' But it was the way he said it, like really soft and calm and totally confident that there *would be* a next time. Freaked me out."

"Sounds terrifying," Will mocked, pleased and relieved to hear she had no interest in Arthur. "I'm sure you could take him."

"I guess." She still seemed distracted. "Anyway, you'll see . . ." Kate tilted her head slightly, considering. "You have a temper, right?"

Will flinched slightly. *Where did that come from?* "I've been accused of that before, yes."

"Yeah. You used to yell a lot and hit the table and throw things and—"

"I *get* it, what's your point?"

"I was never scared that you would hurt me or lie to me or anything. You always got everything out of your system. Maybe it wasn't the perfect solution . . . but in a way it worked. When I saw Arthur the other day, it was like he was holding so much in—he was so reserved. I mean, he's always been quiet, but it never felt so calculated before. It sounds crazy, but I know you already think I'm crazy, so I'm telling you anyway. I have a bad feeling about it." She pointed to her gut.

Will was silent for a few seconds, allowing Kate to gather herself, before replying, "I have an idea . . . You still have access to Arthur's lab, right?" This was the real reason he had texted Kate.

"Why is it that I always go along with all of your 'ideas'? You've never had a single good one." She lifted her shoulders an inch and her eyebrows a millimeter.

"There was that one time in that hot tub up in Vermont. You seemed to like that idea."

Kate snorted. "There *was* that *one* time."

———

Eventually, Kate had to go back into work, so Will spent the afternoon wandering around campus and Cambridge. He walked at a leisurely pace, all the way to his old apartment building on Arlington Street and back again to Winthrop Square. There were students everywhere, headphones, tablets, street shoes in every direction, making Will feel worldly and weary all at once. He ducked into Wagamama for lunch and ordered the chicken katsu curry. It had been years since he had had the familiar dish, and the way that it always tasted exactly the same and would always taste exactly the same was the reason he always ordered it and always would. It wasn't the best food in Cambridge by far, but it was routine and more satisfying than something new *could* be. During lunch, he was able to forget the real reason he was in town and the particular plan he had made for later that night. He was simply enjoying his meal.

When he was finished eating, Will wandered through Harvard Yard. It was just starting to get cold at that time of year, but the sun was out and a gentle chill was only realized in the intermittent pockets of shade between buildings and under particularly robust trees. It was easy for Will to ignore in a light jacket. Bathing in the natural light, he soaked in the bricks. He purposely walked by the famous libraries and each of the undergraduate houses. It was silly—he had never even been into any of the halls before, so it shouldn't have been nostalgic in any way, but his attachment to the institution or to that feeling he had had when he first started his PhD, that he had really made it, nagged at him.

As evening settled in, he became more antsy. He noticed

himself biting the edges of his lips and repeatedly scratching his left eye. He had to consciously avoid wandering over to his old department. If he stopped paying careful attention to where he put his feet, they would automatically start to turn in that direction. In an effort to control himself, he sat down in a bar on Mass Ave. It was a new bar, or at least it had opened since he had left Cambridge, so it was mercifully free of the sentimental prods that had been following him throughout the day. But he only ordered another coffee. *He needed to stay sharp.* Kate had agreed to help him, but they wouldn't meet up again for several more hours. It would be safer to go in the middle of the night. The later they went, the less likely they were to have company. Of course, there was always the chance that someone would be working late in the lab; there was always the chance that that someone would be Arthur. Will shook himself. *Unlikely.* At Harvard he had been accustomed to late, lonely nights in the lab. Back when he was working on his PhD, most everyone else had gone home by midnight, *even Arthur.* Will had often stayed up until dawn to get his work done in peace and then slept through the bulk of the next day.

Halfway through the coffee, Will began to have creeping second thoughts about their plan, but he immediately blamed his anxiety on the caffeine, holding a shaking hand out for proof. Technically, Kate had access to the lab, so there was no reason she shouldn't be there, and there was no reason she shouldn't bring a guest. Still, he knew if Arthur caught them snooping around somehow, there would be hell to pay. Will opened his tablet. He checked his messages reflexively; he hadn't had a notification. He knew there would be nothing new to see and, confirming that, folded it back up again. A few minutes later, he opened it again and loaded one of the papers he was supposed to have read on the train. He skimmed the abstract, but nothing sunk in, so he folded the thing closed and put it away for the second time. Finally, Will decided to give up the vigil, to check into his hotel, and try to force himself to get a few hours of sleep. To his own surprise, he did.

————

He met up with Kate again at half past midnight, back outside ABP. "Hey, thanks for doing this. It means a lot to me." He held Kate's hand. He couldn't stop bullshitting her, even though he knew she was immune to it by now—*probably* because *she was immune.* He didn't like feeling powerless around her.

"You're such a dweeb." She laughed. "Some more advice for you—stop being so predictable all the time. Now let's get this over and done with, and hey, it's not just for you. Let's be honest, eh? I'm wicked curious too." She moved her hand away from his and tugged on his shirt instead, pulling in the direction of his old lab. Will suddenly had the feeling he was being led to the slaughter, but his feet responded quickly, happy to oblige the temptation they had felt all day.

They walked the rest of the way in silence. Will kept trying to think of things to say, but nothing he could come up with in his head seemed worth the effort of speaking out loud. He ran frantically through the mundane possibilities. *Ask her how her work is going. That would be the considerate thing to do, right? No, she wouldn't think it was genuine. She'd probably laugh at me. And she would tell me about her work anyway, if she wanted me to know . . . Maybe ask her if she's dating anyone? No, way too awkward. And she'd laugh at that too. "Why do you care, dweeb?" That's what she'd say. Ask her about her mom. I miss that lady. She was cool. She liked me. I bet she misses me too. I wonder how that dog is doing . . . What if Shugga died? It's been a few years. Shit.* They had arrived outside of Will's old building. He felt that cold surge again, slowly drowning his internal organs, but he shivered it off as they entered using Kate's key card.

It was almost completely dark inside when they first set foot in the building, but all of the lights were on motion sensors, so they clicked on in sections as they moved forward, illuminating a path to the elevators before them and eliminating any chance of discretion. Will's former lab was on the sixth floor. Kate hit the call button, and they intently watched the numbers as the elevator came down, one floor at a time: 5 . . . 4 . . . 3 . . . 2 . . . L. She breathed in as if she was planning to say something, but the doors opened before she could get it out, so they walked in side by side, pressed 6, and watched the numbers in reverse: 2 . . . 3 . . . 4 . . . 5 . . . 6.

On the sixth floor, the doors reopened quietly, but the loud click of the lights coming on made them both jump. Kate laughed feverishly but still spoke in an undertone. "Freaking A, were we always such children? I feel ridiculous right now. Right? Like, where are my leather gloves and ski mask?"

"Come on, you have nothing to worry about. Arthur has such a crush on you. Worst thing that happens if he catches you is you'll have to make good on that date. Maybe let him get to second base though—he's been patient enough."

Kate punched him in the arm. "Gross. I can't think of anything worse than that." She suppressed a laugh. "And

62

what will happen to you? Final showdown to see who has the bigger *graduated cylinder*?"

Hearing her insult Arthur so cruelly gave Will the confidence to move forward. "Come on, let's do this." They hadn't yet exited the elevator and the doors had reclosed, so he pushed the DOOR OPEN button, and the lights clicked on again. This time, he didn't let the sound bother him, and they walked out into the hall. It was a square building, and the hallway followed its shape full circle, with labs on the inside and offices on the outside all the way along. Their destination was on the opposite end to the elevators, so in theory they could reach it going in either direction, but they chose to go left. Arthur's office was to the right.

Kate still had key-card access to the lab as well. Back when Will had been working there, he had convinced someone in HR to add it to her ID card so she could come in and see him after hours and he wouldn't have to get up or disrupt whatever experiment he was doing. He had given the HR officer some other scientific mumbo jumbo reasoning. And because she had never been an official member of the lab—she never officially joined, and therefore she never officially left—no one had ever been instructed to remove her access.

Once they were inside, they looked for Arthur's bench. It didn't take long to find. It was in the same place it had always been, though Will simply couldn't believe it at first. It was an incredible mess. There were used pipette tips and test tubes and vials scattered, unlabeled bottles, crusted and still-wet paper towels, stacks of discarded samples. It looked like Will's desk.

"But he used to be obnoxiously neat. Like, anal retentively

obsessive about everything," Will mused as he checked for Arthur's handwriting on the few items that had actually been labeled.

"I told you he's fucking lost it, didn't I?"

———

Will put on a pair of nitrile gloves and carefully picked through all of the debris, trying to fathom what the hell was going on. He looked through the hood, and the cabinet under the hood. He looked through the cupboards above and below Arthur's bench, and he checked the fridge and freezer for samples. He even sniffed at mystery liquids in unlabeled bottles at the risk of inhaling toxic fumes. From what he could tell, the setup was similar to what he had in his own lab, but there were a few unexplained items that irritated him.

He was frustrated. He tossed a stack of paper-and-pen notes that Kate had gathered in bits and pieces from around Arthur's desk into the nearest waste container. As far as he could tell from the few legible words, it was all gibberish anyway. *There was something he couldn't see.* Whatever was bothering him about all of this, he wasn't going to be able to put it together here. It was too cluttered, too crazed. There was no method to the madness, no rhyme or reason for why Arthur had chosen to put *anything anywhere*. Will had to let it go for the time being. He blamed his mental congestion on the shocking disorderliness and, in the meantime, painstakingly took photos of every single seemingly useless item, in case something occurred to him later. It was a forensic nightmare.

The sound of a block of lights clicking on down the hall

made them freeze. Will threw down the bottle he was examining, and they both dove together behind the neighboring bench. They immediately made eye contact and nearly burst out laughing but held themselves as small as possible, shaking with sudden comedy and stilling with suspense, waiting for the lights in the lab to switch off and conceal them from whatever keen character was wandering the hall in the middle of the night. Will was short of breath. His heart was racing. His mind was racing. *This is cool. This is ridiculous. This is insane. This is awesome. This is stupid. We're going to get caught. Fuck Arthur. No, we're not. It's worth it. Damn, I need to get into shape.* They watched from below the bench as the light coming in from the hallway brightened with another *click*, and they listened intently as someone opened a door somewhere and shut it again. After about three minutes, but what felt like at least twenty, the lights in the lab switched off. In the dark, the air became breathable again, so they allowed themselves to gasp for it.

"Holy shindig," Kate whispered into the dark. "I almost had a heart attack. I've got goose bumps on the soles of my feet, I swear." She giggled with relief.

"Shut up, woman." He pressed his hand against her arm, or what he assumed was her arm in the dark, close space. "Who d'you think is in the hall? What are we going to do if they come in here?" He was sure it was Arthur.

Kate resented him calling her "woman." She knew it was only his apprehension speaking, but she teased him anyway. "Pretend to be making out?"

"Okay." He nodded invisibly, but his voice carried affirmation and assumption.

"What?!" She threw his hand off of her knee. "That was

a joke. *A joke* . . . pervert! What kind of sicko hooks up on the floor of, let's face it, basically a chemical plant, for all intents and purposes?"

Will shrugged. It sounded much worse when she put it like that than it had in his head. Now he started to imagine all of the little slips and spills; accidents had certainly dropped more organic and inorganic waste than the cleaning staff would ever be capable of eliminating. Microscopic mouse droppings and mutated material. He pictured the shower in his hotel room. Somehow he had to get from here to there.

"Never mind," he grumbled. "Come on, if we stay close to the floor, I think the lights will stay off. Let's try to get over to the back door." They crawled on hands and knees out from behind the bench and immediately heard a loud *click*. The lights coming back on startled their senses, and they paused, paralyzed for a moment, blinking to recover.

"Fudge."

"Ummmm . . . run?"

"Walk purposefully. There are cameras." So they walked purposefully, out the back door of the lab, back down the left-hand side of the hallway (which, from their perspective, was now on the right) and down the stairs. They wouldn't risk waiting for the elevator this time. Six flights down and out the front door of the building, Will flinched at every *click, click, click* the entire way, as the motion sensors trapped them in a moving spotlight.

Once outside, Kate continued speed walking along the street. He struggled to keep up as she hung a left and then a right, charging all the way back to the main campus. Finally, he had to stop to catch his breath. She turned back to wait for him. "Come on, grandpa, we weren't even running."

"It's just"—he breathed deeply—"the adrenaline." He paused to pant some more. "And maybe I haven't been to the gym in two years . . ." Panting. "Too busy saving the world," he muttered.

"You're such a nutcase. Hey, I've got to get home. Can't function this late. What with the decaf coffee this afternoon and the excitement over, I'm hitting a major low." She paused. "Good luck with your meeting tomorrow. You *are* meeting Carlos, right? *Just* Carlos?"

"Yes," he lied, but it was only half a lie, he reasoned. He was planning to meet with his old PI, and *who knew* who else he would run into.

She eyed him strangely. *She knew him too well; that's why it would never have worked.* "Let me know what happens, what you find out . . ." Pointing to his tablet, she indicated the photos they had just captured together.

Will nodded.

Kate paused to take a breath, and her tone changed. "I know you didn't come up here to see *me*, but it has been nice to catch up." She looked torn, as if she couldn't decide whether or not to go on. She shrugged. "I guess I always assumed you would eventually become some eminent academic, but I don't think I gave you enough credit. You deserve more."

More? That was all he wanted. "Thank you," he uttered. That seemed like the polite thing to say, whether or not it carried any meaning. *Kate was a good person.* He was more grateful than he could say that she still had his back, whether or not he deserved it. *She* was the kind of person he really *should* listen to. "Have a good night." He smiled. "Couldn't have done it without you."

She laughed at him. "Catch you on the flip side." Throwing down a peace sign with her left hand, she walked off into the darkness.

Chapter Eleven

———

Will's meeting with his old PI went about as he expected. Carlos sat behind a half-empty box of Chinese takeout, performing a balancing act with two sets of chopsticks and chewing three times between every other word. Occasionally he left the end of a chow mein noodle hanging out of the right-hand corner of his mouth while he spoke. Will couldn't actually picture Carlos without a plate of food before him. The image went well with his diminutive round form, but the truth was, he was only ever at his desk when he was forced to sit still by the recurrent necessity of calorie consumption. Today he was rushed, as usual. He only had ten minutes to eat and ten minutes to talk, and they overlapped.

Will immediately tuned out. Carlos was going on about Arthur or George, publishing, conference travel, or possibly fishing? There was a picture, right in the center of the wall behind his desk, of Carlos in full waders and a mesh fishing vest, holding out a two-foot salmon. It had by far the largest dimensions of any picture in the room. He looked prouder in that photo than he had ever looked when one of Will's projects had had a good result, a great result even. Surrounding that centerpiece were pictures of his family—his wife and his two kids. Lots and lots of pictures taken from every age, scattered unsystematically among artwork from every grade.

Professors always had loads of family photos on the wall, Will noted. They had to; there was never any time to see them in person.

Will looked down from the wall of pictures and saw that the box of chow mein was almost empty. It was almost time to go, and Carlos hadn't apologized. *That was no surprise.* Will knew he didn't care what Arthur did as long as his lab got the paper. That was how they all were. Carlos had stopped caring about Will the minute he finished his PhD and left Harvard. And he had always had a soft spot for Arthur. He had kept him on as a postdoc instead of Will. *He probably wasn't intimidated by Arthur.*

Will turned his gaze out the window. He watched a tiny person in a tiny room making lunch across the street. *It didn't matter.* The real reason he had set up the meeting was just for an excuse to be hanging around the lab. He wanted to confront Arthur, but he didn't want to give him any warning. Carlos wiped his face with a napkin, threw his lunch container into the wastebasket, and stood up. It was his way of showing Will the door, and Will eagerly walked through it, free and sanctioned to walk the sixth-floor hall after that brief and meaningless encounter. He drew breath, gathered all the calm he could gather, and rocked up to Arthur's office.

———

Will stood at the door and knocked. He waited for a count of five and then tried again. In between knocks, he reminded himself that it would be futile to argue about the past, even the *very recent* past. What he really needed was to find out what Arthur was planning for the future. He felt impatient.

He counted to five once more and then, immediately following the third and loudest knock, he tried the door. It was unlocked, so he let himself in. Arthur's chair was facing the window, exactly as it had been in his daydream. For four full measures, Will's heart beat a Sousa march as he anticipated the swivel. But no swivel came. At a second glance, the chair was obviously empty.

Will relaxed. He moved forward into the room, sat down in the chair himself, and waited for Arthur to return. While he waited, he looked with suspicion over the bits and pieces scattered around the desk, not that he expected Arthur to leave anything incriminating lying around. The good stuff would be locked inside. For the most part, it was uncluttered, aside from a few books and what Will recognized as Arthur's necessities: a nameplate, a bottle of disinfectant, and a box of tissues. The only thing he noticed that seemed at all out of place was a short stack of brochures and pamphlets from local hospitals. But he supposed Arthur could have picked them up at some seminar or even in person, on the rare occasion he might go in to see patients, to ask for blood samples, or just to remind himself that there was a point to his repetitive work. One of the pamphlets was from the hospital where Will used to volunteer.

Will had planned to be calmly gazing out of the window by the time Arthur arrived so he could turn dramatically to face him as he walked in. But his timing was off. Arthur entered the room swiftly, closing the door behind him before Will was able to rotate even ninety degrees from the desk. So, in the end, he was just awkwardly sitting in Arthur's chair, uninvited. He tried to play it off by holding his right hand under his chin while his elbow perched on the armrest.

His left hand found itself at his waist, making an inelegant forward triangle with his bent arm.

It wasn't ideal, but then Arthur barely seemed to notice him at first. Still standing at the door, he stuffed something hastily into his pocket and then rubbed down the front of his wrinkled shirt, pulling it straight momentarily but at the same time loosening the tuck from his pants, making the overall effect worse. He tugged on his tie and ran the front of each of his glossy leather shoes against the back of the opposite leg. Only then did he pause to glare across the room at Will. Arthur was angry, to be sure, but somehow he didn't seem completely surprised by him being there. Will was more surprised by Arthur. He had the appearance of a look-alike with few resources and little skill trying to impersonate the obnoxiously fastidious rival he once knew. *He looked like a drug addict.*

"Well?" Arthur held his glare. But after ten seconds had passed in silence, he rolled his eyes, grunted, and then looked back at Will with a deadpan expression.

Will had thought something clever would come to him the moment he saw Arthur. *Usually he couldn't help insulting the bastard.* He had planned on giving a speech, but he hadn't bothered with the specifics. It would be scathing, but where would he begin? *He was taking too long.* His mind went blank. He was losing ground, losing respect. He felt uncomfortably warm. All he could come up with was, "What are you *up to?*" And even that *cop-out* didn't come out as gravely as he had intended. Will leaned forward and narrowed his eyes.

"What do you mean? I've already finished what I am up to. I published first; I won. Are you simply here to pick a fight over it?" He spoke quickly and defensively.

It was unusual to see Arthur act guiltily. Will had expected him to brag despite what he had done, or even by virtue (or vice) of it. There was a sheen forming on Arthur's forehead. It reminded Will of his clammy handshake, and it made his stomach turn.

"I'd *love* to pick a fight. I'd wring your fucking neck!" Will breathed. He controlled himself. "What are you up to?" he repeated.

"I don't blame you." Arthur smiled, and it made Will want to kick him in the nuts. "When I gained access to your tablet, it must be five or six years ago now, I never thought I would use it, but . . . you impressed me." He looked wistful, but it was a bead of sweat and not a tear that he wiped from the corner of his eye.

Will picked up the box of tissues from the desk and threw it at the wall behind him. "Fuck you."

Arthur rolled his eyes again. "Look, what's done is done. No one's going to figure it out, or give a shit if they do." He smirked fondly, as if the plagiarism was an old joke, long forgotten. "What are you *really* doing here?" He paused, blinked twice, and deliberately slowed his speech. "You know, I left something in my office last night, came in to get it. It was late . . . quite late, and the light was on in the lab. I thought that was unusual, so I looked in. I didn't see anyone, mind you . . . but the light *was* on."

He's already fucking figured it out. But Will refused to play along. "What did you leave in your office that was so important so late at night? A blow-up doll?"

"It doesn't matter," Arthur spat out angrily. Then immediately he resumed his calm with the same sidelong smile.

Fuck. This guy's a certifiable serial killer, Will realized.

"I asked security to see who swiped in last night," Arthur continued. "Couldn't have been more surprised. Did you know Kate has access to this building? She hasn't worked here for years. Even more surprising is that she has, rather *had*, access to this lab. I wonder why that would be?"

"How should I know?" Will mumbled. He got up from the chair and started to move slowly and at a safe distance, around Arthur and closer to the door.

Arthur sighed, turning with him in orbit. "When did you get so shy? You used to brag to me about *everything*. Every little thing you did well. Every experimental result that looked better than mine, every paper you got on, every party, every girl."

"When did you get so confident?" Will reversed the question. *Forget that, when did you get so fucking cloak-and-dagger?* Kate had been right; Arthur was acting super strange, even for Arthur. He kept picking at his right shirtsleeve, abruptly and repeatedly, like a nervous tic. He was jumpy and irritable and self-assured all at once. And the thin layer of sweat over his flushed brow was collecting into tiny beads, fusing into droplets that had started to give in to gravity and trickle down the edge of his fair hairline. He looked ill.

Arthur drew his left sleeve across his forehead, visibly dampening it. "Maybe we're not so different after all, Dalal." His line of sight hit the floor, and his voice dropped to a mutter. He began speaking fast and low, as if Will were no longer in the room. He had to lean in to catch the words. "I could use help. Could I use help? Things might go smoother. *More smoothly*. Smoother. Who cares, things will be fine. I don't need him. He fucking hates me. He should. No. We're just like them. . . . It's not our fault—they stick us in cages, and we destroy each other." He looked up at Will as if nothing had happened.

"What the fuck is wrong with you?" Will was nervous, but he took a step toward Arthur. He had to *know. But how?*

"Nothing. I think you should go. Maybe I'll call you." Arthur's whole head twitched. "Just don't think *too* poorly of me, not yet." He reached out his hand.

"Too late for that." But Will accepted it. As they shook, he reached out with his left hand as if to bring more warmth to the handshake, but instead he stretched out his fingers to press the crook of Arthur's right arm. *If there was bruising . . .*

Arthur jumped back with pain. "Get out!" he screamed.

Will obliged readily. Despite leaving on instruction, he felt like he was making an escape. He walked far faster than he had the night before. He practically skidded out the front door of the building. Will was tingling from head to foot, but by the time he was a block away from his old department, he could no longer tell if he was scared, or if he was excited.

Chapter Twelve

———

While Will was in Boston, Margot was reading.

She began by reading Arthur's paper. *Just out of curiosity*, she told herself, but despite her own intuition, she cared for Will, and she didn't care for many people. She had been raised by a tight-knit family in the small town of Gatlinburg in eastern Tennessee, and aside from her brother, Jeremy, she had never had more than one or two close friends at any stage in life. She had grown up instead looking up at the Great Smoky Mountains and wandering through woodland by herself and occasionally with Jeremy. That had been enough for her back then. Margot missed the fresh air in her lungs and she desperately missed her brother, but she would never move back to Tennessee. She had left Gatlinburg at eighteen to attend Yale, and she wouldn't move again. She had learned quickly that she didn't care for change. The volumes of the library had replaced the Great Smoky Mountains of her childhood, and the intellectual forays into fields of medical science produced the same temporary gratification that she received surveying the natural beauty of her home state by foot.

When Margot read Arthur's paper, she had the same reaction that Will had had, minus most of the rage, though she did feel a fraction of fury burning on Will's behalf. It was about three-quarters or a little further through the text where the voice changed. As if a sensible run-of-the-mill scientist had, between one sentence and the next, become a mad one. And Margot, who spent all of her time watching and reading and silently critiquing their work, knew there was a fine line between the two. Will, she suspected, was teetering on the edge. Arthur, she had previously assumed, was as straitlaced as they come, at least on paper. She had figured that was the main reason he and Will had never gotten along.

And yet, there, in the discussion section, in particular the paragraph covering future work, was evidence to the contrary. One sentence especially stood out to her: "Though further experimental work must still be completed before a full realization of the potential of this novel therapy can be appreciated, it has become evident that we will soon reach a point from which we may jump forward as a species." Up until that moment, the paper had been focused on a drug being developed for treatment and mitigation of an unavoidable condition that came as a side effect when lives were saved through the regeneration of parts of the brain. The conclusion of the paper, however, set ajar doors for transmogrification and peeked through concealed windows into a different world—a world where perhaps intelligence could be purchased if it was not inherited, or enhanced if it was. Immediately Margot knew it was not a world she would want to live in and not only because she liked feeling special.

She looked up Arthur: his background, his schooling, awards and honors, written work, anything she could find. He seemed to always come second place in everything, but not from a lack of talent or drive. More likely it was due to unpopularity, rivalry, or simple fear, which must have made it smart all the more. In ceremonial photos, he looked cold beneath his shy eyes. He dressed like a lawyer or a politician, in the carefully tailored suits of businesspeople rather than the loosely fitting, lightly wrinkled ensembles most scientists employed as costumes for conferences. *He certainly had an ego*, Margot decided, but he used to cower behind it. She worried about what sentiment or substance had given him the confidence to own it.

Before Will had returned from his trip to Boston she had read every background paper and every book she could find on his and Arthur's overlapping interest. Practical skills aside, she knew more about his project than he did.

Chapter Thirteen

———

After the encounter with Arthur, Will wanted to get on the first train back to New Haven. He had been planning to surprise his parents with a visit while he was in the neighborhood, but he couldn't bear to stay in Boston a minute later than the minute the next train departed South Station. *What they didn't know wouldn't hurt them.* He had already checked out of his hotel that morning, so the only thing he stopped to do before skipping town was drop by Kate's lab with a large regular coffee. He had to try to convince her not to speak to Arthur anymore.

"You were right. That guy is out of control batshit like I don't even know." His hand jerked with feeling, spilling a dribble of coffee as he put it down to form a ring on her desk. "And he knows that you swiped in last night, so if I were you, I'd keep my distance." Will figured she was too curious, too headstrong; she would continue to investigate as long as she remained interested, *but at least he had tried.* He promised to send her the photos and to let her know if he managed to make sense of any of them. He promised to keep in touch. It wouldn't be the first time he didn't keep a promise to her, or the second, but he could tell by the way she spoke to him now that she no longer expected anything more or less than what he was. It was both comforting and dismaying, but *he didn't have time to confront any new fucking feelings.* He hopped on the T and got out of there.

On the train, he thought more carefully about Arthur. Will had suspected that he might be taking the Brill pill, or whatever the hell it was. Of course he was injecting it—the way that he flinched when Will had pushed on his cephalic vein proved that. It must have been a syringeful that he had stuffed in his pocket when he realized Will was sitting in his office. It would wear off every few hours if he didn't keep taking it. Will wondered how much he had been taking, when he had started, and how long he could survive like that. There was no way to know. *That could have been me,* he thought with disgust as he recalled the slimy look across Arthur's face, but he could hear the regret creeping into his condescending words all the same.

When his train arrived at Union Station, he took the Yale shuttle straight to the med campus. He wanted to go into lab. He wasn't planning on doing any work that day. *What the fuck was he supposed to work on now anyway?* But he couldn't stop thinking about the second-to-last packet of powder he had hidden away in his desk drawer. When Will drank, he liked to get drunk. He didn't usually have just one or two. He preferred to have four or five or more. He didn't see the point of doing things in halves. So when he walked off the train, full of emotions he couldn't place or didn't understand, he wanted to drown himself in them. In his lab, they often amplified samples using PCR in order to see results more clearly. In his bewildered state, Will reasoned that if he used the e-potion to amplify his feelings, they would similarly become clearer. Or, at the very least, they would become strong enough to force him into some sort of action. At the moment, he felt like he was trapped in suspended animation while his insides relentlessly churned.

But when he reached his desk, Margot was sitting in his chair. He was genuinely surprised. She had never come to see him before. He hadn't even realized that she knew which room his lab was in, let alone in which bay he worked. He glanced at the two photos on the wall above his desk. There was an old one of his parents that he had printed out years ago, before he left for college. It reminded him of them, but it also reminded him of his old dorm room where it originally hung on the bulletin board over his bed and then a little bit of every place it had traveled with him in the decade or so since. It had its own history. Next to it there was a photo booth shot of Viki and himself. He liked that photo a lot. *He thought it looked cool.* Viki was in some sort of miniature dress, and he had on his charcoal gray suit. They were at a wedding together, and he was holding out a bottle of champagne, pretending to tip it into her mouth while she leaned forward with her left hand on her hip and open, pouting lips. He had always been privately proud of that photo, but with Margot sitting there he was suddenly embarrassed. He imagined she would think it was stupid, childish even.

She didn't think that. She thought it looked fun and care-free. She thought, with a tightening chest, that Will looked happier in the compact world of that single photo than she had ever seen him in person. In fact, she had spent some minutes studying the photo while she waited for him to arrive. But naturally she didn't mention that.

As he cautiously approached, she turned her head to face him. *He didn't have a swivel chair like Arthur; he didn't even have an office.*

"Where have you been?" It came out more anxiously than Margot had intended.

"What are you doing here?" Will countered.

"What have you been doing *not here*?" *What gibberish*, Margot thought.

Will sighed and pulled up a chair. "I was in Boston . . . visiting my old stomping grounds, I guess you could say."

Margot stood slightly to adjust her chair toward him. "Did you see Arthur?"

"Yeah." Will got the distinct feeling that she knew more about what was going on than he did, but he couldn't fathom how locking herself in a library and reading all day had given her such superb intuition. In any case, he needed someone to trust *and she was smart as hell*. He knew he could use her help, so he went on. "I know I have a lot to be angry with him for. But . . ." He paused, trying to think of the right words to convey: *I think he is a comic book–level psycho on brain-enhancing drugs, playing with potentially dangerous materials in a fully funded laboratory and trying to take over the world.* With a deep nod and all of the gravity he could voice, he said, "I think he is up to something."

Margot desperately wanted to reply: *I read his paper, and I looked up photos of him, and he has the craziest eyes, and I'm pretty sure he thinks that injecting people with that smart serum is going to fix some grand problem that I'm not even sure exists outside of his nutball head.* The only two words that left her lips were simply, "I agree."

But the way that she looked at him, showing him the full whites of her eyes and loosely clenched teeth under a trembling upper lip, convinced Will that they were on the same page. "Take a look at these photos with me." Will pulled up the pictures that he and Kate had taken in Arthur's lab and enlarged them on the screen across his desk. Just looking at them made him nervous. He had changed the security information on his tablet, but he was still worried that Arthur would figure out how to log into it somehow. *What wouldn't the crackpot do if given the opportunity?* "They're from Arthur's bench and around the lab he works in. . . . Don't ask how I got them," he added.

"He's a messy son of a bitch, isn't he?" Margot remarked dryly as she began to scroll.

Will was slightly taken aback by her tone at first, but he let it go. "He didn't used to be messy. He used to be . . . well, *shipshape*, in a word. This might sound ridiculous . . . but I think he's been injecting himself . . . with his own samples." Will felt awkward suggesting something quite so outlandish and experienced a renewed pang of guilt for being allured by the serum himself, so he half chuckled and half cringed as he said it.

"I wouldn't be surprised. *Anyone* would be tempted."

That offhand comment made Will feel decidedly akin to a very small insect, so he continued to talk over the uneasy sensation, instinctively and preemptively prodding, "You wouldn't, I bet. Not that you would even need it."

Margot looked up from the pictures that she had been swiping across the desk, but she didn't respond to his predictable provocation. She looked back down at the photo that was currently enlarged and highlighted a bottle of something in the back of the hood, zooming in on it. "What is this?"

Will tilted his head to have a closer look. "Uh, I think that's DMSO, dimethyl sulfoxide. It's usually used in PCR." With this potentially intriguing discovery, his focus returned to the task at hand. "I can't actually think of a good reason they would have that much in the animal-work hood. Unless they're working on something new, like using it as a solvent for a different mode of uptake, which is always possible." He shrugged.

"Check their LabHub to see if they're working on any new projects where it would make sense to have DMSO on hand." She handed Will her tablet so he could look it up and then paused a moment, apparently absorbed in the photo across the desk. "There's one possibility . . ." She maintained her familiar downward gaze as she spoke, but at the moment it seemed out of shyness rather than focus. "DMSO can be used for membrane permeabilization, right?" She sounded hesitant. "I mean, I've read, that is, it has been trialed in certain cases for permeabilizing the blood-brain barrier?"

Margot finally looked up to see whether Will was following or whether he was staring, incredulous, scales fallen from his eyes, regarding her as if she was full-blown mad. He was still with her. "Do you think"—she scratched her nose and swallowed once—"do you think he could be working up something of a more . . . *permanent* nature?" She breathed. She had said the main thing she had wanted to say, what was most important. There were many more things she wanted to ask out loud, but she would need a break first.

Will paused carefully before responding, "It's possible. That would solve a lot of the problems, I guess, from his perspective." He was thinking out loud now. "It would be ideal if he didn't have to keep injecting himself, and if he wanted to make it available to the wider world, a onetime solution would certainly be easier than dosing. I don't know if it would work. Once the brain is developed, it's hard to make changes. Even the zombies—their brains have essentially been cloned. They don't always function exactly right, but I don't think you would be able to control the way that they develop to such an extent, since they are just copies." Will was tapping his fingers against the arm of his chair. He didn't notice Margot's uncharacteristically rapt attention. "If Arthur is on the drug, maybe he *is* more intelligent now. Maybe he's figured out a way—"

"Maybe he's just delusional. What are the side effects of that stuff?" Margot cut in, but Will barely noticed.

"It might work . . . on a brain that is still developing." Lines were being drawn in Will's head; links were being made. "On his desk, on Arthur's desk, when I was visiting him, just this morning, he had a stack of brochures. I didn't think anything of it this morning. Six brochures. They were for hospitals. . . . *Which were they?*" He listed them quietly to himself as he recalled each one, counting them off on his fingers. "All of those hospitals have great obstetrics departments. I wonder . . ." He finally looked at Margot. "It might work on a child's brain, you understand, while it's still developing. Probably have to be very young. Newborn maybe, if not younger."

Will shook his head to dispel his thoughts. He wasn't physically able to accept what he had just said aloud, so his mind reversed to an earlier thread. "What did you say about side effects? To be honest, it's hard to tell with the mice. They don't say a lot. The autopsies don't look great, but they live long enough—that's all you can really hope for from these kinds of long-term treatments." Will breathed. "Judging from Arthur, I'd say the main side effect is annoying the hell out of me. And there's definitely some maniacal tendencies. I think he's secretly always had those though."

Margot nodded. The weight of what he had said didn't escape her, but as with Will, the reality skimmed the surface of her skin, prickling goose bumps up and down her body, but needed time to sink in. She was used to working alone, and she suddenly felt suffocated by the bustling lab, the photo of Viki looking down from the wall, by Will himself sitting across from her. "I better get back to my desk," she floundered. She glanced at her watch. "I've been away for almost an hour." As she stood up, she breathed again. It wasn't the right way to leave, but Will didn't seem to care. They were both at a loss, *but she knew where to find him and he knew where to find her.*

———

Margot went back to the library, and Will finally got what he had come in for—the packet out of his desk drawer. He carried it home with him in his pocket and, as soon as he had closed the door to his room, used the whole bag in a single dose. When he came down from his high, he noticed his pillow was tearstained, a tumbler had been broken, and he had a cut on his left hand. He remembered smashing it against the floor, picking up a small piece of broken glass and squeezing it lightly, dropping it again as soon as he witnessed a clear drop of bright red. *Had he been trying to prove something?* He borrowed two Band-Aids from his housemate, then went out to get a burrito for dinner before going back to sleep.

Chapter Fourteen

————

The morning after, he felt like he had been drained empty, as if the whole of his ability to feel had been used up at once and there was nothing left to distract him. He liked that. He didn't like feeling angry or jealous or lonely or *responsible*. Will knew fresh feelings would flood back in if his mind wandered forward or back, an inch in any direction, so he tried not to think. He looked over the cut on his hand in the morning light. It had mostly dried up and scabbed over; it wasn't as bad as it had seemed after all. The worst part was the hazy memory of determined self-harm, seemingly without reason. Any indication of what had motivated the act escaped him. Like any hangover, memories and emotions would sneak back in slowly and with strength proportionate to their consequence. Reluctantly, Will began to let them in piece by piece, starting with the clearer memories of the day before and the sentiments that followed with them. The morning he spent in Boston, his anger toward Arthur, whatever it was he felt toward Kate—he couldn't put his finger on it, but it made his stomach tilt backward and gave him an uneasy pressure at the base of his throat. His conversation with Margot. He shivered. There was too much to take in at once, ever. He gave up, rolled over, and went back to sleep.

————

When it came to matters that didn't directly involve him, Will's general mantra was live and let live. If he saw Jenny ruining her samples by adding the wrong reagent and causing them to degrade, one after the other, he turned a blind eye. If he were to see someone being mugged across the road, he assumed he would do the same. As he saw it, there was little he was qualified to do that would help. If anything, he was sure he would make the situation worse. So, when he awoke for the second time that morning, and this time got out of bed and dressed, he resolved to do just that—ignore everything. He wondered what had even driven him to visit Boston in the first place. Curiosity and anger, he supposed, but now that he was feeling-free, he was also feeling free. He went off to work, determined to continue with business as usual.

———

"Hey, Jon, think fast." Will tossed a sterile scraper across the hood. They were standing side by side, plating cells, continuing with their work on another project. Science was all about pivoting, always had been. This was part of their normal routine, and Will enjoyed being back. He noted how little he appreciated these small tasks, so seemingly simple yet so important to the project as a whole, and he mused about scientific advancements, improvements, and ingenuity. *In twenty years,* he thought, *this will all be done by robots. The technology exists already. There are just too many goddamn postdocs to keep busy . . . It's a privilege, though, working with one's hands. In twenty years, no one's going to know what a cell scraper is. No one's going to stand for hours leaning into a ventilated box. No one is going to under-*

stand what the hell it is they're actually doing. Furthermore, he considered what a privilege it was to work with Jon. They worked so well together. Jon was so diligent, preparing samples for Will to run. He was so thorough researching and writing background for papers so Will could focus on the *important stuff.* And he was smart—Will could trust him to do a quality job, without having to look over his shoulder. They truly made a perfect team. On more mercurial days, Will would wish for a PhD student, someone he could boss around and, more importantly, someone who could complete all of the practical busywork, leaving Will to the theoretical. But today he could do nothing but the empirical. His capacity for theorizing was at an all-time low.

"Were you really up in Boston the last two days?" Jon had waited until they were about halfway through the stack of petri dishes before bringing it up. Plastic scraped against plastic as he brought the next one forward.

"Yes." Will cringed as he admitted it, but he lifted a gloved finger in the direction of his ear, blaming his instinctive reaction on the sliding sound of the thin, hard plastic.

"Find out anything?" Jon glanced sideways. "Or did you at least punch your old buddy in the face for me?" He mimed half of a right hook, then put his hand back to his task.

"Not really . . ." There was no point in telling Jon what he had found out in Boston if he was trying to ignore it himself, and he had been succeeding for most of the morning. "And almost."

Jon laughed. "Too bad. Eh, we'll get him next time."

Will agreed out loud, but if he was being honest, he wasn't so sure. He knew what Jon couldn't—that Arthur would be untouchable now. They continued plating in silence, but the simple monotonous task left far too much space for Will's thoughts to wander. Their short conversation began to pull at his subconscious. Flashes of righteous reveries snapped through his mind. He had triumphed over Arthur. He had saved someone, or he had prevented something terrible from happening. It didn't really matter what. The point was *he was a savior*. And yet he was no closer to figuring out how he had accomplished the vague feat.

A half hour later, they finished plating, and he left Jon in order to focus on the samples he had prepared at the beginning of the week. He had to finish up with them soon or they would die. There were constant time constraints in his lab work. In biology, things did not last long: cells did not last long, mice did not last long, people did not last long. Occasionally, Will thought perhaps he should have chosen a field of study from among the inorganic sciences. He could leave a mineral sample at his bench for a literal lifetime, and little would have changed. Though he knew it was a fleeting feeling, he smiled at the idea of looking into a microscope and knowing exactly what might be seen—a certain color, a certain shape, a certain size, something reliable, expected. Not the anguish of seeing nothing when there should be colonies, infection when there should be order, cells living, dying, dividing. Of course, there was always a prediction. There was always what one *should* see, what one *hopes to* see, and then *whatever the fuck the universe decides to show you*. It might take a single attempt to produce a conclusive result, or it might take one hundred or one thousand. It simply might not be in the cards, the nature of experiments being that you cannot place bets on them.

Will had, for the first time, reached a stage in his life where he did not have a hypothesis. There was no expected result. He wasn't even sure if he had a preferred result. If he let himself be honest as he had been, somewhere, repressed, during the previous night, he did not know what to wish for. He hated Arthur, *and Arthur was obviously nuts*, but he had been right about one thing. They *were* similar.

Will had resisted taking the Brill pill himself, but only by a hair. He was abruptly sure that if Margot hadn't been in the library that night, he would have gone through with it. Besides, Will bargained, what was so different between that and what he had illicitly taken just the night before? Sure, the e-potion had gone through rigorous testing and had recently been pre-scribed to patients on a trial basis, whereas the Brill pill was highly experimental, with potential addictive and long-term effects. On paper, as in his circulatory system, they would both just be considered illicit drugs. Will recognized a differ-ence between temporary hormonal rebalancing and radical alterations in the chemicals that controlled the brain, but he couldn't help drawing parallels. Despite himself, he had started to admire Arthur. Maybe he had more courage than Will had thought, *more than Will had had*. What was so terribly wrong with wanting to improve the world? It was falling apart. So what if the next generation was smarter, *better*? Was that not what they needed? No one had been able to solve climate change, no one had been able to create peace or stop hunger, or whatever other tens of thousands of problems continually plagued everyone everywhere. There were new viruses mu-tating and spreading every year. That was something Will was able to visualize. And from this valetudinarian perspective, he began to see the world as a cesspool and Arthur's arcane panacea as its only hope.

Will shook his head. "Get back to fucking work, asshole,"

he whispered aloud, scolding himself. If he let his mind wander, there was no telling where it would lead him. He didn't trust himself; he never had. Looking back, he had always gone to someone else for a conscience. Kate had invariably steered him in the right direction with a logical, reasoned response. She had convinced him on more than one occasion not to go over Carlos's head for approval of new animal protocols, and she was right—Carlos could have ruined him. Ethically, Eva had been indecisive and wishy-washy. She had once convinced him to give out test answers in exchange for a pair of shitty concert tickets. Her taste in music was god-awful, but he had agreed, thinking he might at least get a blow job out of it. Then she had had the audacity to go ahead and give his ticket away to her best friend. Admittedly, *he had deserved that.* It only occurred to him now that he had never consulted Viki on moral matters.

———

Around two o'clock, he went out to grab lunch. There were dozens of food carts that stationed themselves outside of the building every day, lining both sides of the main street that ran through the med campus. They started turning up in the morning around nine thirty and slowly built from a sparse smattering to a bustling bazaar by about half past eleven. By two in the afternoon, things had calmed down. Those who had stretched out the last of their supplies had already gone, but the majority remained, and you could still hear a few hawking shouts bouncing off of the brick walls, up and down the road. By three, it would be a ghost town. Between them, they offered pretty much every food you could imagine pan-frying. Will usually went for one of the Asian dishes, a pile of rice or noodles topped with a modest amount of vegetables, a choice of meat, and some somewhat distinguishing sauce all glued together with peanut oil. Today, however, he chose a round, compact arepa and ate it quickly, sitting outside in spite of the chill, on one of the painted white wrought iron benches in the garden space behind his building. It was a charming place to sit amidst a sterile work environment, but more importantly, entering from the back of the building when he was finished meant that he could casually pass by the library on his way back into lab.

———

He stopped outside the entrance to the library for several minutes, opening and closing his tablet while staring blankly down the hall in front of him and debating whether to go in. There was always a History of Medicine exhibit on display in the hallway, something fascinating and grotesque, like war amputees or "circus freaks." But he couldn't see what was showing currently from his perpendicular angle. Anyway, he assumed in a hundred years or so the medicine they practiced now would seem barbaric. *As if it didn't already*. He could picture it on either side as he peered down the hall: sharp, full-color, life-size photographs of brains propagating in jars. *Practically science fiction*.

He turned away from the library entrance toward the front of the building, facing the wall that looked out onto the street. Hanging between two large windows was a lone en-larged photograph of a slide containing stained cells, which had been framed and called art. Will had never stained a slide himself; he just punched in the settings. A machine would wash it with antibodies, and he would simply adjust the filters on the microscope, sending the images straight to his tablet. He could tweak them from there. No wonder Arthur had overtaken them so quickly—Will had kept *everything* on his tablet. He groaned, mentally kicking himself, the acid sick feeling rising slowly through his chest.

But then he thought of his grandfather's speckled paper-and-card-stock composition notebook: unlocked, unconventional, and yet comparatively ironclad. The thought of it calmed him. It made him smile, and in this nostalgia, his fleeting desire for a tête-à-tête seemed suddenly unimportant. Gratefully giving up on the task he had been reluctant to undertake in the first place, he continued past the front of the library and was making his way confidently back to his desk when Margot caught up to him. She must have seen him loitering.

"Hey." She spoke softly, but she reached out and touched his arm to get his attention.

"Hey. Sorry, I was going to come in." Will didn't have an excuse for changing his mind, so he left it at that. "How are you?"

"Fine." She looked at him like that was the weirdest question he could have asked her and then shocked him by saying it out loud. "Why would you ask me that?"

"What? I mean, isn't it like polite, or normal, or something?" He tried to start edging away.

"Excuse me, but I think we're beyond *normal*. What is going *on* with you?" The aggrieved look, a perfect mix of confusion and disappointment, across her face made Will feel instantly guilty. *That expression* was the real reason he had chosen not to go into the library. "Did you get the message I sent you last night?"

Will could barely recall it at first. He had seen the message, but it had been after he had taken the e-potion. Remembering it now brought back a rush of associated feelings that culminated in a burning in his chest so strong he was forced to lean slightly forward. The idea that they could take this information to an authority figure, that the NHPD would give a shit about a blue-blooded lab rat shooting up nameless concoctions when there were criminals supplying the city with actual physical guns and cocaine. Even Ethics would have difficulty stretching the thin evidence without creating several large holes in the case. And going to Carlos with the information—ha! The Goody Two-shoes, high-and-mighty attitude of the whole thing—it was ridiculous. *Puerile.* "I went to sleep pretty early." He breathed out.

Margot shrugged with her entire body, incredulous, pointing out in a single motion that it was well into the afternoon and that even if he had gone to bed early, *which she doubted*, he would have had plenty of time to read it this morning.

"Look, can't we just leave it?" He felt a sudden desperation. Finally, he pleaded, "Que será, será, or whatever."

This was the first time Will had ever seen Margot actually look like a librarian. She paused to take in what he had said, pulled her hair back into a tight bun, and angled her head downward in order to peer at him over her glasses. He would have laughed out loud if he wasn't petrified. But rather than shushing or scolding, she took his hand and firmly led him down the hall to the lounge. She pulled him over to one of the red-and-wood dorm-style couches and sat down across from him.

"My aunt was in a skiing accident a few years ago." She

hesitated. "They have skiing in the winter up in the mountains near where I grew up—in eastern Tennessee . . . we used to go up every year . . ." Margot blushed. In the middle of her lecture, she found herself wanting to share with Will minor unnecessary facts about herself, and she faltered, shaking her head. "It doesn't matter." She swallowed, gathering her thoughts.

Will smiled, encouraging her, despite his fear of where the story was going.

"Anyway, she hit her head. She was in the hospital for months. There was some minor brain damage, and they were able to perform a regenerative transplant for her."

He held his breath for the moral.

"It went really well. She still has physical therapy occasionally, but she's fine and she's herself. Before regenerative medicine, she would have been in a wheelchair, brain damaged. She might not even know me anymore. It's incredible."

"That's great." He wasn't sure what else to say to that.

"I really believe in your work. I just want you to know that." She took a short breath. "But . . . I knew a girl in college. She was a friend. Her grandmother was deteriorating. One organ at a time, she was falling to pieces. It's normal; she was closing in on ninety-five. This girl's mother, the woman's daughter, kept putting her through regenerative treatments. First her kidneys, then her liver, and eventually her heart. Like car parts . . . She might still be alive," Margot reflected. "I met her during graduation. She loved her granddaughter, that was obvious, but she had cried during the ceremony, and I don't think that was the reason. I shook her hand later on in the day. . . it felt like shaking hands with a plastic bag. Her handshake had that disposable feeling to it. She said, 'Congratulations.' And she laughed. 'It's high time for me to grad-uate,' she said, and she looked up into the sky." Margot stared out of the window behind him, not allowing him to look directly into her moist eyes.

Will swallowed. He still didn't know exactly where she was going with all this, but he felt like it was his turn to say something. "Chatty today, aren't you?" he mumbled, turning his head slightly in discomfort. As soon as the insensitive quip had left his lips, he wished he could take it back.

Margot did not reply. He sighed. "I guess that's why I call them 'zombies.' So I don't have to think about the reality. I used to volunteer with the zombies when I was an undergrad." Will lifted his arms out straight, imitating the fictional mon-ster, then immediately put them down again when he realized he was not going to get a response. "The old ones are disgust-ing. I'm sorry, but it's true. You're never going to stop people with money to spend from wasting it on misguided treatments though. That practice goes back as far as medicine does." He shrugged. "And they're harmless. It's the younger ones, the ones like your aunt but the less lucky ones. When they wake up and something is *changed* . . . it was harder to spend time with them. They're crazy, and they know it. It's the worst-case scenario." He debated whether to go on. He *could* go on for hours, detailing every little misapplication and advantage taken that upset him about the business he was in. But he didn't really like talking about it. It depressed him, and he was frustrated with Margot for bringing it up. "So what's your point anyway?"

"I was the first person in my family to go to college." She looked lost in her words, uncertain how to proceed. It pissed him off.

"Oh my God. I get it—you're *so frickin' awesome*, I can barely stand it." He was becoming irritated with all of the apparent smoke screens, and he started to get up to leave.

Margot reached her hand across his path, placing it down firmly on the outside arm of the couch and cutting him off. She laughed. "Sorry. I sound like a fucking after-school special." Her voice wavered over the expletive as she tried to make light of the moment. After he had sat back down, she lifted her hand and pressed it against her forehead with an open palm. "Ah, I'm not even sure if this makes sense to me, but what I am trying to say is . . . it doesn't seem right to make a decision about how someone else has to live their life. Like, my friend's grandmother, that wasn't what she wanted. But she was old, and they declared her unfit to make her own decisions, so what could she do? If Arthur really is devising what we think, an injection that can modify the way the brain develops, he would be completely altering the entire lives of these children without their consent."

Will was taking in slowly what she was trying to get across, and in his hasty desperation to somehow, someway avoid the conversation he was already knee-deep in, he reverted to teasing. "And the part about you being a first-generation Yalie—that was just general bragging rights?" He cringed as he said it. For some reason, he always knew the right words to get under her skin, he always said them out loud, and he always regretted it immediately.

Margot blushed and replied resentfully, "I'm sure the only reason I got in is because I'm from the ass crack of nowhere." She had momentarily been tempted to assume her bragging rights, own them, and stuff them down his throat, but, as usual, her modesty prevailed. She knew his temper.

She had cornered him, and she had expected him to lash out. "No. It was just . . . it was a really big decision for me to come here. The distance doesn't seem very far now, but at the time it was impossibly far. I couldn't conceive of it. I was scared shitless just to get on a plane. Look, I'm glad that I did it, but if someone else had made the decision for me, I think I would always be bitter about it. I would never feel like I was in the right place. If these newborns, when they grow up, *if* they grow up—*and that is an entirely separate conversation*—if they find out what made them the way that they are, don't you think they'll, like, freak out?" She paused, then filled her own silence quickly. "I know this is far from the only issue here, and *I know* it's not a perfect analogy, but honestly, I'm not sure there is one for this situation."

Will thought she was nuts. He thought the whole *situation* was nuts, but she definitely had more than a few screws loose. He desperately wanted to go back to his lab work, to just do the most tedious thing he could think of and let the day go by. Maybe he would finally update the still-empty spreadsheet where he was meant to be carefully listing the two hundred cages with the numbers and sexes of each and every one of the mice inside. That would take at least a few glorious hours. But he always felt compelled to reply to her, like scratching an itch. He knew it would be healthier for the both of them to just leave it be. "You think that giving someone an advantage is taking away their freedom? No one gets to decide whether or not to be born, and that has to be the biggest decision of all. I don't see the difference."

"I don't see why everyone seems to think being clever is an advantage. Being clever doesn't necessarily make you a good person . . . or happy."

"Let me guess—did you get teased in grade school?" He had never felt so bitter toward her, and he didn't understand or care why he should. "I'm willing to bet they didn't tease you for being clever. They teased you for being arrogant about it."

"I guess you'd know from experience," she said quietly. "I wasn't teased. I was barely noticed by most people, but I never minded. As long as I have been able to find someone I can trust, and I have." She glanced into Will's eyes and then looked back toward the window behind him. "I'm still lonely though. You are too. We both spend more time in this building than we spend in our own homes. In our own thoughts, even."

The acid in Will's stomach was rising and falling, burning and releasing and making him seasick. He couldn't figure out how he had gotten to this point, when he had made this friend or whatever she was. He preferred Jon. Jon asked simple questions with, at most, a mild concern. He didn't try to tear Will down from the inside with his words. *Just words.* And yet when he looked at Margot, all he could see was compassion. It made him nauseous. He had to get out of there. *Now.*

"Look, I have a gel running. I have to check on it." Will got up and walked quickly toward the door. The threshold stood like a beacon before him, relief washing over him as he moved to escape. But a nagging feeling in the back of his mind stopped him from leaving without saying something kind. He turned back momentarily. "You know it's not going to happen overnight, right? I can tell that you're worried. We're not going to wake up tomorrow in a deranged new world. You'll still be sitting in the library reading the last book on earth that you haven't read, and I'll still be right down the hall, twiddling my thumbs. Arthur might be somehow enhanced, but he can't speed up time. It will be years before he can develop something like what we are imagining . . . if it's even possible." Will paused, pressing his hand against the doorframe, then pushing off into the hallway. He sighed and wearily saluted. "I'll see you soon."

PART II

Three Years Later

Chapter Fifteen

————

W ill and Jon were working on a new project. They had
made a lot of progress with the zombies in the last three
years. Where Arthur had seemingly gone off the grid, they had
taken over the field. They had finally published a paper on the
use of the Brill pill technology in mice with regenerated brain
tissue, and the drug was undergoing preclinical trials under the
less satisfying title of Einzitec. In addition, they had published a
series of papers on methods and mechanisms regarding drug-
delivery systems crossing the blood-brain barrier and a review
on regenerated brain function.

The new project they were working on involved growing
brain tissue from iPSCs and iMSCs induced from well-cata-
logued samples. The primary focus was to look for changes in
the regeneration potential based on isolation and selection
methods and conditions: pluripotent versus multipotent, carbon dioxide levels, oxygen saturation, and the balance of cofac-
tors in the media. Will had been sequencing each tissue sample
and looking for differences in gene expression from the
source material. Small differences in the RNA levels of certain
genes could help to pinpoint what might be going wrong and
at what stage during regrowth. The regeneration process was
getting faster. It took about forty-eight hours, give or take, to
grow a large enough sample, depending on the tissue type—

glial cells took slightly longer to divide than neuronal cells, for instance—and between him and Jon, they could grow several specimens at a time. So, even though it took only half an hour to sequence a sample now, and they had three working sequencers in the lab, they were always backed up. Of course, they did have to let Jenny have a sequencer to herself so she wouldn't wreck theirs with one of her botched experiments.

This left Will with a lot of downtime compared to usual. He didn't always know what to do with himself when he wasn't staring at the sequencer. It was like waiting for a kettle to boil. If he kept his eyes on it, he became increasingly anxious for the dramatic moment when the whirring would cease, only then to sit through the short dead silence that followed, while data was transferred to the sequencer's computer to be analyzed during the next sample's run. In some ways, his new routine of loitering and lingering was more miserable than having the constant pressure to get things prepped for a specific time. He had to be back at the sequencer to change the sample every half hour, and he couldn't get *anything* done in just half an hour, so he felt like the time was wasted. He would start reading some background paper, then become distracted by a reference and then again by a reference of the first reference, or Jon would swing by and exchange a few words and the time would be gone.

During other thirty-minute spells, he was meant to be looking for new positions. He had stayed on to do a second postdoc in the same lab. Things had been going well, and he had felt an imagined obligation to finish something of what he had started there. But time and funding were running out. Joe had already left. Will found that he was jealous of Joe. Joe was lighthearted, and it made him motile. Will could physically feel himself dragging—his shoes skimmed against the floor as he walked, his very body craving friction.

Often he didn't bother trying to do anything productive between runs. He just walked down the hall to the library to chat with Margot for twenty minutes.

————

They spent a lot of time together without noticing it. That is, Will did not notice it. Margot did. Her life had changed significantly over the past three years, just a little bit at a time, but she was aware of it, and she had let it happen. She was proud of herself for that, no matter the consequences. To an outsider, it probably seemed like nothing. Margot was still Margot. She still worked at the library, she still spent the majority of her time reading, she was still quiet, she was still modest, she was still sitting in the same chair at the same desk every day. But these days, Will dropped by the desk, not once a month or even once a week, but every day. Not to trick her into doing his research for him, but just to say hello or to ask for her opinion or to hear her voice. And while she used to sit at that same desk every evening after her hours were over, now she had started volunteering at the hospital. She had told herself, *Reading is wonderful. It shows you so many things you will never get to see. You spend too much time reading. Do something.* And she had.

Sometimes, when he was free, or when he was waiting, Will came to the hospital with her. They worked with the zombies together. They led them through physical therapy exercises, they retaught them to read, they played memory and word association games. There were more zombies in the ward than ever before, and the numbers were growing. Without volunteers, the program would fall apart. Already these undead were being sent home without proper rehabilitation. Margot could see where it was heading. A disaster was just around the corner. She had always thought carefully about the future—causes and effects, alternate choices, alternate paths, alternate destinies. Perhaps that is what had made it so hard for her to move away from home in the first place. Perhaps that is why she hadn't moved again. But for once in her life, she let it go. The disaster that was just around the corner was more personal than she let on, and she lied ruthlessly to herself to maintain the reverie.

Chapter Sixteen

————

Will was going to pick up the ring that Friday afternoon. He had started looking at rings six months earlier, six months before their five-year anniversary. As five years was approaching, he had thought, *Time to make a decision, one way or the other.* And he didn't like the idea of loss. He wasn't a loser. He couldn't lose someone as special as Viki— she *was* special, *wasn't she?* She was beautiful, he knew, but he was certain that she was smart, and he was *sure* that she was kind. She called him whenever she heard his favorite song on the radio.

And yet he hadn't told Jon about the proposal. He always got the feeling that Jon didn't totally approve of Viki. They got along okay the few times they had met, but they came from different worlds. Jon's wife was down-to-earth. She was pretty, but she was also plain. She wore muted colors, comfortable clothing that hung loosely around her, covering up rather than drawing attention to her features. She was such a "mom." Viki would never be a "mom" no matter how many kids they had. But she would be a wonderful mother; he was *sure* of that too. Will would like to be a "dad," he mused. He wanted to play catch or barbecue steaks or do whatever it was that "dads" did. His kids would be scientists too—girls, he hoped. *They were certainly more manageable.* And one day, somewhere down the line, he would be a grandfather. He hadn't told Margot about the proposal, either. He convinced himself the reason was that he wanted to know what Viki's answer would be before he said anything to anyone. And besides, he was *sure* that Margot wouldn't care.

———

Will took the train down to New York on Friday night. His plan was simple. He didn't want to do anything too elaborate or too public. He had always felt when he saw elaborate proposals on TV, or rather heard about them from Jenny, that if the girl said no, the guy would be left looking unbelievably stupid. On the other hand, if the girl said yes, one could never be totally sure she didn't just feel bad saying no in front of so many people, and after all of the effort and money spent on the thing. So his simple plan was to take her out to a nice dinner and, having dropped off his spare key to her apartment with a friend who would decorate while they were out, return to a flat full of flowers, drop a knee, and wing it.

He booked the kind of place she liked for dinner. The restaurant was loud and crowded, and he had had to book a month in advance for a cramped space where most of the clientele were wearing some form of involved sneakers. But the food was top-notch, if sparse, and the cocktails were, if half the usual size, at least twice the strength. They sat close to each other because of the small table, on a bench side by side. Will appreciated the intimacy—he couldn't have planned it better himself. Looking out into the low-lit room, a perfect perch from which to playfully comment on strangers and their food, they settled into a shared conviviality. A waiter with a knowing smile brought over two flutes of champagne, placing one down in front of each of them.

"Happy anniversary." Will raised a glass.

Viki smiled warmly. "Happy anniversary, babe. I love you."

She kissed him, and he was suddenly caught up in the soft kaleidoscope glitter of the art deco chandelier and the fastidiously bustling tempo of the dinner service, governing the pace of every conversation in the room. He caught the attention of a waiter who was flickering by and ordered a bottle of champagne. A glass was not sufficient—not for her, not tonight. He ordered half the items on the menu, though he knew she wouldn't finish more than half of one, and demanded they be sent out one at a time so that they could be enjoyed fresh. He became who she wanted him to be when he was around her, and he prized this version of himself. He wanted to please her, and he knew how. He had control over his actions. In his day-to-day work, he was successful through intuitive, assured reasoning and in part by chance, but he didn't possess the pompous poise Viki forced upon him. The two days a week he spent in New York, he lived on a high. He wondered if it would be exhausting twenty-four seven.

"I'm just going to wash my hands. I'll be right back." Will stood and walked to the far side of the restaurant, dodging empty plates and swaying martini glasses. Locked in the bathroom, he took out the last bag of the e-potion he had left. He spoke to his reflection. "If there was ever a time . . . it shouldn't have to be now," he admitted. He replaced the packet carefully in his right pants pocket, washed his hands, and returned to join Viki.

———

Sitting in the cab on the way back to her apartment, he became nervous. His heart was beating fast, and his palms were sweating. He kept thinking of words, phrases he had heard before: *I love you. Do you remember that time? All of my life. You know me. I keep thinking. I need you. Forever. Do I make you happy? I want to make you happy.* He tried to filter out the ones that applied to him, that applied to *them*.

"You're being suspiciously quiet tonight." Viki squinted at him like she knew something.

"It's been a long week, that's all." It had been a long week. Will had spent three nights volunteering in the hospital with Margot that week, and each time they had stayed until well past midnight.

Viki unlocked the door to her apartment, and they walked through into the living room. The flowers were gathered on the coffee table and on the side table next to the couch. He had thought $300 would have gone further, but he wasn't disappointed. He was happy that it wasn't over the top. Viki smiled and looked back at him. He walked forward to stand in front of her and got down on one knee. All of the phrases that had been running through his mind in the cab on the way over deserted him.

"You're so beautiful. Will you marry me?"

"Yes, of course!" She giggled. "About damn time," she blurted out gently. She was breathing heavily; she was happy. Will was relieved. *He had done it*, and he had done it well, *or well enough anyway*. It was over. The hard part was over. Now everything else would begin: Viki, stunning in a white dress; his proud parents looking on; the vows; the rings; a big house; a large family to fill it. The rest would be easy.

Viki held out her hand for the ring and waited for him to

stand up before turning her face to be kissed. "Let's open a bottle of wine." She laughed out loud, and the sound of it glanced against her dangling earrings and struck him like Cupid's arrow. He held her close on the couch as they merrily poured out the bottle, talking about how they had met, where they had been, what they had done, what they would do, and where they would go. Then they went to bed together, intoxicated with wine and fantasy.

Chapter Seventeen

———

Back in Cambridge, Arthur, despite a seeming lack of academic presence, was still hard at work. He had barely slept a consecutive five hours in the last three years. He spent nights toiling away at his master plan and days scraping together just enough data so as not to lose his funding. It is a testament to how much money floats, carefree, through the ether surrounding Harvard that no one was particularly bothered by the fact that, on paper, he was spending more than twice the cost of what he was producing.

Every night, as soon as everyone else in the lab had packed up and gone home, Arthur rolled up one sleeve, took out a small sample of the smart serum, and injected it into his right arm. He had been improving it. It no longer gave him the sweats, and it no longer made him quite so edgy, though perhaps he had merely developed a tolerance. He often discovered, as he lifted the syringe to his vein, that he had incrementally increased the dose. After administering this injection, he waited about half an hour for it to fully kick in. As he waited, he ate a bag of Fritos from the vending machine and downed a twenty-ounce Diet Coke to keep himself awake for the coming hours. At first, all he felt was mild dry mouth. The Fritos began to stick to the sides of his tongue and scrape the insides of his cheeks, but the flavor was sensational washed down with the tingling, sweet, fizzy crack-pop of the Coke. He figured if he was going to endanger his body for his mind's sake, he might as well eat junk food too. It was guilt-free and saccharine-salty heaven.

Gradually his thoughts began to move faster, jerking, jumping, skidding as they picked up momentum. Eventually they sped through his mind, racing forward and careening backward, bypassing each other like cars shooting up and down an eight-lane freeway. And his consciousness grew larger, ballooning to the size of the room he stood small in. He could see every corner plainly. He had the volume to catalogue every thought and the capacity to recall each of them at will. Arthur *loved* this feeling. It was so much better even than the hard-earned accomplishment of an ambition that had been difficult to achieve. It was the feeling of having no limits, or at least not knowing of them—like learning the basics of a new language, before the nuances and the arbitrary rules, singular declensions, and rare tenses are realized. Arthur had never struggled to pick up such tedious yet vital details, but there were several instances in his career where he could have chosen an easier path. He never did, and now he would never have to.

He spent the remainder of each night tinkering, testing, trialing, and theorizing. He rode the elevator down to the basement to visit the mice often. Although practically speaking they were his test subjects, the truth was that they had also been his closest companions during those three years. By the end of the first year, Arthur had come up with a rudimentary version of what he wanted: a permanent solution to his own issues of brain lust. He gave the newborn mice the formula that would change their tiny minds and their short lives, and he watched them grow up together, to see how they would interact.

In Arthur's warped mind, he had expected a heightened intelligence to bring a heightened civility to the creatures. And, surprisingly, no amount of enhancement to his own intelligence was able to show him that he was dead wrong. He injected and observed the mice for six months to discover that they were as vile and homicidal as ever. They simply went about it in a more convoluted way. They teamed up. They went after each other in their sleep. They devised schemes and strategies, cornering each other in the playful igloos that were the central and sole structures in their cages.

So Arthur had been forced to get more creative. He would not give up on them, his friends, his comrades, struggling right before his eyes. He dispatched with the lot of them, breaking neck after neck, leaving a pile of small furry corpses, which, once tipped into a bag marked BIOHAZARD, disappeared from the world and his mind. He ordered a new batch of cronies. The next batch he was ever certain would be better. They would be cleaner; they would be kinder—he would *make sure of that.*

Employing knowledge gained from the work on the e-potion that he had done with Will years before, and that had been continued by others in his lab, Arthur spent the next two years of nights fiddling with traits. Using a similar gene-manipulation therapy to the one he had developed to permanently enhance brain function, he now played with the variables of emotions and behavioral characteristics. In the past, his research had been undertaken with the intention of imparting feeling in the case of a brain that had lost the link of empathy. But now, with loftier goals in mind, he was also able to remove feeling. He could grow a sociopathic mind if that was what he wanted, or he could pick and choose, with an adequate degree of accuracy, which key features he thought most valuable and disregard those that he viewed as inferior or damaging. There were certainly traits he would forego in himself if it were possible, though in a catch-22 the traits that worsened the quality of his life were the traits he would choose to keep by virtue of them. In his mind, Arthur surveyed the pointed faces of each of his compadres, beginning with the two black-and-white splotched sisters he had owned as pets in his childhood and leading up to the last soft brown wretch he had snapped the life out of. And he chose carefully, as he saw fit.

With a few small slices and dices and several iterations, he rewired the neuronal circuitry. He took away traits associated with aggression, carefully wiping away the anger, the cruelty, the predatory nature, the urge to hunt, the survival instinct to kill or be killed. And he enhanced the traits that promoted caring, kindness, goodwill—the traits of good mothers and good neighbors. Of course, the genes were not specifically labeled as such, but the data existed—data that associated different expression patterns with different attributes, and he had compiled it and analyzed it and done his very best.

The long and short of it was that at the end of three years, Arthur was very close to putting into action his particular plan. He lorded over his cages of well-behaved specimens. Not one of them had sunk claws or teeth into another, not one of them had devoured their own young or torn the ear from a sibling or ripped the genitals from a cousin. They were quiet, peaceful even. In the still, Arthur considered his next steps.

In the daytime, Arthur did not take the injections. He knew his body could not sustain being on the drugs twenty-four hours a day. If he allowed himself constant access, he would deteriorate quickly, and in any case, the compounds weren't inherently addictive. They only became addictive when he succumbed to the overwhelming feeling of helplessness that accompanied the hours between waking and starting his night's work. So, during the day, he switched off. He was no one in particular and nowhere in particular and, though he couldn't realize it in his state, his purported project and once-cherished career suffered. Each time he tuned out the people around him, he lost a little bit of humanity and he gained a little bit of insanity. He was creeping slowly, day by day, into the world he was creating, night by night.

Chapter Eighteen

————

Will returned from New York in a daze. The ground swam before his feet as he stepped onto the platform, but it hardly mattered; he was light enough to skip across it. It was after dark, but the streetlamps shone brighter than usual. They twinkled back and forth like Christmas lights, dazzling his eyes, while an unending string of senseless tickled thoughts ran through the back of his mind. Even the shuttle from the train station seemed to speed along. Usually it stopped for a tiresome ten minutes every two to three blocks, but this time, Will was home before he knew it. When his bedroom door clicked shut behind him, he felt liberated. He looked across the disheveled, dreary room he had inhabited for the last five years, and it dissolved before him. For once since he had moved to Yale, it wasn't the only thing in his view. There was something concrete in his future to look forward to.

Though it was late, he called his parents to tell them the good news. They were proud as ever, wishing him all the best, sending their love to Viki, asking when they could expect to see the both of them again, and when they would set a date. Will was contented to hear affirmation and endorsement from the two most important people in his life. It didn't matter that they had only met Viki a handful of times. It didn't matter that since he had moved to Yale they only saw

him three or four times a year, and then only on his best behavior.

———

He took his good attitude to work with him the next day. In
between prepping and sequencing, he read diligently, he
planned new experiments, he helped train Julie, the new PhD
student. He was being productive, and as a result, he stood
slightly taller than usual. At lunchtime, he found Jon and convinced him to take a break from running genotyping gels so
they could eat together. They walked down the street to the
hospital cafeteria. Will wanted to tell Jon his good news. He
was excited that he *wanted* to share it, now that it was official. *After telling Jon, it would be easy to tell Margot.*

In the canteen, Will carried his tray uncertainly around
the food stations, bypassing the suspicious sushi and the salad
bar and going for a solid slice of pizza instead. He paid, then
walked over and placed his choice down across from Jon, who
had already gone through ahead of him and claimed a table.
Jon always knew exactly what he wanted, and he only ever
ordered one of a few ostensibly nutritious items. But instead
of commenting as he normally would, Will dove straight in.
"You'll never guess what I did this weekend." He grinned.

"Viki."

"No. I mean, yeah." Will rolled his eyes assuredly. "But
guess again."

"Uh, I have no idea, man. Come on, just tell me."

"It has to do with Viki—"

"Fuck no. You proposed?!"

"How the hell did you guess?" Will shook his head, unbelieving. "And what is this 'fuck no' about?" He tried to take it as a joke.

"Oh, come on, you've been planning your wedding since you were a little girl." Jon laughed. "I'm just surprised, you bastard. Can't believe you didn't tell me what you were up to." He played it off as a joke more successfully than Will did. "Congratulations, mister!" He hit Will hard on the arm with an open palm. "When can I start planning this bachelor shindig? *Gonna get wild.*" He raised the roof, but even Jon could see he was taking it a little too far. He quickly threw down his hands and then held the right one forward.

"Seriously though, congrats, man." They shook on it, but Jon's grasp felt heavy, and the gravity of the motion hit Will abruptly with a shallow, sinking feeling.

Of course it was far too late to cut and run from the interaction, so Will pressed on, trying to ignore the subtle tension. What else could he do? *This was his life; Jon was his friend.* He described the short and sweet proposal story, scene by scene. He smiled gratefully as Jon applauded and congratulated again and again. It was an act, so he embellished, and Jon, he supposed, embellished as well. They both played their parts to a T, and their lunch ended cheerily over facile conversations concerning party locales and booze selections.

Will was relieved when it was over. As they walked back to the lab, their discussion slipped naturally back into the comfortable work-related listing of tasks and targets, and the dialogue came more readily. Will relaxed. He rallied. He began his instinctive subconscious habit of glossing over notable details, sweeping things irretrievably under the rug. Still, he couldn't help feeling queerly bereft, as if he had left something prized behind in the cafeteria. He certainly wasn't in a hurry to tell *anyone else* his good news.

Once Will returned to the routine of his lab work, the fine point to which all of the matter in his stomach had seemed to be slowly converging soon stabilized. He often found tranquility, or rather numbness, in repetition. The rest of the afternoon passed by quickly. In between running the sequencer, Will looked at departments he might join in New York, and his good mood cautiously returned. Truth be told, he couldn't recognize precisely what had caused it to falter in the first place. That was part of what had made him uneasy, but he assumed that it had to do with Jon. And while Jon was a good friend, Viki rarely came up to New Haven. Jon hadn't had the opportunity to spend all that much time with her. So he left it at that.

———

Margot was waiting for him in the library, pretending to read something on her desk. In fact, she had been legitimately trying to read a paper on chimeric antigen receptor therapies, but she kept glancing up toward the doorway and losing her place. So, at this point, she was carrying on just for show. She had been doing this for half an hour at least, since six thirty, and it had been getting progressively worse.

Will sauntered unconvincingly in at ten past seven. "Sorry I'm late. Experiment just ran over," he mumbled. That, and he had spent half an hour debating his reflection in his tablet whether or not to cancel on volunteering with her that night. He knew after lunch that he didn't have the courage to tell her. With Jon, he had just faced disappointment. With Margot, there was a hidden guilt he couldn't seem to uncover. But he couldn't avoid her forever, *and he didn't want to.* So his reflection had won out, and he had made his way slowly to the library. In reality, he was not all that much later than usual. The only difference was his awareness. *There's nothing wrong with being a private person,* he mentally assured himself as he walked up to Margot's desk, *and it doesn't alter our relationship. Just act like nothing has changed. Nothing has changed.*

He doesn't look any different, Margot thought when Will walked in at ten past seven. *Though he is late.* She looked at her watch, surprised and a little embarrassed to find that he was in fact only a few minutes later than usual. She supposed she couldn't help paying particular attention tonight, though it irked her that she couldn't. Margot, in her infinite wisdom, did not let slide her dedication to reading all forms of media, including social, and she had been keeping up in that specific field more and more studiously over the last three years. It hadn't been difficult for her to discern within a few swipes what had happened over the weekend. But as Will approached her desk, she reminded herself, *It's not your business, really. He wasn't single before; he's not single now. Just act like nothing has changed. Nothing has changed.*

"Well?" Will took a final step forward toward the desk. Margot hadn't moved. She had just been staring straight at him from the moment he had entered the room. The look she had fixed on him had made his hands go numb. As he teetered at the end of her gaze, waiting for her to snap out of it, he felt a sweet shooting sensation moving from just between his eyes to the pit of his stomach, catching slightly on the way down in his throat and producing a dripping umami at the back of it. He swallowed, she smiled, and he relaxed.

"Let's go." She threw her things in her bag and brushed past him, her friction bridging the inches between them and dragging him along beside her.

―――――

Before starting their shift, they ate a quick dinner in the hospital cafeteria. Margot always packed a sandwich, and Will almost always bought something cheap and unhealthy. But since he had already been to the cafeteria once that day, he chose dubiously from the salad bar. She followed behind him, as usual, giving tips and keeping him company.

"I'd go for the cucumbers; the lettuce is always wilted by this time of day." She pointed at the crisp round disks. "And you should get some protein—beans, or they do grilled chicken behind the counter."

"I don't want any of your freaking beans, lady. What do you think I am, a rabbit?" He held the tongs up like ears and scrunched his nose. It was easy to fall back into the short, lighthearted sketches they played out each day as they went through the familiar routine. It was impossible not to. "Let's find that chicken you were talking about." He looked down tragically at the handful of cucumbers and three broccoli florets on his plate. "This is sad. I gotta get you to start making me some of those killer sandwiches you're always packing." He smiled slyly.

"You wish."

"Come on, I'll make it worth your while." He had lost where he was going with this but decided he better play it off like he meant it, so he raised the pitch of his voice at the end to imply he knew not what.

"What can you give me that I would want?" Margot replied from the heart. The words had come out involuntarily, straight up and serious, but she shook her head playfully to ease her tension.

Still, it hit him like a gust of wind, blowing through his body and rocking every one of the things he was sure of. He dropped the subject and picked up a spoonful of beans. "I don't think rabbits eat beans, actually." He tipped them out onto his plate.

They sat mechanically at the same table where they always sat. It was in the corner of the room, by the window. Will went to the cafeteria often with other people, but he never sat at that table with anyone else. Margot went to the cafeteria often by herself, but she never sat at that table alone. They began to eat in silence, an easy silence that Will had gotten used to over the years. Margot could be chatty, but she was sometimes quiet for long stretches. He wondered what she was thinking about all the time. He probably should have figured it out, but instead he imagined she was thinking about the world, and her books, and her family back in Tennessee, and the mountains she grew up in the shadow of, and what to put in the next glorious sandwich she planned to make. He peeked over and watched as she took a large bite. Today it was turkey and cheese, avocado, and peppers. He imagined that when she put together everything she had learned in her life, it fit like a puzzle and became the key to a secret she wouldn't ever share with him. *He probably wouldn't understand it.*

But in the wake of the weekend, the silence was unsatisfying. He wanted to reach her, and he didn't feel the usual patience he had trained in himself. Even subconsciously, he used the backward logic he was so fond of. Now that he was officially taken, he felt more open than ever before. There was no more risk, and so he unwittingly relaxed enough to create one. He finished all of the food on his plate aside from the small pile of beans and then pushed the plate across the table, smiling like a jerk. But she had seen that grin so many times, he knew it wouldn't bother her. He would never smile at Viki like that. She would probably roll her eyes, or worse, ignore him. But to Margot, it was contagious. The corners of her mouth would twitch, her lips would come apart just slightly, and her small nose would lift almost imperceptibly. Will craved the feeling of anticipation it raised over the soft skin on the back of his hands.

And Margot couldn't help herself. She smiled as she always did, as she knew she always would. But then she rolled her eyes too, and as punishment, she baited him with a question she did not want to hear the answer to. "How was your weekend?" It came out in a steady, mid-pitch monotone, and she looked down at the plate in front of her directly after she said it. She picked up his used fork and stabbed the closest bean, eating them one by one.

"Really great. It's great to get out of here for a few days. New York is great. Great food. Great shopping. I mean, I'm not really into shopping, but there's just so much there. Compared to, well . . ." He lifted his arms at the city surrounding them. "Anyway, it was great." He paused, but the unanticipated agitation compelled him to tag more words onto the short silence. "You should come down sometime." He paused again for just enough time to note to himself, *Why the fuck would you say that?* then finished lamely with, "It would be fun." The image of Margot and Viki struggling through a conversation flashed through his mind. *No, actually, it would be torture.*

Margot laughed; she liked to make him uncomfortable. It made her feel less invisible, as if for once in her life she had enough pull on someone that they might notice if she fell out of their orbit. "Don't worry—you're there to see Viki. I am sure it would be too awkward to have a third wheel hanging around." She put him at ease, but silently, she couldn't help questioning, *Do you know* why *it would be awkward?*

Margot sighed involuntarily, then moved on. "I've never been much of a city girl, anyway. . . . When I was in under-grad, I used to go to New York with friends. Or we used to be friends. I haven't kept in touch." She looked off to the side as if they could be seen standing in the distance, and she wondered for a moment if she was embarrassing herself. *Well, who gives a shit?* she thought, then she jerked her head back into the conversation. "Anyway, they always wanted to go to the club or to the lounge or one of those brunch parties, some *scene.* I never understood the difference. What *is* a brunch party?" She shook her head. "I wanted to go to museums. Of course." She shrugged. "I spent hours in the public library. It's such a beautiful building. And when the museums and the libraries closed, I would meet them at a restaurant or a bar and spend the night soberly waiting for them to drink too much or get tired enough to leave . . . I'm sure it sounds lame to you. The truth is, I couldn't have afforded to party with them if I had wanted to. And they liked me because I was always there to take care of them when they overdid it." It sounded pathetic to her when she said it out loud, but it was the truth. And though she had told herself nothing had changed between them, *something had.* Her fear was gone—

her fear of saying the wrong thing, her fear of giving too much away, her fear that sharing too much about herself would cause him to sprint out of the gate. He was no longer even on the track.

"Shit, girl, you used to have *friends*!? What the hell happened?" Will stuck out his tongue and smiled while scrunching his nose. It was a gut reaction, but he knew from experience that it was difficult for her to share, and he knew he could make it easier with affectionate teasing. If nothing else, she would pretend to be angry with him. At the moment, she seemed sad, and he *couldn't stand that.*

"Developed an incurable allergy to assholes." She glared at him and began scratching her arm pointedly.

Will smiled. "I'm just kidding. I would love to see you clubbing though. You probably looked like you were proctoring an exam. I can just imagine it." He folded his arms in front of him and gave a sweeping scan across the room. "While everyone else is like . . ." He pumped his head and his left hand forward and back to some imaginary dubstep anthem. Margot laughed, but a shade of sadness promptly returned to her demeanor. "Come on." He reached across the table toward the few strands of hair straying in front of her face but caught himself before brushing them back and let his hand fall flat. "Going to museums and libraries in your spare time between classes is way more badass than drinking $30 cocktails and dancing to some washed-up 2010s DJ."

"It's not that. I know I'm pretty awesome." She brushed off a shoulder quickly and quietly and then blushed. "I wish I had known somebody like you in college. I think things would have turned out differently."

"I was an asshole in college." She had made him uncomfortable again, so he spat out a truth himself.

"I guess not too much has changed." She smirked, reveling in what she could—minor and meaningless victories.

Chapter Nineteen

———

There were new patients every week. They came off of life support with different problems and different personas than they had had when they went on. Will sometimes longed for the days when taking a person off of life support had meant only one permanent thing. It was so much simpler, pulling the plug, when everyone knew the outcome. Once the decision was made, there wasn't this long struggle to return to some supposed salvaged being; there was peace. Sure, it was a failure in the most basic sense, Will admitted, *but could you call the current alternative a success?* The thing Will hated the most was observing the families. The loved ones of each patient were always so hopeful, so determined to right all of the wrongs, to fix, to correct, to wash clean. But there was no reset button, no option to restore to default settings. No matter what was explained or how it was stated, there were no words that could puncture the minds that had sealed themselves around perceived recognition. For them, seeing was believing.

The new patient that Will and Margot met that week was called Milton. Despite having undergone brain regeneration, he still seemed fairly sharp in his mind, and at first Will was disposed to like him. His speech and his conversation were refreshingly competent. It was rare to work with a fresh zombie who could keep up with the highs and lows, the subtleties of sarcasm and sweetness, who possessed the requisite short-term memory that made chatting with Margot worthwhile. Milton was a welcome relief from the other dejected convalescents who slogged through the exercises as if they truly were soulless monsters bound to this halfway existence for eternity. He made rehabilitation seem like what it was meant to be—a rewarding challenge. To be fair, he was improving rapidly. He had been kept in the ward solely for physical therapy, foremost to regain the use of his legs and, less urgently, the use of the fine motor skills required to, say, drink from a glass without spilling and without using a straw. And he was already standing, with the aid of his right hand and the wall, after only a day of practice.

Having taken a break from the arduous but successful task of remaining vertical for a full minute, Milton was sitting back down in his wheelchair, slowly lifting one-pound weights while Margot and Will encouraged him and carefully watched his form.

"Well, I guess you've already been briefed on me. What is it that you two do?" Milton used to be a hedge fund manager, before he had gotten into the car accident. He had been speeding, he had been high, and he had had a prostitute with him in the passenger seat. She was dead. He had shelled out the exorbitant sum to have his extra organs synthesized and perpetually kept on ice while she did not have the money for that sort of insurance. Seconds before the car crashed, moments before everything went black, Milton had thought to himself, *What an excellent investment*, and mentally patted himself on the back.

If Will had known the circumstances under which he had come to meet Milton, he would have thought, *Fucking predictable bastard*. He would have noticed Milton's pointed nose and pale, see-through skin, his tiny pupils concealing the light from his boring-to-the-point-of-inscrutability eyes. He would have noticed that he seemed to stand taller than he was, even though he was only five foot seven and could barely stay upright. But Will made a point of never finding out the backstory of the patients he worked with. There was no point in judging someone based on who they had been when everything had already changed. He glanced at Milton's dark brown scruffy stubble just starting to gray and his mess of hospital hair. "I'm a postdoc at Yale. I work in a lab just . . . back there." He lifted his right index finger to stab at the air behind his head.

"I work in the medical library," Margot chimed in softly.

"Lucky me. Two brainiacs at my disposal." He stared at Will's forehead for a second. "I suppose you're solving all of this shit." He pointed in a circle to the other patients in the room with them. "Ha. I guess that makes *me* the lab rat." There was an almost imperceptible moment of silence before he broke it with laughter.

It made Will uneasy. He wasn't sure how to respond, so he kept his eyes low and focused on watching the weight in Milton's hand, his arm moving it up and down, up and down.

Milton continued, this time to Margot, "And what on earth do you do in the library? Haven't we finished with fucking books?" He laughed again, a millisecond too late.

Will tilted his head slightly. He continued to watch Milton's arm. The weight moved quickly, easily, with no apparent expended effort. "Doing pretty well there." He pointed it out to Milton, and his eyes narrowed to scrutinize his reaction.

"I'm tired. Can we switch arms?" Milton dropped the words like small stones in the sand and looked him right in the eyes. Will suddenly noticed how small his pupils were, how thin his lips were, stretched, pink and premeditative. He nodded and moved the weight into Milton's other hand.

"It's mostly database work. Organization, managing accessibility, and making sure there are no glitches when downloading the material. Mostly I answer a lot of ignorant emails from esteemed, aka old, professors." Margot brought the conversation back.

"If it were me, I'd make the trip to see you *in person*." It came out a decibel too loud as Milton smiled at her with just a hint of teeth. "That's what *you* do, no doubt?" This time a decibel too soft as he looked back at Will.

"Yeah, well, most of the time she is busy *reading*." Will teased her and blocked himself at the same time. He glanced at the clock on the wall. Milton made him nervous. His skin chilled as minuscule beads of sweat evaporated from his pores to join the thickening air. *How much longer could be left?* "Hey, what do you say we try standing up again? Maybe you can even take a few steps if we both support you."

"Sure." Milton smiled flatly, complacently, and rose slowly with one arm draped over each of them. With their support, he took three slow steps forward. "Will . . ." Milton waited for an acknowledgment but didn't receive any. "It *is* Will, isn't it?" he coerced.

"Yes."

"What are you doing here, caring for an old crab apple like me in your free time? Don't you have a nice *young* wife to get home to?" He paused for a response.

Will blushed but didn't answer his question. He looked at the ground. "Try to keep your feet facing forward."

"There must be *someone*?" Milton persisted. He peered

sideways at the faint rouge forming under Margot's skin, then turned back to Will.

"*There is.*" Margot was curious to see where this conversation was headed, and with Milton as a shield between them, her flushed cheeks were safely concealed.

"I suspect you have a long-distance girlfriend somewhere in the world. Am I right?" He didn't wait for Will to reply. His voice was liquid. "She's easy, man, out of sight, out of mind, but she's there when you need her." Milton smirked at the ground as he continued to shuffle forward. "Question is, *do you?*"

"How did you guess all of that?" It slipped out before Margot could stop herself. "I mean, the part about the long-distance, not the rest of it," she added, not wanting to cause offense or give any of her own suspicions away.

Milton laughed. For once it seemed genuine. "These things tend to sort themselves out . . ." He shifted his head from side to side. "I like it in here. These walls, they keep the crazies out. They keep the crazies in." He raised his eyebrows at both of them in turn, but, standing on either side of him, they couldn't see. "I'm lucky, you know, lucky like lemons. Here I am alive, fresh like sunshine, just souring everyone who squeezes me."

Will couldn't tell if he was still loopy from the procedure or if he was trying to sound deranged on purpose. *Maybe he was faking the whole damn thing.* He loosened his support suddenly, and Milton caught himself. "Sorry, man." Will reinforced his body under Milton's arm. "That was really good though. You're improving at an *unprecedented* rate." He threw the word out like a lure. "Keep on like this, and you'll be out of here in no time!"

"I want to lie down. I'm done for today. I'm expecting visitors. Take me back to my bed." The warmth had disappeared from Milton's voice. He went limp in their arms and collapsed back into his wheelchair. Will wheeled him back to his hospital bed and helped him into it without saying a word. "How extraordinarily kind of you." Milton scowled as he said it, then his eyes quickly relaxed. "Come back to see me soon." Will leaned forward, close to Milton's face as he arranged the pillows behind his head. Milton smiled. "And bring Margot."

Will felt cold as he walked out of the room. He had wanted to add a note to Milton's chart, but only doctors and nurses had access to the tablets at the foot of the hospital beds. He didn't feel like confronting a medical doctor in person with the petty concerns of a philosophical doctor, but he walked out slowly in the hopes of running into a nurse. Instead, he ran into a family member. So Milton *was* expecting visitors.

"Hi. Do you work here? Were you just in to see Milton?" She spoke hurriedly, as if someone might catch her in the act of secret spreading, and pointed at the door to his room. Her face looked worried beyond the standard fear of loss, Will thought. It bore the lines of a concerned citizen. *Or perhaps it was simply age.* She was probably about as old as Milton, he surmised, and something about her was akin to him. They both seemed out of place somehow, but she seemed kind. She must have been a sister. *Or a cousin?* She could have been his wife, Will supposed, but he didn't get the feeling that she was.

"I'm just a volunteer." Will nodded and then tried to move past her.

She grabbed his arm. "I'm really sorry. Can I just ask you something?"

"Sure. But . . ." Will felt uncomfortable and unqualified giving medical advice. "It's really much better for you to talk to his doctor. *Seriously*." He tried to look serious, but he noted that he had himself been intimidated to speak with the doctor. *He shouldn't blame her.*

"He's different. Milton is." Will didn't roll his eyes, but he wanted to. *They all said shit like this.* "I know that's normal; they said it was normal. But. There's something wrong. Look, he passed all the tests for psychosis or whatever. So he's not a certifiable nutcase." She giggled to relieve some tension. "I don't know how to explain it. I think he's hiding something. Have you noticed anything strange about him?"

"Look." Will checked his watch. He agreed with her, but he wasn't sure how much to say. It was dangerous to lead family members on with theories or personal insights. Whether it gave them false hope or swept it away, altering the way they perceived their loved ones inevitably created problems. It wasn't his place, and he had gotten in trouble for it in the past. "I have to get going. I'm not really permitted to help . . . You should *really* tell the doctor about how you feel. *It could be important*." He gave the words gravity and looked at her imploringly.

Dumping the responsibility onto her, Will shirked it. He hoped she would follow through, though he could tell from her dilute expression that it wasn't likely. Soon Milton would be out on the streets. But it didn't matter what either of them did, he told himself. Doctors didn't listen to anyone anymore, *and why should they?*

———

He met Margot back at the entrance to the hospital, and they walked out across the street together to wait for the blue line shuttle that circled between the medical campus and up north to East Rock. As they came to a halt at the med school stop, a heaviness grew throughout Will's body. He had a strange and disagreeable sensation in the pit of his stomach, as if soap bubbles were forming, one by one, filling his gut, bit by bit, and he would need to choose carefully the right words in order to pop them and free himself before he eventually choked. "That guy was *strange*, right?"

"Hmm? I guess." Margot was thinking more about what Milton had said rather than the eerily disciplined way in which he had said it. "He was funny."

"Funny, *like* . . . he was a fucking weirdo?" Will sounded hopeful, but it wasn't clear to him whether he was hoping that she agreed with him or whether he was hoping Milton's creepy-as-all-hell vibe was just in his head.

"Funny, like he seemed to know a lot about us . . . Like, he knew about Viki . . . is it hard, the long distance?" Margot surprised herself. She had never asked even an indirect question about Viki before.

This was not at all the conversation Will had envisioned having. Every one of the nervous bubbles in his stomach had popped at once, but now it just felt as if he had swallowed the whole bottle of soap. "Yeah, I mean . . . it's not *ideal*, but it's fine." Her sincerity pressed at him. "Honestly, sometimes it's good. Just because I am so busy with lab work all the time. She would hate it . . . and I wouldn't blame her."

"Do you miss her?" Margot looked up into the sky. The

words fell out of her mouth like they were nothing more than a low breath.

Will absolutely hated Margot at times. He was sure he didn't know her so well as she seemed to think he did. She would be nice and normal for months at a time, then out of nowhere . . . *Why did it always get so personal?* He really enjoyed talking to her, he had to remind himself. They could spend hours discussing scientific papers or movies or which was the best New Haven apizza (*obviously Sally's*). But these ten-minute, out-of-the-deep-blue conversations were a *horror*. Whenever this happened, he had the urge to be mean. He imagined what he would say to her: *Why do you need to know? Because you've never had any firsthand experience? Isn't it all research to you? Read a fucking book.* But he didn't say any of that out loud. Not because he was afraid to be mean to her, but because he was afraid of what her real reaction would be. He had an inkling that, whatever it was, it would change everything somehow. Instead, in these situations, Will gave short answers, answers that meant little to him but still gave away more than he thought. "Of course I do." He said it as a matter of fact, a dependent variable that followed, simply by definition.

"But you're sure she's *the one*. Or 'a' one. Or whatever." Margot's voice had started quiet and subsequently decomposed into a low mumble, but she was sure that he had heard her.

Will reeled. He very nearly leaned forward and puked into the gutter, but thankfully he spied the shuttle arriving around the corner, and he relaxed. "Yes, I'm sure." He nodded, but he didn't look at her as he said it. Instead, he signaled the driver and the end of the conversation.

As they moved forward toward the approaching bus, Margot whispered under her breath, too quietly for him to hear, "How do you *know*?"

Chapter Twenty

——————

George strolled through the lab the next morning, dropping his customary not-entirely-inspirational messages. "Looking sharp, Julie. Don't let the rest of these decrepits get you down. That's right, Jon, I'm talking about you." He slapped Jon on the back. "Now, don't fuss. The tortoise can still take the cake with a little conditioning and a big head start—just look at me!" He laughed loudly and then stopped short. "Don't forget, we're meeting at one. I assume you have plenty of new data to show me this time." George coughed quietly, then glided over to Will's desk.

"Will." George took a striking stance, peering down at Will from the side as he sat, leaning over his tablet.

"Yes?" Will turned his chair ninety degrees to face him.

"You heard me just now—meeting at one, yes?"

"Yep. All systems go." Will often found himself speaking to George in offbeat idioms without control.

"Good. I wanted to talk to you about something else."

"Shoot." He couldn't stop himself.

George put on a serious face. "Have you been looking for new jobs?"

It was common knowledge that Will's postdoc was coming to a close, but he was surprised by the question. It hadn't occurred to him that George would give a fraction of a shit where he went next. He shrugged. "I've been looking. Sent a few applications last week. And there are a few more I want to send out this week. None of them are exactly . . . Well, I'm hoping to move to New York, or that direction."

"New York? Don't tell me, *Dr. Dalal* . . . it's about a girl? Ha!"

Will blushed. Personal accomplishments always embarrassed him in front of professional colleagues.

"Don't be embarrassed. Lord knows it happens to the best of us." George paused. "You need to branch out. Get some more managerial experience. You've been here too long. The cautious cat catches only caterpillars."

"I . . . see." Will had no idea what he was talking about.

"Jon, he's been here for just as long as you. He's settled down; he's married. More importantly, he's satisfied. Get out of here before you are too. See you at one." George walked off.

Before Will had a chance to try to deconstruct and decipher exactly what he intended to take away from George's mini lecture, he had to change his sample. He picked up a fresh sequencing chip that he had loaded with cDNA earlier that morning from the ice bucket at his bench and carried it over to the sequencer, swapping it out for the finished one. While he was recalibrating and placing it into the machine, George swung by for a second pass, startling him, but all he said was, "Back in my day, some of these things"—he gestured at the sequencer—"took up a whole room!" He winked at Will and moved on. Will was pretty sure that was considerably before his day, but he didn't want to touch on anything that would bring up George's age, so he didn't mention it. In fact, he had no idea how old George was. On some days, he looked a healthy sixty. On other days, he looked a dyspeptic ninety-five. Either way, despite his baffling metaphors, when it came to evaluating their research, his mind was as sharp as a nineteen-year-old's, with seemingly the same amount of unused space ready and willing to be filled. Will envied and admired him. He secretly hoped one day to emulate him.

———

It only took Will ten minutes to set up each run, but by the time he had finished, his thoughts had already become sidetracked. He was thinking about wedding planning. He didn't like to admit it, even to himself, but he *liked* thinking about wedding stuff. Most of his daydreams now were taken up with the little details that made memories special, that made something good into something significant. There were pictures in his mind, both vague and vivid: the sun, the sea, white tablecloths, blue flowers, yellow champagne, green grass.

The previous summer, he had taken Viki to the seaside. It was customary in the Northeast to flee the city and run for the shores when the temperature reached eighty degrees and the humidity reached 80 percent. They had watched, as bystanders, a small wedding at a small hotel in a small town on the Connecticut coast, and he had been struck by the scene. It was hard not to be. The weather was perfect. The sun spotlighted the fresh setting from above, and delicate, bright flower arrangements swayed in perfect harmony with the subtle sound of low waves washing over the sand. The couple were joyous beyond inhibition, and the guests were a flawless extension of their rejoicing. They sang aloud. A college fight song or drinking ballad, a performance Will would normally dismiss, played ardently in his memory. Everything in the spyglass view took on a vibrancy in the tiny space between the past and the future. Will had never before witnessed a perfect moment, even in the weddings he had attended as an invited guest. He didn't stop to question whether perfection was merely perspective.

And so now, at work, on the shuttle, or staring at the ceiling while waiting to fall asleep at night, Will contemplated wine varietals and wisteria, cake toppers and cummerbunds, set lists and sabrage. The self-important streak that had both compelled him to act like a jerk in high school and a dick in college, and propelled him into the graduate program at Harvard, longed to dazzle and awe. He fantasized through nearly every superficial detail that would make the wedding of the century, neglecting the sole important one.

Besides, when he wasn't thinking about wedding stuff, his mind drifted to snippets and bits of the conversation he had had with Margot standing at the shuttle stop the other night. He found it impossible not to dwell on the inexplicable look she had given him that entire evening—the look that gave him honeyed twinges down the backs of his legs and made him want to dematerialize before she opened her mouth to say something he would regret having heard.

He didn't want to admit it, but he had been avoiding her. He had been taking slightly more care with his samples, adding extra minutes onto his experiments that leaked into his breaks. He had started setting up more meetings than usual, and he had already decided that he would spend the rest of the morning at his desk, browsing job postings and researching other labs where he might look for a new position. They had previously made plans to volunteer again at the end of the week and he was already creating excuses, setting himself work goals that he would never be able to reach without putting in a significant number of extra evening hours.

———

Will sat down at his desk and brought up his CV on his tablet. He projected it onto the larger desk space and angled the screen forward so it would be easy to edit. He hadn't looked at his resume in years, and he became sentimental as he scrolled through his accomplishments, recalling them proudly one by one and mentally calculating how many researchers in the country were as qualified as he was at his age. No more than a handful, he was sure, possibly fewer than three. Coming across the project he had worked on with Arthur, he shivered instinctively. This knee-jerk reaction surprised him, and he glanced over his shoulder as if Arthur might be standing behind him, waiting to pounce. In a way, that had always been his stance. But now that it had been three years since he had heard from Arthur, Will had let go of most of the rage he felt toward his rival, and in its place had gained some measure of curiosity. Three years ago, he had broken into Arthur's lab and confronted him in his office. It was still shocking for Will to think about. But what was more shocking, he realized, was that he had been waiting to hear from him.

Arthur's strange words had been ringing in his ears for the last three years: "Maybe we're not so different after all . . . I could use help . . . We're just like them. It's not our fault. . . . Just don't think too poorly of me, not yet . . . Maybe I'll call you." They had been haunting Will's subconscious thoughts, making inroads where Will couldn't see them, couldn't fight them, and they had grown into questions. What had Arthur been up to? What was taking so freaking long? Was he close to completing some tour de force, or had he truly gone over the edge? *Possibly both.* Was he a hero? Was he a villain? Had the Brill pill serum driven him down this path, or was it merely a facilitator? Had it all just blown over?

Will had been trying unsuccessfully to ignore these questions these three years, but even with the welcome and unwelcome distractions of late, he was never quite able to put them out of his mind. Though Arthur had largely disappeared from the academic world in which Will chose to hide and strove to thrive, he couldn't shake the feeling that he was biding his time, waiting for the perfect moment to show his hand. Still, despite remaining constant in the volatile train of Will's thoughts, Arthur's next move came as a surprise to him. Whether by fate or simply fluke, in the same single week that Will would later deny had defined him, he finally received a message.

———

It appeared on his tablet, encrypted, from an unknown account. Will wouldn't have expected any less. It read: "Hi there. It's your old *pal* from Harvard." This was followed by a string of emojis. "🗡️/🐍😀. Funny how time flies. Do you remember what we discussed three years ago? I have a feeling you *do* know, so I won't treat you as if you are *stupid* 🗃️💀/ 😀💯. I told you once we were similar, and I still believe that. Nothing is going to happen right away. But if you agree with me, please reply. If you don't agree with me, I suspect it is out of some sort of arrogance or cowardice rather than some kind of moral stance, so I don't expect you will share this. Please simply ignore. Thank you for listening to me, though you *may* think I am crazy 👽👍."

Will closed the message, erasing it as soon as he had finished reading. He sat back in his seat with his full weight, rocking the chair backward and then allowing it to push him forward again. He stared at his screen. He brought up a document so that it would appear he was reading, but he continued to stare until the meeting at one. During the meeting, he stared at the wall as Jon took care of the presentation and fielded George's questions with great trained skill and only a few cross sidelong glances in Will's direction. When the meeting was over, Will returned to his desk and stared at the screen some more. Finally, he put his quandary into words as he said out loud to no one in particular, "I should tell her."

He stowed the screen and stood up slowly. He walked up to the door that led into the hallway and squeezed the handle, turning it about twenty degrees before releasing his grip and letting it spring back. Though no one was watching, he made a face to imply he had forgotten something and doubled back to his desk, this time using his fingerprint to open the drawer and then clicking it shut again—once, twice, three times. He stalled. The fourth time, he picked up a stylus that was designed to look like a fountain pen, twirled it between his fingers, and then put it back before shutting the drawer again. He walked over to Jon's bench and stood next to him as he worked, carefully moving the micropipette forward and backward, two inches at a time, precisely, as if he had a mechanical arm. "Sorry about earlier," Will apologized. "I have a lot on my mind. I guess it's finally getting to me." He said it sarcastically, like it wasn't a big deal.

Jon looked up sharply, like he was about to say something cutting or at least perceptive, but seeing Will's anxious features, he looked back down at his work and only said, "Don't worry, man, we all have our days." He added, "You can make it up to me by checking on my mice this weekend. I'm taking the wifey up to Boston. Think she's impatient for the snow. Psycho."

"I check on your mice *every* weekend. Let me know if there's anything else I can help you out with." He put his hand down on Jon's shoulder, making his arm shake out of the two-inch pipetting range, but he recovered quickly. Will chuckled at the tensing motion and then walked away, toward the door again. He turned back to Jon as he reached for the handle. "Nice guns, by the way. You're pipetting the shit out of that." He nodded and then walked through, into the corridor.

Now there was just the hallway to contend with. It seemed longer than ever, not least because he had been avoiding it for the last several days. Now that he had made the decision to walk it, he felt nervous. It reminded him of the very first time he had cautiously entered that building, as a visitor coming in for an interview; he had felt like he didn't belong. He couldn't stand outside of the door forever though. *He'd look like an idiot.* So he made his way down to the library, one foot in front of the other, one step at a time. In about two and a half drawn-out minutes, he rounded the door to the library and ambled up to the desk as if it were just a normal day. "Hey, girl."

"Hey, boy." Her tone was dry, but she didn't seem displeased to see him.

"Whatcha reading?"

"A novel algorithmic approach to in-silico modeling of PD-L1 deficient squamous cell carcinomas."

"Phew." Will fanned his hand in front of his face, and put on a feminine southern timbre. "Isn't that a mouthful?"

Margot half smirked, then caught herself and changed tack to a classic eye roll. "What do you want?" The words hung in the air, sharp and light, but there was a flat melancholy hiding behind them, pulling them taut.

"Who says I want anything? I stop by here all the time. Why would today be any different?" Will tried to speak with a genial tone, but he couldn't entirely hide the defensive edge in his voice.

"Sorry, but 'Hey, girl' is your tell." She said it bluntly, still focused on the last sentence she had been reading. She looked up after a pause. "You haven't been by since we volunteered last week. I hope I didn't offend you." These words were soft and sincere.

"Naw." Will, caught between two conversations he dreaded, found that discussing Arthur and his debatably demented schemes suddenly seemed like a walk in the park. So he went for it. "I do want something. That is . . . I want to tell you something." He had her full attention. Margot's pupils seemed to grow so wide and deep at these words, he got the impression he could slip and fall into them. Will cautiously peered inside. There was an expectation written in the bottom that made him tremble. He spat out the next words before any vague notions floating through the back of his mind about where this expectation might originate could be clarified. "It's about Arthur."

"Oh . . . Oh?" Her pupils shot back down to normal size.

"I think he sent me a message. I mean, he *did* . . . Do you remember, years ago, when he published that paper, and we thought he was trying to infect the world with intelligence or some bullshit? Well, I think he may be getting close . . . or, just as likely, he's gone off the deep end." Will tried to add some levity on the off chance that he himself had started to sound crazy. "I don't know. I don't know what to say to him, or whether I should even reply. I wanted your advice."

Margot's face went slack. It was too much. The roller coaster of emotions was, in the space of a few minutes, more than she had dealt with in the entire rest of her life. After all he had done, he still wanted *her goddamn advice. As if he had ever or would ever listen to it.* But she came to quickly, with the desperate, baseless resolution that if Will *did* listen to her advice, she still had a part to play—even if, at the moment, it felt like an achingly inconsequential one. "You have to tell someone. I mean, like the police, or the greater scientific community, or his department chair, or his PI, or whoever has power over him . . ." She heard the words coming from her own mouth, the same words she had stood firmly by three years ago, but now they were softer somehow, muted, an echo of former convictions.

Will heard the same advice and flashed back to three years ago. He cringed. Back then it had all seemed so ridiculous. But three years had passed, and here they were again. Should he listen to her now? He silently considered and dismissed her suggestions for a second time. Going to his department head, telling Carlos—it would still do no more than possibly get him fired. And Arthur would find a way to carry on. He would have to go to the Ethics Committee. *He hated the Ethics Committee.* Will rapidly rationalized and justified. He wriggled. He pivoted. He didn't respond.

But Margot barely noticed the silence. "Do you really think he's going to do something *crazy*? It's been so long; it doesn't seem real anymore. It never seemed real . . ." She shrugged her shoulders. It was uncanny. There had been a time when she had felt so strongly about this. She could recall the feeling of certainty, but she could no longer embrace it. In comparison to what, just seconds before, she had let herself dream she might hear, it all fell hollow. Still, she told herself it was important. She sighed.

"Is it crazy to want to make the world a better place?" Will reasoned with himself in her presence. It was the only way to stay balanced. If he reasoned with himself alone, he tilted, he lost his equilibrium, he fell sober into Arthur's disoriented perception. "Is it so wrong to give someone a head start? They may not live to deserve it, but let's be honest, how many of us do?"

Margot was stunned. She felt sick. She knew she couldn't win an argument against a lunatic, but it occurred to her that she was losing much more than that. If Will continued down this path, the illusory ambitions that had nurtured her over the past three years would cease to exist. Her voice faintly trembled. "He could *kill* someone. A lot of someones. What are the chances it would even work?"

She was the pessimist. Will carried on, playing devil's advocate. The itching desire to discover a fault in her perfect brain was convincing him Arthur was right. *He wanted to be convinced.* "He could change *everything*. People die every day. They'll never allow that sort of testing on infants. There *are no* proper channels. But do the risks outweigh the rewards?"

"*Potential* rewards," she corrected—disgusted with him, *disgusted with herself.* "And yes, they do. Besides, it's not just the risks. It's the choice of whether to take them."

Here she goes again. The repulsed look she had given him had made Will momentarily uneasy, but he bulldozed that feeling with irascibility and sarcasm. "If you had had the choice, you would have dumbed yourself down, wouldn't you? You would have stayed close to home, gone to state school. You'd probably be married with three kids by now. You'd be *oh so happy*. None of this librarian-savant crap."

"And what would you do?" she spat back without thinking. "Probably be a fucking prodigy . . . Don't you ever think there are more important things than being smart? It's not going to fix anything, you know. Some people are already too smart for their own good." *And no, I'm not talking about you.* She was careful not to insult him out loud, but she was sure he would take what she had said as a twisted personal compliment. She glanced at the wall behind him, at the promotional posters perpetually mocking her from across the room: ARE YOU A RISK TAKER? WHEN YOU NEED TO BE RIGHT, ASK YOUR MEDICAL LIBRARIAN . . . BECAUSE THE BEST SEARCH ENGINE IN THE LIBRARY IS THE LIBRARIAN. *What a load of crap.* And yet she couldn't stop herself from looking up at them. *Every damn day.* "You're not responsible for saving the world. No single person is." Margot spoke these words in the same level, metered voice she would use to explain why libraries were still relevant or to tell him what time to meet her after work.

Will was agitated, and he couldn't see why, which made him more agitated still. "I just don't think you understand what a *huge* thing this is. Maybe it's *hard to see* from behind all of these bookshelves." He spoke the last sentence casually as he waved at the walls, but he knew it would piss her off. He wanted to piss her off and then walk out the door, back to work where she couldn't follow him. He wanted her to stew.

"I do understand. That's the whole point." She said it softly. He had touched a nerve, but she didn't want to fight. She wanted to give up—she didn't care who won anymore. It was insignificant to her. All she wanted was to freeze time. To keep Will safe from his future, to keep herself safe, to keep her heart safe. *It throbbed.* If only she could freeze time. Over the last three years, while she hadn't been looking, all of her principles and convictions had melted into worries and fears. In a moment, she saw Will's life flash before her eyes, and she understood how people grow old. How affection crumbled ideals, how attachments cracked decisions, how paranoia came to rule, how exhausting the whole thing was. She was finished for today. It was enough for now. Tomorrow she would try a different tactic. Will was almost at the door. She pleaded, "Don't do anything yet, okay?"

His feet stopped and his body rocked to a standstill for a few seconds before he turned around to face her. His voice came out unintentionally flat. "Almost forgot, I can't make it on Thursday to volunteer. Got a lot of samples to run for next week. So I'll be working late." He started to move again toward the door and then sighed and turned once more, his hand on the wall, keeping him momentarily from moving either forward or back. "*Please* don't worry. I won't do anything . . . *yet.*"

Chapter Twenty-One

———

The next thing that happened, happened so quickly that Will would not be able to build up the courage to totally blame himself for it until it was too late.

———

On Thursday, while he was in lab preparing samples, thawing reagents, making up buffer solutions, waiting for samples to run, recalibrating, and running again and again, Will felt guilty. In his head, it was easy to argue that he shouldn't feel guilty. After all, he had work to do and he was doing it. But in his gut, he couldn't quite settle the sinking, swirling eddies. It wasn't as if he had never skipped out on volunteer work before, so he wondered what it was that was bothering him. Was it the way he had left things the other day? Was he worried about her? He had meant to say something to someone about Milton. *He didn't trust that guy.* But with everything else that had been going on in reality and in the infinite imagined scenarios plaguing the corners of his consciousness, he had forgotten. Or had he chosen to ignore the way Milton's cold eyes had carved through the space between them, or how the woman he had met outside Milton's door had quivered?

Will didn't like getting into other people's business. He

had an unwritten rule against it. But in theory, this rule would never put someone *he knew* in danger, only nameless, faceless entities. Those pixelated sacrifices that were required to maintain the unjust balance between good and bad. Ironically, his interest in Arthur's private project made a complete hypocrite out of him, and he knew it. He told himself, "It's on a much bigger scale. It could actually make a difference. It could tip the balance." *If that wasn't a good cause, nothing was.*

And beyond that limited justification, he had to admit there was another, more fundamental part of him that was purely interested in the science. He had so many questions. Could it work? Would it work? *How* would it work? He wanted, rather *needed*, to know what Arthur had accomplished, whether he had made leaps and bounds or whether he was plain demented. Were the injections he had been taking working for him or against him? Will wondered what he would do with the information, but he didn't allow himself to wonder far. He needed to get his hands on the data before he could consider where it might lead him. As far as Will could tell, there was only one way he could achieve that.

He considered how disappointed Margot would be in the weakness he incurred from elemental curiosity. He felt selfish, and for once it bothered him. His guilt redoubled, but he stood up from his bench, walked around the room, drank a glass of water, and shook it off. *Don't be ridiculous,* he told himself. *You haven't done anything wrong. Not yet. Nothing bad is going to happen tonight. Or tomorrow. Stop acting like such a fucking wacko.* His thoughts strayed darker again at the word "wacko," but he reassured himself. *Milton is just a little off—what else can you expect with a brain grown in a* jar? *Besides,* Will reflected, *he seemed to like Margot. She certainly seemed to enjoy what he had to say about* me. He heard his own voice turn bitter inside his head. He let his fist down on the nearest countertop, perhaps harder than he intended. Then he finished his work and went home to try to sleep everything off.

The next morning, Will went to the library. He thought he went to apologize, or maybe not apologize but to say something nice, or at the very least to *listen.* He had managed to sleep off much of the anger and annoyance of the past week, and at the risk of rekindling that anger by bringing up the same sore subject again, he was eager to be on better terms. In his sleep, he had realized that leaving things the way they were was slowly crippling him.

When he walked through the door into the library, he didn't see her. She wasn't there. Instead, in her place, there was a cop, standing at *her desk, messing with her things.* Picking each item up slowly and placing them into a box, methodically, packing it bottom to top like a grocery bag. Will's face numbed as he began to comprehend. Goose bumps prickled the palm of each hand. His head went a thousand places at once, and yet all of those places, he knew, were better than where he was.

Still, his feet stepped forward. They moved as their own entity. His mind was now out of control, blood was ripping through his ears, protecting him from the words he would hear as soon as he was able to open his mouth, to ask the question. He hesitated. His throat had gone thin as a thread, taut like a rubber band; it would sting like a bitch when he let it go. But he had to know. "What happened?" He choked it out. The band snapped, slapping him in the small space behind his nose. It smarted like he had been flicked hard from the inside.

The cop looked up. She was petite, blonde. She had a kind face. Will wanted to punch it, to pull her hair, to kick her in the ovaries for what she was about to say. "Did you know"—she looked down at her tablet, and Will cursed her incompetence—"Margot Brandt?"

"Yes. She was a friend. I work down . . ." He gestured toward the hallway. "We used to . . ." He couldn't find the words to go on as he realized he was already speaking in the past tense. The desire to punch the cop in the face melted along with every cell contained within his skin.

"Will you sit down with me?" She pointed to a chair. As she sat down across from the empty seat, he glanced at the name on her uniform. It was Ann.

"Okay, Ann. I'm Will." He didn't shake hands but sat slowly in the chair, careful not to put his weight on either corner, for fear the thin skin sack holding him together would burst and he would ooze all over the carpet.

"Did you know she volunteered over at Yale New Haven?" Ann looked at him keenly, keeping him focused.

"Yes. . . I did also, sometimes . . . I couldn't yesterday . . . I . . ." His shape had slowly returned as he had sat, but now it felt as if small termites were nibbling, or acid was etching away, at every one of the bones in his body.

Ann sighed. For her, it was time to get it over with. "I'm really sorry." She placed her hand on his motionless arm. "There was a patient she was working with yesterday. No one thought he was dangerous." She sighed. "He managed to get a hold of a scalpel. We aren't sure how yet. We think he had it hidden in his bed, and when Ms. Brandt took him back to his room, he attacked her. Unfortunately, she didn't make it."

"I thought everything was lasers now." It came out as a whisper. It was all he could think of to say.

"You should go home, get some rest. Do you have a friend you can call and make plans for dinner? Make sure that you eat . . . If I can just get your contact details?" She placed her tablet in his hands, with the blank contact form up. "That way we can reach you if necessary, if we have any questions."

"Sure." He numbly entered his details and handed the tablet back over. He stood up from the chair. He glanced around. He looked back at Margot's desk. He saw himself leaning over it, telling bad jokes, making fun, teasing, laughing, smiling, but there was no one behind the desk anymore. The library was empty. He wouldn't come back.

Chapter Twenty-Two

———

He nodded at Ann and stalked out of the library, turning automatically down the hall. He paused outside of his lab but then kept walking. Time stood still inside him as his body carried out the only response it could conjure. He was in the sky bridge that connected the hall of medicine to the hospital, and he looked down at the busy street of wanderers below. *How many were secretly monsters?* Somewhere deep down, were they all?

He continued on, into the hospital, up the elevator, down the corridor. There were police crowded around Milton's door, but he grabbed a lab coat from the next room and walked straight through. Milton was confined to the bed with two zip ties, each one binding a wrist to the bars on either side, but he looked comfortable. His elbows were propped up under two pillows, and his head was reclined. He looked as if he might have been about to drift off to sleep, but his eyes opened with interest as he noticed Will's arrival.

Milton smiled sincerely. His eyes were clear as glacial melt. If you cut his expression out of the crime scene, he was the stock photo in an unused picture frame. "I told you these things tended to *sort themselves out.*" He closed his eyes and returned to his restful position. Will felt Milton's smile like an anvil on his chest. His peaceful demeanor was a two-by-four to the gut, winding him. He noticed the dried blood on Milton's gown, and his hands were shaking. Will's whole body was shaking. He imagined jumping across the room, soaring onto the bed, and ripping Milton's head clean off. Or maybe he would slit his wrists and watch him bleed out slowly. But Will couldn't soar. He wasn't strong enough to rip him apart. He could barely stand; he could barely breathe. He was gasping for air.

The police finally noticed him. When they looked at his face and not at the lab coat, it was obvious he didn't belong. One of them took him by the arm and supported him back out into the hallway. "Go on home, son." He patted Will on the shoulder.

More words followed, inquiries or input, but they faded into static. Will wandered back through the hospital, back in the direction of his building, but he took the outside route this time. It was November, and it was starting to get cold. Will wished it were colder. His feverish emotions cut through the wind, but all he wanted was to succumb, to be numb. He tried to work, but there was no distracting himself. His fingers fumbled, and his mind wandered to good moments that now seemed perfect, and to bad moments that now seemed precious.

He found himself going word for word through conversations, the familiar calls and responses: "Hey, girl," "Hey, boy." Then there were *the infinite unformed questions* to which there would *never* be an answer. There was no escaping the void, the vacuum that was sucking away a part of who he was or who he *might have been*. Everywhere he turned, there was a sign flashing, burning into him the fact that something amorphous and sublime had been lost forever. He thought about asking Jon if he was free for dinner. Ann had suggested that. He thought about telling Viki what had happened. Common sense told him he should talk to someone, and common sense also told him that she should be his first choice. But as he brought up her number on his tablet, he felt immediately repulsed and instinctively slid it across his desk, away from him.

He didn't want to see *anyone*. He opened his desk drawer and pulled out the last packet of powder, the one he had nearly consumed in the restaurant bathroom before proposing to Viki. He was relieved he hadn't used it then. He clutched it tightly in his hand and then pocketed it before mechanically packing up his belongings to walk home. Refusing to put on a jacket against the parched bald wind, he felt sick with desolation. The little pieces of warmth he had stored away in Margot's mannerisms, in the patterns of speech she used, in the number of times per minute she blinked or touched her hair or her face, in every detail, were turning cold one by one, making him nauseous with panic. He was helpless. The familiar physical feeling of soft, clear plastic as he compulsively touched the small pouch in his pocket was the only thing that kept him from giving up and huddling on the ground. When he reached home he would flush it all out, *everything*.

Chapter Twenty-Three

———

The next several days did not exist. The sun presumably rose and set, but Will did not know this for a fact. It was only an assumption, based on years of experience. Inside his mind, there was white noise. There was fog as thick as custard. It was raining in every direction, and the torrents soaked through cerebral matter, waterlogging, filling it like a sponge. It expanded, squeezing into the edges of his skull. There was molasses dripping down the folds of his brain, slowly, creating oozing rivers and thick waterfalls. There was gelatin leaking in, setting up in the cold. It slowed his thoughts as they tried to creep through the wobbling mess.

When he awoke from this vegetative state, he couldn't be sure whether he had eaten, whether he had slept, whether he had been into work or, if he had, whether he had accomplished anything. Had he simply gone on? Had he even left his room? There was a prickling fire burning, itching, annoying. It had started in his foot, maybe, or the tips of his fingers. It was what had woken him. It tingled at first to get his attention, reminding him that he was still a living and breathing organism, reminding him that he *would* continue, whether or not he wanted to. And as he became aware of this failing, it stung. The sting was bitter, the harsh bite of what had been lost and yet had never been realized. Will did not like losing, and he didn't do well with admissions, either. To say that he had loved her would have caused his own throat to tear.

So the bitterness turned to heat, as grief and loneliness were boxed away, compartmentalized. Something had to give, and the flames that grew in their place were of vengeance. Will had no anger left for Milton or the rest of the zombies living on borrowed time. It wasn't their fault that they were the way they were. Though he would most likely throw Milton from the roof of the hospital if he happened to see him again, it wouldn't be out of retribution, but out of a concern for nature and balance and some other fictitious worldly causes. The anger that had laid hold of him had originated in the mirror, but it was easily misdirected, and the vendetta he had taken up was against everyone and everything that caused the world to be what it was. A vendetta against evil and good and sadness and joy, and against the mice in their cages, eating and shitting and fighting all day. A vendetta against existence. Arthur had given him the cause, and Arthur had presented him with a solution. It was all becoming clear.

Will got out of bed, got dressed, and ate half a box of his roommate's dry cereal. He would have eaten the whole box if it had been more than half full. He had been starving. The immediate aching sickness he felt at having a full stomach indicated to him that he hadn't eaten much in the last week, and the implication was even worse than the sudden nausea. He was briefly tempted to just throw it all up again and return to his room, to the protection of the black-out curtains, to his warm, isolated bed. But he stood tall to keep it down and walked out the front door. The light burned spots over his eyes, and he blinked to adjust. There was snow on the ground. He was freezing. *What day was it?* He went back inside to grab a heavy coat and then resumed his journey. The walk would do him good.

Back at his desk, he felt safe. Looking at the playful picture of himself standing next to Viki, holding the bottle of champagne, made it seem for an instant as if nothing had happened. *Shit,* he thought, *when is the last time I called her?* He checked his tablet. It had been three days since he had texted Viki, six days since he had been into work, six days since *that* day. He remembered with relief that Viki was traveling. He sent her a nothing text and then put his tablet down. He breathed. He picked it up again. He scrolled through his messages. There were about ten from Jon asking if he was okay. Apparently he had written back, "Ok." He couldn't remember sending it. Then he found what he had really been looking for, the anonymous account from which he had received the encrypted message from Arthur. He hit REPLY on the empty thread, and before he let himself think or deliberate or care about the fact that Margot would have been pissed, he sent, "Whatever the fuck you are up to, you crazy son of a bitch—*count me in.*"

———

A hand fell on Will's shoulder, and he jumped and dropped his tablet, startled in the midst of his furtive task. Jon was standing next to him, an irritatingly thankful look on his face. *Great, my other motherfucking conscience is here. Perfect timing,* Will thought, but he felt a small trickle of warmth penetrate his chest. "Hey."

"Hey! It's *good to see you.*" It was all Jon had to say, but it was enough. Will was grateful he didn't need to reply. If he

163

had moved any muscle in his face at that moment, the seal would have broken and the droplets that had been welling and seeping uncontrollably for days would have escaped.

Chapter Twenty-Four

———

Will told Jon and the rest of his lab that he was going down to New York to see Viki the following weekend. *Thank God,* Jon thought. Jon told himself that it would be good for Will to talk to someone outside of work and to have some physical human contact, but he knew that the relief he felt was largely on his own behalf. News about the librarian's murder had traveled fast, and he had been anxious around Will all week. Nevertheless, he had managed to muster the courage to say about ten words to Will each day, and he had managed to do so every day without fail. By the end of the week, he'd gotten up to about fifteen. Jon would spend most of the weekend thinking of harmless topics with which to engage Will on Monday.

In fact, Will did not go to New York. If Jon had known that Will was planning to go to Boston to see Arthur, he would have upped his number of words to at least two hundred, in an effort to dissuade him. But Will wouldn't be dissuaded, and besides, it was a secret mission north, so Jon would never know. No one would.

———

Will was meeting Arthur in one of the several small second-story restaurants on Tyler Street. The area was familiar to him. When he was growing up, he used to come to Chinatown occasionally for dim sum with friends or with family. The sights and smells running down each block were, objectively, exactly as he remembered. But as he walked up the stairs to the entrance, he didn't feel like he was back in his hometown. He felt uncomfortable and out of place. *He might as well have* actually *been in China.*

He had arrived first and, failing to locate a host, sat himself at one of the square metal tables for two. The shrill screech of his chair against the linoleum floor as he pulled it in startled the only other customer sitting at the opposite end of the room. But it failed to register through the psychological diving helmet Will now wore day in and day out in order to appear sane. A waiter, who also seemed to be part of the kitchen staff, appeared at the sound, dropped a menu, and then disappeared again just as suddenly. Will turned the menu back and forth without reading it. It was a perfect moment for daydreaming, but for once, his mind was resolutely blank. He couldn't even focus on the words. The waiter had purposefully given him an English menu, but it could have been in Chinese, or it could have been in Wingdings; it would have made no difference. He was still flipping the thing over and back again six minutes later when Arthur came in.

Striding toward Will, he quickly waved the waiter over and ordered for both of them in what Will assumed was Mandarin . . . *or was it Cantonese?* Will couldn't tell the difference, even though Joe had taught him to count to seven in one or the other. When he had finished ordering, Arthur took the menu out of Will's hands and handed it back to the waiter before sitting down across from him. He adjusted his seat for several seconds, shifting his weight in a nearly obsessive manner four or five times before speaking.

"So. You and me." Arthur feigned skepticism, but his excitement to have a partner in crime that wasn't furry and four inches long, plus a tail, shone through.

"Us." Will nodded, still unsure.

"Here." Arthur nodded back.

"Here we are." Will continued to nod.

"Yes, we are." The nodding had become a sort of trance.

"Me and you." Will paused mid-nod and shook his head quickly to break free. "Look, you tell me. This is your game. Some crazy shit has been happening in my life and I need a distraction, so I'm just here to play it."

"It's more than that." Arthur stated it as a fact, but his expression was questioning.

"Maybe." Will tilted his head slightly to his left. "It doesn't matter. I don't back out of my commitments. You know that." Will swallowed.

"Okay. I'll tell you a story then." Arthur raised the small porcelain cup of jasmine tea that had recently materialized at his right elbow. His hand shook slightly as he lifted it to his mouth to take a preparative sip before carefully placing it back down. "Where to begin? Hm. When I was nine years old—no, it isn't important. How we came to be where we are is meaningless. The point is that we are here, and *where will we go*? Or is it?" Arthur sighed as if a weight was pushing down on his chest, forcing out a slow stream of air.

"Sorry, what was that?" Will was exhausted and didn't give a shit about Arthur's childhood, but he *needed* Arthur. He didn't want Arthur to pull away, so he did his very best to

be polite while bringing him back around to the point, whatever that point was.

Arthur leaned two inches to the right and then two inches
to the left before centering himself again. "In the times between, when I'm not . . ." He inhaled. He motioned to the
crook of his arm where Will had physically pressed him for
evidence three years ago. He exhaled. "It's fucking fuzzy.
Everything is just fucking fuzzy." He inhaled. "It's impossible
to change shit. I mean *real* shit. Big picture. But big pictures
are for the romantics, up on the big screen. The 'one day'-ers.
I'm over all that by now. There's no infrastructure. They built
the infrastructure for living and for dying and for feeding and
taking shits, and of course for prolonging the poop parade but
never for salvation. God isn't opening any more windows, not
without consent." He hit the table. A few drops of tea
slopped delicately over the edge of his cup as it trembled.
"This whole affair is just for me and for you." He pointed at
Will and then back at himself. "*A spoonful of hope.* Just
enough for the two of us. So that I can die with an addled
sense of righteousness and so that you can go on with the
comforting knowledge that you aren't the only *crazy son of a
bitch* on this planet."

Now Will was actually beginning to wonder about
Arthur's screwed-up childhood. He was willing to bet it was
fascinating—a real Lifetime masterpiece. Somewhere behind
it all, Will understood that he had reached this point in a
rage. He was choosing consciously to fall into ruin, where
Arthur had clearly been set up from the start. Certainly this
distinguished Will, but he wasn't convinced it put him at an
advantage. If anything, it made him all the screwier. At least
his hand didn't shake when he lifted a tiny teacup between

his finger and thumb. At least he wasn't fuzzy, not mentally fuzzy. Emotionally fuzzy, maybe, but emotions came and went. Even in his present state, he knew he would forget about Margot one day. She would become simply a turning point, an excuse for bad behavior. A justification for everything and anything that happened next. A free pass. Will's mind had started to wander again. *That was a good sign.* He was moving forward, getting back to normal. He had been nodding slowly, deliberately. Arthur had been speaking genius or nonsense for ten minutes, maybe more.

Finally, Will gave it up, the feigned interest, and just spat out the question he had been dying to ask since Arthur had walked through door. "So come on, what's your research? Tell me what you've been doing for the past three years." It occurred to Will that this was all he had really wanted to know—purely information. Information he was pretty certain he would never have been able to uncover for himself, *or at least not for decades.* It made him all kinds of desperate.

And Arthur understood. They *were* similar, after all. He immediately dropped the conversation about outcomes and objectives, ethics and enlightenment, and dove into the science. At first, Will had difficulty following all of the details obscured by Arthur's drug-dependent brain. When Arthur wasn't in a sharpened state, it seemed he could still recall the words to describe his work, but the connections that normally flowed through his mind like swift water, linking each individual pool, dribbled to a halt. The explanations became stilted, disparate. Yet each motley slice of information was invaluable. Will had to focus keenly to take it all in, but as he built the picture in his mind, his fascination and admiration grew.

By the time he had left the restaurant, following a few awkward handshakes and copious nods from Arthur, everything had changed. Whether he chose to admit it outright or to allow it to sneak and sew itself into his subconscious, he was all in. He *needed* to be a part of this. *Consequences, good or bad, be damned.* Still, he stayed lingering on Tyler Street for several minutes after Arthur had driven away, watching shop owners move merchandise and restaurateurs accept deliveries, wondering uselessly if a single sideways plan could make a pointless life worth living, wondering if there had *ever* been *any* meaning to *any* life at all. He shrugged, then turned and trudged back toward the T.

———

Will stopped by his parents' house for dinner before returning to New Haven on the last train. He was hopelessly withdrawn, his mind still a jumble with spanking new scientific thoughts heaped hodgepodge around the unremitting pain. A world of possibilities key to the future, and a world of possibilities lost to the past. He had never told his parents about Margot. *Why should he have?* And obviously he would never in a million years attempt to describe to them his meeting with Arthur. So there was no reason to explain his strange spirits. *No reason to worry them.*

He sat largely silent through a meal of *rajma* and rice as his mother and father twittered on about his upcoming nuptials, his potential new jobs, and new living situations—the important things he emailed them about regularly. The passionless things he emailed them about to please them and to please himself. They were already planning a trip down to New York

City. Perhaps Ann had been right about having dinner with company. If he kept pretending everything was okay, perhaps one day soon he would wake up and it would be.

Chapter Twenty-Five

———

Over the next several months, Arthur and Will planned. They scouted. They invented projects that would take them to some hospitals. They volunteered at others. They were each so comfortable in their respective labs that they began to feel invincible. There was a confidence that came with being at a single institution for too long, especially one at the top of its field, and the fact that they were working toward the same goal and not competing as they had for years gave them both the freedom to self-inflate, unchecked.

Since the Monday Will had returned to work following his meeting with Arthur, it seemed, from what Jon could tell, as if he hadn't left. And Jon wasn't far from the truth. Aside from a few showers and changes of clothing, and a couple of long naps, Will had only left the lab to pursue hospital connections. Despite the inherent time constraints of his experimental work, he was flying through it.

Will figured the more work he did, the less suspicious he would look because, frankly, when did he have the time for extracurricular activities? Besides, keeping constantly busy was keeping constantly distracted. As Margot's death receded into the past, he was forced to see it from infinite, continuous angles of perspective, and the only way not to overthink every one of them was to stay perpetually sidetracked.

It was about five months before they were ready or, rather, before Arthur was on the verge of totally losing the fine motor skills necessary to complete their task. He was deteriorating quickly, as were both their mental states. Even without Arthur's handicap, it wouldn't have been long before they just said, "Fuck it. Now or never." They each had the responsibility of three hospitals, three obstetric wards, where they would each inject two infants with the serum, and two with a control—four randomized syringes labeled 1, 2, 3, 4. More than that would be way too risky; four was risky enough. So, in the end, if all went to plan, they would have a total of twelve subjects and twelve controls spread throughout the New England area.

———

For Arthur's part, everything went exactly and easily to plan, or at least that is what he told Will. Arthur was adept at being unapproachable. He easily assumed one of the blank personalities that was deliberately ignored in a hospital—one of those inordinately absorbed "doctor types," though no one ever knew for sure if they were actually a medical doctor or merely wore a white coat. He made sure he was seen often so that he didn't seem out of place. But he also made sure to give off a cantankerous vibe so that no one wanted particularly to know what he was up to, or in fact to take any interest in him whatsoever. This was not a difficult feat for Arthur. His whole life, he had been putting people off, dissuading interest. So, with the indispensable help of a handful of quietly borrowed and copied key cards, he simply walked into each ward, syringes easily concealed in his pockets, administered them quickly and quietly, and slipped out. If it happened that someone came in while he was at work, a simple excuse set him free. "Hi there. Just a little routine testing. Stool samples for the lab, you know." He would gesture vaguely. "Wonderful, beautiful, excellent, miracles, eh? My roommate's sister's friend's cousin just had a boy." He would tap his watch and hurry out.

———

Will's approach was much more convoluted. He scammed HR, ordered unauthorized key cards. He gained fraudulent credentials, volunteering under false names. He requested human samples using different lab accounts and then flashed his Yale ID, threw around some big names in the research world, and hoped no one would be the wiser. He flirted with all of the nurses, male and female, as well as the doctors, the other volunteers, and the administrative staff. He wandered into rooms and perused charts, striking up conversations with patients and even changing the occasional bedpan. He liked playing a part. It was far easier than being himself at the moment, and he desperately filled every spare second that he wasn't in his own lab working, working, working, to make it seem like he was never anywhere else.

Even Will knew that he had overdone it. If he ever did complete his mission, he would have to keep coming back and hanging around, like the sad and lonely and desperate man that he frequently reminded himself he was, just to keep anyone from becoming suspicious. Not only that, but he had begun to feel a nagging responsibility. Not such a deep responsibility as might be felt by one human changing forever the course of another, or up to six others, but the conceited responsibility of an overeducated asshole who assumes that after a few short months, he has become indispensable. He saw it as a matter of course that he had surpassed the laypeople to whom he had come to lend a hand, and that each of the hospitals he now frequented would suffer if he were to leave. Nonetheless, it was exactly this brand of conceit that allowed Will to feel necessary, to mentally remove himself from the masses who struggled only to keep their own heads above water and find the drive to *try*.

It was this conceit that had put him on this path from the start. It had whispered in his ear that getting good grades in high school was okay, as long as he kept it to himself, that college wasn't a degree to be completed and afterward flown like a flag but just one slightly higher step on the way up the staircase. It showed the majority of his peers in a poor light, following dim trails toward achievable goals, certain accomplishments that would keep them satisfied, *content*, *cringeworthy*. Will, when he looked in the mirror, saw ability, potential, and neglect. Somewhere in the back of his mind, there was yet even greater genius lurking, if only he could unearth the key to unlocking it. So he had worked harder and harder, physically ruined himself to get to his current position. And still it wasn't enough. Few who find themselves sunk in academia discover they truly have the patience to live on the timescale of research. Margot had had it, but Will had lost it.

And so here he was, sidling along the aisles of newborn babies, legs and arms flailing softly with newfound freedom in the sterile air of the ward. He had uttered the same generic phrase to the nurse as Arthur had when he entered.

"Miracles . . . every one." And he had swiped a finger carefully under his dry eye, blinking two or four times as he did so.

Marta, the nurse on duty, was so *very touched* by this show of emotion that she left Will in charge while she went out to make a phone call, buy a bag of Ruffles from the vending machine, consume them sitting at the back of the waiting room, and then take a smoke break. "Just for one minute. I'll be back in no time, sweetheart, just a two-minute phone call and to rest my feet for a second. Just three minutes, and if anything *does* go wrong, here's the bell." She pointed to a call button by the doorway. "Docs will come rushing over . . . but, well, unless it's really bad, just wait for me, *okay*? I shouldn't— well, never mind, it's just a bit of crying at most, really. You'll be just fine." She patted him on the arm before going out.

As he prepared to dose his four subjects, Will thought, *Two of you are lucky bastards.* It was easier than he had expected. His greatest fear had been that he would hear Margot's voice creeping in from the past, telling him he was fucking things up, that he was using her death as an excuse to behave shamefully, or simply that he was being a *huge jerk.* It was worse than that. He could no longer hear her at all. He couldn't recall the tone of her voice. He tried to replicate her speech pattern in his mind. *You never listen to me about* really *important things.* That wasn't it. *You just choose not to* hear me *when I try to tell you something serious.* Maybe she wouldn't have said anything. It would have all been conveyed in a sharp glance.

But even her face was fading. The quick pain of these realizations made him feel weak. He looked around him again, up and down the rows of bassinets. "*You're weak, babies.*" *He sounded completely stupid.* "That's right, you heard me." He sighed and located his first subject. "I'm jealous of you." He stuck the tiny pink body in the thigh and released the full contents of the syringe.

Jamie Barden didn't cry. He didn't make a sound. He yawned and looked at Will (or so Will thought) and then closed his eyes again. Will took a quick photo of the name and the rest of the information carried on the tablet next to the tiny bed. "I'm so fucking jealous."

The other three babies cried. Loudly. Will didn't know what to do. He petted them on their heads and uncertainly poked their small bellies, and then he sat down in a chair in the corner and waited for Marta to return. She came in smelling slightly of sour cream and onion, and cigarette smoke, and strongly of Febreze.

Will stood. "I don't know what happened." He gestured toward the sounds of crying but found he couldn't think of anything clever to explain the cacophony.

"Don't worry, sweetheart. That's just what they do. One starts for one reason or whatever, and then the others get going. You'll find it out one day." She glanced at his left hand. "You got a girlfriend?"

"Fiancée." Will thought of Viki for the first time in the last couple of crazy days.

"Soon enough then." Marta nodded knowingly with slightly pursed lips. "When's the big day?"

"July 10. Three months from this Saturday." The date came out of him like clockwork.

———

The remainder of Will's assignments were carried out, if not quite as smoothly, without major incident. With their immediate mission accomplished, all there was for Will and Arthur to do now was to sit and wait—wait with anticipation for whatever data, good or bad, would present itself in the upcoming years, and *who knew how many years it would take*? Will was already impatient, anxious to acquire every detail, itching to sift through every last annotation. He was curious how Arthur had gained access to the medical records of each of the selected patients, but he had decided to just accept it. The important thing was that the twelve subjects and the twelve controls could be monitored remotely, at least to some extent. In any case, they would soon know whether or not the tots would make it to their first birthdays.

Chapter Twenty-Six

———

The wedding was perfect. The weather was perfect. Even the cake tasted better than it looked, and it looked good.

In the three months leading up to the wedding, Will had found himself lacking in extracurricular activities to fill in the time he had previously been spending on his project with Arthur. *Arthur's project, really*, he would tell himself, and his head would drop an inch toward his desk. And he still wasn't sleeping well. So he threw himself, headlong, into wedding planning. It was hard keeping up with Viki at first. She had started months earlier, and she knew by rote every detail that had to be seen to, every minor decision that had to be made. Watching her at work, Will saw her in a new light. She was calm, in control. *She was better than him at something.* It was unexpected, and it was sexy.

Those three months he spent every weekend in New York and during the week, he diligently sent applications to NYU and Columbia, Rockefeller and MSK, Sinai and every other *respectable* institution he could think of in close proximity to Viki. They went to see a florist one Sunday, and Will stood silently for the hour, marveling at her simple ability to choose. He couldn't understand how she could know with such confidence blue over red, green over white, hydrangeas, gardenias, or peonies. The only flower he could come up with the name of was a rose. While Will had ideas and daydreams and pink-tinted visions of the hypothetical day, Viki knew exactly what she wanted, and one of the things she wanted, Will supposed, was him. *That made him feel special.* He had always suspected he was special.

By one month before the wedding, Will was madly in love again. Viki was just as alluring as when he had first met her—shiny and new, accessorized beyond recognition. But not with hoop earrings and a statement necklace—this time she was adorned with the mere fact that she had agreed to spend the rest of her life with him. She, so slim and stylish, she who could trick *any man* into being her husband. He lost himself inside of her every weekend. In bed, she was pretty as a picture and somehow volatile. If he let her go, her celestial body might wisp away into the dark abyss above them. He *had to have her* two or three times a night. And during the week, it was all he could think about. She wasn't even *that good* in bed, and he knew it. Objectively, Kate had been better, but with her, he had never felt the gravitational pull, the absolute fundamental brass tacks *need.* In fact, it occurred to him now that he hadn't really thought of Eva or Kate in months, maybe even a year. *Since just around the time he had become engaged. Surely that was it.* Of course, excepting the last several weeks, he hadn't really thought of Viki much since then, either, but he let that fact slip his mind.

In his weekday fantasies between his weekend rendezvous, the ones that seemed to consume all of his waking focus, he would walk through the front door, and without so much as a "Honey, I'm home!" (or maybe he would say it, but *seductively*), he would confidently stride over to Viki. She would be sitting on one of the artisan wooden stools he also fantasized about owning, at the granite countertop they would one day have, in a short flowing skirt, her delicate legs held just comfortably apart. He would slip his right hand between them, holding his left against the small of her back. She would hold onto his neck with both of her hands, and she would make the soft chirring noises that coaxed him further in. Or she was doing the laundry. She had decided she had better wash the clothes she had been wearing; after all, they only did laundry every other week. So he would come across her, leaning over, pulling fresh clothes out of the dryer, in her underwear, no bra, her small breasts pointing toward the ground, the smell of Tide in the warm, dry air. Needless to say, the laundry would have to be redone. In all of his weekday fantasies, they were already married.

———

Perhaps that is why the wedding went so splendidly. Will was obsessed. He got caught up in every detail: The way the gentle wind blew the tears flat against her father's face as he walked her down the aisle, giving her to Will; the way his vows were just slightly better than hers. *But hers were sweet, weren't they?* The way the crowd applauded as they returned back down the aisle together. He had never been applauded for his work before. Crowds of friends and family didn't stand up and cheer when he had a paper accepted or on the rare occasion that the data turned out to be exactly what it was predicted to be.

Walking down the aisle was an unfamiliar feeling. It wasn't the rush of vindication, the satisfaction and self-love that came from being right or making progress; it was simple approval. For once in his life, his accomplishment was recognized by everyone. He had achieved a standardized goal, *and wasn't she desirable?*

During the ceremony, Will's parents sat in the first row, beaming. When the ceremony had finished, his father shook hands with him. "Congratulations, my son. I wish you every happiness."

His mother kissed him on either cheek. "Isn't she an *absolute dream* in that dress?"

Will had always felt warm in their presence, and today he basked in it. Nothing could make the day more special than having the two of them there beside him. In his parents, Will saw marital success, and he wanted what they had, and he wanted *so much more.* In the bleaching light of celebration, he couldn't see that their success had been wanting nothing more than one another, and in the swift twinkling moments, diluted by gossamer and champagne flutes, it seemed possible.

———

The rest of the night, Viki glided around the reception in her long, sleek dress, and Will watched her from the bar while he got drunk with his friends. Even Jon had one or two too many, to mark the momentous occasion. At the end of the night, after the dancing and the lip-syncing, while Viki was saying dutiful goodbyes to the straggling guests, Jon sat down across from Will. Will was just about holding himself steady, momentarily alone at one of the tables that had been swept to the side to make room for the dance floor.

He leaned in. "Congratulations, man." Jon then proceeded to tap his bottle of beer lightly against the glass of wine Will was staring into the depths of. It overturned and rolled off the side of the table, missing Will's suit by an inch. "Whoa!" His eyes went wide for a second. He blinked and looked up at Will imploringly, as if unsure what action to take. But a moment later he seemed to have completely forgotten what had happened.

Will looked up from the spot where the wineglass had been. "Hey, Jon." He blinked heavily. "You're a really good friend. I don't think I ever tell you that, but you're a really good friend. Really, like, really good." He moved his right hand forward to place it firmly on Jon's shoulder but miscalculated. His hand slid down Jon's arm and hit the table. He laughed. "I'm fucked."

"Don't say that, man. I know you've had a hard year with, you know . . . I mean, I always thought . . . Hey, I don't know how to say this, all right? I've been trying to say it for months. All these *effing* months. And it's your *wedding day*!" Jon took a large swig of beer, and Will stared at him, petrified, like Jon was holding a gun to his head and Will couldn't decide whether or not he wanted him to shoot. "I'm *not* a good friend. Shit, I'm a groomsman. I should have talked to you sooner, but *all this*"—he gestured toward the ceiling—"I know you've been with Viki forever . . ." He swallowed; he shifted. "You know, you never go to the library anymore. You used to go *all the time*. Do you *miss going to the library*?" Jon was bright red and not just from the drink.

"All I meant by 'I'm fucked' was I'm drunk." This sentence came out cold and sober.

Jon fumbled. "Of course. Yeah. Obviously. I, well, congratulations again, I have to . . ." He pointed toward his wife who was sitting patiently a few tables away and then looked longingly at the door. He sighed. "See you at work, I guess."

Will wanted to say, "See you at work," back. He wasn't really all that angry with Jon, though he knew he should have been. But his vocal cords had tied themselves into a tight, painful knot and he couldn't speak. He could barely breathe, and the rage in his eyes was not directed at Jon but at the possibility that this familiar feeling might *never* completely disappear.

———

Will moved his limited wardrobe and immoderate library into Viki's small Manhattan apartment a few weeks later and commuted to Yale until he started his new position at Columbia in the fall. With the help of her parents, the following January they moved into a newer, larger apartment in Long Island City. They didn't have granite countertops or artisan stools, but they had a fresh space to start their lives together, living together full-time, married and working in the city, just like they had always planned.

PART III

Thirty Years Later

Chapter Twenty-Seven

———

CONTROLS:

i. Maria Newsom—sous chef at a local restaurant in Providence, RI. Associates degree in culinary arts from Johnson and Wales.

ii. Abigail Chan—pharmaceutical rep. BS Trinity College, biology. Was premed in undergrad.

iii. Remy Mendoza—secretary. BA Southern Connecticut State University, communications.

iv. Carling Kim—waitress. High school diploma and two semesters at Bunker Hull Community College. No major.

v. Julie Tangeman—stay-at-home mother. BS Boston College, history.

vi. Shannon Stuber—registered nurse. BS Quinnipiac University, nursing.

vii. Brianna Dominguez—teacher. BA Providence College, psychology. MEd University of Massachusetts Boston.

viii. Max Bousaid—cardiology fellow, Georgetown. BS Cornell, human biology. MD Duke University.

ix. Branden Kemp—security guard. Dropped out of high school.

x. Alana Castro—certified public accountant. BA Clark University, management. MS Clark University, accounting.

xi. Elizabeth Brooke—receptionist. High school diploma.

xii. Maria Moravec—salesperson. BA Albertus Magnus, philosophy and religion.

SUBJECTS:

i. Jamie Barden—classics professor, Cambridge University. BA Princeton, graduated age 19. DPhil Oxford.

   Comments: Impressive but then again, *Classics*. And I had high hopes for this one.

ii. Alison Marcher—astrophysicist, Stanford University. BS Stanford, graduated age 19. PhD Stanford. Postdoctoral fellow Stanford.

   Comments: *Theoretically* interesting . . . practically, not so much.

iii. Nancy Nguyen—novelist. BA Brown University, creative writing. MA Columbia, creative writing. Literary Prizes: National Book Critic's Circle Award, PEN/Faulkner Award for Fiction, Nebula Award.

   Comments: Unbelievable.

iv. Ben Gold—deceased: Childhood illness (undetermined encephalopathy), unclear if related to injection. Age 4.

   Comments: Probably unrelated.

v. Carly Brown—working at the local supermarket stocking shelves. Two years of undergraduate studies at Yale before dropping out, never chose a major. Mixed grades —As in several classes; however, failed a majority of pass/fail classes. Spent six years in and out of mental institutions. Currently living at home with parents.

Comments: No comment.

vi. Mike Hart—actor, unsuccessful. Does odd jobs (house-sitting, sperm donation, focus groups) and borrows money to stay afloat. Dropped out of high school. Suspected drug addiction.

Comments: Fucking useless.

vii. Alfonso Bennet—deceased: Drunk driving accident. Age 17. Didn't complete high school. Previously: Average grades, well above average test scores, no history of mental illness. Popular it seemed, according to social media.

Comments: Too bad. This one could have been a winner.

viii. Felix Long—blogger, *The Good, the Bad, and the Tasteless*. Reviews of all forms of media, restaurants, design, travel, anything worth complaining about. BS Vassar, chemistry. Functioning alcoholic.

Comments: What the hell happened to the chemistry? Why are blogs still *a thing*?

ix. Christopher Xu—paleontologist. Two years of community college before transferring to Northeastern and then transferring to the University of Michigan to complete BS. PhD University of Chicago.

Comments: That's a lot of fucking effort to study fossils . . .

x. Austin Vail—programmer. BS UC Berkeley, EECS. Graduated age 18, top of his class. No graduate school. Highly successful entrepreneur and philanthropist. Former CEO Muula, former CEO PanGO, former CTO BroadEn. Has his own foundation: PreVAIL, gives millions of dollars to various charities with no apparent discrimination based on what they deliver.

Comments: Maybe I should have studied CS.   •

xi. Simone Fitzgerald—pediatric oncologist. Head of Pediatric Oncology at Mass General by age 30. BS Harvard, graduated age 16. MD-PhD Harvard. Cover story in *Scientific American*. Profile in *Time*.

Comments: Fair enough.

xii. Ashley Barnes—climate scientist at Lawrence Berkeley National Laboratory. BS UCLA, Geophysics. PhD MIT, atmospheric science.

Comments: At least one in twelve might actually do something *useful*.

Overall comments: *Clearly* the stuff works . . .

Chapter Twenty-Eight

———

Twenty years ago, Will had attended Arthur's funeral. He had intended to stand at the back, unnoticed, but there had only been eight people present, so he had ended up in the front row along with everyone else, each of them leaning back slightly in order to avoid being confused with one of his closer acquaintances. No one had ever explained exactly what Arthur had died of. A cousin had mumbled to an aunt who had mumbled to a colleague that it was some vague, unknown, neurological, degenerative illness, that it hadn't been treated properly, that he had ignored the symptoms for too long, stubbornly refused to see a doctor. No one knew Arthur intimately, but everyone knew he had been a stubborn son of a bitch.

———

As they lowered the casket, Will pictured the familiar mini twitch of all of the mice he had injected over the years. His mind conjured images of the teeny glassy eyes, the shriveling limbs, the limp tails. When they became like that, he would snap their necks, put them out of their misery. Occasionally, one would slip through, deteriorating quickly throughout the weekend or even overnight. He found their wretched bodies in the morning, paralyzed, bared teeth, tiny monsters he picked up lightly and carried away, out of sight and out of mind. It was hard for him not to imagine Arthur in just the same way. But instead, he imagined a mouse laid out in a miniature suit, enclosed in a small wooden box, no bigger than the pocket bible in the hands of the minister. Something about seeing the compact chunky volume was comforting, even though Will himself had never read a leather-bound book. The pages were thin and yellowed, as delicate as insect wings. The book was older than Will, much older than Arthur would ever be. It was cinematic; it reminded him of fantastic tales, of magic spells. It reminded him that Arthur, as everyone, had been, would become, nothing more than slugs and snails, stardust.

At the end of the service, it started to rain hard. As the rest of the party moved obediently back toward the church, Will peeled off. He had already begun to feel the cold trickling around his heart when the sudden downpour closed in. He preferred to face the storm alone rather than sit safely inside with strangers, strangers who didn't know him from the person they had just buried. Only he and Arthur had understood each other. He hunched over. Within the sheets of water there was nowhere to turn, so he made himself smaller, inching away across the street. He hid under the eaves of a shuttered antiques shop. There was a bell on the door, but the lights were off inside, and a continuous layer of dust had collected over the old junk.

Will turned back toward the street to watch for a break in the rain. Inside him there was an eddying mix of guilt and sorrow and fear, but it wasn't over Arthur. Arthur had been brave. Will had come to idolize him. He had literally given years of his life to science and gotten back more than Will could possibly hope to achieve in *his* lifetime. Hiding from the elements, Will knew he would never be able to do it. He was desperately self-preserving; he couldn't help it. When he considered his existence, he didn't see all that much worth saving, but the fear of fading away was *simply dreadful.* Will even argued with himself that this was just an evolutionary trait, meaningless in the big picture. *He should be able to out-smart it,* but he couldn't.

He felt nauseous. Yet another reminder of his inescapable *humanity.* Despite his best efforts to justify and suppress, despite more than ten years having passed, the burden lingered. Every time he attended a funeral, he felt the guilt of the one he had missed. He hadn't gone to Margot's funeral. *It was in Tennessee, for fuck's sake,* he told himself. *Tenne-fuck-ing-ssee. And besides, ceremonies were meaningless. Just look at your beautiful fucking wedding.* He snorted.

An imperceptible tear leaked out of the corner of his eye, but he laughed it off, and the sky gave up on the waterworks as well. He straightened himself, standing tall and fixing his coat to shield himself from the elements. As the rain slowed to a drizzle, he walked back past the cemetery, gazing across the scene but choosing not to see what was happening.

———

A few days after the funeral, Will had received a secured email from Arthur's lawyer. A few days after that, all of Arthur's research, down to every last footnote and voice memo, arrived to Will's office by private courier on an external drive. Will understood Arthur had been too paranoid to upload it. He would have done the same, kept everything se-cured in an isolated, disconnected box. The entire thing was no bigger than a cigarette case. He held it in his hand for a few minutes. It seemed so light and small to be carrying all that he was imagining.

Chapter Twenty-Nine

––––––

In the last twenty years, things had moved quickly—that is, the things that Will could keep track of, that had clear if not contenting benchmarks. Professionally, with the help of Arthur's bequest, Will had produced dozens of papers, many of them well known and frequently cited. Within five years of receiving Arthur's notes, he had investigated and published enough of the theoretical work to be offered an endowed chair at UCSF, and he had left his tenure-approved position at Columbia to head west. A few years after that, he was made head of the Neurogenetics Department. He had minions: technicians, PhD students, and postdocs, and he had funding. He had reached the top of the ladder at forty-five and had begun the real struggle of pushing his own boundaries.

Personally, things had moved along too, but not with the same rush his professional life gave him. It had taken some effort to persuade Viki to move to San Francisco, or more precisely, to move away from New York. She didn't have many family members or close friends left in the city, but the city itself seemed, in the wake of lost connections, to be a closer relation than her parents had been. Will's parents had passed within a year of each other, before Will was offered the position at UCSF. He wasn't sure if he would have taken it otherwise, or perhaps he would have moved them out to California. *That was a sunny thought.* But they hadn't ever left Boston. Even as they grew older, they insisted upon assisted living rather than inconveniencing Will, and he had agreed. Though he had always assumed he would take them in as they had his grandfather, when the time came, it was impractical. He was never home. They would have been living with Viki, and Will wasn't convinced either party would be comfortable, so he had never suggested it.

There had been moments when he truly didn't think Viki would join him in San Francisco, but to his own surprise, he didn't lose sleep over it. Whenever he hit a wall with her, he jumped to the simplest conclusion. He thought, *Oh well, I guess this is it.* He would sigh and think, *What a damn, damn shame,* and then his mind would turn back to his lab. *Who was doing what, and were they working as quickly as they could? Was he forgetting something important?* But she had caved. She hadn't given up on them, and for some reason, he admired that. Right after they had moved, they had two children, one straight after the other, a girl and a boy. Then Viki had had her tubes tied and her tummy tucked as she immersed herself in her new surroundings. She proved adept at adaptation, diving headfirst into the full-time occupation of modish aerobics classes and buffalo-milk drinking that it took to be a proper yummy mummy in a world of men and women who were still stuck in just another version of the same stereotype.

Viki was in fact reasonably happy. In a way, she had everything she wanted: money, beautiful children, a hot body at fifty-five, and a full social calendar. The fact that Will wasn't home all that often didn't bother her too much. She found equanimity in solitude, so long as she had the right objects and amusements at her disposal. For all of her high-maintenance proclivities, her dreams had always been simple and material. She wanted physical things, and she got them.

Will, on the other hand, had become insatiable. Whenever he published a paper, it immediately became yesterday's news. It was *great* until it was done, and then suddenly it *wasn't good enough*. Real progress was always looming just around the next corner. And the older Will got, the worse this notion became. In the reality of the day, sixty was still considered relatively young—life expectancy was around one hundred or so *at least*, likely longer with enough artificial replacements, and Will reminded himself of this point every single day. But he was plagued by thoughts of being hit by a runaway bus, caught in the crossfire of a drive-by, or crushed under a building during the next big earthquake. Latent, imagined aneurysms drove him out of his mind. He would never see it coming, and he was sure that the stress caused in worrying about the unseen threat would only increase the chances of occurrence. The worst part was that Will considered himself to be scientifically minded; he *knew* he ought to know better. "Statistics," he would whisper to himself under his breath during weak moments. "Statistics. *Statistics*."

In his lab, they were now growing brains, full-sized human brains. Many of them were exposed in jars, personal aquariums, the way they had always been grown. But now, in the back corner of the room, over by the window, there existed a set of tanks where cerebral matter was being propagated inside of synthetically cultivated human skulls, the idea being the constraint would help to create the right forms and folds.

After all, proper structure was critical at every level of development. But sometimes the mere sight of them made Will shudder. When he looked into that corner of the room, he began to believe he truly *was* a mad scientist and that nothing in his wacky world was really real. Yet despite or perhaps due to this disquiet, he was drawn in. Occasionally, late at night when he didn't have the common sense to pack up and go home, he would wander over to that corner, almost involuntarily. He would find himself striking up conversations with the two specimens on the end.

———

"Hey, pal." He put his hand against the first glass cylinder and then removed it casually. "Hi, you." He touched the second lightly and quickly pulled away.

Chapter Thirty

———

"*They're* turning thirty this month." Will turned to the right-hand jar. "Are you proud?" He paused. "*Well?*" The floating skull gave no response. He glanced at the second jar, into the empty eye sockets, then down at the ground. He breathed out slowly. "Nothing all that bad has happened . . . Nothing *all that good* has happened, either." He tapped the base of the first jar absentmindedly. "What am I supposed to do with the information? *It's boring, you know*. What did we expect to happen? Create the next president? The next Linus Pauling or Marie Curie?" He looked longingly into the first jar. "Fucking novelists and paleontologists." He kicked the air. When he spoke to the specimens, they took on the personas of Arthur and Margot, the devil and the angel on his shoulders, both lost to him, both leaving him lost. But they were gone. They remained only as imperfect labels to the different shades of Will.

"Did I tell you? I let them do it to my own kids, Marla and Arbor. They didn't make them smart. They made them pretty. They're fourteen and fifteen, and they're *pretty*. They should be snotty and pimple-infested. They should be miserable and angry and studying as hard as they can to get *the fuck out of high school and into college*. We've messed with the *order of things*." He looked at Margot. "I know, you didn't. You *love* the order of things. Everything in its place; everything as it should be, as *God* created it. Well, *let me tell you*, things were fucked up then, and they're fucked up now. It doesn't make a damn bit of difference if zombies rule the world. Pretty soon they'll be *better than we are*. We keep making them stronger. They're not stupid anymore. Soon they'll be smarter than they started off. Some of them *already are*." He chuckled. "They'll become classics professors! They'll make video games!" He was laughing hard now, but he stopped short. "I met a few of the twelve, you know. I probably shouldn't have, and I didn't tell you. Because you're dead. But I had to *see them*. I ran into them on campus, in coffee shops. I accosted them at conferences, even at work." He paused. Will's eyes were moist. "They were smart . . . Certainly they were smart. But they were all so . . . so . . . complacent. *Yuck*, am I right?" His eyes darted back and forth between Margot and Arthur, searching himself for confirmation. "All of their seemingly great achievements were so easy for them. I swear, Simone felt finishing med school was tantamount to taking the GED.

"Don't you *see*? They aren't going to change anything. Twelve average people with eleven hundred SAT scores and a quality inferiority complex could do more. Not to say that the control group isn't just as shamelessly indifferent. But where do we find the gene for *giving a shit*? Where do people come from that are both *good and angry*? And clever, on top of that . . . "Still," he mused, "in a basic sense, the experiment was a success. *Perchance* it is just a question of scale." Will forced a deluded half smile at his two advisors, bowed half an inch, then got the hell out of there. Even he could tell he was utterly raving.

Chapter Thirty-One

These days, Will tried not to think about the zombies. He still felt a remote responsibility toward them, but he hadn't bothered to visit the ward at Columbia or at UCSF. He hadn't deliberately seen a patient face-to-face in thirty years, since the last time he had volunteered with Margot. In the interim, he had made a universal decision that he did far more productive work when he didn't know any of the patients personally.

But the zombies were everywhere. There was no room left for them to stay, so they were rushed out of their hospital beds just a week or two post-surgery. Now they roamed the streets. New rehabilitation centers were being built, but it was impossible to keep up with the sheer numbers. As Will walked through the crowded, bustling streets of the Dogpatch, he glanced at every face that swept by. He wondered, *Are they really supposed to be here?* He thought that sounded bigoted, but he didn't care. When he imagined he recognized one, he would gloat silently. *I might have made your life possible, you undead fuck.* He loathed and pitied them all at the same time, and in his bitterness, he used them for self-glorification.

Once, he recognized the familiar traits on a dog-walker being pushed and pulled by a handful of mismatched charges. *Mush!* He laughed out loud, seemingly at nothing. He caught his own reflection in a window. *You're the crazy one.* In his darkest moments, he was convinced that one of them would take his place. Not his position—he didn't fear competition—but his place on earth. Despite countless attempts to employ logic, Will couldn't shake the feeling that there were more applicants than there were posts and, as usual, contestants would be chosen at random, by a lottery system rather than on merit. He was sure he wouldn't be called.

Worse still than the zombies were the Vikis of the world. True, he hadn't tried very hard to stop her. It was hard to see straight about your own kids, so naturally it wasn't *his* fault. When he had decided to publish Arthur's work on the permanent possibilities of what at the time was loosely referred to as "Expression Patterning Therapy," or "EPT," he had overestimated *people.* He had thought, *People will want this—a smarter and better future.* At this point in time, the test subjects had been about ten. They were all, *save the one who didn't make it past four,* excelling in school. They had no behavioral issues whatsoever. Will had had high, high hopes. But somehow, through the channels of research and design, endorsement and delivery, the message had gotten lost. The use of EPT technology to alter mental ability and stability had been banned, and instead, regulators had let slip through its use to enhance physical features. Suddenly it was paramount in the "war on obesity," but of course the extremely expensive treatments had only given wealthy people the opportunity to endow their descendants with longer lives and longer legs and done little else.

That was when Will had begun selling the Brill pill. He was pissed off. He couldn't stand the fact that something *he* had created was being regulated by nincompoops. Everything was wrong; *they* were wrong. *Ignorant, imbecilic, idiotic . . . Why did everything good he tried to accomplish always turn out for the worse?* He didn't have time to think about it. Somehow he had to balance out everything he had done. Everything *they* had done. He had given the world a beautiful gift, and the world was squandering it. So he would find another way. He would need funding, and he would need secrecy. He couldn't have research management checking up on his work, investigating where every dollar was being spent. He could get away with a lot, but *why have any constraints?* He felt reckless.

So he had turned to dealing drugs. That was *all it was*, and he knew it. It was an easy drug to peddle. None of the canines had been sniffing for *that* the first time he packed it in prescription bottles on his way to the conference in Singapore. But that was just the beginning. Now he outsourced. Someone else did the synthesizing, someone else did the packaging and the posting, and the packages were sent *all over the world*. Will didn't do much, aside from collect. And he collected *a lot*. He was the head of a drug cartel with no competition.

Perhaps there was a time in his life when he would have felt guilty. Sometimes he had flashbacks to Arthur's premature funeral and some form of remorse would begin to materialize, but when he considered all of the things Arthur had done in his short life, he was able to brush it off. He had improved the formula since then, and the ingested dosages were smaller, much smaller than what Arthur had been injecting. The risks were *relatively* low, and though the rewards were somewhat proportional, the ability to comprehend was an *unbelievable offering*. Will even went so far as to feel magnanimous at times.

He hid the money in plain sight, in the form of large grants and awards. He made up false foundations, he invented obscure institutes, and when he spent the money, he felt justified. These overflowing resources would allow him the freedom to come up with a new plan, a fresh plan, a plan to make a difference before the zombies took over and it was too late.

Chapter Thirty-Two

———

Jon was going to be in town over the coming weekend. *Good old Jon.* Will hadn't seen much of him since he had left Yale. When Will had still been living on the East Coast, Jon had come down to New York every so often, and Will had gone up to New Haven even less so. They had had a coffee if it was before noon and a beer if it was after noon, and they would chat about work mostly and sometimes wives, renovations, or household appliances. Then they would laugh about how old they both had become and how suddenly. But aside from running into one another at a conference in Austin ten years ago, they hadn't seen each other since Will had moved to San Francisco.

Jon was still living in New Haven. He had left academia and gone to work for one of the biotech firms that had headquartered themselves around the university. He oversaw research and production, got home at six thirty, ate dinner with his family, and slept a full eight hours every night. Will was always tempted to offer him a place in his lab at UCSF, but he knew Jon wouldn't have taken it. He was another one of *those*—contented types. He told himself that he pitied Jon, but the twinge he felt as he said it left him with an easily ignored inkling that his pity was just another warped form of jealousy.

———

Toward the end of the week, Will became nostalgic. The prospect of seeing Jon in a few days brought him back to another time. As he walked through his lab during his weekly Thursday roundup, he thought of George, barking mad comments to anyone in earshot, motivating by confusion. Will had always assumed he would make a better PI than George. Back then, he had thought to himself on several occasions, *I'll explain everything carefully. I'll make time. I'll give a shit.* But he didn't have to look far to see that he didn't.

Will flinched as he noticed a young girl coming up to him, marching determinedly straight down the center of the laboratory, ignoring PCR blocks humming on either side. She had a tablet in her hands, holding it up as if she were going to show him something, ask him for an opinion or an answer. She looked familiar, but he couldn't remember her name. Was she a PhD student? Was she a postdoc? An exchange student? She could have been a high school intern for all he knew; everyone under thirty looked the same to him these days. Will promptly took a fake call on his own tablet. He tapped his ear, held up a finger, adjusted his glasses, and made a sharp turn, dodging her and heading back to his office across the hall. He shut the door behind him.

But locked inside his office, all he could do was daydream about the past. That was the problem with no longer doing his own lab work—he didn't have any distractions. And he was still manipulating Arthur's oeuvre. Arthur had a seemingly unending supply of experimental plans that he had never had the time to carry out. Will *could* come up with his own procedures, but it seemed impractical to ignore the gold mine he had in his possession, *irresponsible* even. So he built on Arthur's ideas, mixing them with his own, updating them with new methods that had been developed over the years, *improving them*. Still, he was left with plenty of time to ruminate on other issues, big and small.

He contemplated moments in time, words he had said on a whim and what the rest of the room had thought of him. Like the time he and Viki were at dinner with Viki's friend and her husband, or maybe the husband was the friend and she was the wife. *Whatever.* They were up on Nob Hill, packed into one of those tiny restaurants that seem exclusive only because a seating of over twenty could be classified as a fire hazard. One of those restaurants that all had the same name—Garland, or Turf, or Beech. He had been asked some nonsense about his busy work schedule.

"Well, at least it gets me out of *yoga and book club*," he had replied. Did they find him funny? Or was it just awkward? *It was a rude question anyway.* Will was beginning to suspect that every time he said something he thought was funny, everyone else just felt *awkward*.

He turned his thoughts away from his increasingly inept social interactions. *They made him cringe*, but this only left room for far more unsettling considerations. As he so often did these days, Will began to contemplate the moments in time when decisions were made. Sometimes he felt that large decisions, like the decision to move to New York and marry Viki, had minor outcomes. If he had left her at the altar, Will assumed he would have gone on to marry someone practically identical. *Viki might have wound up better off*, he supposed. On the other hand, small decisions, like the decision not to volunteer that very last time with Margot, could have major outcomes. *Where would he be if she were still alive? Would he have ever connected with Arthur?* Did the universe diverge every time he made a choice, or did all paths eventually lead to the same place? He was almost certain that *everything* would be different, though he wasn't at all sure how.

Will spent hours pondering fate. He didn't believe in fate, but he wanted to. If fate existed, if the series of poor decisions leading to foreseeable and forewarned consequences he had made were just the cog-and-wheel workings of some universal clock, then he was off the hook. But he didn't believe in fate. Will imagined his life like a ball of yarn unraveling. The longer he lived, the more unspun yarn there was to keep in order, and the more twists and turns that he took, the more tangled it all became. The only way to untangle the mess was to somehow reverse the turns. He had to start from the beginning and try to make right everything that had gone wrong. The danger was the possibility of tangling things further. Some would cut off the string where it was and start fresh, but Will couldn't give up the past. He still couldn't stand losing. He could fix everything, and he would start with Jon. For once, he would be honest with him—a little.

———

On Saturday morning, Will met Jon down by the Embarcadero. The biweekly farmers market was going on in front of the Ferry Building, and Will had thought, *That seems like a touristy enough activity.* It amused him that in an age where, without so much as opening your tablet, you could have a sack of potatoes, a bunch of carrots, a case of wine, or an entire four-course meal delivered to your door in under an hour, people still succumbed to this novelty. They streamed to it. It was probably more popular now than it had ever been. People apparently wanted to know where their food was being grown, down to the specific plot of land, and they wanted to meet the human being that had reared it for months before they whisked it through a blender in seconds and passed it in a matter of hours. It wasn't just crackpots, either. In fact, one of Will's PhD students had recommended it to him a few years ago. He had come within twenty feet of the thing to see what all the fuss was about and then decided it was too crowded and left. This time, he braved the crowds and walked with Jon, side by side, into the first aisle.

It was a rare crisp morning in San Francisco. The customary layer of fog was nowhere to be seen, replaced by a quick breeze. The sun was bright and, though strolling between the dense market stands it could hardly be felt, it brought out the rich organic hues of the diverse fruits and vegetables. Will, and he assumed anyone with half a brain, didn't believe in all that "GMO free" bullshit, but he felt the sharp contrast to his daily life of splicing and dicing, growing the unnatural in media, on plates, in jars, taking tiny furry life and distorting it. *All for the greater good.*

He turned to Jon, musing, "Can you imagine being a farmer? Take a seed, put it in the ground, and *shit grows.* No pluripotent stem cells, no gene overexpression, no test tubes and petri dishes, no nutrient agar. Just dirt and water, and you care for it and you harvest it and you do it again." It was an oversimplification of the mass-production agricultural methods in place over most of the world, but he assumed the farmers market providers stuck to traditional methods. He popped a Fuji apple sample into his mouth and chewed on it. It burst with flavor, juicy, crispy, absolutely delicious.

"And you've made something essential to life," Jon pointed out. "Whatever you might say, it's more important to eat than it is to have three kidneys or a brain transplant, or whatever it is you are working on these days." He smiled and nibbled on a perfect slice of pluot.

They walked through the remainder of the stalls, snacking and keeping largely silent aside from the occasional reminder that they were participating in a shared experience: "Mmm, you have to try this one," or "Nice weather—chilly, but usually it's foggy until at least noon." Then they wandered away from the market and sat down inside the Ferry Building to have a coffee.

Will opened up his tablet first. The coffee shop had appeared on his sidebar when they were in range, but Jon stopped him, insistent on paying. "What would you like?" Jon opened his own tablet and plugged in a kava latte for himself. Will protested briefly but soon gave up and requested a black coffee with two sugars. He had never been any good at arguing with Jon, and that hadn't changed in thirty years, so he compliantly went to find a seat while Jon waited at the counter for their drinks. The café wasn't busy—everyone was still out enjoying the market—but all of the furniture was precisely mismatched. He would pick out a decent-looking table and then see that the chairs were unfairly paired: one taller, one shorter, one comfortable, one austere. Will sighed. He would take the hard-plastic pink stool and let Jon have the armchair. The main thing was not to be too close to the entrance—too many people milling around, trying to decide which caffeine to consume.

Once seated, Will silently mused, *You can order from your*

tablet and pay by fingerprint, but it still takes a real human being ten minutes to make a good latte. He smiled, deliberately taking pleasure in the simple notion. Then he reluctantly turned his mind to the task at hand. *What was he going to talk to Jon about all day?* It had been so many years. There was a lot he *could* say. There were a lot of new truths to unload and a lot of old lies to dispel, but what was *the point* exactly? Will had wanted to be honest. Maybe he *needed* to be honest, but as the time came, he wasn't sure what good it would do either of them.

Before Will could put half his thoughts in order, Jon turned from the counter to face him, holding the drinks up like trophies won. He moved toward the table where Will was waiting and handed over his two-sugared coffee. Then he sat down slowly, taking a sip of the kava before setting it down carefully in front of him. "I'm sorry it has been so long, Will. Work. Kids. All of that. We both keep busy, I know, but all the same, I'm sorry. We used to be close, didn't we?" Jon was smiling, and his lightly playful tone implied that what he had said was rhetorical, but still it made Will uncomfortable. For half a second, his throat filled with the dread that Jon was going to tell him he was dying. *He couldn't handle it.* He knew he couldn't. Will started to panic. He could feel the sweat breaching the surface of his skin, loading the base of each pore.

Luckily, like most everything Will felt these days, it passed in a matter of seconds. He forced out a strained chortle and moved forward. "Of course we did. We still are. Time and distance are just constructs and so forth. So how is work? How are your kids? *Please,* let's talk about that." The words rushed themselves out of his mouth before he could pause to take a breath.

"Work is the same, the beauty of industry. For the most part, we just make one product, and we aim for consistency. I do miss real research sometimes, being on the cutting edge, even if it takes years of long, lonely hours to cut." Jon moved an invisible knife forward and back with his hand to underline the wordplay. "But there is something to be said for the humdrum. Let's just say I don't miss the disappointments. It isn't for you, God knows, but then you rarely seem to be disappointed. I read your papers sometimes. There are almost too many to keep up with." Jon had a strange look on his face, but he continued. "The kids, well, they aren't kids anymore. They're all grown up."

Will nodded. "It happens fast." That seemed like the thing to say at first, but then he remembered his vow to untangle himself. He would *try* to be honest with Jon for once, even if it was another decade before they saw each other, even if they never saw each other again. As Will made the decision, he knew it was a selfish one. It wouldn't do Jon any good to hear his problems *now*, but *oh fucking well.* "Honestly, I barely see my kids. Marla and Arbor. *Cool names*, right?" Will chuckled uncertainly. "I've watched them grow up on a screen. New pictures come up on the tablet every day, and when I see them, I think, *Hell, they're fine; I don't need to go home tonight.*"

At noon, Will and Jon left the coffee shop. They moved outside to have lunch at one of the bayside restaurants, looking out across the water, past the ferry terminal and under the Bay Bridge. It had warmed up considerably since the morning, and they celebrated with two cold beers. "Cheers." Jon lifted his bottle, and Will mirrored him.

He was lost in his thoughts, getting deeper and darker. It

had felt good to let go of a truth and he wanted to dump more of them, get them out into the open so that at least one *good person* would understand what a smoldering mess he was. He suspected that Jon had always silently judged him, as any good friend should, but now he *craved judgment.* "You were right, you know." The food hadn't arrived yet, so Will found himself dropping weighted chitchat between sips of beer. "About Viki. You never liked her. I was *obsessed* with her. I thought she was *fucking cool* . . . but now she's old. She keeps it tight for an old lady, with all that Zumbalates rigmarole though, *damn.* But that isn't the point." Will shook his head and took another sip of beer. He angled the butt of the bottle toward his chest. "*I'm an old man.* Five years older than she is, though I look at least fifteen. When we were young, it was easy to overlook things. It wasn't even compromise, really. We would get so caught up in things that didn't matter. We're not cool anymore. *I* never really was. And that's it." Will shrugged his shoulders. "I hope she's having an affair. Sometimes I have dark fantasies about her leaving me . . . She walks in like, 'Fuck you!' There's bags packed, and she storms out, and some handsome thirty-six-year-old sous chef with a six-pack picks them up, like he's lifting a cup of coffee, and follows her out. And I'm alone in my house. All alone." Will blinked. "In the fantasy, the kids are in boarding school," he explained. Then he took another long sip of his beer, enjoying it.

Jon drank deeply before replying, "And it's never the other way around? You and a twenty-five-year-old surfing-champion-slash-marine-biologist?" He laughed tentatively.

"I'd do a lot of things, but I'd never cheat on her. Somehow I think I've even turned that policy into a selfish thing." He lifted his beer to his mouth, killing it, then hailed the waiter for two more. They sat in silence until the next round arrived. Will had on a gloomy expression out of decorum, but inside, his heart was beating a meter faster. He felt a lift in his chest. Speaking these words out loud, releasing them to an upright and unlucky listener, had felt indulgent and gratifying. Will basked quietly for a minute.

"Can I ask you something?" Jon turned his attention away from a seagull bobbing in the bay to face him.

"Shoot." Will was ready to spill.

"Or actually, tell you something." Jon swallowed. "I was kind of a shitty friend back when the librarian . . . when Margot died. I know it's decades too late, but I always wanted to say that it wasn't your fault. I guess I didn't think you'd believe me, or you'd think it was *so cliché*, or I don't know." Jon swirled the end of his first beer around in the bottom of the bottle, staring down into it.

Will had not been ready for that. "It was and it wasn't," he mumbled.

"It *wasn't*."

Will nodded. "*Plenty of things are*. I sometimes . . ." He paused, considered changing the outcome of the sentence, then took another swig and carried on. "I sometimes have dreams about her. Or maybe not about her, but I'm sure she's in them. I don't remember what they're about, but I have *that gut feeling* in the morning that I was talking to her about something." He drank deeply again. "Annoyance, I think it is." He snorted. "Maybe it's time to start keeping a dream journal."

"There's an app for that."

"Heh. Honestly, I think I don't want to know." Will shook his head.

After lunch, they shook hands. Will thought, *He deserves a hug for listening to all of my bullshit,* but he didn't go in for it.

As they parted ways, Jon paused. "It's never too late, buddy. If you need anything, I'm here . . . Well, there." He pointed to the east.

————

Too late for what? Will couldn't get the words out of his head as he walked back through the FiDi in the direction of home. He had thought that, for once, he had left Jon with more to think about, but it always went the other way. Jon knew him better than he knew Jon, yet another proof of his selfish behavior.

Chapter Thirty-Three

———

Will had been more honest in his conversation with Jon than he'd been with anyone in a long time—maybe ever. But he hadn't been *totally honest*. He did remember bits and pieces of the dream. The *dreams*.

———

He would walk into the medical library at Yale. It was just as it had been thirty years ago. Margot was there at her desk, but she was hiding something. As he walked in, she quickly pulled down her left sleeve. He knew she must be injecting herself with the serum, but why? Where had she gotten it? Had she made a deal with Arthur? He was angry. He didn't want to see her hands begin to shake, her mind scattered and shattered between doses. She was *smart enough already* for fuck's sake. He didn't want to watch her die.

Then suddenly, it was a few years later. She had done something incredible. It wasn't clear in his dream exactly what she had achieved, but he figured it was probably cold fusion or time travel. Someone handed her a Lombardi Trophy and someone else hung an Olympic gold medal around her neck. It was crowded, and there were bright flashes in front of his eyes from camera bulbs going off. Will wasn't even sure where he'd seen such huge cameras like that. Everything was chaos, but through the crowd she somehow managed to look straight at him and be heard. "Told you so," was all she said, and then she fainted.

Everyone disappeared. She was sick and alone in a bed, but she was far away, up a mountain. He tried to climb it, but it was too hard, so he gave up and walked home. But everywhere he looked, there were billboards, screens with her face on it, praising her for whatever it was she had done. When he walked through the door to his old apartment in East Rock, Margot was sitting on the couch watching TV with his old roommates. She laughed and pointed at him. "Gotcha!"

––––––

Will woke up. *Where was he?* He was back in his bed, back in his house in California. He turned sideways to check on the color of the walls, the shape of the room, the framed family photos as confirmation. Then he sighed and flipped over out of habit to stare blankly at the time, the temperature, the humidity, the pollen count, and the UV exposure. It was almost as if chatting with Jon the other day had made the dreams more vivid, *worse*. He thought bitterly, *Why hasn't anyone figured out what the hell the deal is with dreams yet? Hundreds of years of research, and a soothsayer could still tell me more than a scientist.*

He threw off the covers, and the chill arising from the thin layer of sweat that coated his lower legs filled him with the compulsion to shower *immediately*. But he could hear the water running. Viki was already in there. He considered joining her for half a minute but instead did ten push-ups on the bedroom floor. He paced back and forth across the room, then did ten more. He picked up his tablet out of his workbag and sat down on the edge of the bed to search the ten names, the ten that were left of the twelve. He checked on them every morning, compulsively, despite the fact that nothing ever seemed to change anymore, despite the fact that it frustrated the hell out of him day in and day out. They had all been stagnant for years.

Jamie Barden appeared on the screen at the foot of the bed, his smug picture next to a stack of old bound paper books on the Cambridge Classics Department homepage. *Books, hah.* Will hardly even looked at Jamie anymore; it was too disappointing. Today his photo was accompanied by the news that he had translated some text that was fifteen hundred years old and had surely been translated fifteen hundred times before. Will closed the page.

Next up was Alison. But as he brought up the new search, there was a knock on the bedroom door, and, without waiting for a reply, Marla came in. He reflexively swiped the results off of the screen, minimizing them.

"Hi, honey." Will sat up straighter. "What's going on?" He couldn't help staring at her. She looked natural enough, standing there with teenage posture, still in her pajamas and bed hair, but he knew there was something made-up about her. She was *too symmetrical.* They hadn't told the kids what they had done, though he was sure they would figure it out if they hadn't already. The older they got, the more of their friends were just the same. They weren't stupid. *They weren't* that *stupid.* Would they be upset? Would *he* be upset if they were pleased? Wasn't it the job of parents to make their children's lives easier, *by any means*? Will felt ashamed all the same. It was just one of the reasons he stayed late at work.

"We're out of milk." She leaned against the doorframe self-indulgently as if it was too early in the morning to expect her to support herself.

"No problem. I'll order it now." A few taps of his tablet and the order was complete. He waited momentarily for notification that a drone was on its way. "It'll be here in five minutes."

"Thanks, Daddy." She rotated back into the hallway, still leaning one arm against the doorframe, then shuffled back down the hall. Will waited to hear her footsteps down the stairs before reopening the search window and turning his attention back to Alison. Alison Marcher. She was always discovering *something*. Some extra-solar planet or distant star system that would come to be known as the "Marcher this" or the "Marcher that" or more likely "planet number ten bazillion and fifteen." Will didn't think it was fair to call them discoveries. He knew it was the accepted language, but he didn't think they ought to be compared to the discoveries made in a lab on the basis of months of evidence-stimulated research. He imagined a large telescope tracking data points through the sky, following an unending code of precise locations. And when, in the vast, dark vacuum, an object appeared, Alison happened to be in the room, and there the credit went. Will believed in these cases they should instead be called "uncoveries," or perhaps "stumbled upons."

He rolled his eyes and moved on. Nancy, Carly, Mike, Felix, Christopher—all of them still chugging along, doing whatever it was that they did. The number of hours that Will had spent poring over their medical histories and transcripts, curricula vitae, and online profiles far exceeded the number of hours he had spent looking over his own kids' homework or progress reports. *To be fair, his kids had only been around half as long.* Despite year after year of largely disappointing results, he had remained obsessed with the ten. He was determined to find *a reason* for their existence. Not even ten reasons—just *one* would do. If he could find one good reason for their existence, then perhaps it would extend beyond them. Certainly it would extend to the person who had given them the ability to exist as they were. True, that person was Arthur, but Arthur was gone, and in his absence, he and Will had become so entwined that Will could barely separate them anymore.

Nothing was new with Austin, either. He was probably building a company or selling it out. He always was. Will felt the most animosity toward Austin, though even he recognized that behind this trumped-up disdain was your basic, straightforward jealousy. Austin was always grinning. Will didn't think anyone over the age of twenty should be allowed to grin *like that*. But the worst thing about Austin was that he didn't have a single good reason for existing, and yet he didn't give a *flying fuck*. He happily brought trinkets and trifles to the world and sold them for good—scratch that, *fantastic*—sums of money, and it didn't bother him one crumb. He traveled the globe, he worked when he wanted, and he didn't work when he *didn't feel like it*. He was married, and his husband, Gerome, ran their foundation, PreVAIL, throwing money at sick puppies, performance art, and, obligatorily, cancer research. And that made them feel good about themselves. It was *ludicrous*.

In disgust, Will turned to the next name on his list, Simone

THE BRILL PILL

Fitzgerald. Simone was receiving some award for some break-through or another. The headlines always splashed something dramatic like she had cured cancer, but the news always exaggerated scientific achievements while underplaying the work and innovation that went into them. How many times could a single person cure cancer? *There were always plenty of cancers left to cure.* But Will respected Simone. It may be a cakewalk for her, but her job was still *saving children*, for goodness' sake. He liked to read her research. It was impressive, the work she had done by the age of thirty, and he looked forward to observing her future accomplishments. There was a time when he would have thought she was *the best* of the lot. But in the last thirty years, things had changed—since Margot and Arthur had died, since he had seen zombie after zombie take their places in the world. His perspective had changed. He knew that not everyone could be saved, but also, that they *should be*. What he struggled with was whether everyone was meant to be.

Will stretched his hands out forward, extending his cramped fingers. He leaned back onto his pillow and looked up at the ceiling. There was only one name left to try. But he had heard the water go off in the shower. He lowered his gaze, watching distractedly as Viki came out of the bathroom wearing a towel. She removed it without looking at him, roughly drying her hair as she moved, naked, toward the walk-in closet to dress herself. At the foot of the bed, she came into sudden focus, along with the rare realization that he was aroused. But as he made a move toward her, he felt the thin layer of dried sweat slip softly between his skin and the clean white sheets. He lost it. He jumped out of bed to take the shower he had been desperate for all morning, leav-

221

ing Viki where she had left him, behind the door of the closet.

A hot shower had been just what he needed. He had the water preset to 110 degrees. It burned his skin, cooking, disinfecting the tiny microbes, searing off the crawling feeling that invariably tormented him when stalking his artificially astute subjects—the feeling that justification would never, ever come. When he got out of the shower, Viki had already gone downstairs to make one of her awful green breakfasts, or out to one of the early morning social-gatherings-cum-calisthenics-cults she frequented. He dried off and dressed himself in the same closet she had, facing the opposite side, where GRETA™ hung his fresh-pressed suits. Will chuckled at what his younger self would have thought as he pulled on the trousers and buttoned up the stiff-collared shirt, tugged taut the jacket and tie, and laced tight the chestnut brown oxfords. Whatever advancements had been made in cloth and care, nothing could replace the bolstering feeling of a simple, secure necktie.

He heard the doorbell ring and then Marla shout, "I got it!" from downstairs. *It must be the milk,* he thought. *It's a few minutes late. Hmph.* Will wandered out into the hallway with the thought of registering a complaint but heard the front door close before he had reached the top of the stairs. He turned on his heel and went back to his tablet. Sitting up in the armchair at the far side of his nightstand, he brought up the final name: Ashley Barnes. His eyes glazed over as he attempted to read the newsreel running like a ticker on the left-hand side of the LBL homepage. He had always had a hard time with physical science—not with comprehension, but with feigning an interest. Whatever his credentials, he was seldom able to overcome that glassy-eyed look that gave

him away to fellow scientists in different fields and profes-
sionals the world over. The same look that so often gave him
away to his students when they pitched what they considered
legitimate ideas, or to his wife, children, and friends when
they started speaking in too much depth about topics that
didn't catch his interest. He could nod and grunt at all of the
right moments, but still *they knew*. Yet another one of his
many shortcomings, though daydreaming remained the most
persistent. He figured the two were probably related.

But *there she was*. His eyes refocused on the page in front
of him as he saw Ashley's name come up along the ticker. For
all of his grumblings, Will was ever hopeful, and seeing her
work advertised on the lab's press feed sparked an inevitable
optimism he didn't like to acknowledge. He nervously clicked
on the news article, trying to manage his expectations in the
split second it took to load. The article explained, in slightly
plainer words and including a few colorful quotes and anec-
dotal references, the research that she had recently published
in *Nature*.

Will read it once through without taking in a thing and
then reread it a second and a third time. He blinked slowly.
He opened and skimmed the *Nature* paper, and then he
glanced through the article one last time to be certain. He just
about had the gist of it, and *it was big*. It certainly *seemed* big
to Will, anyway.

Ashley had invented a box. Not just any box . . . This box
could take in atmospheric gases and, using sunlight as energy,
convert these gases into a solid hydrocarbon. It was a process
analogous to photosynthesis. Only much, *much* more efficient.
The device could sequester carbon dioxide at an unprecedented rate. It was a major breakthrough, *apparently*, in what

was termed "direct air capture." The hydrocarbon the box produced could even be used as a fuel source (though Will wondered whether this wouldn't just defeat the purpose). It was an expensive box, no doubt, but it wouldn't remain expensive forever. And it could, *theoretically*, be reproduced on any scale. *Now that was something.*

Will nearly pissed himself. The stiff, arrogant feeling that came with every good data set the minions produced under his tutelage, with every paper they published with his name on it, and, goodness knows why, every time he looked in the mirror, melted away like a spring frost midmorning compared with the even more conceited thought that *he* had made this happen.

Chapter Thirty-Four

——————

On his way to work, he felt different. There was an edge of attitude about him, a spring to his step, if you will, an additional smidge of self-worth to his walk. For one thing, he did *walk* to work. On most days, he used a ride service, though it was only a half-hour walk and the weather rarely warranted more than a lightweight jacket. When he arrived at the lab, he didn't go straight through to his office as usual. He stopped at each bench, smiling at samples already underway and nodding his approval to the stacks and stacks of empty plates and empty racks, all eagerly waiting to be filled. He lightly touched the cold white countertops, lined up two by two down the length of the room, one hand on either side as he strode up the center, turning left to gaze out of the window at the misty blue sky and then right to admire the wall of priceless, precise machinery. He even said hello to all of the postdocs and to one of the two PhD students, the one who wasn't asleep at her desk.

Eventually, he made it to his office, situated across a hallway from the far entrance to the lab, and sat down in his leather swivel chair. He rolled over to the window and looked out. From this vantage point, he could just barely identify the San Francisco Bay in the near distance, a few shining slivers caught between the neighboring sky-high buildings. The university buildings and the biotechs had been there for as long as Will could remember, but the vertical shopping centers and the multistory arcades had cropped up recently and abruptly, filling in what little had been left of the horizon. Will found the popularity of arcades amusing. Why anyone would pay to play games in a public place when you could play them in the privacy of your own home, on your tablet even, at a fraction of the cost, was beyond him. He thought video games were silly, or rather, he liked playing them but he had the decency to be embarrassed by it. Will had only set foot in one of the arcades once before. He had walked in off the street on a whim and left shortly thereafter. Everything was in 3D. It had given him a headache.

He sighed and looked back at his desk. It was piled high, metaphorically speaking. There were about ten thousand documents open and about twenty thousand unopened emails. He wasn't going to get much work done today though. He could tell. He glanced out the window again, this time in the direction of home. He wondered what was happening there. Was Viki back? He was tempted to look at the surveillance feeds, but he didn't really like the idea of checking up on her. Besides, he wasn't particularly worried about what he would see. It was just a dim curiosity about what she was having for lunch or what she was reading, because he used to ask her and he didn't anymore. It occurred to him for the first time that Viki was the *better* one. That *he* didn't deserve *her*. Will focused on a small bright-blue bit of bay and imagined himself on a boat on the water. He had brought Viki on a romantic cruise. The air smelled of salt. Her hair was blowing in the wind. They drank champagne straight out of the bottle, just like the good old days. He smiled to himself. Maybe he *would* take her on that cruise. *What would she say to that?*

He rolled his chair away from the window and turned to face the east wall of his office. It was in that direction that he saw the past. His eye was caught, momentarily, by the diploma, hanging steadily in its elegant frame. In a largely paperless world, these embossed vellum certificates seemed even more significant than they once did, true treasures. His mind wandered back to that graduation day, when he had received his PhD from Harvard. His parents had been there. They were all dressed up, better dressed than they had been for his wedding. They had saved up and bought him a fancy new band for his watch. He still kept it in his desk drawer even now, though the leather had long since cracked and faded from years of exposure. They had been so proud of him. He had been so proud of himself. *Doctor Dalal.* At that moment in time, he had felt that he could take on *anything*.

The diploma came back into sharp focus before him, and it occurred to Will that paper was only used at one or the other end of the spectrum anymore. Aside from children's books, trashy waiting room magazines, and art supplies, it was either reserved for significant, official, important documents, or criminal activities. With increasing cyber surveillance, both real and imagined, Will refused to send messages electronically, encrypted or not. He didn't trust burner devices. If they had a signal, they were connected, and if they were connected, they were vulnerable. *He had been hacked before.*

He chose instead to send all below-board communications on the backs of greeting cards and gum wrappers, to be literally burned once read. He knew it wasn't illegal to have a cabinet full of torn-out coloring book pages and old journals, though he could possibly have them confiscated by the university as a fire hazard, but it still worried him that someone would discover his secret. Will had read somewhere that a long, long time ago people used to send messages via pigeon. Now *that was ridiculous*. He absentmindedly tapped his fingers on the top of his desk and a song that had been popular some thirty years ago started playing at full volume. He shivered and switched it off after only a few bars, but not before it could trigger a fresh transition from one rumination to the next.

The day went on like this, filled with the sustenance upon which Will existed—fond memories and *what-ifs*. But in the back of his mind, at the very bottom, in a corner somewhere, things were racing. There was excitement on the verge of running away with itself and taking with it the principle of purpose. There was *very nearly* conviction. But mostly, there was *that buzz*. Not the one he felt twice daily after the three gorilla-fat fingers of Scotch he swallowed precisely at half past eleven in the morning and again at four fifteen in the afternoon—*even the price of the Scotch couldn't make that look classy*—but the buzz he hadn't felt in years. The naturally occurring buzz that strolled hand in hand with cheesy words like "possibility" and "hope." It was a feeling that both invigorated Will and filled him with dread. It gave him chills and pit-of-the-stomach aches and cold sweats and hot flushes. *It was worse than having a crush*. The problem with high highs was *anything* that fell short.

———

Will stayed in his office the whole day. Around four thirty, just after his second tumblerful of Scotch, one of the postdocs came in to ask him a question. Jenny—he remembered her name because he had hired her for it. It made him think of Jenny from Yale, though in actuality her name was Jiang-li. She just insisted Will call her Jenny, he assumed due to the fact that he butchered the pronunciation. Aside from the name, Jenny and Jenny had little in common. They were born halfway across the globe from each other, and Chinese Jenny was *actually competent.* But Will always took a little extra time to help her out all the same.

She knocked softly and gradually pushed open the door that was already ajar. "Hello, Professor Dalal?"

"Please, call me William." Will liked the way he sounded when he said that. He tasted the whisky on his breath, and he smiled warmly. "Have a seat."

"Thank you." She sat. She glanced up at his Harvard diploma on the wall and then far out of the window as she brought up her tablet. "I'm having some trouble tracking the morphology of the specimens. I think, maybe, the cell-staining is off—we are not using the right antibodies, or . . ." She projected her most recent results onto the desk in front of him.

They spent the better part of thirty minutes going over her data, thinking up different ways to interpret it and devising new experiments to clarify the results she was seeing. Chinese Jenny was so curious, so engaged. Will thought that maybe she reminded him a little bit of himself. Maybe she reminded him of someone better: a younger, fresher, naiver Jon. He was fond of Chinese Jenny. He was legitimately interested to see where her career would lead. He had no idea where in the world American Jenny had ended up, but he assumed she had left academia and, God willing, science altogether.

The rest of the evening passed without incident. Will kept an eye on the light coming in from under his office door. The hall outside never went fully dark, but it dimmed throughout the night to save energy when the lab was empty. He waited for the space between the bottom of the door and the floor to go gray and the thin crack lining the left-hand side to disappear. Then he waited thirty minutes more. When he was sure that everyone had gone home, he walked out of his office and into the lab. The lights powered back on; there was no way to avoid it.

The room was empty, but Will still shunned the center aisle that led, in the most direct path, straight through to the back of the lab. He skirted the ghosts still hard at work, the flasks rotating in their warm chambers, gently mixing their secret contents. Of course, *Will knew all the secrets*. He sidestepped the low-humming machines running sample after sample throughout what seemed eternity, and the life-less robotic arms that animated the after-hours spectacle of preparation, a nightly ritual dance. Lab work was so efficient now. And precise. Lasers, auto-pipetters, movers, shakers—scientists didn't require a careful hand anymore, just a cursory knowledge of computer science—aka which buttons to push when. Will knew what all of the equipment did, but he didn't know how to use any of it. He didn't need to anymore. He delegated.

He peered out the windows along the right-hand wall, and keeping his eyes shifted from his forward view, edged across the lab toward the back corner. As he got closer, he began to feel shy, embarrassed by his recurrent urge to visit. He paused to admire the moon, but the moon was in another direction, out another window, so he turned his gaze to street level. He watched a stranger get into his car and drive away. He watched a couple meet on a corner and a stray cat disappear behind a dumpster. Finally, Will carried on to his destination, clearing his throat as he crossed the last few yards.

———

"Here I am again." Will said this half to announce his presence to the floating idols of Margot and Arthur, and half to remind himself of what he was in fact doing, *yet again*. But he knew it couldn't be helped. He needed advice, and there were only two figures from this world that he felt he could turn to. So he dove in. "There's something I need to tell you, Arthur." He glanced at Margot and a shade of shame cast quickly across his features, but he turned resolutely back to the first specimen. "Something good has happened." He spoke slowly. "Maybe it's a sign. I *know* I don't believe in *fucking signs*." His eyes darted back to Margot again momentarily as if she had challenged him.

"Ashley. She did it." He paused. *What exactly was* it? "After thirty years. One out of twelve. That's not bad odds really, if you think about it. What with nurture versus nature. Bad parenting. Good parenting. *Whatever*." He put his hand against the thick glass that was holding Arthur at a half-foot distance and a world away from him. For a minute, he became desperate. "What was the long-term plan? Was there a plan, if everything went the way we wanted? *What did you want?* I remember something you said. 'A spoonful of hope,' barely enough for the two of us." He breathed out. "Maybe it was enough then. You never got to age; you made yourself sick, and you died young."

He turned back to Margot. "And you . . ." Will couldn't finish the sentence. He had never, in thirty years, been able to name the tragedy aloud. "Maybe you two just don't *understand*. The older I get, the more *ridiculous*, the more *heedless* I am. The more *indifferent* I feel toward individuals. The more *urgent* and yet *meaningless* I find every accomplishment. I could have fifty good years in front of me, or I could have a single day . . .

"But that was always true, wasn't it? *What changed?* You left me at a delicate time. A time when *I* felt unbreakable. You probably wouldn't even recognize me now." He smiled at Margot. "Good fucking riddance to that guy. He was *never* going to make you happy anyway." Will felt bilious chills prickling the back of his neck, running down his spine. His stomach pitched forward. A cold sweat cracked across his brow. He turned his back on both of them and walked up to the window again, glaring into the moonless sky. He searched for a beacon, but the stars were too weak to stand up to the city lights, so his gaze sank deep into the navy dark. After a few long seconds, he turned sharply back to face them, finally ready to admit to himself what he had *really* come to discuss. "There's only one way to go out. Am I right? With a bang." The nausea passed.

———

Will peered into the four dark sockets. He peered into Arthur to imagine what advice he would give going forward, and he peered into Margot to imagine what reproach she would give if he never looked back. *Would she even be speaking to him now?* As he stared at the dreadful totem that could never be

Margot, it occurred to Will that it no longer mattered. He had crossed that line thirty years ago. There was no redemption in his current purgatory—one had to surrender completely before one could be rebuilt. *He had read that somewhere*—probably on Viki's tablet. She subscribed to all kinds of bullshit self-improvement pages. In truth, Margot was so long gone that Will no longer craved redemption, merely recognition of the inextinguishable variety. With his conscience successfully blotted out, Will turned to Arthur to discuss more practical matters.

"The main issue is scale. We would have to affect a substantial number of subjects to make an impact. *Af*-fect, *in*-fect. I could barely reach six patients on my own with months of planning. And I'm much more *well recognized* these days." Will caught his distorted reflection in the curved glass. "It's too cumbersome. Regulations are even more strict now than they used to be. How do we get around it?" He began to pace in a small figure eight in front of the two specimens, holding his chin in his left hand—he was pretty sure that helped him come up with good ideas.

"Aerosolize it. Yes. And then have tiny drones sprinkle it over the maternity ward. No. *Maybe* . . . somehow genetically engineer a highly contagious but mostly harmless childhood virus to infect the population? Possibly . . . *Unlikely*. It would take far too much time. Nano-diamonds in the formula? Ridiculous. What about the drinking water? *I think I saw that in a movie once.* But infants don't drink water. *Do they?* Shit. Stupid . . . Who knows if it even works when ingested? No! You're only going to have *one shot*. Don't fuck it up by changing the delivery . . . Delivery rooms. There's something there. *Is there?* Vaccinations! But they need those fucking vaccinations, don't they? That would certainly backfire . . . Too bad babies don't take steroids, or do heroin, or use Botox. *It's almost shocking that they don't, really, come to think of it.* What else do we *inject?* Fucking hospital regulations; no one *trusts* anyone anymore." Will strode in silence for several more minutes, carefully tracing his footsteps back and forth around and across the infinity sign. "*I know* . . . I've got it!" He stopped his pacing and looked up directly at Arthur as if Margot had never existed. "It's simple—you would approve."

———

That was the last time that Will consulted his two confidantes. It wasn't the last time he would walk down to that corner of the lab. It wasn't the last time he would see them, conjured into existence by his need for a genuine mirror or his obstinate lack of a true peer. He would further talk, yell, whine, spout at their deaf ears, but Will no longer sought a moral compass.

Chapter Thirty-Five

———

The next day, Will wrote out a long procedure over six separate portions of paper that he had fished out of his fingerprint-release cabinet. When he was finished, the entire side of his right hand was covered in smudged blue ink. He hastened to wash it off with the quick-wipe sanitizer he used to spray his desk each morning. After he had removed that bit of evidence and cracked a window to let out the antiseptic smell, he hid five of the scraps of paper in his desk drawer and put the last one in a small plastic bag and then into a Chinese take-out box, weighing it down with a few scoops of rice, fresh from the hospital cafeteria across the street. He picked up his secondary tablet from the chair in the far corner of his office and dialed a number that he knew by heart but didn't have stored. When the line picked up, he didn't wait for a greeting. He said directly, "Can I have one order of ginger chicken and an extra order of rice? Thanks." He hung up.

Twenty minutes later, a delivery boy knocked on his office door. He took an order of ginger chicken and an order of rice out of his insulated bag and put them down on the desk, carefully picking up the take-out box Will had packed in preparation and placing it where Will's order had been. Will prayed it wasn't too hot inside. If the ink smeared, it could be disastrous. How unreliable. He hated ink. It was *so messy.*

The delivery boy looked at him expectantly, until Will instructed, "The usual." Then he walked out, closing the door behind him.

Will opened the two take-out containers. He carefully moved half of the chicken into the rice container and half of the rice into the chicken container, then ate them both methodically in quick succession. One container was thrown, still greasy, into the waste bin that would be picked up the next day and, Will presumed, sucked down some tube to be sorted into either compost or recycling—he *still* couldn't understand the exact rules on food-contaminated paper products. The other container was carefully cleaned and placed back in his cabinet.

Over the next five weeks, the remaining five scraps of paper were shipped off. All to the same *usual* place or person. Will was patient. He understood that discretion took time, but with each delivery, he became more anxious for the next. Until the sixth and last came up, because once the last memo was sent, everything would begin, and he wouldn't be able to recall it.

————

Once the final dispatch was discharged, done and dusted, Will exhaled. He left work early for the first time in years. He couldn't stand the thought of faking it throughout the day, robotically responding to the garden variety queries of his workforce. He couldn't stand the thought of planning novel experiments when his greatest one to date was nearly in the works. *He deserved a break.* He hoped that the house would be empty. He would take a long, lonely bath. He would *relax*—but he didn't bother to check.

Marla and Arbor would be out; they were always out. If it wasn't soccer or swimming or piano or flute practice, it was community service or debate. Will had purchased a silver Audi wagon a few years back, a family car, but aside from the test drives, he'd only sat down in it two or three times. It was constantly shuttling the kids back and forth between school and extracurriculars. Soon he would have to get a second car so they could each have their own chauffeur. There wasn't a moment to rest if they wanted to grow up to be functioning members of society, and *Marla did*, though he wasn't convinced about Arbor. Will occasionally found he was doing their schoolwork himself because they weren't physically present to manage it before the deadlines that cropped up at all hours of the day. "Submit part I by 16:00." And then shortly after four, "Submit part II by 18:00." He generally enjoyed the schoolwork. It was like a game, where he could win parental points without being a present parent. But sometimes it was frustrating. They hadn't taught computer science as a full subject when he had been in school, and by the time the kids reached the age of eight, they were too far advanced for him to muddle his way through anymore. Still, he would find himself *trying*, looking up answers, sitting through online lessons, sneaking quick peeks at their class notes. That was another thing he couldn't understand. *Why was he secretly competitive with them?*

When he walked through the front door and noticed Viki's purse hanging on the far-left coat hook, he wasn't disappointed. He had been planning to brew a hot pot of coffee, put on some music, do some reading sprawled across the living room sofa with a highball in hand. But, realizing she was at home, it occurred to him that he wouldn't mind a little company. Despite any buried feelings of self-destruction the send-off of the final puzzle piece had incurred, a weight had been lifted. He didn't know if his plan would succeed or fail or even make a ripple, but the certainty of uncertainty was far better than the stagnation that had been badgering him ever since the ten remaining participants had graduated high school. He closed the front door behind him and hung his jacket purposefully in the place right next to Viki's handbag, smiling, then he headed through the swinging door on the right, into the kitchen.

"Good God!" Viki jumped a foot in the air. She was standing on the far side of the kitchen island making a snack and listening to one of her podcasts. With her headphones in, she hadn't heard Will come into the house. She paused for a moment, hand on her chest, catching her breath. Then she laughed. It started as a laugh of relief, a modest thankful release, but as she lost control, it grew into a restrained chortle and then an open cackle, and soon she was cracking up in front of him, holding onto the counter for support.

Will chuckled lightly, not wanting to feel left out, then waited patiently for her to finish, observing her from across the room, enjoying the spectacle. It was a *revelation* to watch her laugh, a window into another time, the past, or, for half a second, Will imagined, an alternate present. Then, for less than half a second, he let himself go so far as to blink into the future. In the split seconds that made up what was only an instant, she was again as enchanting as when he had first met her. In those split seconds, he wanted to fix things, right wrongs. He was overcome with a painfully sweet nostalgia that blurred itself into *hope*. As he moved forward with his plan, as he no longer sat in suspended animation, feeling returned to his body, and the romantic rush that perpetually left him lost in love and in life pervaded him again.

Viki finally caught her breath. "You scared the shit out of me, honey. When is the last time you came home at *three* in the afternoon?" She raised her shoulders incredulously, and her stylish arms followed deftly, rising in time with them. "I very nearly screamed at you, 'What the fuck are you doing home!?'" She had been holding a carrot in her hand the entire time, and now she dipped it in something gray green and brought it to her mouth. The hollow sound of crunching echoed in Will's ears.

"Sorry I scared the crap out of you," he mumbled, suddenly embarrassed. *Should he have warned her he was on his way home?* He glanced at the green muck she was dipping into. "You have to admit it was a *little bit* funny." He considered her outburst of laughter. It was still there, somewhere deep in her eyes. Will shifted his weight back and forth, undecided for a moment, then he confidently stepped forward. "Have a glass of wine with me." He stated it as a command, but his eyes were full of query.

Viki hesitated. She seemed unsure in this distantly familiar situation. "I have a class . . ." She looked down at her watch and dipped another carrot. But, abruptly, she looked up again, her face bright with curiosity. "Fuck it. Sure, let's." She smiled warmly, then popped the end of the carrot into her mouth and turned behind her, reaching up into the cupboard for two wineglasses.

Chapter Thirty-Six

———

Somewhere in South Korea, on the outskirts of Seoul, not far off of the train line that connects the capital to the Incheon International Airport, is a pharmaceutical company called Nacera. Nacera touts itself as a small-scale company with a global reach, their success deeply rooted in science, technology, and, of course, concern. When asked what their main product and source of income is, they have been known to say, "Well-being." And when asked who their target consumers are, they commonly reply, "Each and every Tom, Dick, and Harry."

Across the street from Nacera is a much smaller building, just four stories to Nacera's twenty-eight. It is approximately square in shape and more or less off-white, though it looks as though it could use a fresh coat of paint. There is a single usable entrance around the western side of the squat building, indicated by a thin and faded pink arrow, and, peering through the dusty glass door, it appears to be some sort of storage facility. That is in fact what Nacera claims it to be, which explains why, on occasion, scientists and lab technicians can be seen walking between the two buildings. Rarely, though, are they seen carrying anything across.

———

Sharon had moved to Seoul from Manchester about ten years ago to oversee operations in the humble four-story. She arrived daily at 8:00 a.m. sharp and entered through the dusty door by fingerprint access. Inside were pallets upon pallets of expired aspirin and acetaminophen, penicillin and hydrocodone, and all manner of erectile dysfunction remedies, all covered in dust. The packages were stacked higgledy-piggledy, looking as if they hadn't been seen in years. But every morning, Sharon walked assuredly between the nearest two pallets and followed the concealed path created by the heaps of prepped, packed, and useless tablets around hedge-maze-like twists and turns. They were piled too high for her to see out or for anyone looking in to see which way she was being led. At the end of the maze, she would speak the words, "Hey, let me in," or "Knock, knock," in an audible monotone. In fact, she could just as easily say, "Bite me," or "I like apples," as long as she used her own voice. Some days, when she was *really* bored, she would tell a fart joke or belt out her favorite pop rock songs. At the sound of her speech, a trapdoor would open at her feet, leading the way down into the basement.

The four aboveground stories were divided into two warehouse floors, the second floor looking nearly identical to the ground floor: dusty, storage-like, and useless. But belowground, where Sharon worked, shrouded in concrete, under fluorescent lights, there was a bustling assembly line running. Robotic arms swished back and forth, making, measuring, mixing, purifying, synthesizing, dispensing. At the end of the line, a white powder was being mechanically poured, bit by bit, into gallon-sized plastic bags, which, once full, were then sealed up and dropped into a large bin at the end of the room. Sharon didn't do much during the day. She watched, in person, or on her tablet, to make sure that everything was running smoothly, that nothing was getting stuck or jammed up. Most days, she got through a considerable amount of TV. Occasionally, if something went really wrong, she had to call across the street for help. Otherwise, she spent her days alone.

———

Will had never met Sharon in person. He had only ever seen an animated avatar. He doubted she had created it to look like herself, and even if she had, personal projections rarely captured attributes accurately. In any case, Will had decided it was better not to know what she looked like. *If she's hot, I'll think she's too hot. If she's not, I'll think she's not hot enough.* On the rare occasion, he knew himself well. He had found her profile online, though he couldn't remember the exact site—he had looked over so many. Portals that matched vetted hands to unorthodox jobs with no exchange of labels or personal details. Based on her psych evaluation, she was intelligent and loyal. She seemed lonely and, most importantly, she didn't come across as totally evil. *A hell of a lot of them did.* Better yet, she had lived a third of the world away, and the job was based a third farther. Will had wanted to keep as much distance as possible.

When he had first reached out to her, he hadn't honestly expected a reply. His side business was still in the early stages. Things had moved so quickly following his first sale that within a few months he wasn't able to keep up with the demand. It would be impossible to produce that kind of volume discreetly in a university facility. Will had figured he might as well quit while he was ahead, but on a whim, he considered the possibility of a partner. He skimmed profiles for freelancers with a suitable set of morals and a necessary set of skills. There were thousands advertising across the Internet, if one knew where to look.

Sharon was the perfect candidate. She had a PharmD and some five years of experience in drug development, but an oversight or blame game had gotten her fired from her last position, and she was on the outs with the industry.

Sharon had responded straight away. She had been craving a change, and this timely stranger who went by the name of "George" provided the perfect, fully funded opportunity. She had nothing to lose. After a few informal background checks on both sides, "George" had fronted the cash and the formula, and she got everything up and running. The operation had been running smoothly ever since.

———

As it had been business as usual for nearly ten years since they had started production, Sharon was surprised to find a courier waiting outside when she arrived at the four-story on a Monday morning. He handed her a plate of dumplings. "No need to return the plate today," he said in Korean, then promptly walked off, back to his scooter, which was double-parked on the street.

Sharon hadn't bothered with making breakfast that morning, so despite her confusion, she gratefully scooped up the first dumpling and began munching hungrily as she strode up to the building. At the entrance, her print didn't immediately register through the thin layer of grease. She wiped her hand across her skirt, ran her sleeve over the access pad, and tried again. When she reached the trapdoor hidden among the pallets, she paused for a few seconds to chew and swallow. "Mum always said, 'Never speak with a full mouth.' Or was it just 'Never speak'?" Sharon tilted her head, stretching her neck, as the trapdoor slid open. She tossed another dumpling into her mouth and climbed in.

By the time she reached her desk down on the basement level, the dumplings were gone. She wiped her hands clean again and lifted the opaque plastic sheet covering the bottom of the plate to reach the message waiting below. Carefully removing the square piece of paper, she held it up and began to read.

"Are you joking?" She spoke out loud to the powdered chemicals and purpose-built machinery, the inanimate objects that composed her company. She swallowed carefully, as if the information might cause her to choke on the dumplings that had long since disappeared. Sharon turned the scrap of paper over and back again. It was written in code, so she considered for a minute that perhaps she had misunderstood. She muttered as she read and reread the note, making certain that she was indeed comprehending.

Increase production now . . . Stock up . . . Change the formula . . .

"If it works, why screw with it? Right?"

This is what you will need . . .

"Injections? Don't move it? Holy what?"

The rest of the procedure will be on its way over the next five weeks . . .

"The bloody cheek!"

The last few lines instructed her to reply once the final message had been received, to inform "George" what the timeline would be for completion. *As if he expected her to just blindly follow whatever whim came into his eccentric egghead.* She inhaled. She exhaled. She copied the information into her offline tablet and then ripped the paper into tiny pieces and scattered them between the four trash cans in the building.

Sharon was incensed at first, but she only struggled briefly with the news. After all, the reminder that she had allowed herself to settle down, become complacent—content even—was more upsetting than the orders themselves. Although she didn't in fact know her employer's name, she knew it was *his* lab. He had paid for everything, and though she had worked hard to set it up, she had been unreasonably lucky to receive the opportunity. She *was* loyal. Besides, she had made a good chunk of money, and possibly she could use a change again. For Sharon, ten years was practically an eternity. She closed her work tablet, opened her personal tablet, and put on a couple of episodes of the show she had left hanging the previous night, letting it all sink in. She needed that idle hour to digest what she already knew she had committed to.

While the credits were running at the end of the second episode, Sharon went to the control room to increase the rate of production. Then she called up her suppliers to order the materials for the new mystery product so that everything would be ready and waiting when the remaining pages of procedure arrived.

Chapter Thirty-Seven

———

The next step of Will's plan involved infrastructure. It would take some time to develop the means and organization necessary to distribute the product, if Sharon indeed took care of the manufacturing. Will had been 90 percent sure she would pull through, but that percentage was dropping steadily with each paranoid thought. He was hoping to hear from her soon with a timeline. *Any day now.* He was *sure* the last of his messages *must* have been delivered. The hours, the minutes, *the seconds* that passed while he waited for confirmation became agony if they weren't filled. Sitting at his desk, reading routine papers, answering uninspired emails, devising alternative experiments wasn't enough. He had to be active.

There was an energy that surrounded his newfound goal or conceivably just the incidence of having one. For the first time in decades, he began to look forward instead of perpetually, relentlessly *back*. Will didn't usually leave his desk much during the day. At lunchtime, he generally picked at and threw out whatever "health food" the cafeteria had been peddling, and ordered a pizza. He would finish it, slice by slice, while reading whatever garbage mass midday blurbs the university sent out about free outdoor yoga or those masochistic core-strengthening chairs that threw the weak-obliqued sprawling across the floor. But on an impromptu Tuesday afternoon, he checked his tablet to make sure that Viki was in, hailed the fastest ride home, and talked her into bed. He surprised himself. *It hadn't even taken much cajoling.* On his way back to work, a blurb appeared on his tablet. "Try a full-body plank during this lunch hour to strengthen mind and body."

"Done." He smirked, enjoying the inside joke alone in the self-driving vehicle.

On a Wednesday and a Thursday, Will used up a few of the frenetic hours riding along with his children to and from school. Shocked by his company, they made him sleep his tablet so they could tell him about What's-her-name and Whose-his-face and Mr. So-and-so and Ms. Miller. He remembered Ms. Miller from the parent-teacher videoconference. Will had never been very good with names, but he listened to the stories: lunchtime gossip about who sat where and endless complaints about their teachers that boiled down to either lack of discipline, or abuse of power.

Will found relief in the reminder that some things never changed. Of course, *some things* had. After leaving them at school, Will mused over the endless possible childish pranks that could be played in this day and age. It was a fragile time, when lives could be ruined by a few keystrokes, and not particularly clever ones if you had the right equipment. More than ever, the world was being *barely* held together by a declining majority of individuals deciding to be good. His children were more mature than he had been at their age. *Thank God.*

On a Friday afternoon, just around four thirty, one and a half fingers through his Scotch, Will picked up his tablet and called Jon. It was nearing the end of November, so he had "the holidays" and wishing for them to be happy ones ready as an excuse for his spontaneous outreach. Not that Jon had asked.

"Hey, William, long time no see." Jon's face slid onto the screen from the left. "I trust everything is going well out in sunny California?"

"Yes . . . well, I just wanted to give you a call to wish you a happy holidays." Will was honestly having trouble remembering why he had called. Maybe that *had* been all he had wanted to do. "And to the wife. And to the kids. Of course." He followed up, unsure of what to say next.

"It's a little early for Christmas . . . late for Thanksgiving." Jon made light of the fact that they almost never spoke. "Early for Chanukah too, this year, but maybe shoot for that next time. At least there's eight days, so you're more likely to land on one of them, eh?" Jon's half-assed joke didn't entirely hit, so he moved on. "Well, how have you been?"

"Good, really good. Just chugging along." Will furrowed his brow at his own use of that expression. "Uh . . . how are you?"

"Fine. Good, yeah. Actually, can you hold on for just one second?" The sound of several small objects being tossed across the floor came over the microphone. "Grandchildren." Jon rolled his eyes and then shifted out of the view of the camera.

Will, confused about what he had been hoping to communicate when he had started this conversation, reached for the half-finished Scotch and downed it quickly in one go. For some reason, he didn't want Jon to see him drinking it. They had been drunk many times together, *but that was a hell of a long time ago.* As Jon reappeared on the screen, Will swallowed, coughing once loudly into his hand as the strong liquor singed his throat. Jon smiled at him, apologizing for the brief disappearance, but Will could discern the pity around the edges of his lips, and it stung more than the whisky.

"Do you ever think all of the shit we started," Will blurted out, "back whenever that was—the Styrofoam Age or the Stone Age, even—that it might eventually backfire? Or that it already has? I guess we made life a lot easier for a lot of people, a lot better," he mused. "But sometimes . . ." *Always.* "I feel like the whole thing is going to come crashing down on us, like some sort of collapsing shitstorm. And we're at the point of implosion." Will had thought, *I am at the point of implosion*, but had said "we're" because it sounded more inclusive, because it shared the blame.

Jon stared at the lower corner of the screen for a few seconds, contemplating his response. Finally, he let out a short laugh. "You gotta quit the day drinking, friend." But he couldn't keep his smile from twisting slightly. "If *we* hadn't published then someone else would have. Just look at what went down with your pal Arthur . . . There's no way to prevent what's going to happen from happening. There's only mitigation."

Will cringed. He nodded slowly, then turned the conversation back to grandchildren and Christmas with as much of an unceremonious about-face as his previous outburst. Jon had gotten out of the game decades ago; he wasn't entitled to a piece of Will's guilty conscience. He didn't deserve it.

In the hours when he was bound to his desk, overseeing the projects and research that went toward his lesser but more legitimate source of income, Will obsessed over statistics. Crime statistics, mental health statistics, economic, homelessness, and disease—every number was a piece of the puzzle. He was convinced if he could only find a way to plot them simultaneously, a pattern would emerge that would disfigure every one of his past achievements and reveal either *a solution or a curse*. What Jon had said was true: in the absence of a magical crystal ball, all that existed was risk and mitigation.

Violent crimes in America had increased in number over the last fifty years, but the per capita rate had remained, with some minor fluctuations, significantly steady. Historical downward trends, it seemed, had leveled out in an equilibrium between mortals and non-mortals. But soon, Will was confident, *they* would tip the balance. Disease was still an issue in the first world, but so much of the illness faced now had been created by science. Not only did the increase in average life span lead to the prevalence of late-age disorders, but in some cases, the cure to one problem was the birth of the next: the cure for one cancer causing another, more dastardly; the regrowth of organs resulting in minor physical and mental defects, small enough to dismiss but significant enough to alter the minute functions that medically distinguish one human from another. Will considered a time and place in the future where the leading cause of death would be tripping over a sidewalk and diving headfirst into a fire hydrant, or plane crashes. Of course they would never overtake heart disease or diabetes, the diseases of people who had made themselves sick. Or *murder*—no treatment existed for *that*.

Homelessness was at an all-time high. Zombies, having made an unforeseen recovery, often returned to work to discover that they had been replaced. Some returned to find they couldn't perform the same functions that they used to. Then again, a lucky few had been rebuilt better than before. They were so good at the jobs they had slogged through previously that they caused dissent among their peers. A tragedy turned into a happy accident that made them better than the rest, and it was *unfair*. There was no winning. Will scoured the numbers and looked for a light, any general change in widespread behavior that would prove his point one way or the other. *What was his point again?* But when he looked with a detached eye, every dredged-up detail pointed to one immutable truth. The zombies were just as fucked up as natural humans, or maybe natural humans were just as fucked up as zombies. Perhaps the test tube and the womb produced identical results, a range of monsters from the least bad to the very worst.

And yet, he had seen it with his own eyes. Milton, strapped to the hospital bed cold as ice, cool as a cucumber, bitter as the base *son of a bitch* he was. The time Will had spent in the ward—he *knew* the numbers, the proportions, the profiles of the patients that came in, and the characters of the convalescents that walked out. There was a perfectly good explanation for everything. There weren't yet enough "successful" cases to string together a pattern. The significance was too low, the greater population too monstrous. The procedure was expensive, and the subjects nearly all came from middle- to upper-class backgrounds. Did their advantage allow them to get away with new character flaws, minor and *major*? Was Milton somewhere roaming the world, free and clear?

Will adjusted the numbers, played with statistical assumptions, accounted for this and adapted for that, twisted, turned, and transformed the data until he could see the results that he deeply desired. Laid bare, they told him a story of a small, elite, and heartless subset of society that had no regard for community, no interest in humanity, and no moral or emotional boundary in which to contain itself. The e-potion was a joke. It was prescribed regularly, but nine out of ten times it was never refilled. It turned out that when given the choice, no one wanted compassion dragging them down. It was just another shitty feeling to add to the pain and the fear and the rest of the unbearable, insufferable crap that came flooding in after a major accident. No amount of smiling reunions, friendships, joy written on the faces of family members was worth it. There was no contentment found in bouncing between the highs and the lows that compared to the relieving sensation of nothing at all.

As medical improvements continued to be made, this small subset was growing in number and likewise in intelligence. They would continue to grow and grow and grow, into significance, into consequence, into importance, and eventually, down the line, they would overtake everything and everyone, the whole kit and caboodle, all and sundry. *Numbers didn't lie.*

———

But always at the back of his mind there was the small seed of hope he held on to—*the optimistic streak that wouldn't surrender.* Will was still trying to fix something that had occurred over thirty years ago, as if a random misfortune could be balanced out by an equally arbitrary fixed obsession. In his head, though he would never admit to this simplification, one was the force of *good*, and the other had been the force of *evil*.

He didn't want to get ahead of himself, but he refused to fall behind. After all, big picture, everything he had ever attempted to accomplish boiled down to one simple, clichéd race against time. He had to press on, and he returned his focus to the next step, to the problem of infrastructure. It wasn't an insurmountable issue by any means, but it had to be done delicately so as not to raise too many suspicions, at least not up front. If suspicions were raised in the aftermath, he would either accept the consequences or outrun them. Will couldn't see beyond the completion of his short-term plan.

When it came to distribution, it had occurred to Will that he knew just the right person for the job. Austin was nearly perfect. He was perhaps a little too clever, but his lack of true interest in anyone other than himself and his general lack of curiosity about the world or drive to change anything in it outweighed Will's concern. His indifference made his intelligence irrelevant. Will doubted if his proposed and, admittedly, slightly far-fetched cover story would even be questioned. Still, there was something unnerving in the idea of approaching one of *the things* that he had created. But, Will reasoned, he might as well make use of it. *Waste not, want not.* Austin had his own self-branded foundation, PreVAIL. That was the key.

He drafted a message to Austin's husband, Gerome, who ran the foundation. It was carefully worded, flattering, and just detailed enough. Will had the commodities; the foundation had the connections—they would be partners in crime. Will even used those exact words, only his new partner didn't take them literally.

Chapter Thirty-Eight

———

Sharon was getting worried. Despite the push to increase production of the Brill pill before she had switched over to manufacturing the new mystery product, her reserves were starting to run low. In just a few short weeks, even rationing carefully with all of the best late-delivery excuses she could conjure, she would have sold the very last dose remaining. She didn't have the equipment necessary to produce both drugs at once, and her employer, "George," or whatever his name truly was, didn't seem to care. Sharon knew enough about synthesis to create substance from formula but she wasn't able to grasp what this new concoction was capable of, what its purpose could be. She recognized some similarities with the Brill pill, but it was far more elaborate. *Would this new product somehow replace the need for the old one?* It was wildly expensive to make; she couldn't fathom who on earth would buy it.

So far he had given her instructions only to make the stuff and to store it. If everything went to plan, the total request would be ready and waiting two months hence and she had sent back a message saying as much. Sharon was confident in her ability to deliver on time. When the two months were over, she planned to return production to the Brill pill and carry on as if nothing had happened, or pack up and quit if that wasn't an option. *Maybe she would quit either way.* What really worried her was the month and a half in between. They weren't in a particularly forgiving business, and being "temporarily out of stock" wasn't generally acceptable.

Over the next few weeks, as regular deliveries stalled and then finally came to a full halt, the online and street dealers, those in direct contact with now-desperate customers, those whose livelihoods depended on each individual sell, became agitated. They couldn't find a substitute for such a niche product, and they lost sales, money in their pockets. They went to their suppliers, and their suppliers went to their higher-ups. Their direct superiors didn't have the answers to the simple, essential question they posed, so they turned around to their bosses to repeat the same concerns. And up and up it went. There was a chain of command in the organization, but it wasn't infinite. Time was running out.

Finally, the question arrived at the consortium's head of distribution. The head of distribution ran so many different drugs across the globe, she hadn't noticed one was missing from the set. Despite the fact that no one else seemed aware of her ineptitude, the personal embarrassment of having let that element slip by *taunted her.* Lana knew better than *anyone* that she wasn't to be trifled with. She determined to take on the case herself. She would track down whoever it was that was so poorly running production of this "brilliance pill," destroy them, and subsume their facility. Or, if it was an overly complicated procedure, she supposed she would just have to force them into working *for her.*

But first, she needed to find out just who this person or these people were. Lana went carefully through the logs and discovered the global delivery service that was being used. It was a private service, but it wasn't a criminal one. The Brill pill, in many ways a perfect product, was largely unknown to the police and therefore unrecognized by canine officers. Using a below-board delivery service would only create more suspicion. The powder was shipped in organic baking powder containers and detergent boxes, or packaged as artisan flour, sugar, protein powder, or pancake mix. Lana had a lot of influence with the illicit delivery networks in the northern hemisphere, but obtaining information from a legitimate service would take slightly more time. It was a question of finding the right people to bribe, and that would take a little research and a little finesse.

Sharon was counting on it taking at least a few more weeks.

Chapter Thirty-Nine

Will wasn't oblivious to the dangers of some pissed-off drug lord coming after him in a fit of flawed righteous demand. He had even considered purchasing some sort of weapon in case it really came down to it. He imagined being grabbed in the parking lot in the dark or being tricked into getting into an unregistered service car. Inside the car, he pulled out a gun, and three thugs simultaneously stabbed him to death while he fumbled at the trigger. He thought maybe a better alternative would be to invest in protective armor, a full-body suit. But instead, he did nothing. It didn't matter how prepared he was. He *had* to finish his project before they got to him. Whatever happened after, *happened after.* If he did get iced one night down a dark alleyway, he had contingency plans in place for his family, protection arranged, relocation even, if necessary, but it was a precaution. It was unlikely they would go after Viki. She knew nothing, literally nothing. *What would be the point?* His only real cause for concern then was Sharon, but he assumed she would give him up and survive. She wasn't *that* loyal; she had no reason to be. That was the one problem that came from organized crime that didn't include a family element, or perhaps it was a blessing.

The fear of this confrontation pushed him forward. Will certainly didn't want to die, but it wasn't the fear of death or even pain, not the emotional suffering of his family or the public shame of his double life being revealed, that egged him on. It was the same drive that came with the rush to publish. That greatest fear that all of the work, all of the effort, all of the intelligence and pride, *one's very worth* could be denied in an instant, simply by the mere fact that someone else said it first. In this case, the prospective confrontation was not a danger but a devastating nuisance, a floating chance that one day late would be meaningless, but one day early would be catastrophic.

———

Will held the message from Sharon tightly in his hand. He just had to wait it out for two more months. Two more months and the product would be finished, packaged, all ready to go. She would send him a sample when it was ready. Will *longed* to see the elixir with his own eyes. It was risky to send a physical sample, but it seemed riskier not to. If something had gone wrong in the formula, he would have to put a stop to the whole thing, much as it *pained him* to imagine.

In spite of his hopeless impatience, time moved forward. On the one hand, two months seemed excruciatingly long, but on the other hand, it was barely any time at all. Working with Gerome to set up phase two was slower than Will had anticipated. There were a lot of hoops to jump through, regulatory figures to be satisfied. Will had to make up a false sample of what he was offering, what he was peddling for no apparent gain. He didn't want to order vitamins through the university. What if some clerical clone had an overdose of cold-press coffee one morning and opened their eyes to the multitude of unnecessary items passing through the budget? He went to the corner drugstore, bought a pack of multivit-amin drips, and dissolved them into a saline solution. Then he filled up a handful of randomly marked standard syringes and handed them over for evaluation along with a few files of fudged paperwork. Of course there was nothing toxic or con-tentious about the substance, so it passed the screen. There was little interest in whether or not the stuff was truly effec-tive or simply a waste of money and resources, so long as the cost-benefit analysis retained an overall surplus of good PR.

Once the product was satisfactorily vetted, they moved on to logistics. First of all, *where*—where was the most benefit to be gained upon receiving this gift? Which country, which cities *deserved* it the most? Which places were also easy enough to get into, easy enough to operate in? A region with high birth rates and low living standards, decent roads and name recognition. Next, advertise. Contact the hospitals, contact the clinics, gather volunteers, inform expectant par-ticipants of the benefits, of the opportunity not to be missed. Register everyone; get it *in writing*.

Finally, the board members of PreVAIL signed off. The foundation director took charge of validating delivery and distribution. The channels were set up, and the overstock of neonatal vitamin injections, designed by researchers in Amer-ica, manufactured in Korea, and then rebranded and left to gather dust, was ready to be sent off to Bangladesh. It only had to be picked up from the warehouse in Seoul where it was being stored and, once transported, distributed to the destitute newborns in the dozens of obstetric clinics by the volunteer nursing staff engaged by PreVAIL.

Chapter Forty

———

Lana had told herself she was on a seek-and-destroy mission, but she was becoming increasingly impatient with the seeking part. She had noticed her impatience growing ever since *the accident. Was it an accident,* she wondered, *or was it a gift?* Lana shook off the moody rumination before she sank too deep, but she couldn't help pondering her restlessness. She figured it made logical sense; her instincts had been shaken up. Coming that close to death had left her with a certain urgency surrounding the new life she led. *There was nothing peculiar about that.* But then there were other things that seemed occasionally off. She'd pick up her tablet, and sometimes her fingers didn't quite follow the instructions her brain had set out. They hesitated, hit the wrong keys. She was sporadically and utterly *clumsy.* A balanced cup of coffee would suddenly fall from her hands, as if she had momentarily forgotten she had been holding it, and embarrassingly crash, smash, splash all over the floor. Now and then, her mind would wander. She hadn't lost her memories, but still she experienced sudden flashbacks—urgent, inane thoughts that occurred to her out of nowhere and wouldn't be quelled. There was all of that, and then there was the fact that she had inexplicably found herself chin-deep in a criminal organization. But she brushed off these details. She focused on the task at hand. Her ability to focus had increased enormously.

She was sitting up in her king-size bed in Tuscany, reading the *New York Times* and sipping an Americano, when word came to her via a trusted employee from the private delivery company. She wasn't bothered with *how* the information had been gathered, whether it had been swindled, bribed, or blackmailed. Her interest began and ended with orders sent and intelligence returned.

The source that had *finally* been tracked down was a manager at the delivery service. He knew nothing of the product or the manufacturers, but he could electronically trace the start of each shipment to within a confined radius. They came through deliberately differentiated channels with pickup locations spread across the metropolis, but he had a hunch that the deliveries all originated at a particular third-party packing establishment. The manager had only heard about it in whispers, but based on dispatch patterns and the size, weight, and content of the packages being delivered, he had his suspicions. This rumored enterprise took any product of any degree of legality and repackaged it to look like something as boring as baking soda or flour, for the purposes of drug running. Not many customers spent the little bit extra on his shipping service for the security of shipping items as banal as laundry detergent.

A below-board institution Lana could legitimately, illegally approach. She immediately called up her assistant from downstairs and sent out feelers, purporting to have need of their services herself. Then she got dressed, packed an overnight bag, and went downstairs to have the rest of her breakfast in the rustic open-plan kitchen. She expected to hear back before she was finished eating.

Chapter Forty-One

Once everything had been arranged, Will was surprised to feel an unprecedented lack of responsibility. There was nothing he could do for the time being and therefore nothing he needed to worry about. The short time between setting up an experiment and acquiring the results revealed a window of certitude. He had done what could be done, and he didn't regret one ounce. During this interlude, he returned to his frenzied state wherein every moment urgently needed filling. There were only a few weeks left of limbo, and the passage of time was magnified within them. Throughout the two months, since the day he had first set the wheels in motion, he had been spending more time with Viki, more time with Marla and Arbor, more time participating, and less time daydreaming. And, as the days passed, as the realization of his plan loomed closer and closer on the horizon, this behavior redoubled.

The four of them were in the living room, spread across the two sofas, watching a movie together as a family. Will wasn't paying attention to the plot though. He had never seen the film before, but he was sure he would get the gist of it. *The backstory wasn't what was important anyway.* He gazed upward. The light from the projector was shimmering against the tiny pieces of dust floating in the air above Will's head, giving form to the beam of light. What was important was that he was there, visibly present, just like the beam of light. He glanced at his wife and his two children. He wanted to know if they had noticed him, if they had noted his prevailing presence, or if the surround sound had drowned him into only a background figurine. Of course they had, but then they pretended they hadn't. They pretended for his sake and for their own that things had always been this way.

At the back of his mind, thoughts rushed by, mainly questions. Would this be the last time they would all sit here and watch a movie together? Would this bore fest be the last movie he ever watched? Were they all really enjoying it, or were they just being polite? How was it possible that his own son didn't like popcorn? Was there anyone else in the *whole world* who didn't like popcorn? A year from now, would he still be living here? Would he be in prison? Would he be on the run? *Would he even be alive?*

The last few questions were the ones that had prompted him to be present. Fear of mortality had finally caused value and priority to align when it came to family. The late-in-life crisis that so often affects those who put their careers first had come early, sudden, and urgent with the typical realization that if something didn't change soon, no one would cry at his funeral. So, abruptly, Will was *there*, with the caveat that he secretly expected, just as abruptly, to leave again. He highly suspected his relationship with Viki was totally repaired. It seemed to him that they were having sex probably three or four times a week. He had cooked her a five-course dinner one starry evening, and they had stopped in a hotel bar and gotten tipsy on sparkling white wine one sunny afternoon. To top it off, he found he was genuinely enjoying listening to her personal problems as well as the personal problems of all of her friends and acquaintances for the first time in years. *Maybe ever.* Belittling them was a great distraction from his own.

The long and short of it was that Will was on a high. Everything was set up, production was running, distribution was waiting, gears were whirring, clocks were ticking. There was motion in the air, and an end in sight. And no matter what the end would eventually bring, Will desperately craved the sense of finality that he was sure would come with it.

———

He was expecting the sample from Sharon any day now. They were a week out from the deadline, and the anxiety to test the sample and confirm its legitimacy, to have his final mortal task over and done with, woke him promptly, with no hope of returning to sleep, at 5:26 in the morning. He stared at the ceiling for ten sedate minutes, watching the wind create changing patterns as leaves rustled in the dim light. He wanted to shower, but he didn't want to wake Viki. He *had* showered the night before, just six hours earlier. He always showered before getting into bed, unless he was blackout drunk, and he hadn't been blackout drunk in far too long, in his opinion. So he got up and pulled his clothes on, shuddering as he dragged them quietly over the outermost layer of dead skin cells that he knew had sloughed off through the night. Then he headed to the only other place he knew to go—his lab.

Through the tall windows of the lab, there was no direct view of the sun rising, but the clear pale glow dawning across the sky bounced over the buildings across the street, glinting against glass and lustrous metals. Early morning light stretched into the long room, casting shadows over many of the instruments and shining spotlights onto others. Will hadn't intended to seek out Margot and Arthur, his former friends, but he couldn't help being drawn in by the shade obscuring them from his sight. He didn't say anything out loud or to himself. For once, he didn't want any confirmation that he was *just short of mad*, no matter how special it made him feel. Now was not the time. He simply stood, gazing into the darkness for a minute, then nodded, turning and walking the length of the room to the far exit. There was nothing left to be said.

When he reached his office, he noticed a small envelope had been left in the mailbox attached to his door, enclosing what looked to be a greeting card. Will grabbed it and took it inside, sliding his finger under the flap to open it as he sat down at his desk. The words "Happy Birthday" flashed across the front of the card, then disappeared, returning upside down at the top and then skidding across the bottom as tiny balloons floated across the background. A not-quite-familiar tune played in a miniature electronic bagpipe tone, startling his ears in the otherwise silent building.

His birthday wasn't for another two months, and besides, he never celebrated anymore. He didn't even acknowledge it. Very few people outside of his immediate family knew when it was. In fact, there were many years it had passed by, and *he* had barely even noticed. But he used to celebrate. *Way back whenever.* There had always been drinks and food and friends and then, of course, more drinks. Even in slightly later years, Viki took him out to dinner, made him breakfast, brought him lunch. Little things he had once dismissed as unnecessary that now flooded his memory at the sight of a few dancing words. The swift recollection brought with it the abrupt, sweeping feeling of a sinkhole forming at the back of his throat. The whole back half of his head was likely to collapse into it if he didn't think about something else soon.

He hastily opened the card, shaking off the paper-thin screen as well as the sickening feeling. But it was directly replaced by a new sensation at the pit of his stomach. The card at a glance was simply and anonymously signed, "Your Friend," but a small slip of "burn after reading" paper lay against the left-hand page as he opened it. Turning it over, he translated from the code:

"To: Subscriber

Expecting minor delay (weather).

Apologies. Partial refund to arrive with delivery."

The new feeling was fear. What would happen if the sample didn't arrive on time? *Must the show go on?*

"Fucking climate change." Will took the slip of paper down the hall, switched on the nearest Bunsen burner, and held it over the flame until it was nothing but ash.

Chapter Forty-Two

———

Sharon wasn't sure what to do. With one week remaining before the new drug was meant to be picked up for delivery, *whatever that really meant*, she had finished production early. Every last one of the injections had been synthesized, allotted, and packaged as vitamin supplements—just as she had been instructed. She had barely raised an eyebrow at the counterfeit packaging request, and she thought she had done quite well with the design. They looked nice and neat all consolidated into pallets, save the one sample specimen she had sent off the previous week. *She really had done a superb job.* The thousands of ultrathin needles attached to the thousands of syringes carrying thousands of samples of serum, ready to be administered, were waiting upstairs in the storage space under a carefully deposited layer of dust designed to match the rest of the warehouse wares. Now, while Sharon waited for this literal burden to be lifted, she was forced to consider her next plan of action.

Her first thought was to return to the old production line as if nothing had happened. But there was no guarantee of new materials, and little chance that she could get back into the distribution ring smoothly without some serious retribution coming her way. Option two would be to double-cross her employer. She could bring the issue to whoever would listen, cut "George" out, and offer to keep running the place. After all, she knew the formula, she knew the procedure, she knew the machines, and she knew she was dealing in a specialized product. She *knew* she carried enough value to save herself. Then again, she *didn't know* who or where "George" really was, and *then again*, there was the not-so-slight guilt brought on by the fact that she had just received an unexpected and rather large bonus. The third option, she supposed, was just to cut and run. Find a new part of the world to loiter in. But she had grown attached to Seoul. She wasn't sure why; she hadn't made any particularly close friends, and her apartment was barely the size of an Easy-Bake Oven. Maybe it was the soju. Nothing was so disgusting and yet so drinkable. At the very least, Sharon was determined to see through what was most likely her final job in this position and to earn the bonus she had received, even if, as she suspected, that was the only reason she had received it.

———

She was still patiently puttering around the four-story, task-less, debating what to do, when a dark sedan pulled up outside, just three days out from the pickup date. At first, Sharon prayed that it was a fluke, that the car had broken down or that the uninvited visitors had become lost on their way to Incheon by some incredibly unlikely satnav malfunction, but *she knew better*. She watched the three skulkers from the safety of her basement office, switching between the camera angles on her tablet, following them as they circled the building with purpose. They didn't look lost. Sharon didn't know who any of the three strangers were, but it was obvious that the petite yet strong-looking brunette was leading the pack, despite the fact that she lagged slightly behind. She had forced-flat, shoulder-length dark hair, careful and conscious eyebrows, and a mouth that perhaps hadn't developed a natural sharpness but had been urged into it with small, detailed pencil lines and brushstrokes. Her eyes were hidden behind a pair of glaringly deliberate tortoiseshell cat-eye sunglasses. She was perfectly in costume. Walking side by side, just ahead of her, more artlessly daunting, were a tall, lean man and an expressionless woman of middling height but dense build.

"Shite," Sharon swore, out loud for herself to hear. She wasn't scared, though she was pretty sure she knew what they were there for. If they found her hiding, they would undoubtedly torture out of her any information she did know and probably a few things she didn't. She was pissed off because she was forced to make a decision. She could hit the alarms. The three lurkers would most likely buzz off for the time being, and she could get out, run in the opposite direction, and never come back. Or, rather than being tortured for information, she could simply climb upstairs and hand it over to them—offer up everything she knew and hope for a little charity in return.

She paced. "George," or whatever his name *actually* was, was certainly fucked one way or another. *What the hell was he up to anyway?* She had been trying hard the last few months not to pose that question, a question that assuredly had an answer, and yet a question that she wasn't *allowed* to ask. Suddenly, under the pressure, it seemed to Sharon that he had played her. *Why shouldn't she play him? She didn't owe him anything; she had never even met the son of a bitch.* And then there was the nagging notion in the back of her head— she knew if she ran, she couldn't come back. Cooperating with them was the only way she was going to finish what she had started. *When had she become so goddamn devoted? And to what, exactly?*

Sharon kept her eyes glued on her tablet as the trio moved back around to the front door. She watched closely as the brunette peered through the grubby glass doubtfully and knocked, rolling her eyes wearily as her knuckles struck lightly against the metal frame. After only three half-assed rap-tap-taps, she shrugged her shoulders and stood aside, nodding in the direction of the tall man who obediently stepped forward, presumably to try a more assertive approach.

Sharon tensed as he reached into his coat and brought out an ordinary crowbar. He crouched down for leverage. In just a few moments, an alarm would go off. *It was now or never.* In that instant, Sharon realized that she had already made up her mind and was simply stretching out the moment for love of indolence or adrenaline.

She moved quickly. Before any damage was done, she scrambled up through the trapdoor and rushed out from behind the stacks and into view. Halting just a few yards from the entrance, she paused and took a long look at the sharply dressed woman standing before her. Did she look reasonable? *It didn't freaking matter at this point, did it?* The man had stopped whatever it was he had started and stood back up straight, glaring through the thick Plexiglas, defiant and intimidating. The second woman remained inscrutable. Sharon scratched her head and glanced involuntarily at the one pallet in the room that had a purpose, albeit an unknown one. She jerked her eyes away, mentally kicking herself, pulled one of her thick curls straight, let it spring back, sighed, and moved forward to open the door.

"I suspect I know why you're here." Sharon did her best to appear nonchalant. It came across as bored.

The woman in charge pulled down her dark glasses and moved forward, passing between her two bodyguards and through the door, right into Sharon's personal space. "Do you?"

"I'll tell you whatever you want to know. That is, if I know it." Sharon held her ground and continued to sound relaxed. She found that she was. It seemed to her that she had done what she had done, and it was out of her control now.

"*Will you?*"

"Yeah. I mean, I'll try. I'll do my best." Sharon shrugged. "To be honest, I don't know all that much." But she quickly added, "I do know some things though. You'd be well wise to keep me around." Out of the corner of her eye she noticed the brunette make an almost imperceptible motion with her left hand. The stout woman, now standing to her right, seemed to let go of something she had been holding tightly in her pocket.

"Holy shit, girl, I'm not going to *murder* you." The brunette rolled her eyes. "Not *now*, not here," she continued. She looked almost disappointed, as if she had been hoping that Sharon would resist. As if she had been hoping she might be forced to do something more unseemly in this abandoned warehouse than accumulate a thin layer of dirt on her stilettos. "Look. Can we sit down?"

Sharon glanced from side to side across the dusty floor. "There are a couple of boxes . . . only three," she apologized, looking up at the four persons present, including herself.

The woman narrowed her eyes, glancing at Sharon, then scanning the room. "Forget it, you can come *with us*. Let's grab a drink. Are you hungry?" She waved her hand dismissively before Sharon could respond. "Whatever, it doesn't matter." She nodded toward the door, and the three of them obediently followed her out to the car.

Sharon tried to keep stride with the hostile brunette as they approached the dark sedan, but the woman resolutely remained a step ahead. When they reached the vehicle, the female bodyguard automatically stepped into the driver's seat, turned on the engine, and quietly set the destination. The man got into the passenger seat, and the brunette finally let Sharon advance, ushering her into the back and getting in behind her. They drove toward the center of the city in silence. Sharon's captor stared out of her window, seemingly lost in thought, and Sharon stared out her own window because there was nowhere else to comfortably direct her gaze.

———

The thoughts that had lost Lana were habitual and, as usual, disjointed. This time they were brought on by the young woman sitting just a seat away from her. *She was brave, wasn't she? What did it take to walk up to a perfectly dangerous stranger and remain so calm and collected?* Lana was brave now, if brave was the right word, but she hadn't been born brave. That was *one thing* she remembered clearly. She remembered dodging certain people at school, ditching certain events if they were going to be present. Then, later in life, avoiding dark alleyways and walking quickly and determinedly past abandoned shops with broken windows as though, if she dawdled, they would swallow her whole. *But fear wasn't all she had lost, was it?* The self-inflicted question taunted her, day in and day out—ever since the day she had woken up in the hospital.

They had told her that she had been in an accident, on a train that derailed, that she had been in a coma for months. She had been lucky. Many of the passengers, including the woman she had been traveling with, had died. But none of it sounded familiar. If anything, the event was a dull play that she had watched years ago and without paying much attention. To her, on that very first day of her new life, before the memories began to creep back in, the world had been something totally new.

Of course, she still knew what everything was. They had brought in childish picture cards with simple drawings: a cat, a house, a hat, a horse. She spoke, she read, she wrote. She had even recognized the few faces that stopped by the foot of her hospital bed to say, "Get well soon," to chat about the weather, to wish her well, though they had worn different expressions than she could recall. Everything, familiar and unfamiliar, that she came across she saw from a new angle—in a sharper, if harsher, light. The world hadn't changed, but her view of it had, and as she had regained memories from before the accident, she was keenly conscious of a lingering hunch that she couldn't feel the same way about them as she suspected she once had. *What had she felt, for instance, for Devin, the woman on the train?* They had traveled together before. They had had dinner, coffee, read books, played tennis. Throughout the years, she played and replayed the memories in her head like individual reels of film. She studied them. But she had a terrible, angering suspicion that she had woken up from the accident lacking whatever intuitive instrument or gut-guiding gizmo was necessary to a full understanding.

Better not to speculate. Lana pushed away the gnawing thoughts once again. They had reached their destination. She gave the girl a sharp look, and the four of them exited the car and crossed the street, disappearing into a small shopping center.

———

In the basement of the center, under the upstairs food market, was a corridor lined with restaurants. Rounding the first corner, Sharon followed the two women into an unassuming dumpling house, the tall man walking close behind her. Ten antiquated, light pink, Formica-topped tables served for the entire interior decor of the nearly square space. Nine of the ten were already taken. Without checking in with a hostess or putting their names down in a tablet, the four of them walked across the room to the only free table, farthest from the door, and took a seat. There was a full container of kimchi already ready and waiting. The tall man withdrew a pair of metal chopsticks from the communal holder and picked up a piece of the cabbage. "I'm Aaron." He placed the fermented leaf in his mouth.

"Abra," the other woman chimed in. Then she grabbed the attention of a passing waiter and ordered two sets of dumplings and two large Hites for herself and Aaron. That was all either of them said for the duration of the meal.

Sharon's eyes flicked to and fro between the three as they stared back at her expectantly. "Sharon," she blurted out.

"Lana." Lana muttered her name. She placed her hand lightly on her chest to indicate herself, then turned to the hovering waiter and ordered a tea and another plate of dumplings. Gesturing toward Sharon, she added, "To share."

Before the waiter could turn back toward the kitchen, Sharon hastily added a Cass beer to the order. She was still trying to appear bolder than she felt, and, if it was possibly going to be her *last drink*, it was definitely going to be an *alcoholic* one. She was tempted to order an additional plate of *mandu*, too, rather than share a last meal with this stranger, but her confidence would only stretch so far. Besides, Lana had a trim figure, and the dumplings that she had glimpsed passing by atop the moving trays looked nearly the size of Aaron's fists. So she left it at that and resumed her silence, snacking on *banchan* and waiting patiently for Lana to make the first move.

Finally, after the tea had arrived and she had taken a long sip, Lana spoke. "Okay. You tell me what *you* want, and then I will tell you what *I* want."

Sharon's Cass rolled in immediately afterward, just in time. She took a swig. "Are you sure it shouldn't be the other way round? What you want is quite likely to inform what I want." Sharon couldn't believe what she was saying out loud. She returned to sipping the beer, if only to keep herself from saying anything *even stupider*.

Lana pushed her hair back behind her ears out of habit, dragging her left index finger against the small scar at the edge of her hairline. She quickly pulled her hair forward again. "Absolutely. Fucking. Positive." The words came out separately, in a light, almost playful tone, but no one at the table mistook it for playfulness. "Go ahead." She nodded.

"Fine." This response came out far more petulantly than Sharon would have wished, but she quickly recovered. "Look, first I'll tell you what I *do*. I make the stuff, and I send it off.

You know the rest. It's that simple. I'm not going to tell you *how or where*, not just yet." She paused. "The person you want, I suppose, is the guy with the formula. He hired me online, and I moved here for the job. I've *never* met the guy. I *don't know* where he lives. I *don't know* what his real name is. I call him George. Or rather, that is the name he gave me."

"Fantastic." Lana raised her eyebrows, but kept her expression blank.

"It *is* bloody *fantastic*. You have a gap in the market now, right? I can fill it. I know everything you'll need, and I know how to make the product. Just get me the materials, and you're sorted. You'll have a much better margin this way, really; it's a win-win." Lana didn't reply for several seconds. It made Sharon nervous, so she carried on, starting to ramble. "You don't need George or whatever his name is—he never really did anything much . . . and to be completely honest, he seems like a bit of a strange character." She was grasping. When it came to the point, she wanted to protect him. It wasn't that she cared for him particularly. She didn't find in the moment that he needed to be spared. *She didn't know him; he hadn't spared her.* She found that she needed to spare herself from doing one blatantly bad thing in a lifetime of veiled indiscretions.

"I like strange characters. When I was a girl, I used to have this . . . *friend*?" Lana paused, staring intently over Sharon's right shoulder. "Yes. A friend. She wore the most bizarre things. Cutoff socks on her arms, hats with a huge bobble at the top." Lana lifted her hand over her head absentmindedly.

Sharon waited for the punch line, but it didn't come. Lana seemed to descend into another daze, so she used the opportunity to pick up a fresh *mandu* as it arrived on the table. She took a bite. The tender skin burst, releasing rich and savory flavor with a satisfying crunch. If it was her last meal, it was a delicious one. She gulped her beer to wash it down. It was perfectly light and thin beer for the purpose. She picked up a second dumpling and a third, seeing how many she could get away with "sharing."

———

Lana was lost, falling through a rabbit hole. Chasing down, thread by thread, link by link, something that no longer existed. The memory of her childhood brought to the surface afresh that perpetual sense that she was one shade short of a full set. Her pre-accident memories had a different hue to them, a color she couldn't create with the limited palette she had been left with. When she had first been released from the hospital, physically fit as a fiddle, she had been required to see a psychologist, just two one-hour sessions for assessment and diagnosis. He had prescribed for her a small pink pill that he stated "may help you come to terms with what has happened in a healthy, *normal* way."

She had only taken it once, and *holy shit*, had it made her feel sick. Not sick to her stomach. She hadn't had a fever or cough; she didn't sneeze once. But she had had chills in her chest, she had felt she could hardly breathe, there had been a thick lava rising through her neck all the way up to her ears, making them numb to every sound. Her legs hadn't been weakened, and yet she had fallen to her knees, curled herself into a ball on the floor. She had tasted dust at the back of her mouth and gagged on it. She had wept. She had wanted to run screaming into the arms of a friend, a relative, anyone, but she was terrified of leaving the house. *How could that be healthy? How could that be normal?* She had left the rest of the bottle hidden at the back of her medicine cabinet until the day she had sold it. It still bewildered her that anyone would pay good money for *that*.

Lana shook her head slightly as she became conscious of how much time had passed during her reminiscences. She glanced at Aaron and at Abra in turn, but they respectfully acted as if nothing was out of the ordinary and continued into their second round of dumplings and Hite. *She knew it wasn't normal. She knew they knew it wasn't normal.* She looked down at her own plate. The plucky girl sitting across from her was picking up the last dumpling, using *her fingers*.

———

"*Hey!*" Lana blurted out, suddenly forgetting her manners in the onrush of background noise coming from the nine lively tables.

Startled by Lana's emphatic return to the conversation, Sharon mumbled an apology and moved to put the dumpling back onto the plate.

"*Don't.*" Lana rolled her eyes. "You've touched it now." She pressed the button at the corner of the table to call over a waiter and, when one arrived, simply pointed at the empty plate. He nodded quickly and disappeared.

"So . . ." Sharon thought she had better get the conversation going again or they would be there all night. Now that she had eaten, there wasn't much point in dragging it out any longer. Unfortunately, she wasn't really sure what was appropriate to follow up with. She hesitated for a second, then went with her gut. "Do we have a deal?"

"Nearly there." The fresh plate arrived and Lana started in on her first *mandu*, tearing it apart carefully into bite-sized pieces with her chopsticks. She continued without looking up from her dumpling dissection. "I know I don't have to spell it out for you, so don't make me."

Sharon pressed her thumbs into the crooks of her index fingers, making the nails go white. She breathed in through her nose and let the air out easily along with the remainder of her integrity. "Can . . ." She swallowed. "May I order another beer?"

Lana reached for the call button again, but she miscalculated. The thin metal cup of tea tipped over at her elbow, skidding a few inches and falling onto the floor. *It had happened again.* She blinked twice, her hand frozen in midair for a distinct moment. Then she pressed the button, pointed at the waiter, pointed at Sharon's empty glass, pointed at the mess she had just made, and continued to eat.

Sharon couldn't stop her eyes from widening as the teacup crashed, but as soon as the show was over, she turned back to Lana and deliberately carried on as if nothing had happened. The hubbub in the restaurant, which had died down as everyone turned to look at the sudden noise, picked up again. "There's a service we use to send messages and to make deliveries. That is how I got the formula and the procedure in the first place, and then I would send back samples from each batch for testing . . . in the beginning, when I was new. Of course, I don't need checking anymore." She hesitated, but anxiety pushed her to continue. She tried to anticipate what Lana would want to hear. "I can set up a pickup if you like. Then you can—"

Lana put up a hand. She didn't necessarily like to hear out loud what she could or would do. "Yes. That will do it." She chewed. "Now where is the facility? I want to send someone over later this week." She nodded to Abra who made a note in her tablet. "And in the meantime, you can make a list of everything you need to get going."

"Okay. They can meet me at the storage space." Sharon agreed to the appointment, but she was suddenly too intimidated to propose a date and time. Following all of the dangers of the afternoon, she had at last begun to feel the nerves she had been suppressing all day. Her heart was picking up speed. After weeks of uncertainty, things were finally happening.

Lana was mildly annoyed by the vague answer but moved on. "Okay . . ." She reached for the tablet in Abra's hand, glancing quickly over the display. "Day after tomorrow, or day after that. You won't be busy, *will you*?"

Sharon shook her head mechanically from side to side.

Lana's eyes narrowed. "All right then, tell me about yourself. Make it up if you have to."

Sharon stared.

"What's your favorite color? To look at or to wear. Who's your role model? Dream vacation? Favorite dog breed? Sexual fantasy? Any fucking thing. I'm not going to take a photo, so go on, or I won't remember which one you are." She brought out her own tablet to take notes.

———

After dinner, they dropped Sharon off outside of her apartment building. They had insisted. She had considered giving a false address but figured *what was the point*? They clearly had their ways of figuring these things out; it was best if they weren't made to use them.

As Sharon got out, Lana gave a perfunctory wave from the car window. "See you soon." The words fell into the air, not lifting as a friendly farewell or stabbing as a threat but dropping solidly as a simple truth.

To her surprise, Sharon found that she liked Lana. She was clearly a strong woman, but then there was certainly something awkward about her that put people *falsely* at ease. It was dangerous but endearing all the same. Sharon was looking forward to working with her. There was just one thing she had to get out of the way first, and she preferred it be sooner rather than later. She had her tablet at home synced with her work tablet, and when she got upstairs to her cubicle flat, she looked up the contact information for the company that was meant to be picking up the new product in three days' time. She composed and sent the following message:

"To Whom It May Concern: Unfortunately, due to a family emergency I will need to leave the country the day after tomorrow. I am the only person with access to the storage space and keep the only key. Could you please arrange for someone to come *tomorrow* to pick up the shipment? Everything is ready and waiting as ordered. Thanks in advance for your help, S."

Chapter Forty-Three

———

W ill was lying in bed, looking up at the ceiling. It was the middle of the night. The stupid digital clock was *ticking*, as if that was a feature *anyone really wanted*. He rolled over and rolled over again, got up and flossed his teeth for the second time that night, and then lay back down. It didn't matter what he did—he wasn't going to sleep soundly until the sample came, and he tested it, and it was confirmed A-OK. The rest of the injections were scheduled for pickup the *following day*. If the test sample didn't arrive by the end of the day today, he would have to postpone, even call the whole thing off—whatever it took. No matter his good intentions, his self-reassurances, a small kernel of sanity in his soul had begun to fear the consequences. At the very least, he had to be certain of what he was prescribing.

He turned onto his side and began picking up the splayed strands of Viki's hair, one by one, and placing them in a row down her back. When he had finished, he picked up the entire bunch and carefully fanned it out again. Some nights, he used the end of her ponytail to brush her cheek, applying a midnight blush. He would test himself to see how softly he could pull it across her skin, disturbing her just enough to relish the relieving recognition that he wasn't alone, without fully waking her.

Over the last few nights when he *had* fallen asleep, he had found some stranger in navy blue scrubs standing a few yards away, back toward him, injecting infants with a bright, sparkling purple liquid as they came through, one by one, in a parade of prams. In the dream, Will needed to stop them. Something had gone terribly wrong. But he was behind the glass, outside of the ward, and he couldn't get the stranger's attention, as hard as he tried. The prams were labeled with names: Margot, Arthur, Kate, Eva, Jon, Joe, even freaking Jenny. He *had* to tell them they had forgotten something, *someone*, important. They had left him out. *Left him behind.* He would wake up with his right hand clenched tightly around a fistful of bedsheets, pulling them in toward his chest. *Better not to sleep than to deal with trying to interpret that one*, Will surmised about the whole thing.

When morning finally came, he had the temptation to jump out of bed and immediately run off to work and check his mail slot. But he knew it was silly to think a delivery of that importance would be left in the door. If it came that day, it would come around lunchtime in a box of tandoori chicken or a falafel wrap. Will hoped that for once it would be a bacon cheeseburger with extra fries. So he left Viki sleeping soundly while he took an unnecessarily long shower. He then meticulously carried out the rest of his regular morning routine— brushing his teeth for one and a half minutes and fixing his hair for two. He got dressed in one of the same striped button-down shirts he wore every day, taking extra care to minimize creasing. He tied his tie with a half Windsor knot.

Walking down the hall and down the stairs to the kitchen, he took deliberate steps, watching each of his feet, wondering whether that was his normal gait, or whether being conscious of his stride had altered it. Once in the kitchen, he pulled out plates, a bowl, a pan, flour, eggs, milk, butter; he started whisking up pancakes. He heated up the pan with a drizzle of melted butter and cooked them, one by one, until perfectly golden brown. The house smelled like heaven. Marla and Arbor filtered in, following the scent. They had gotten used to this unusual routine over the last few weeks and didn't want to do or say anything that would alter it. So, smiling angelically, they grabbed plates and pancakes and sat down at the island counter to stuff their faces. Will watched them eat while picking at the corners of a slightly overdone pancake that he had saved for himself. He dipped a piece into the maple syrup on Marla's plate, but she didn't complain. She just refilled the space he had made with fresh syrup out of the bottle. When they were finished eating, they dropped the plates in the sink, kissed him on the cheek, and left for school. He cleaned the dishes by hand. And when he couldn't come up with another task to further stretch the morning, he picked up his things and went into work.

———

As one o'clock drew near, Will began to fuss with his tablet, rearranging applications, grouping some, ungrouping others. He opened one of the little games Viki liked to play. The screen filled with a stack of colored blobs and he drew lines through them, making connections, recognizing patterns, until the colors had all disappeared. He hadn't eaten yet, hoping for his much-anticipated meal delivery, and he was growing rather hungry, though he wasn't completely sure if it was a hunger for food or for information that he felt. When two o'clock rolled around, he went to the cafeteria and grabbed a vegetarian protein patty on a hardtack bun, hoping a proper meal would be waiting for him when he returned, but he was doubly disappointed. No delivery came, and the cafeteria food tasted as if it were compressed from a powder. Sometimes he really regretted his lab being attached to a hospital.

By three o'clock, he had all but given up on the sample arriving. It wasn't too late for a lunch delivery, but with each passing minute, he was feeling more and more unlucky. Karma wasn't going to let him have this one. He could wait it out for another few hours before calling the whole thing off, but *why?* The mammoth failure was already unbearable. He wanted nothing more than to throw a hissy fit. He reached for his tablet, ready to bail, when a flag came up: a new message from Gerome and Austin at PreVAIL.

The succinctly worded subject read simply, "Great work, everyone!" Will was used to receiving generic spam from the foundation now that he was on their mailing list, and he very nearly deleted it instantaneously. But just before he had fully swiped it away, he noticed that attached below was an intriguing and frankly, to Will, shocking news story featuring the foundation. He pulled the article back into focus. At first, he just peripherally caught a few words in the headline: "Aid," "Children," "Health," "Rangpur." At the mention of Bangladesh, Will's heart began skipping rope in his chest. He dragged his eyes back over the headline, and it escalated into double Dutch. There was no mistaking it. Somehow, someway, the delivery had come early. The injections were out. They had landed. They were being distributed to hospitals as he sat there, like an idiot, wishing he could stop time and just *think*. Was it too late to recall everything? *Could he stand that?*

Of course, he knew he couldn't. Besides, it wasn't very scientific to halt an experiment halfway through just because it *might* fail. All data, even bad data, was *useful data*. Will stared at the wall, imagining each life-altering measure of tonic on its journey from his mind into reality, through the stages of production, and out into the clinics and the wards, administered like any test to the thousands of *necessary* participants. It was stunning, how the few words he had jotted down mere months ago would have such a capacity to lift up, *or fuck up*, so many lives. As he thought, perhaps for the first time, about the sheer enormity of the operation, he felt impressed and ill all at the same time.

Maybe it was perspective, his test subjects being half a world away, but in his mind they became tiny, smaller even than the infants that they were. They fit in the palm of his hand. They misbehaved; they bit and they scratched like animals. He pushed the metaphor further—*he had to*. They sprouted fur and then tails. They were nothing more or less than the millions of mice he had already expended, chucked out, and incinerated after they had given their pocket-sized gift to the human world.

———

Daylight melted into night. The lab cleared out as eight o'clock rolled around, and the last of his fresh-faced students and still-expectant postdocs had put a pin in their experiments for the evening. Eventually, Will shuffled out of his office, across the hall, and down to the far corner of the lab. There was something he felt compelled to do. It was silly. It wouldn't change anything and he knew it but, all the same, he thought it would have been meaningful to her. Or, at the very least, it might help *ease his conscience*. So, sheepishly, he sidled up to Margot for the last time, to apologize for the first time.

"I *am* sorry . . ." He stared.

"Yeah, you *are looking pretty fucking sorry* from where I sit," she replied.

"I never was much good at taking your advice. I always *needed it* though." Will felt a wet, warm, unwelcome bead forming at the corner of his right eye, growing with every honest word he spoke. "If you were here now . . . if you had been here. I wonder . . ." He looked down at the floor and reached a hand forward. The tips of his fingers grazed the glass and a pulse of pressure surged from his chest up into the space behind his eyes. He let it fall. "Well, you aren't here. What's happening is happening." Will shook his head slowly from one side to the other. "Not *exactly* to plan," he admitted.

"You know you're feeling guilty about fucking up, not about the fact that you thoroughly trashed my words of *infinite* wisdom. Why you would choose a conscience that disagrees with you on so many levels beats me." She was cold, colder than she had ever been in life.

"Who said I fucked up?"

"Just a hunch."

"Screw you; I said I was sorry."

"Sorry for what?"

"Nothing . . . Everything. For never listening to what you said, for talking to you in the first place, for teasing you when I did, for being stupid or selfish or scared, for canceling on you *that time*. That one goddamn time. I don't know. Do I really have to be specific? Can't it just be sort of a blanket apology?"

"Sure, why not? *Do you feel any better?*"

"No." He shook his head. The tears that had been welling a few moments before had sunk back down. He wiped his face with the back of his hand. Suddenly he was feeling defensive. "You're judging me."

"No, no, I can't actually judge you from beyond the grave. You're going to need a *mirror* for that. And by the way, don't confuse the guilt you're feeling now with the guilt from thirty years ago. Not everything is tied together in some magnificent all-encompassing slipknot. Pulling hard enough on the right thread won't unconditionally disentangle you."

"Why not?"

"That's just not the way shit is. Chaos. Entropy. The universe is ultimately screwed."

"Well, if chaos is the way forward, I guess I'm right on track!" He laughed.

"You're twisting my words. If chaos is an inevitability, isn't it your job as a moralizing megalomaniac to hold everything together as long as possible?"

"And by whatever means possible. Don't you see *that's what I've been trying to do?*" He sighed. He ran his hand through his thinning hair. Margot was silent. "Yes. *That* is what I am doing."

He turned away from her and stalked out of the lab before she could put in another word. But there was a corner of his heart that knew he *never* would have won an argument against the genuine article. He would have turned and walked away just the same but feeling petulant and ashamed rather than vaguely and twistedly triumphant. He didn't go home. He slept in his office, and, for the first time in days, he slept soundly.

Chapter Forty-Four

———

Will woke, half scrunched up and half splayed out, on the short couch in his office the next day with a sore neck and a feeling of deep disgust. He longed to shower, but he didn't have any desire to shower at work. He wouldn't be one of *those people*. When he checked his watch, he was surprised to see that it was already 11:00 a.m. For a second, he worried that someone might have looked in and seen him passed out there. *God, that would be embarrassing.* But he shrugged it off; after all, he hadn't slept for days, and who really gave a crap? *He was the boss.*

There was a clean, pressed shirt and a basic set of travel toiletries that he kept in his desk drawer for just this sort of occasion. He pulled out the button-down and swapped it for the one he had slept in, leaning over slightly to sniff his armpits and applying deodorant as needed. He stuffed the dirty shirt into his satchel and was just buttoning up the collar on the fresh one when there was a knock at the door. Will passed his tongue over his unclean teeth, breathed out into his palm and in through his nose. He grimaced, then sighed and moved to open it.

"Bento delivery for a Mr., ah, William?"

"Freaking A." He whispered under his breath as he forced half a smile and nodded in affirmation. "Thanks." He grabbed the plastic box out of the delivery man's hand and shut the door, opening it as he walked back to his desk. The sample was inside, tucked between a few rolls of *futomaki*. He couldn't believe it. A day late, two days late—it made all the difference in the world. Yesterday morning, he would have sprinted to the lab to run tests. Today, he wasn't so sure he wanted to know what was truly trapped inside that vial. He tipped it back and forth in his hand and then placed it in the mini fridge under his desk while he finished the bento slowly, chewing, cogitating, contemplating. When he could stand the curiosity no longer, he pulled the sample out again and walked across the hall with it.

Will hadn't run an experiment himself in years, but if his students thought it was strange to see him fumbling with the modern equipment, they gave no sign. The tests would take a few hours to run. Everything was mechanized; the results would even be sent directly to his tablet. All he had to do was drop it in and wait. But waiting was the hard part. And he had done a lot of it lately.

———

Waiting, waiting. And all for something he didn't really care to know. *Or did he? Was it his instinctual curiosity, his thirst for knowledge, his desire—no, his* need—*for information that had made him a scientific success?* Self-important thoughts floated through his head. *He was a success, certainly.* On paper. Of course there were things he hadn't achieved. *A Nobel Prize. Was that in his future? Did he even have a future?* It occurred to him that he had done it. The thing he had set out to accomplish. The thing about which he had told himself, whatever happens after, *happens after*. Now *was* after. *And, shit, had it come quickly.*

It had been years since he had done any of his own lab work, years since he had spent those uncertain hours with nothing to do but wait for the final buzzer, the *ding* signaling the cake was ready to come out of the oven. Only upon opening would one know if it had stood up to the heat or fallen flat. *Life was kind of like that*, Will mused in his reflective state. *Was it really? Yes, I think so.* A piece of cake. Ha. Actually, that sounded delicious. Will checked his watch. There were, at minimum, thirty minutes left before the sample would be finished running. He grabbed his tablet and a sweater and walked out into the hall, locking his office door behind him. Rather than taking his usual shortcut, he followed the corridor around the outside of his lab, waving exaggerated hellos to juniors and peers bustling up and down the busy hallway. Exiting the building, he turned the corner and walked two blocks to his favorite bakery in the 'Patch.

————

The bakery had a calming effect on Will. Not only did the employed alchemists conjure innumerable delectable delights from boring basic ingredients such as flour and sugar, a chemistry he would never understand, but the space itself affected him. As he approached, he was soothed by the familiar stark red awning stretching out from above French windows. Delicate wooden chairs, informally arranged around pointlessly tiny circular tables, each wobbling a touch as if by design, perfectly affected a Parisian café. When he entered, the smell of baked butter overwhelmed his senses. His eyes dwelled on the intricate mosaic floor, drifted to the wine-bottle chandelier suspended from the ceiling, and rested on the lacquered oak bar. In this bijou escape, he could focus on minor decisions and simple pleasures. He could leave a little bit of the rest of the world behind.

Chocolate or carrot? He couldn't decide on which cake to order. If he were at home, he would have had both. *It was one of those kinds of days.* But he was in public, so he thought he'd better just pick one. A party of three, two short-to-average-height women and one abnormally tall guy, walked in behind him as he deliberated, so he made a split-second decision and stepped up to the counter, eager to order straight away before he found himself three orders behind in line. "I'll have a slice of the . . . chocolate cake, please, thank you, and, ah, how about a cup of tea . . . any tea . . . black tea. . . um, large, please . . . No, no milk." He preferred ordering from a tablet as was customary at most of the chain coffee shops, but for some reason, the best places always associated themselves with *personal* service. They got the orders wrong a hell of a lot more often though.

Will sat down at the nearest table to wait for his order. While he waited, he brought out his tablet to check on the sample back in his lab. The process was 95 percent complete. He was merely 5 percent away from knowing the composition once and for all. Still, there was nothing to see. Until the analysis had run its course, there was *nothing to do* but stare at the progress bar. In the background, he could hear the tall man ordering. "Three medium coffees, black." It was the kind of order people made when they just wanted to use the bathroom. Will thought it was funny that anyone would come to a fantastic place like this and not get a pastry, at least to go.

But, he reasoned, *people are funny.* What he didn't expect was that the three of them would pick up their three black coffees, then walk over and sit down at *his* table. There were plenty of empty tables. *Wtf.*

———

"So, Dr. Dalal . . . It's William, isn't it?" The small brunette had taken the seat across from him. The tall man sat next to him, blocking any chance of exit, and the other woman occupied the remaining chair. "My name is Lana, and these are my associates, Aaron and Abra. Would you mind coming with us?" Will noticed that they had ordered their three medium black coffees to go. The leader, Lana, looked briefly as if she was going to explain further but left it as a wasted effort. She nodded to the door and then glanced at the other two in turn. She didn't need to voice a threat or parade a weapon. He understood the ultimatum.

So here they were, not too early and yet too late. They hadn't accosted him in UCSF parking lot G or in an unregistered service car after all. They had disturbed him in his local locale, his only oasis. *What a bunch of bastards.* Will glanced around the café. It was reasonably busy, and he really was craving that slice of cake. "I ordered *for here.*" He shrugged his shoulders.

Lana smiled in spite of herself and settled into her coffee. "Very well. We can enjoy our drinks, but we can't stay here forever. Abra, please, would you order me an almond croissant? And bring some sugar." She pointed to her cup.

A waiter brought Will's tea, along with a thick slice of chocolate cake. He was about to dig eagerly into the only pleasure he had left in this quickly declining day when he re-membered his manners. He would offer a taste to his surprise guest. It probably wouldn't do much good, but it didn't hurt to try. There was a chance when the progress bar on his tablet had reached completion that he would happily climb into a body bag in the trunk of this woman's car, but there was also a chance he would need to bargain.

He raised the plate toward Lana and affected an inquisi-tive look. She hesitated for a moment, then shook her head stiffly. Her eyes narrowed a hair, but she didn't speak. When her croissant came back with Abra, she began methodically pulling it apart, consuming it piece by piece, while continuing to watch him in silence. It made him uneasy, but she was *try-ing* to make him uneasy. *What could he do about it?* He shrugged again and started eating. Slowly.

The cake was divine. The dense sponge and ganache frosting melted together into a bittersweet spread that filled his mouth with bliss. It amazed him in such a fraught situation that he could still taste such joy. He savored every mouthful. At the end of each bite, the rich flavor dissipated pleasantly with just a hint of salt and a pleasing sweet conclusion. *He didn't want to die*—not with cakes like this in the world. He sipped his tea thoughtfully. There was one other thing he needed to check before leaving the café with these irksome strangers. Surely it was almost time. He finished the slice of cake, down to the last crumb, taking small sips of tea to wash down each morsel in harmony. Earthy, malty, smoky, deeply bitter tannins cut through and mingled with the rich, smooth, sugary treat.

When the hefty wedge was gone and he had scraped the last of the frosting off of his plate, he brought forward his tablet. "I'm not calling anyone." He showed the screen to Lana. He didn't have anyone to call. He unlocked it and there, full-screen, was the complete molecular structure of the sample.

In a split second, everything and nothing changed. Will sank to the bottom of the room. He was two feet tall, then he grew to the size of a giant. The world was at his feet. Then, just as suddenly, he was back again, sitting all alone at a table with three strangers who likely held his future in the palms of their hands. They didn't know anything *about anything*.

———

What he read in the structure was a small error, a minor error really. If it had been an assigned task to synthesize this chemical on a test or as a lab assignment, the result would most likely have still gotten an A, or at least an A-. The individual atoms, the elements, were all there. There had only been a structural swapping in one location. *An isomer of the original formula, as he was an isomer of the person he had once been. Shut up*, he scolded himself. *Now is not the time for that ruminative bullshit*. The main thing, he noted, was that it probably wasn't going to kill anyone. Probably. Of course there always was and always had been the risk that he would wind up with the deaths of truckloads of babies on his conscience. *Could he live with that?* A few hours ago—shit, twenty minutes ago—he would have said no. But faced with imminent danger sitting across from him now, he wasn't sure. As his fight-or-flight instincts kicked in, he reasoned, *If I could live with myself after that, was I ever anything but a monster? Why not just give in?*

But he didn't *really* think they were going to die. Sure,

lots of them would, but lots of them would die anyway; they were living in fucking Bangladesh, after all. But that wasn't the problem with the serum. He had pored over Arthur's experimental notes, memorized every trial, every element in every compound that had been tested, every stereo-sibling and chiral twin that Arthur had run through before he had been satisfied with the final formula. His best guess, and it would remain a guess until the little rug rats had matured, was that the isomeric difference would affect docility. The additional work Arthur had put into making the first twelve subjects less aggressive, nicer, *more complacent*, was slightly askew. *What did it mean?* Would they turn out to be monsters? Worse than the worst zombies he could imagine? Hyperintelligent with a cold, cutthroat attitude and no remorse? Or would they have souls and, to go with them, the spark of anger necessary to drive change in the world? Will guessed the former, but he wasn't feeling particularly optimistic in that moment.

One way or the other, he had done *something*. Made an effort. *Tried, at the very least. What was that worth?* Would he even find out, or was he about to be thrown into the compost bin behind the bakery?

———

"What is that?" Lana glanced with curiosity at the molecule rotating before them on the screen, but it was meaningless to her.

"It doesn't matter." He shook his head. "It doesn't fucking matter." Will looked directly at her for the first time since she had sat down. He noticed a small and familiar scar just above her left ear. It was almost impossible to see, but she had a habit of brushing her hair back, then pulling it forward again to hide the damage. He caught it in the half second between. Will immediately felt the aggravation rising in his chest. *Of all of the crooked, nasty, ironic, poetic, dirty, rotten tricks fate had played.* He smiled and nodded to her, looking at the door. "Let's go." At the back of his mind, he added, *You undead bitch.*

Will decided, in that moment, that he wasn't going down without a fight. Not a physical fight—he reckoned they would kick the living shit out of him—but a rational one. All of the melodramatic tendencies that had pressed him to sow his scintillant seeds in the world and just let the chips fall as they may shattered in the face of the reality before him. *He could convince them to keep him around; he could work for them if he had to.* He would manipulate, he would bargain, he would lie, but he wouldn't succumb. *If you can't beat them, join them. There will always be an opportunity to turn on them later.*

He followed Lana out of the café, with Aaron and Abra shadowing closely behind him. Two blocks down the street, they all got into an unmarked car, a nondescript, dark gray SUV. They drove south along the water, away from the biotechs and the arcades, *away from the witnesses*, eventually pulling into an abandoned lot, right at the edge of the bay. The second they were out of the car, Lana pulled a gun on him.

She stepped forward, waving him on, and awkwardly picked up the conversation. She had never been very good at the blunt explanations and one-liners that came before a hit. "Sorry, you understand. I've taken over your operation.

Sharon works for me now. I can't have you around dabbling or whatever. Competing. Of course, you understand." She raised the gun higher and walked him toward the edge of the lot, backing him up against the water.

It had happened much faster than Will had expected. A minute ago he was eating cake, and now he was looking down the barrel of a gun. *How did he get here? What was his plan?* Would they find chocolate crammed between his teeth when his corpse washed up onshore, or would he be lost forever, eaten by sharks? *Did sharks like the taste of chocolate? Breathe*, he told himself. *Bargain; find an in.* He wasn't nearly as composed under pressure as he had imagined he might be, but he had to do something. Say something. *Now.*

"What happened to you?" He asked her point-blank, brushing his temple, mirroring the spot where she hid her scar. "Is this who you really are?" It sounded unbearably clichéd, but for once, Will thought, it was totally appropriate. She knew it, and he knew it. She hadn't been born like this. *She wasn't natural.*

Lana's mouth formed the familiar shape of the word "no" before her mind caught up to stop her from voicing it. One of the things she knew she didn't do was reveal anything—particularly weakness. She hated him for bringing it out of her. She moved to pull the trigger.

He winced. "I can help you, you know." A quick and desperate plea—Will had no idea if she wanted help. Maybe she was perfectly happy in the body of someone she used to love. But based on the zombies he had volunteered with way back when, it was a confusing transition. In any case, he had to keep the conversation going.

She hesitated, but her hand remained steady. "How?"

Will relaxed a fraction. His hands were still shaking, but she was allowing him to speak. Now was his chance to make his case. It wasn't as eloquent as he had hoped, but he got in everything he could think of, as quickly he could. *Before she changed her mind.* "I've worked with people like you. That is, with people who have gone through what you have, before. In my lab, we do research. Maybe you've looked it up already? No? Okay, well, research to better the process"—he pointed to his head—"so fewer . . . *issues* occur. And there are other drugs, lots of them, for managing, for coping with what maybe you might be feeling." He paused. "Or not feeling . . ." Will swallowed. He switched tactics, broadening his value, just in case what he had put on the table so far wasn't *her thing.* "And anyway, besides, the Brill pill you've been selling is decades behind. It was cheap to make, so I never changed it, but I can design new products for you. All kinds of things. You name it." This was a stretch, but he went with it. He had to put all of his cards on the table. Surely she would pick a card, *any card.* He could feel his voice starting to crack. That was all he would be able to say in his defense.

As he waited for Lana to make up her mind, he didn't think of Viki. He didn't think of Marla and Arbor. He didn't think of Arthur or of Margot. His mind wandered to the future, in which, at this point, there was just a glimmering hope of his existence. Lana was everywhere, and Milton was with her. Tearing through cities, gnawing at the corners of society, consuming and defecating, they took whatever they wanted, leaving chaos in their wake. In his daydream, he locked them up, he fed them, he starved them, he poisoned them by the dozen. *If he couldn't fix them*, he would toss them out with the trash. They were garbage, after all—bits and pieces cobbled together like a shitty patchwork quilt. He looked into Lana's eyes and imagined he saw the outline of her soul. The good stuff had been poured away, and all that was left was an empty tumbler, a vague reminder of what it was designed to hold. It wasn't her fault she remained behind, but she belonged in a better place, with her better half, wherever it had gone. She *needed* him. He would make sure that she got there. That is, if he didn't get there first.

Will smiled at her. Lana lowered the gun a half inch.

PART IV

Ten Years Later

Chapter Forty-Five

———

It wasn't that Lana didn't like who she was. It wasn't that she wanted to be someone else or that she was trapped in another person's body, tied to this earth by some ungodly act. It wasn't as if she had somehow misplaced her soul, leaving it behind in the wreckage of the train, or whatever Will seemed to think. And he did think it, whatever *it* was; she could see it in his eyes. But she *had let him live*. There had to be an explanation for that. Lana wasn't a vindictive person. She didn't enjoy killing for sport, but she was every kind of practical, and it simply hadn't been practical to keep him around. A logical explanation for her behavior was what she mused over now. Logically, she thought, it all made sense. She wasn't disappointed with her lot in life. Surely she thought she had everything anyone, anywhere, ever could desire. But she *had changed*. That couldn't be denied. So it was logical to want an explanation. She deserved an understanding. *Knowledge is power*, she reminded herself. But it must have been ten years ago that she had spared him. What wasn't logical was *why she was still thinking about that specific moment right now*.

Will *had* explained a few things to her, a lot of things, really. He had described, in more than enough detail, chemistry and structure, neural plate folds, balances and imbalances of neurotransmitters, synaptic clefts, electrochemical gradients. He even took scans of her brain and showed them to her. There was more than enough cold, hard scientific evidence to explain why one small regrowth issue could easily alter a personality beyond recognition. And yet still it bothered her; she still felt unresolved. It had been so long now, she couldn't even picture the faces of the people she once knew in that former life— family members, friends, whoever bore the visages that blurred in her waking mind but still occasionally snuck into her dreams at night. That's why she kept him around. One day he would make all of that disappear, cut cleanly between *before the accident* and *what came after*, so she could finally let go of the past. *Or it could let go of her, goddamn it.* She was afraid that it would haunt her forever, that it fogged her judgment, that it already constantly caused her to make minor and major mistakes. If Lana had still understood the meaning of the word "fear," she might have realized that completely letting go of her former self was the only thing she was really scared of anymore.

In any case, Will was working for her now. Or at least, she thought so. He had produced new and improved follow-ups to the Brill pill, and they consistently outcompeted rivals in terms of effectiveness and production costs. But she wondered whether he stretched out the timelines—if he sometimes, or often, exaggerated the slow pace with which he revealed new formulae. The truth was that she never really knew what he was up to. She didn't understand enough biochemistry to know whether he was producing an intelligence-enhancing drug or a Tic Tac. But she had grown fond of him, if being fond of a person was something she was indeed capable of. She thought of him tottering around his lab, stirring and shaking tinted liquids in glass bottles. In her mind, he wasn't much more than a glorified mixologist. Harmless, really.

———

In reality, no one did any stirring or shaking. Everything in the lab was automated now—almost everything. The one thing the robots couldn't reliably handle was the ever-growing population of mice down in the basement. Will appreciated this fact. If it weren't for his small furry friends, no one would bother coming into lab. There was no other reason to come in; virtually everything else could be done remotely. Of course, he would have insisted they come in anyway. There were already far too many people in the world getting away with this *work from home bullshit*. That was for consultants and statisticians, not scientists. Lab work *should* be grueling; it was a rite of passage. Standing at your bench for twelve hours at a time, squeezing endless microliters of liquid into row after row of tiny tubes, was character building. Will was old-school, he told himself, and he liked the sound of that.

Alone in his office—his door shut to the minions across the hall sitting at their desks, working on screens, not samples—Will still caught himself daydreaming. *Some things never change.* Two dusty, dry skulls sat on an old shelf across the room with other bygone trinkets, including Will's PhD diploma. He didn't look over at them very often; usually they just faded into the background. But when he did catch a glimpse of them, he thought of Shakespeare. *What a fucking legacy that guy created.* What was Will's legacy? This had become the focus of many of his daydreams, but over the last ten years, his daydreams had become more and more like waking nightmares.

He shook himself before falling into another one. He didn't have time to daydream anymore. He wouldn't allow himself time. Immediately following that afternoon ten years ago when he had stood at gunpoint, not knowing whether he would live another day on this earth, he had changed. He had made a schedule, looked himself in the eye, and told himself to stick to it. He had. He was home by seven o'clock every night, in time for dinner. Before Marla and Arbor had gone off to college, he had spent the evenings after dinner asking them unwelcome questions about academics and applications, significant others and social activities. Now he spent his evenings alone with Viki. He wasn't entirely sure how Viki felt about it, if he was being honest, but it was the right thing to do. When your life was threatened, Will thought, you make changes. You focus on what is most important in your life. That *should* be family. He saved the daydreaming for the evening, to fill the hours before he went to sleep, when he was sitting with Viki eating dinner or watching TV or doing jigsaw puzzles. It simply couldn't be helped.

During the day, the emails flooded in. It seemed to him that he spent all day every day replying to emails. Every day except for Friday, that is. On Fridays, Will went to see Lana in whatever high-rise apartment or hotel suite she was working from in a given week. He gave her a brain scan and updated her with some garbage about how her memory-erasing scheme was going. He had no interest in helping her. If anything, she deserved whatever shadow of her former self remained, reminding her of what empathy was, haunting her. He took the scans, and he studied them for his own purposes. The more he knew about the zombies, the better armed he would be. He didn't often get the chance to study one so consistently over such a long period of time or so far into its life cycle.

Of course, she would ask about progress at least twice a year, and Will would make up some jargon about neurochemical modulation and synaptic remodeling. Then he would launch into a rant about how "Everyone watches *one goddamn film* and thinks you can just throw"—air quotes—"'*science*' at a problem and, whoop-de-doo, cut to the next scene, *bam*, there's a monkey in space. Well, let me tell you the same goddamn thing I tell you every time you ask, *so you don't have to ask me again*—science is slow. As fuck." The truth was, he doubted if he could come up with anything, even if he tried. Memory was a tricky thing. It certainly wasn't linear, so cutting it off at a specific date sounded to him as ridiculous as trying to sweep dust out of the air with a broom.

It didn't matter. Lana was never fazed by his performances. She would counter with her own rehearsed lines. "I've read up about you. You've done more in the last thirty years than the next ten best researchers in the field have done in their lifetimes put together. I think you're just stalling, in case I decide that when you're finished, I don't need to keep you around anymore." He was no longer worried that she would have him killed though. These exchanges had become more like a familiar game they would play, desultory bickering rather than any sort of genuine threat. Sometimes he even thought she had an awkward crush on him. It made him shudder to consider her blank mind filled with two-dimensional thoughts of him—puzzle pieces sliding into place.

He wasn't going to kill Lana, either. His silent threats as

she held him at gunpoint all those years ago were nothing more than that. He didn't have it in him, he knew it, and he *should have* been proud of it. It was too personal. He had loved that feeling though; the pure anger and conviction he had experienced in that moment had been a rush to his system. He had never felt so sure of himself as he had in those fleeting seconds. He wasn't certain he would ever feel at all sure of himself again. It was a foreign and fabulous sensation that he would continue to cherish, and in a way, he had Lana to thank for it.

Chapter Forty-Six

———

Will turned back to his emails. He stared at his desktop. He would try to get through a dozen today. Just twelve. It had been at least five years, and he still struggled with the constant correspondence. It wasn't that he wasn't interested or that he didn't want to engage, but all of the little tiresome social customs, the polite questions and the sincere sign-offs, overwhelmed him. He took a deep breath.

He had a couple hundred pen pals now. It amused Will that they were still called "pen pals." In fact, one of the only things that encouraged him to reply to the emails was the much more terrible thought of having to handwrite a letter. But despite his reluctance to write, he was proud of his "pals." *What a fantastic scheme it was!* He had looked for years after the injections were administered for a letter-writing program in those districts of northwestern Bangladesh. Finally, he had thought, *How silly. I will just set one up myself.* Ten years ago, when the vitamins were just delivered, he had made one innocent request to obtain the list of subjects from Gerome, and now he was making use of it. He had carefully reached out to their families with a harmless, character-building, culturally enhancing—not to mention free—program to build writing skills and relationships with a professional, honest-to-God, world-renowned scientist. *And it had worked!*

Naturally he made up slightly different identities for himself, a slightly different backstory for each handful of pals. But they were all related to the medical field, connected in some way or another to that most prominent area of medicine, *in Will's opinion*—regeneration. He had started writing to his "flock" when they were only five years old. He wrote to them via their parents at first, building his integrity and getting a sense for how quickly they were progressing. The children were learning at an unprecedented rate. Their families were overwhelmed; they had no idea what to do with the tiny geniuses. This made it much easier for Will to entrench himself.

By five, the tykes were already picking up English, and with a few translational aids, it was easy to tell they were advanced enough to produce complicated and thoughtful correspondence. But they were still very young, so five years down the line they trusted him. Will had been a ready and available outlet for minds quickly outgrowing their surroundings, and in more cases than not, he helped to mold them. He endeavored to shape their interests around his own work. He let them in on "little secrets" he had picked up here and there from the memory he had spun out of Arthur's notes. He sprinkled righteousness over their spanking new understanding of scientific medicine and handed them a good helping of pride. These small, eager, and boundless minds craved sustenance, and he gave them every scrap he had, one letter at a time.

In the back of his mind, Will entertained the preposterous notion that they were here to save the world as—and this didn't hurt the perception—was he by association. Soon they would be far out of his reach, too clever for him to be of any further consequence. But until then, he would do his best to prepare them. A few were already on their way. Using their wits to change their surroundings, they had taken every opportunity, every scholarship, and with a little direction from Will's sleight of hand encouragement, they were beginning to pop up at recognized institutions. Today, Will was writing to one of his favorites. Asim had just graduated from Harvard summa cum laude and was starting an MD–PhD program at UPenn. *How exciting.* A regular wunderkind, though there was no way to know whether this early progress would translate into tangible results. *What will he accomplish?* he wondered. *What have I accomplished?*

It would still be a few years before Asim could really get into the zombie business. There were still several hurdles to overcome, but Will had hope that he would find his way. In the meantime, he regularly included a couple of Lana's scans in his emails, trying to keep him interested, nudging him into the field. Will was less willing to admit that he was desperate to know what Asim saw in the scans, how he would analyze them, what he could tell Will about them that Will didn't already know. He wasn't jealous of the boy's intelligence; after all, *he had created it.* He was worried for the moment when Asim realized his superiority, when the scales would fall from his eyes, and Will would mean nothing to him. He was proud of him. He did wonder sometimes if he was supposed to feel that way about Arbor. But Arbor was studying French literature. *Good God.*

He awkwardly signed off, "Your Pal." He couldn't think of anything less childish without sounding too formal or somehow inappropriate, and he did think about it for some time. Then he had an idea. It wasn't a new idea; in fact, it had been a solid idea knocking around in his mind for a few years.

He just wasn't sure when he could put it into motion, and when—or whether—he should. They seemed balanced enough so far, but if even one of them was just slightly deranged, it could be dangerous. There were three of them now in the United States and a handful in Europe, one or two in Canada, a set of twins in Hong Kong, and more on their way into colleges or universities or technical schools around the world. Not to mention the few thousand or so he hadn't managed to start up a correspondence with. Will paused for a moment, then he jotted down a postscript: "P.S. I have a friend who participates in this pen pal program. I recently discovered that his pal, Jhillika, is from the same district as you! In fact, just like you did a few years ago, she has moved to the U.S. to start an undergraduate program. Let me know if you would be interested in getting in touch with her. It might be fun." He hesitated, considering whether it really was a good idea to introduce them. They would certainly deduce that something had happened to them in that small part of the world. Maybe they already suspected. Surely someone must suspect such an anomaly.

He shrugged and sent off the email. It was just one potential introduction . . . for now. So what if they figured it out, *why they were the way they were*. They should count themselves lucky. No one else was entitled to that luxury. Statistically speaking, some of them had probably already met, possibly even grown up together. Eventually they would all get wise. Eventually they would all meet. This was just a first trial. Two brains were better than one, and so on.

Chapter Forty-Seven

———

When he had finished his twelve emails, Will rewarded himself with a delivery of Detroit-style pizza and a tumbler of Scotch, the same three fingers he had grown accustomed to a decade ago. But now he limited himself to only one portion a day, and he didn't allow himself any at all if he hadn't accomplished what he had set out to do. The trick was to minimize the benchmarks so that a few dispatched correspondences would suffice to warrant an allotment, and the allocation often slipped past three fingers into four, but that was the gratuitous thickness of the glass and the unpredictable curve of the bottle for you.

He wondered if Lana drank much, or if she needed to. Perhaps drowning one's feelings was inessential when one didn't have any feelings left to drown. Not that this was the reason Will drank. Sometimes he drank just to pass the time. No one visited him in his office anymore. His students these days didn't seem to covet that face-to-face mentorship that was once so treasured. They wanted his name on their papers, they wanted his clout and his capital, but they didn't want to learn from him—not directly. All queries came via email or voice memo, and he spent so much time responding to his preferred protégés that he rarely had any effort left to bestow on his paid pupils. That's what postdocs were for.

Besides, Will had other matters to attend to. *Bigger mat-*

ters. The world had been falling into disarray all around him all his life, and the window for restitution was closing.

———

But how were they going to do it? He and his pals—how were they going to save the world? What exactly were they saving it from? Will tried to put into words the growing threat of the undead, the regenerated, but the words fell through his mind, hiding in the deepest, darkest corners.

Over the last ten years, things had only worsened. No matter what improvements he made in the growing process, he could never restore their *humanity.* They became cleverer, their memories improved, their reflexes sharpened. But the vast majority of zombies still woke up *broken.* They were no longer themselves. They knew it, and everyone around them did too. Many people vowed they would rather die than wake up that way, and yet, when it came down to the final pitch, not one of them didn't swing for the miss.

But that was still just the basic problem. Then there was everything else on top of that. *Everything else.* Will had convinced himself that they were taking over the world. As soon as he started pondering problems, he dove quickly into worst-case scenarios. Those counterfeit, dummy, fake forgeries of human beings were running the government, taking control of big business, exploiting their new gifts and fresh lack of compunction. They were banding together, growing in numbers, becoming organized, plotting. Surely, they were plotting. *But what in God's name were they plotting?*

Will's fears weren't unsubstantiated. It wasn't simply an overpopulation issue anymore. Sure, there were still shelters being built. There were clinics, support groups, help lines, religions, cults. More homeless than ever, zombie and human, roamed the streets. They made up a large enough percentage of the population now that people had coined an actual term for them. It wasn't "zombies," of course, but "re-gens." The world was bursting with excess numbers, creepers or crawlers destined to knock Will out of his place. In fact, there was one right down the hall, only two doors' distant, relaxing in its office, twiddling its thumbs, scratching its ass, biding its time: Dr. Bruce W. Hale. As soon as he had shown up, *Will had suspected*. And he had done his research. Before an attempted suicide, *Dr. Bruce* was a washed-up professor at Boise State. Before the *tragedy*, he hadn't published more than a handful of papers, in shitty journals Will hadn't even heard of. Whether or not whatever research professor Hale was working on just two doors down was worthwhile, revolutionary, or absolute bunk, Will had created this *impostor*.

Zombies, sporting brand-new brains, fresh from the propagation tank, *had* found their way into positions of power. Will was able to tell them apart easily now. A few didn't try to hide it; even celebrated the fact. The fact was that it was his fault. In his long struggle to improve the process, to grow brains into the best brains they could be, he had given them an advantage he couldn't take back. *Or could he?* The rate at which zombies were replacing humans in the workforce was slowly but surely increasing. There were instances of people intentionally injuring themselves, throwing themselves head-first onto the pavement, diving for a second chance. *Dr. Bruce* had almost certainly been among these idiots. Others, with money to burn, actually walked into hospitals demanding transplants. It was only a matter of time before they got what they wanted. Will was absolutely disgusted. *How could any-one choose to warp themselves like that?* The world was be-coming a goddamn hall of mirrors. Soon, nothing would be what it seemed. Sometimes he fantasized about setting up a private company where he would spend his time curating brains for transplant. There would be a consultation with some dithering multimillionaire too giddy to understand his own demands. Then Will would take those demands and carefully turn them on themselves. A desire for increased motor function would turn into Parkinson's-like convulsions. An eidetic memory might come with the added bonus of ob-sessive-compulsive disorder, or an attention deficit. Maybe instead he would just swap their brains out for those of an-other patient, new memories and new motives, or better yet, just leave them empty-headed.

Will reached down into the small fingerprint-accessible fridge under his desk. He pulled out a vial. It was something he had worked on feverishly for the first five years following the incident with Lana, while he had still been very angry. It was also one of the few things he had created in the past thirty or so years without Arthur's posthumous help, so he was pretty proud of it. Still, he wasn't sure what to do with the thing. He tipped it from side to side very slowly and watched the near-clear potion swish back and forth, trapped in the unreactive glass. "You'll do a number on them," he whispered. It was safely contained, but only a few millimeters from his bare skin, and he recoiled at the thought of what it could do. There had been a time in his life when it would have been the worst thing he could imagine.

It wasn't too late to put a stop to everything. Will was pretty sure. Whatever alterations had occurred in each specimen before transplant weren't transmissible. *Will chuckled at the thought of Dr. Bruce's dumb-as-a-brick kid.* It wasn't quite an epidemic. Not yet. They were only growing at the rate of head injuries, and only those that didn't result in sudden or even relatively rapid death. Will relaxed. He had *some* time.

He looked down at the vial in his palm and found himself whispering aloud again, "Restoring balance. That's all it is, really." He sighed. "Not that I will *ever* figure out a way to administer it. Fuck." He reopened the fridge and placed the vial carefully back where he had picked it up from, camouflaged among vials of water and mouse anesthetics, as if it were just another reagent.

————

Will often walked the two doors down the hall to visit his antagonist in his office. When he felt particularly frustrated or craved vindication, he simply couldn't sit still. He used to go up to the rooftop and pace in a deliberate rectangle over the square space or walk into the 'Patch, pick out a place he had never been in before, and give it a five-star review from his tablet as he criticized the storefront from the street. Talking to Bruce Hale, he decided, was much more satisfying. Will baited him with questions about the Boise State football team or vocational track, things he considered no self-respecting university would brag about. *Dr. Bruce* would color at his insinuations: he knew *now*, even if he hadn't known *then*, to be embarrassed. And what could *the bastard* say? There was no room for him to admit that it had all been a fluke, no self-respect in acknowledging that the auspicious error that had carried him here had been the handiwork of the very asshole provoking him now. Will would have hated him more for confessing to it. If Will was forced to reconcile this metamorphosis with life's other foibles, he might lose faith in the whole system. The research Professor Hale had conducted since his accident may have been admirable, pioneering even, but it didn't *count*.

Will walked down to his office now. He was full from his heavy lunch, and the pungent, peaty liquor was sitting smoky on top of the grease in his stomach, floating too close to his thoughts, sharpening some and clouding others. The walls of his own office had been leaning too close, trying to crowd his good and bad judgment into a single trivial hunch.

Dr. Bruce was always busy after lunch. He was busy before lunch too, and in the hours of the late afternoon, working with the ambitious optimism that Will had once had. Will took a secret delight in interrupting this earnest energy. He called it a cruel pleasure, but a part of him hoped he might capture a bit of the fervor for himself as it shattered with Professor Hale's concentration.

Will knocked. He waited four or five seconds, then pushed open the door.

"Excuse me, Bruce." He cleared his throat, but his colleague had headphones placed resolutely over his ears and was either inadvertently or willfully oblivious to the obtrusion. Will knocked again on the door, now behind him as he stood in the doorway, with greater and greater force, until he was heard.

Professor Hale pulled the clunky, outdated headgear down around his neck. He looked up but didn't say anything. It had been many too many times for him to feign politeness for this little charade any longer.

Will didn't care. "Why do you still wear those?" He pointed to his own ear. "Aren't they uncomfortable?"

"Kept losing my buds." Professor Hale shrugged then turned back to his tablet.

"I keep a spare pair in my desk," Will lied. "You're welcome to borrow them." He smiled. *The impostor wouldn't dare ask.*

Professor Hale nodded. He was already weary of the encounter, up to his eyes before it had even begun. It only encouraged Will to hang around longer. He stepped forward, picked up a stylus off of the desk, and began twirling it between his fingers. "I read your paper on basal ganglia reprogramming." He had read he abstract anyway. "Impressive stuff."

"Cheers." Professor Hale reached for the stylus. Will handed it back absentmindedly, and he replaced it in the exact unspecified spot from which Will had removed it.

"Hey, do you ever think about it? The suicide attempt. Do you ever . . . regret it?" Will was blunt, blunter than he had ever been. His tone had conveyed all the gravity of a rhetorical weather report, but *Dr. Bruce* would understand, whether or not he chose to. Besides, sooner or later, Will needed to know. The details were important, after all. If he was ever going to go through with his plan, it would be much easier to punish the audacious or the duplicitous. There was no other rationale. He could ask Lana, but Lana was too attached. She would say whatever she thought he wanted to hear or whatever would piss him off the most. Bruce W. Hale represented a demographic, a world of people who owed Will everything and yet nothing.

Professor Hale looked as though he might willfully misunderstand for a moment, feign offense, and kick Will out of his office, maybe even for good. He had every right to do it and certainly had only been waiting for this perfect excuse. But his eyes flickered with the temptation of honesty. Will was someone so infuriatingly obtuse, he could say anything he might never repeat to someone more intimate or less provoking. Will watched closely as he made his decision, imagining he saw the outline of a conscience or the shedding of a cloak.

"Never."

"Never . . ." Will repeated. "Not once? And what if it simply hadn't worked out?"

"The rewards outweighed the risk." He was forthright, sincere. "I'm half surprised *you* haven't given it a shot, Professor Dalal." He smiled suddenly. "Is it crazy to want to make the world a better place? To want to give yourself a leg up?"

The distantly familiar words, now turned against him, made Will hesitate. He felt uncomfortable, replying instinctively, unintentionally, "You think you deserve it?"

"Does it matter?" Professor Hale's smile twisted.

"'Course not." His cool admission infuriated Will, but he was right. Still, it couldn't have been that easy from the other side. *Dr. Bruce* must have debated, deliberated while he still had beliefs to defend. He could easily have gone too far, left his career in the shambles it was, permanently irretrievable; his son, fatherless, somewhere in Idaho. "How *is* little Bruce Junior?" Will switched subjects.

"It's 'Kyle.' He's doing all right, enjoying the new school, I think," he mumbled, reassuming his uninviting demeanor as Will tried to remember why the youngster had switched schools. "He's happy."

Will nodded, satisfied. "Good."

Chapter Forty-Eight

————

Will collected his things and left the office at six thirty. He walked home through the Dogpatch. It hadn't changed much in ten years. Restaurants and shops came and went, but the good ones tended to stick around. On his way, he stopped in the same French bakery where he had met Lana for the first time. He wanted to pick up a surprise treat to bring home to Viki, but he wasn't sure what to get for her. He pondered as he waited in line. She never seemed entirely happy with anything he picked out, but he was sure that eventually he would choose the *right thing*. It was just a matter of statistics really, trial and error, an experiment that one day he was sure would all make sense. By this point, he could usually gauge outcomes. The mechanisms were what still evaded him. Ah well, they had been married for forty years. That was something to be proud of.

When he reached the front of the line, he still hadn't decided, so he ordered a slice of chocolate cake for himself. That was another thing he did since the near-death incident. He ate twice as much cake—just couldn't get the taste out of his mouth. He sat down with it and finished quickly, then purchased a slice of carrot cake to bring home. Viki liked healthy things; carrots were healthy, and besides, he usually ended up eating half or more of any dessert item she picked at, so he might as well get something *he liked* too.

When he entered the kitchen, Viki was making dinner. That is, she was unpacking dinner from that strange thermal-insulated box that arrived right around seven fifteen every evening. Will wondered for half a second how much *that* cost, then realized he didn't care. Lana had let him keep the money he had made before he had started working for her, and he wasn't likely to run out in this lifetime. What was money for, aside from convenience? There was no reason Viki should have to *use* their sleek stainless steel kitchen appliances. If she ever did, she would also have to *clean* them. Or someone would. "What's for dinner?" he asked.

"Roasted quail and sorghum puffs. It's just about ready." She had one more canister to open. "Table's all set; have a seat." She rummaged around the cupboards for an appropriately sized serving plate, then laid everything out on the table in front of him. She poured out a glass of red wine for Will and opened a beer for herself, setting it down next to the empty plate in front of her seat. "I just have to change the laundry. It'll be quick. Go ahead and start without me." She swung around the island toward the far kitchen door.

Will couldn't help being impressed by her activity. Setting the table at lightning speed, running up and down the stairs carrying baskets of laundry at their age. He didn't want her to leave the room just yet. He stalled her. "Hey."

"Yep?" Viki caught herself on the doorframe. She hung mid-motion.

"I picked up a slice of carrot cake on my way home."

"Oh thanks, sweetie . . . We can share it after you finish your dinner." She unfroze from the doorframe and disappeared down the stairs into laundry land.

"Well, I guess carrot cake wasn't the thing, either," Will

said matter-of-factly to himself as he tucked into the small bird.

Viki was still fussing around the house when he finished dinner, so he moved on to the carrot cake alone. He knew he wouldn't have to apologize for finishing it. She didn't want it; *she never did.* When the cake was reduced to crumbs that he could no longer be bothered to press together into morsels, Will poured himself another glass of wine. He had never been skinny, but for most of his life he hadn't been fat. Now he was fat. *But what was the point of diet and exercise if you were just going to be shot dead and tossed over the side of a pier?* He patted his stomach, sipped his wine, and took a deep breath. It hadn't affected him really. The incident. He was still the same Will. He thought, *I'm still the same old guy. Same brain equals same guy. Remember back when I used to be cool? Ha. Feels like a fucking century ago.* But his eyes darkened at the thought of the incident, and the top layer of skin on the back of his hands suddenly felt cool. He swallowed a large slug of wine, temporarily washing down the quick feeling.

Will stared at Viki's fresh plate. She still wasn't back from the laundry or whatever it was she had moved on to now. He could hear her puttering around. *Was he supposed to wait for her?* He got up slowly from his seat. It was hard to move quickly these days, but he managed to put his weight onto his two legs while carrying his tablet in one hand and balancing a fresh glass of wine in the other. He shuffled into the next room and sat down on the sofa, switching on the TV from his tablet as his rear plunged comfortably into the soft seat. He hardly knew what to watch these days, there were so many options tiled across his tablet. He turned to a basketball game. That was one thing that would never change. There would always be sports on TV.

Will watched a few baskets swing the score back and forth, but he wasn't engaged. In his peripheral vision, he caught Viki walking through the room on her way hither or thither. "Why don't you have your dinner in here while we watch the game?" he suggested idly.

"What game is it?"

Will didn't have a response ready for such a digging question. He looked up toward the score on the TV but by the time he had the answer, she was gone again. He wished she would come sit next to him. She used to sit next to him when he had first started coming home early, right after the incident. Of course, he had never told her about the incident. Maybe, when he had started coming home on time like that, out of the blue, she had thought he was dying, at least for a few years. They *did* spend a lot of time together, or at least confined within the same four-thousand-square-foot space, but he felt that he missed her. It was a nice feeling, to miss someone special. *Or maybe he simply had too much free time away from his work now, and he was just plain lonely.*

At halftime, Will became restless again. He began searching through articles on his tablet, sifting through headlines. He was constantly nervous to discover what was happening in the news, but at the same time, it drove him. He had to know what was coming. When he had finished scanning the day's big stories, he began casually looking up the latest serial murder cases. That was what he was convinced *they* all were, after all: psychopathic killers. They either were already or they were going to become killers, given the right set of circumstances. It was all Lana was, in reality—whatever business-related excuse she hid behind.

If Will had been totally honest or had even bothered to think logically about the matter, he would find that he didn't really know for sure if serial killers *were* on the rise, but it certainly *seemed* like it since he had started searching for them. *And he was scientifically minded, so he was probably right.* On the occasion that one of these killers was caught, he looked for signs. Was there a terrible accident in this person's history? Were old friends and acquaintances shocked by the unfamiliar behavior of this person they thought they knew so well? *They used to know so well.* The important thing was that he had to figure out a way to track them, to analyze their behavior over time. If only he could tag them all.

While Will was deep in thought considering the treatment of zombies as dangerous animals, the TV began to ring. It was Marla. Will picked up the call and immediately glanced back and forth across the living room. He called to Viki, hoping she was near enough to join the conversation, but she didn't seem to be in hearing range, so he turned back to the screen.

"Hi, Dad."

"Hi, Marla. . . . How's school?"

"Okay . . ."

"Great. Good to hear."

"Is Mom there?"

"She's around here somewhere." He moved his head barely, back and forth again. "I think she's doing the laundry. Maybe."

Marla laughed. "You need to get off the couch a little more often, Dad. Haven't you heard how bad it is for you not to do forty jumping jacks, ten squats, and nineteen toe touches every thirty seconds while you watch TV?" She joked, but at the same time, she eyed the empty wineglass sitting on the coffee table in front of him.

Will noticed her line of sight. "It's good for the heart."

"That's an old wives' tale."

"Who cares? I'll just grow myself a new one."

"And a new liver, and a new kidney, and a new *brain*?" The last word came over the TV speakers with a nagging inflection.

"No!" Will replied swiftly and sharply. "I won't be a z—" He stopped himself. "Re-gen. And you won't, either!" Oh God. He had made things awkward, *and he had been doing so well.*

Marla rolled her eyes and moved on. "I got an A in my chemistry class."

"Good job."

"I figured you would be proud of that." She smirked. "Hey, Mom!" Viki had appeared at the back of the room, moving forward to join the conversation. "Can I ask you a favor?"

Will sighed in relief and hoisted himself up. He waved goodbye to Marla as the two of them chatted, then he moseyed into the next room with his tablet still open, gloomy news stories still filling up the screen. He pondered as he wandered slowly through the house. He was proud of Marla's A, certainly. When he was younger, he had always assumed his children would follow in his footsteps. He had thought he would be such a central figure in their lives that they wouldn't dream of pursuing anything but science or medicine.

But for some reason, he felt uneasy about it now. It

wasn't as clear-cut as it had seemed back then. *Back when was that?* In any case, it wouldn't be easy. The competition was steeper than ever. Will figured at least half the student body of most top universities were on the Brill pill or had at least taken it at some point. Lana was moving it like crazy. He felt sick at the thought of Marla tossing one back right before her orgo final. It drove him mad.

Worse still was the future. Opportunities snatched away from her by greedy, unfeeling hands. What if there wasn't room for her in what was once a wide world? It was narrowing rapidly, as was Will's field of vision. In many ways he hardly knew Marla, and yet the obvious interpretation that she was a part of him caused him to feel fiercely protective. There were no lengths to which he wouldn't go in order to save her from the coming plague. The monsters on his tablet would *pay*; after all, they owed him. He had given them reasoning and respiration. He was entitled to take some of that back. As Will's mind plunged Marla into the most unlikely and dreadful situations, his resolve hardened. He would sit by no longer. Something had to be done.

Will waddled upstairs and brushed his teeth. He couldn't even be bothered to shower. He lay in bed, ostensibly reading papers on his tablet, but his thoughts were elsewhere.

Chapter Forty-Nine

———

O ver the years, Will had deliberately been dropping tiny, and then little, and then noticeable, hints into the electronic letters he sent to his pen pals. These carefully worded hints were intended to nudge his young friends into the *right* field of study. To his pleasant surprise, though most probably due to the fact that the majority hadn't been exposed to much else within the broad interpretation of what can be classified as a liberal art, it had worked an outstanding 40 percent of the time. What Will hadn't noticed were the more nuanced cues that came through unintentionally, the slight changes in tone or word choice that would easily be picked up and noted upon by the set of child intellectuals. Minor implications, inadvertent and yet ingrained, that re-gens were not wholly human: "Unfortunately, *they* return lacking basic connectivity"; "It isn't *their* fault, naturally . . ."; "*They* are not capable of forming bonds in the way that you and I can, that you and I *have*"; "This makes *them* unpredictable . . . unstable." *A potential threat.* In Will's occasionally unrestrained words, the re-gens needed help, certainly, not out of pity for them but out of protection for everyone else. *At least he had never explicitly referred to them as "zombies."*

———

Asim had emailed him back.

Will lingered over his inbox, dancing through spam, wondering distractedly if he should join his alumni traveling group after all. Skimming through a closeout sale on designer watches, pondering whether he could possibly use a gua sha face crystal or if he might even bother to learn what it was. Buying a hand cycle studio membership would be a waste of time and money, but it would surely be easier than opening the latest missive from Asim. His emails were generally harmless, a bit boring for someone as astute as he was purported to be, if Will was honest. But Will had started a line of questioning that he couldn't take back, and now he wasn't sure he felt entirely ready to accept the consequences.

He wavered tentatively over the unopened message again. He had now gone back through his inbox and either opened or deleted everything else from that day. If he were to go back any further, it would be hours before he got around to the task at hand—hours *wasted*. If he just opened this *one* email. If he just read it through and formulated a response in his head, he might reward himself with a quick drink before the onerous task of putting his careful answer down in words. The problem was, this time Will was more anxious about reading the message than replying to it. Suddenly, the act of a single click seemed tied to the outcome of so many years of suspense. *He was being dramatic.* There was probably nothing out of the ordinary in the message. But if there *was*, would he have to *deal* with it? If he just left it alone, was there a chance it all might just *leave him alone* as well?

Will sighed and clicked.

"Hi, Dr. Dalal! Good to hear from you!" Will wondered whether it really was. "I've just finished my neuro rotation—I loved it!" He always used a lot of exclamation points. For all of his brains, that was one translation he couldn't seem to get right. Asim seemed to think that in American English, you added an exclamation point at the end of every single blasted sentence. "Anywho"—*there was another thing he did*—"I thought you would be excited to hear that!" Will, in fact, was excited. UPenn had a great neurology department; he could do a lot there. "Speaking of excitement!!" The exclamations were out of control. "There's another student out here from my neck of the woods?!" Now this was beginning to sound disingenuous, even for Asim. "I would LOVE to meet her!" It went on like this.

Will wondered if Asim already knew about his female counterpart. Perhaps they all knew. Perhaps they had figured it out ages ago. They knew they were special, and they knew Will, or whatever name he had given each of them, was responsible. Would they be grateful if they knew? Would they be angry? *They should be fucking grateful. They would be nothing without him.* It didn't much matter what they should or shouldn't be though. He was probably just reading too much into things. *As usual.* He had gotten toward the end of the email now, past all of the updates on the best Philly cheesesteak in town (!!) and "What is *up* with the Liberty Bell?"

It seemed to finally be getting more interesting. "You know, I have been spending some time analyzing the scans you've been sending. What a treat to get to look at your data! And I think I have noticed something pretty freaking (excuse the French haha—why is that a thing??) interesting! I don't want to get your hopes up—and don't tell anyone, of course, why would you? ;)—but it seems like we may have found a solution to your problem, well *our* problem, I guess, universally speaking, LOL. It appears that there may be a weak link, a chink in the armor, let's say, leaving the zombies (Ha! Do you like that name for them?) vulnerable. Do you think you could take a focused scan of just the basilar pons region? I would love to have a closer look at it, thanks!"

The text went on to explain the details, but the gist of it was an overlooked flaw in the blood–brain barrier. In the regenerated models, there was a small but consistent defect in the design of that defense system that protected natural-grown human brains from infection and toxins. It wasn't so much of a fault that they were subject to disease in the natural world, but someone with the right know-how and tools could trick the system, creating a nanoparticular vehicle that could penetrate the barrier at a particular point in the brain stem. The bottom line was that if Asim was right, zombies could be selectively targeted with anything the nanoparticles could deliver.

————

Will felt somewhat sick for a second at the fact that Asim had called them "zombies." He was *sure* he had never mentioned the pet name to him. *97 percent sure.* But it passed quickly. He didn't blink at the fact that a ten-year-old boy had just described to him the potential for a bioweapon that could target and take out one one-thousandth of the population. It was a small percentage, but it was *a large number.* After all, this was the opening that Will was hoping for. This was the justification for the very existence of his young chums, the means by which they were going to save the world together. He had to tell Asim about the carefully disguised vial he kept locked in the fridge beneath his desk, and he had to tell him now. It was time to get it off his chest and onto the table.

Will closed his email and opened an encrypted messaging app. The idea that he could now just barely form and was anxious to communicate would certainly result in the spelling out of words that he wouldn't want recorded. He opened a blank message template, then immediately flipped back to his email to double-check that he had read everything completely correctly. It was gone.

Had it all been a crazed dream? Had he become desperate to the point of delusion? Was he finally losing it? No. He was sure he had read it. He flipped back to the messenger and moved on. He just had to figure out how to put it exactly.

"Hello, Asim. I was just reading your email. I wanted to check on something, but it seems to have disappeared?" Will pressed SEND and waited for a reply to pop up. *It could take hours.* But it didn't. Asim replied within the minute.

"Hi there! Oh yeah! I did that on purpose—sensitive information, burn after reading, you know (but more efficient!)."

Cool trick. "I see. Cool trick."

"I know!"

Will wasn't sure if he was supposed to respond. He found himself just pressing random keys to make it appear that he was still engaged.

Asim didn't keep him waiting long. "So what did you think about the stuff at the end?"

"That is what I wanted to ask you about . . ."

"Ok, shoot!"

"Do you think, if you're right about what you said, that is, do you think it would be possible to deliver a targeted dose of small-molecule inhibitors?"

"Well, you know as well as I do . . ."

The rascal. "Yes, obviously, of course, well . . ." *How to put it?* "There's something I started working on about ten years ago. A sort of a fail-safe, I guess. We have—" He backspaced and rewrote, "The technology exists to develop more intelligent brains."

"Well, I am very aware of that!"

What the hell did he mean by that? Will shook his head, but he was committed. He had no choice but to continue. "Yes. You see, that is part of the issue with the zom"—he quickly deleted the three letters—"the re-gens today. We've worked so hard to improve their lives, their *minds*, and now they are taking advantage. There's an imbalance. Slowly but surely, I can see it happening, and we're losing ground."

"I agree. Something needs to be done."

The sober words surprised Will. Asim hardly ever seemed serious. It made him nervous, but he kept going. He was almost there. "I have designed a drug cocktail. What it does is basically the reverse process." Will cringed at the idea. The one-dose plunge into oblivion. *Things were so much easier to break than they were to make.* "It should remove their artificially enhanced intelligence, bring them back down. Maybe it will help to restore the balance."

"Interesting. That is one idea."

Will's face flushed. "There's a professor down the hall from me that I'm pretty sure used to teach high school chemistry before his 'accident.' He didn't *deserve* this gift. I'm sure of that." He was getting slightly angry. He wanted Asim to agree with him, to back him up. Suddenly he needed someone to tell him in writing that he wasn't just being a crazy asshole. He needed someone to tell him that something he had done in his life had mattered. Anything. *Why was everyone so sympathetic to these bastards?*

The boy was typing again. Will stared, waiting for the words to appear.

"Stupid or smart, they're still redundant." Asim allowed the six words to float for a minute, then dropped a flimsy excuse and left the conversation.

Will gratefully closed the messaging app. He had felt a dreadful obligation to say something, but *what on God's green earth could he possibly reply to that?* He gulped. He poured out his three fingers of whisky, but he didn't touch it. He turned to a peer review he would normally have passed on to one of his postdocs, a tedious task to distract himself from whatever meaning hid behind Asim's words, but he couldn't ignore the goose bumps prickling up and down his forearms.

Chapter Fifty

———

Will sat in the back of the room as one of his PhD students was giving his thesis defense. It was a big deal, a big deal for Walter Wiggins. It was probably the single most significant day of his so far insignificant life. He was shaking slightly as he indicated the highlights of his presentation with a laser pointer. The small dot danced a few centimeters in every direction as it hovered over a heat map, disappearing over the dark red clusters and flashing again in front of the adjacent pale space. Of course they wouldn't fail him, not unless he really fucked up.

Will had overseen, or at least seen, his research. In theory, Walter presented his project to Will every month. He had answered the occasional question, made the occasional suggestion or connection. He could have done more, he supposed, but how else would Walter learn? Will rarely taught anymore, but a large part of his job description was still this mentorship aspect of academia, for the sake of science and cheap labor. It was only on days like this that he started to wonder if he could have done as much with this cohort of probationers as he could with Asim and the others, if he had *really* put in the effort. They lacked the potential, but as he considered the last message he had received from Asim, he wondered whether potential might be a double-edged sword.

Will quickly lost faith in this notion as he watched Walter fumble with his slide animations. He felt anxious himself, a feeling so constant he barely recognized it standing out from his baseline level of agitation. It was almost a relief to discover he still had a concern left for something other than the underside of his double life, though he would be lying if he tried to convince himself that the concern extended to poor Walter. If the kid didn't have his PowerPoint in order, that was on him, but if his research was shoddy, that reflected on Will too. He was one of the examiners, but he couldn't help wondering what the other people in the room were thinking. *Dr. Bruce* was antagonistically sitting in on the talk, two rows forward, probably making snide comments inside his *defective* head. Will tried to think of some softball questions to pepper in after the presentation was over to make Walter look good, but he soon got distracted thinking about the questions he had been asked however many years ago.

Will remembered his own defense clearly. In his memory, he was older than the child standing before him. Twenty-six-year-olds were tiny. Walter was scarcely old enough to drive. He probably still had his parents do his laundry. When Will thought back to his own defense, he felt the same age as he was now, only physically and emotionally lighter. Only he had made far fewer dubious decisions, and fewer people bothered to listen to him—that was the main difference. If he were as young now as the PhD hopeful standing before him, there would be an excuse for all he had done. In fact, if he ever *had been* that ignorant and naive, maybe he could trace his problems back as far and deflate them on that point in time. People were meant to learn from their mistakes, but Will had gotten away with everything he had ever tried.

He turned his attention to the front of the room again. He watched as Walter gained confidence following the first few slides. It was going okay after all, and the best part was coming up, the needle of good data in the haystack of frustrations, the big reveal. Will stayed focused during the rest of the presentation, pleased that he wouldn't have to defend his own student's defense or shamefully avoid Professor Hale when it was over. Walter began smiling as he moved into the final stretch. He even made a few lighthearted jokes. It was good work that he had done, and he knew it. He was proud of it. When the questions came, he met each one with a succinct and strict riposte. He seemed older already, facing the room like an ace, not a rookie. Will's newfound calm faltered. They shouldn't tell idiots like that they could change the world— that they could do whatever they wanted to do, be whatever they wanted to be. It was *irresponsible.*

When it was finally finished, Will shook hands with Walter. He said, "Well done," or something to that effect, then trundled over to the long table that had been set up by the door to get a cookie before the chocolate chips were all gone. He had had a few ideas during the talk, the kind of ideas that still snuck up on him, that he didn't used to be able to ignore, that had gotten him into this whole *fucking* mess in the first place. Improvements, innovations. Ideas that used to seem like pure gold, somehow tarnished over the years. Nothing was quite as straightforward as it had seemed when he had been in Walter's place, when he still had the unaffected confidence of youth, not the reckless confidence of senescence and desperation.

Will should have stayed and mingled, nodded at all the right people, half-smiled at the rest, but he couldn't bear it.

The chocolate chips were gone. He took a snickerdoodle and an oatmeal raisin and walked out of the room and down the hall, taking the elevator and the emergency stairs up to the roof where he used to pace, but he stood still. He sat down on an abandoned chair and looked at the edge of the bay in the distance until it was time to go home to Viki.

———

Chapter Fifty-One

T he following Friday, Will had his weekly meeting with Lana. This week, she was staying in some modish penthouse apartment in Hayes Valley. *Parking would be a nightmare.* Will couldn't wait to be finished with the tiresome ordeal and back from the bustling streets, back by himself, safely locked away in his office. In the car on the way over, he wondered if he *should* send the focused scan that Asim had asked for. He would, obviously, take the scan for himself. He had to know whether what Asim had predicted was actually true. *And what if it were?* In any case, he was sure the boy genius would be able to get hold of a similar scan somewhere at UPenn with only a little bit of cunning, and he had plenty. In fact, now that he thought about it, Will wasn't sure why he had bothered asking him to take the scan at all. Why reveal anything he didn't have to? He had certainly had the opportunity to keep all of the information to himself. Maybe it was all a test. *Those child Einsteins really were conniving; chances are they've all been working together for years. Hmph.*

Lana answered the door. She was wearing all black, a collared sleeveless shirt, and cigarette pants with some kind of thick sandal, almost orthopedic but somehow stylish on her small, pedicured feet. She looked absolutely in charge of herself, as always, which always made Will smile. *How could she be so sure of herself when she wasn't herself at all?* Lana, as always, misunderstood the meaning behind it and smiled back at him.

"Good morning, Will. Nice to see you."

"Mm-hm." He walked into the apartment past her. It seemed she wasn't alone this morning. Then again, she was never alone, but it wasn't just her security team in residence today. He didn't look back to see whether she would blush. "Is everything set up?"

"Yes. All ready to go. Would you like some coffee before we begin?"

"Sure." He sighed. He knew she wasn't nice to most people, but he wished she wasn't nice to him. As she was getting the coffee ready, her guest from the previous night moved past Will toward the door. He paused. Will wished he hadn't.

"Good morning."

"Morning . . ." Will nodded and glanced around the room. The generic man kept standing there. "Nice to meet you," Will mumbled.

"What great weather we're having."

"Yes."

"Have a good day." He walked out the door.

Will sighed with relief. *Poor guy. He seemed friendly,* Will thought. *I hope he's not planning to come back. She would eat him alive.* Lana returned, mug in hand, no milk but more sugar than he liked to admit. She always remembered.

"Thanks. Well, have a seat." Will set the machine to scan in detail the areas he wanted to study, pressed START, and then relaxed with his coffee. To be honest, he didn't really need to be there. Lana could probably manage it herself by now, or he could even set it up remotely. They used to talk business during these little consultations. How could they improve the Brill pill? Make it better? Stronger? Lower the cost of production? Reduce the side effects? But lately Lana seemed to have lost interest. Maybe she was bored by her success; maybe she needed a new challenge. *Maybe she was just bored by life with no one and nothing to live for.*

Will sipped his coffee and eyed the images on his tablet as the machine went through its motions. "That seemed like a nice gentleman." He was never sure whether teasing her was a good idea, but he was always just curious enough to find out.

"Are you jealous?" She asked directly.

"Nope."

She raised an eyebrow.

"Stay still," Will commanded. "Do you even know what jealousy is?"

"Was that meant to hurt my feelings?" She smirked. "You know I don't have any left." Her eyes narrowed.

Will, disgusted, turned back to sipping his coffee and looking through the images one by one as they appeared on his tablet. *Flick, flick, flick.* He squinted. If he could just find the "chink in the armor," she wouldn't be so goddamn clever anymore. He would see to that. Maybe it sounded cruel, but at least one person in this world ought to get what they deserved. She would be first. Then the rest of them—he would take care of them all. *Cut them down a peg or two.* It might not be perfect, but they would be less dangerous. Maybe they would even be happier that way—*someone had once told him some nonsense like that.* He looked over at Lana and tilted his head.

"What is it?" she demanded.

"Nothing."

He returned to the images. It wasn't worth fantasizing about grand plans until he discovered the weakness, if it really was there. Maybe Asim had just played him. *To what end? What the fuck was that boy up to?* The goose bumps had started to creep under his skin again, so Will shook it from his mind. He knew he wouldn't see any indication of the weakness here flashing before him. He would have to look at the images more closely, analyze the data more carefully. But still, he stared at the scans if only for something, *anything* to do that wasn't engaging with Lana. He heard her breathe in, to make another inane comment, no doubt, and began instinctively to wince, but in that instant, something caught his eye. He froze, and his tensing stopped her mid-breath.

Will brought the image that had startled him back up on his screen and zoomed in on what he thought he had seen. It was almost nothing, a small shadow in a sea of gradients. *But it was out of place, wasn't it?* Enhanced, it grew into a tiny, dark pool. Almost microscopic, and yet it had the power to swallow everything, all at once. Will confirmed his diagnosis through two sets of filters. It was nothing more or less than a swell, a meager balloon of blood threatening to leak at any moment and rain total destruction with a few deadly drops. In all of his knowledge of medicine and science, it was still a wonder to Will that a thing so beautifully vital as the very blood running through our veins could turn on us in an instant.

He looked up at Lana. She might live ten years with that ominous bubble in her head; she might live ten seconds. *Was it operable?* Possibly. But it wasn't the most likely scenario. The most likely scenario involved a handful of stem cells cultivating in a jar. *Was it fair for someone to cheat death?*

Twice? What *thing* would be reborn from her seconds' seconds? Will speculated on characters in the world worse than a drug lord. *Pedophiles? Fascists? Terrorists?* He couldn't bear the thought of bringing her back again. Surely it was a sign from God or nature that she was well past her time. That mistress Fate, who Will struggled to believe in, was on his side for once. She shouldn't be ignored, *not again.*

And yet there was a twinge in his gut, a thin silhouette left standing of the ideals of youth *and the thought of that fucking Hippocratic oath.* The first signs of regret showed before he had even completed the act worth regretting, it had become such a familiar sensation. It was too perverse to make a decision right here, right now. Lana was in front of him. He couldn't be impartial with her sitting there. He wasn't even confident about which way her presence would sway him. He would take a day or two and decide. Certainly he would have come to a decision by next Friday. He could let her know, or *not* let her know then. In the meantime, she was looking at him expectantly.

"Have you found something yet to make me forget it all?"

Yes. He shook his head.

———

On his way back from Lana's, Will came to at least one decision. He would not send the scan to Asim. What would the kid do if he found the lurking aneurysm? *What would he not do?* Will wondered if it would influence him, or *how* it would. The strange conversation they had had the other day made him wonder whether their interests were truly aligned or whether, as he had always feared, Asim had a dark side that he had kept hidden. *At least up until now.* Will was frightened that if he found the aneurysm and did nothing, Will would agree with him, and he was horrified by the possibility that if Asim chose to warn Lana, he would disagree. Either way, he got the feeling that he would have a hard time looking in the mirror for at least a couple of years. *It wasn't easy as it was.* And if Will did decide to tell her, and Asim found out . . . that worried him too, although he wasn't entirely sure why.

He needed to keep Asim's respect, to hold onto whatever influence he still had over the boy, *if he still had any.* If he didn't, how could he go through with his plan? Asim's help was essential. He had figured out the key to delivering the concoction Will kept under his desk, the next antidote to the last mess he had made. Will couldn't help thinking of names for it to parallel the Brill pill, but nothing was as catchy. Stupid serum. Dumb drug. Brain drain. It couldn't have the same ring to it, because no one wanted it or *would* want it. Ever.

But there was something else too, something Will longed to forget but wasn't able to disregard. It wasn't just that his latest plan *needed* to be carried out; there were times, pretty frequently in fact, that he doubted its integrity. The best remedies were rarely such an obvious and contrived reversal. It was the final words from Asim: "Stupid or smart, they're still redundant." At the bottom of his heart, or the back of his stomach, or the tip of his spine, or wherever instincts show themselves, Will knew that if Asim didn't like *his plan,* the boy had something much worse in mind.

Whatever happened, one way or another, it was all Will's fault.

Chapter Fifty-Two

———

A t home over the weekend, Will was alone in his thoughts. Viki flitted in and out of the physical space around him. They even went for a long walk together, up and down the Embarcadero. Will moved slowly, and she dashed in and out of shops and bounced back and forth across the sidewalk between the glistening San Francisco Bay and the high-rises and boutique markets that dotted the inside arc of the esplanade. He sat down on a bench to catch his breath and watched her run circles through the Ferry Building farmers market, gathering leaves and bulbs, pastes and pastilles for him to carry home and let spoil in the large decorative bowl on their kitchen countertop.

But while he looked at her, he didn't see her. He saw Jon and himself, ten or more years ago. Two ghosts walking through the market, tasting the fruit and chewing the fat. They were having drinks looking out under the Bay Bridge while sailboats sailed and dolphins dove in the distance, and who knew what was going on below the rolling surface. There had been a time or an age when, on paper, they had looked so similar. They had lived in the same city, had possessed the same degrees. They had worked together on the same project in the same lab. They even drank the same beer. *But one of them was sane, and the other was not.* Jon was out there somewhere, but it was too late to ask for his help. It had been ten years since Will had spoken to possibly the only person left in the world whom he had totally trusted. *But why in God's name should he be thinking of him now?* He subconsciously groped for his moral compass, only to realize that he had let it slip.

The remainder of his turmoil, sandwiched between conflicting concepts of right and wrong or good and evil, had been plaguing him for years, showing up in subdued and latent feelings. They weren't clear-cut. They weren't even recognizable, but the dull pain they had caused over time had been a great deal more strangulating than the sharp stab had been. The other voice of reason in his life, the one he might have listened to, was long since gone, and no number of flashbacks or trips down memory lane would bring her back.

Viki returned with full bags and, dropping them off on the bench for him to manage, she skipped on down the Embarcadero. Will hoisted himself out of his seat, pushing on the back of the bench for leverage, and plodded along behind her, moving forward at his own steady pace. But he could still feel the drag as his thoughts strayed behind him. Will tried to forget the past; the problems he was facing were in the future, but he couldn't or wouldn't understand why his mind always seemed to wander back to a certain time.

———

They cobbled a veritable feast together from the boxes of farm-fresh prepared produce Viki had lifted from the various stalls and storefronts. She always picked up more than she could manage, but the excess was part of the charm, especially when they could put it all down the compost bin in the name of supporting local business.

As the time between the previous Friday and the next plotted itself, Will knew that the week would pass quickly, but as a proportion he was only 15 percent of the way there. He decided to put Lana aside for an hour and return to her fate with redoubled effort when that hour was up. Food tasted sweeter in the interim. The medley of mixed, maimed vegetables, a jumble of flavors he would normally pick through, pecking at familiar shapes and colors and discarding the rest, became palatable. Every taste was enhanced by ignorance. If he chose not to see the dark edge of an eggplant spear, clinging to the end of his fork, it took on its own subtle sweetness, soft and not squishy; savory, not sickly.

When he set aside Lana, he set aside the rest of his troubles. After all, everything was inextricably linked. He couldn't think of one problem without the other, and he couldn't ignore the bubble in Lana's head without Asim, the Brain drain, the very zombies themselves dissolving into an alternate reality where he was nothing more than a megalomaniacal sim hobbyist. He could get up and leave the hypothetical exactly where it belonged. *And where would he go?* Back to where it all began? To run a new and improved simulation with a few major tweaks? Or to the TV in the den with the biodynamic pét-nat Viki had guilt-bought from a natural winery pop-up after starting a two-and-a-half-minute conversation with the proprietor about organic grape varietals?

An hour quickly turned into three, and he hadn't used the spare time to engage with Viki or even get a start on his taxes. He basked selfishly in the provisional exemption a quick change in mindset afforded. He binge-watched a murder mystery series and criticized the detective for never seeing what was coming just around the corner. Sure it made for good drama, but even an imbecile could have told him to start with the affair. The heart was always the true motivator of atrocity.

At eleven o'clock, he turned in. It was too late to address this week's moral dilemma now, but a good night's sleep was sure to clear his thoughts. He'd easily come to a decision in the morning. Will had great faith in his subconscious. Relaxed as he was, everything was sure to order itself in the peaceful void. All he needed was a little refresh, and finally he felt the tranquility to receive it.

But as soon as his head touched the pillow, the quiet betrayed him. The sublime vacuum of surrender filled, thread by thread, with the ambitions that had haunted Will all his life. Only now, they looked less like aspirations and more like regrets. He couldn't stop himself from tracking each one, looking for some kernel of charity beneath the wreckage. As he lay in bed, he retraced each intention and found a map leading backward instead of forward. The roads had all diverged behind him, and every alternate path lay far out of reach. There was only one future now, obscured by one final decision that would do nothing more than color everything drab or dismal gray.

Chapter Fifty-Three

———

B y Wednesday, he had gotten nowhere with his decision concerning Lana, and there were only forty-eight hours remaining in which to make up his mind before he saw her again—forty-eight more hours in which to mentally play out every sick scenario.

What he *did* get was another encrypted message from Asim. *I guess we chat now,* Will thought. The message was concerning the scan and whether Will had managed to take it and would he *please* send it over when he had the chance?

Will supposed he had known this was coming, but still he hadn't prepared an excuse. He scrambled to answer promptly and managed a succinct, "Canceled, sorry." He had intended to say something more, but he couldn't think fast enough, and he didn't want Asim to see him typing for a long time and then coming up with something useless, or worse, insipid.

Asim pressed. "Will you be able get it this week? I can most likely obtain a scan from the hospital here if you don't have the time to take one . . ." He was still typing. "Or if you'd *rather not* send it."

Will cringed. He formulated and jotted down a reply on a notepad and then copied and pasted it in. "I should be able to take the scan in the next month or so. Sorry, my patient has had another medical issue come up that took priority. If you do get a scan from the hospital over at Penn, I would love to have a look." Will nearly added an exclamation point there, but he couldn't bear it. "By the way"—here came the awkward bit—"if it turns out that what you suspect is true, did you have something in mind going forward with this information, or is it purely academic?" His body prickled with nerves as he gingerly pressed SEND.

"Academic? No, I don't think so."

Will inhaled through his nose and exhaled through his mouth. He cast out the end of his rope. "Maybe we can work on something together?"

There was a long pause before Asim replied. Will stared at his tablet as the minutes passed by. He swiped through old pictures of himself and Viki, of Marla and Arbor growing up in the time lapse of digital photo scrolling. Viki used to send out annual Christmas cards featuring the four of them, posed somewhere on a holiday or dressed up on the living room sofa, but it had been a few years. They were rarely all in the same place anymore. Will thought perhaps it was time to start it up again. He would convince the kids to come home for Thanksgiving; they could take the photo then. Or if not, there was always Photoshop. Logically, he knew traditions were stupid, but he liked holding onto them. He couldn't help himself. Asim's reply appeared at the top of his screen.

"So you have gotten to the point."

Will felt a chill. His fingers hovered over the keyboard, as if there were anything he could say to put a stop to whatever was coming.

"Ok. I'll tell you everything," Asim continued, "but don't go running to anyone with this information. It won't do anyone any good, especially not you."

Will helplessly watched the three ominous dots.

"First of all, thank you for putting me in touch with Jhillika. I hadn't seen her in a while, and it is always nice to spend time with someone *like me*."

Someone like me. Will silently repeated the words. *He knew.* He had known for a long time.

"There *are* quite a few of us, *aren't there*? I suppose you are somehow responsible for this anomaly . . ."

Will stared blankly. What should he say? *What could he say?* Asim was typing again. He said nothing.

"You must think we are lucky. Maybe you wish you were in our shoes? Maybe it was all an experiment . . ."

Will was sweating now. *What had he done?*

"We *are* lucky. When people see me, a child in glad rags walking the halls, they think I'm lonely. I'm not. So if you were worried about me (which, by the way, I doubt), don't be. I have a feeling we see the world in a similar way. Possibly by your design, but *why* isn't significant. What counts is how we proceed.

"If my preliminary findings are confirmed, what we have on our hands is what we might consider a tool, though others may call it a weapon. The world is changing. I believe that people can feel it, you and I know it, but as usual, it is being ignored. Your idea is to slow down this change, to enforce a handicap on those who are causing it. I'm afraid this isn't enough."

Will swallowed. This was not going as he had hoped. The weight of his actions pressed against his temples and swamped his clearest convictions, giving him a headache. But at the same time, he felt a significant if unwelcome rush, a nervous tremor in his chest. There was a small but undeniable light associated with the awful, disgusting, *dreadful*, *ghastly*, *sickening* thought of just starting all over with a blank slate. *Somehow* he would get it right next time. *If you have the chance to rid the world of murderers and rapists and you don't do it, what does that make you?* Will couldn't find any sort of reply in himself yet. He waited to see what more was coming, not that there was anything more to say, really.

"There are a few of us, myself and Jhil included, that have a plan in place. We *will* proceed. That said, access to a facility such as your lab would be *very useful.* No need to reply right away. Think about it . . . and send me that scan when you have it." The string of messages disappeared.

Since Will had in fact taken the scan the previous Friday, he had also made time to analyze it. With Asim's previous guidance about what to look for and where to look, he had confirmed the boy's suspicions. Everything that Asim had just suggested seemed imminently possible. And Will was pretty convinced that he already knew it.

———

Will felt betrayed, impressed, and ultimately overwhelmed by his young correspondents. They knew about him, they were already working together, and they were plotting genocide. *But was it gen-ocide if they weren't really people? If the targeted population had already died?* The zombies were living on borrowed time as it was. Perhaps the kids' little scheme was just nature's way of picking up the slack. Will quickly returned to the theme that fate would excuse his actions.

He took a breath. *Were all children psychopaths, or had he custom-made these devils?* It didn't really matter if they had been born and bred that way, or if a syringeful of poison had done the trick. What he had given them was the ability to do what they wanted with what morals they had. But he hadn't *meant* to give them that, or he hadn't meant for them to use it in such a way. He didn't know specifically what he wanted, but he knew that Arthur would have come up with something if he were in Will's place and Will were in his. *Will suddenly wished he were in Arthur's place*—just a harmless pile of dust, six feet underground.

He had just wanted everyone to go back to the way they were. *Was it an impossible task? Why, in nearly fifty years of research, could he not manage it?* Well, they would be brain-dead. That *was* back to the way they were—just not as far back as he had imagined. Was what they had become a fate worse than death? If he truly believed that, then there wasn't really anything worth arguing about. And, truly, he did. But still there was something that didn't sit right, something that made him feel as if the walls were edging closer. *Could they be?* Was it anything more than the selfish fear he might be personally affected by this mess? That the bread-crumb trails would all lead back to him, and he wouldn't be able to hide behind Arthur's notes any longer? Someone might find a flaw in his reasoning. *If that was all it was, who gives a shit? No one anywhere, ever, in the world had thought as much about this as he had.*

The bottom line was that you couldn't kill someone who was already dead. No one would blink twice if they were the zombies of film and television. More than that, he would be a hero. *They* were *the zombies of film and television really, only clever, only worse.* The bottom line was that it was out of his control.

Will's heart was racing as if the entire population of zombies were about to drop dead at the push of a button. As if it could happen at any moment, as completely unpredictable as the treacherous bubble in Lana's head. Maybe he should have at least warned her not to do anything strenuous for a while, until he had figured it all out—what was right and what was wrong, what was up and what was down. The room had started to spin slightly. He leaned against the edge of his desk for support as his thoughts spiraled uncontrollably.

———

At six thirty, Will's watch buzzed, rousing him. It was time to leave. He stood slowly and gathered his things. He would definitely buy a slice of cake on his way home tonight. He might even buy a whole one.

Chapter Fifty-Four

———

It was Friday. Will had had too much to think about since Wednesday, and so he had thought about nothing instead. Or, more specifically, he had thought about insignificant curiosities, such as: Why did Viki go to the grocery store every week when all of their meals seemed to be delivered? Or why did he feel the need to close the bathroom door now when he got undressed at night? But he knew the answer to that—*he saw it in the mirror every morning.* When he was younger, he had thought that men could get fat and it didn't matter. To his credit, he had also thought Viki could get fat and he wouldn't care, *not that he would ever face that challenge.* But lately he found himself cringing every time he caught sight of his reflection. Maybe it was being fat *and* old; maybe it was something else altogether.

So he arrived at Lana's residence of the week without a prepared decision. In the car on the way over, he had mused: On the one hand, if he chose to save her, and the horror children he had created had their way, she was likely doomed in any case. So why not play the Good Samaritan for the interlude, however brief? On the other hand, why put her through all of that again? *Why put himself through it?* From a scientific approach, he had some amount of curiosity to see what might be regrown from an already regenerated brain. Would it develop in the same way, or would it become something worse? Could it possibly be better? *It might be worth finding out, so long as whatever was produced were to be put down quickly.* He shrugged and got out of the car.

Will had never visited Lana in this location before. He had never before set foot on this particular street in his life, but as he shut the car door behind him and made his way across the road, he experienced a familiar sensation. He couldn't place it at first. He tried to ignore it. But the feeling grew stronger as he walked up the front steps, and his stomach dropped a half inch as he slowly reached for the bell. It was a peculiar physical condition, a ring right around the center of the gut pushing upward on the heart and lungs and in the same moment sinking into a deep stomachache. It was unmistakable déjà vu but distant, so long ago he could hardly remember. He grasped. *Something had happened, and he would soon find out what it was.* Will shivered and pulled his hand back from the doorbell. He was nervous but also intrigued, so drawn in by the feeling that he hadn't even noticed the ambulance parked on the street, a dead giveaway.

Shaking himself, he forced his hand to the bell again. But as his finger grazed the switch, he abruptly recalled when and where he had felt this nervous cramp before. The recollection made his stomach lurch forward and shimmy back. The last time he had experienced this specific nausea, he had been in a very familiar place, somewhere he used to visit almost every day. Here in this unknown corner of San Francisco, he suddenly knew what had happened. He disregarded the bell and reached for the doorknob. The door was unlocked, as he suspected. He took a deep breath and then entered.

People were milling around; things were being inspected.

On the surface, everything was just as orderly as it had been the last time, all those years ago. Will wasn't sure *why* he was so affected. Someone who he knew was going to die had died, and he hadn't even liked her enough to try and save her. He might have tried to save a dog in a similar situation. Still, he was shocked. *Had he killed her?* Despite blaming himself for Margot's death all these years, he was vaguely aware of a distinction. Margot wouldn't have been killed if he had been there, but he hadn't known she was going to die and then *chosen* to let it happen. *Margot wouldn't have blamed him for her own death, but she absolutely would have blamed him for this.* He could run in circles through his morning's logic— *Lana was dead anyway; this was certainly a nicer way to go—* but none of it mattered anymore. And honestly, it came down to what Will had or hadn't done more than what Lana would or wouldn't have suffered.

In the entryway, he shook hands with her head of security. "What happened?"

Abra pointed to her head and made a quick motion with one hand, indicating the instant catastrophe. "Stroke. You never saw it?"

"No." He lied, but to be fair, he had likely missed it for years, so he didn't really feel like he was lying.

"Do you want to see her?" She pointed upstairs.

Will definitely didn't want to see her, but he felt either rude or weak admitting that, so he nodded. He followed the woman upstairs. He had only ever said a few words to her in all of these years, though he saw her every week and though they were probably the two people in existence who had known Lana best. *Not that that was saying anything.*

Behind the bedroom door, Lana was awkwardly positioned on the bed. She looked anything but peaceful. She had probably fallen mid-sentence, surely on the verge of sealing some poor sucker's fate, and toppled over her open dresser drawer, landing, facedown, *ass up*, over the footstool at the end of her bed. *How embarrassing.* No wonder they had moved her. The team of paramedics was hovering around the bed, getting ready to carry the body down the stairs and out the door, anywhere away from here. But Will didn't see her anymore.

He had never seen Margot's body, but he pictured it now in Lana's place. She was pristine, lying flat in that same sweater she always wore, uninjured yet still. She was so young. Of course, she would always be that young. Will had gotten old without her. *Would she even recognize him now?* He resisted the urge to stride across the room toward her. *If he so much as shifted his feet, she might disappear again.* If Margot were able to move, if she were able to speak, if she were able even to open her eyes, they would fall on him like a thousand-ton weight. If there were ever a way in the wacky world of science and sorcery to bring her back, he would never be able to face her. It occurred to him, as her presence filled the room, that he was definitely going to hell. For all of the good intentions, for all of the grand plans intended to make the world a better place, he had become a Faustian tragedy.

Lana—limp, lifeless Lana—was scooped up and carried out the door. She had made him a murderer. She had turned him into *one of them.* But only a portion of the blame could be wasted on her. There was a polymeric chain of events, an intricate and tightly bound structure, leading up to his downfall. He had to admit it had started before Lana. It went back further than his experiment with the impecunious brainiacs. He could trace it earlier even than his receipt of Arthur's wretched notes. There was the first batch of infants, the twelve that had started it all. Had that really been the beginning, or had he long since been doomed to this conclusion by a grandfather he had barely known? *Could she have saved him?* He stared at the imprint left in the sheets where he had just seen Margot, cold and dead at twenty-eight years old. *What in God's name could have filled all of that pitch-black space stretching after her?* He couldn't ask her. Even *she* didn't know, clever as she had been, and besides, she had left the room with Lana. Will struggled to bring to mind her face once again, but there was nothing.

He was ready to go. *There was no fucking way he was going to stick around chatting to this monotone brick wall of a woman. She was most likely devastated about her boss or at least about losing her job, but who could even tell? It certainly wasn't going to help her having him loitering around.* Will nodded in Abra's direction and then turned toward the bedroom door. He rushed out and down the stairs, only pausing at the front entrance to fiddle with the lock. But before he could break free from that stifling residence and inhale fresh air again, he heard the sturdy woman clearing her throat on the landing. Will sighed and looked up at her.

"Yes?" he queried, wearily.

"She left everything to you."

"What?"

"You're my boss now."

He stared, stunned for a few seconds, then turned slowly back toward the door without speaking. There was a mirror above the shoe rack, next to the hooks on the wall where

Lana had hung her coat. He caught sight of himself in it, head-on. He couldn't help wincing just a little, but behind his personal mortification, the source of which he had yet to riddle out, he saw a normal-looking guy, an average Joe. In his life, Will had envisioned himself as a lot of things but unexceptional was never one of them. *How could the bland man looking back at him have the gall to do the things he had done? That basic son of a bitch didn't have the right to poke his nose into what color tile his wife chose for the bathroom floor, let alone tamper with life and death, with genetics, intelligence, and fucking human nature. The zombies were god-awful, but so was everyone and everything else in this miserable world.* He felt a childish sob rising quickly through the dense weight of his conscience. *Why couldn't he have listened? Just once.*

Will flailed his hand wildly behind him, unlocked the door, and escaped out into the street. But the air wasn't fresh. The cool fog that enveloped the city, which Will usually found bracing, was smothering him. Outside, alone with his swirling, discordant thoughts, it was almost worse than it had been in there. *At least he would avoid looking into another mirror.* The car was still sitting there, just across the street, waiting for him as if nothing had happened. In a daze, he opened the door and got back in. He turned on the radio. Will didn't recognize any of the music on the radio these days, but he didn't care what was playing as long as it was playing at full volume. He checked the time. It was still early in the afternoon. He didn't know where else to go, so he went back to work.

———

The afternoon sun had burned through the blanket of fog and shone a light across Will's office, casting shadows over his accomplishments and highlighting his abominations. He sat at his desk and mentally listed all of the things he had done and all of the things that were still to come as a result of his experimental handiwork. He separated them into pros and cons. He weighted them according to their short-term and long-term effects, their degrees of despicability. Many items seemed to be pros *and* cons, so he moved them back and forth, and back and forth. But no matter what reasoning he used, one list always ended up significantly longer than the other.

A chill filled his chest, but his mind was hot on the brink of explosion. There were so many winning ideas and losing defenses knocking about, gaining kinetic energy and smashing against his skull. *Will it ever stop?* Will reached below his desk and pulled the vial out from the back of the small refrigerator. Turning it left and right, up and down, he warmed it in his hands. He wondered at the crystal liquid inside, beautiful in its way. He smiled, thinking of something Margot once said, the gist of it anyway—he couldn't quite remember the words or the voice that had spoken them. *Good God, if she could see him now.* He filled a syringe and took it to his arm.

Epilogue

———

An empty lawn chair and a six-pack of beer beckoned from across the road. He locked up the house and made his way, barefoot, down the wooden porch steps, across the single sand-dusted lane, and onto the small soft dunes that fell away under each stride. His seat was right where he had left it last night and right where he had left it the night before, right next to hers. He leaned over to kiss Viki on the cheek, then sat down beside her.

"It's not such a bad life, is it?" He put his arm around her.

"Not bad at all," she replied with warmth.

Waves swept up and down the beach before them as they sat, side by side, watching the sun glow red and dip below the horizon. He raised a beer and drank deeply without knowing or caring exactly what it was he was toasting. It just felt good in the salty air, in the mild evening breeze, under the water-color sky, the satisfying malty flavor on his tongue. He was looking forward to tomorrow. He might go for a walk into town, maybe take a drive along the coast. It didn't really matter much.

He picked up a second beer and sighed with relief. He had read an article in the local paper that afternoon, front-page news even in this summer-home backwater. An epidemic was sweeping the nation; soon it would spread worldwide.

But there was nothing *Will* could do about it. In any case, it wouldn't affect him or his family. They were all-natural, A-OK.

THE END

Acknowledgments

I would have nowhere and nothing to write without the support of my parents. THANK YOU, Mom and Dad. Thank you to all of my friends pursuing careers in academia and to all of those who have chosen not to. To the medical library at Yale for providing a quiet corner and a wealth of inspiration. To friends and family who read drafts and provided much-appreciated feedback: Andrew, Noodles, Rob, Robbie, Sidney, and Aria to name a few. To Henri for your unwavering belief in me. To Kayo for always being Kayo. And a special thank-you to my sister Lauren, unflinching optimist and first reader of everything I write, and to my husband, Christian, who painstakingly helped fill in the many blank spaces I had originally left labeled "science stuff." You truly deserve coauthor on this paper.

About the Author

Credit: Lauren Brodsky

AKEMI C. BRODSKY grew up in the Bay Area, went to college at Brown University, and lived in the UK and New Haven for a few years before eventually returning home. She studied geochemistry in school but started writing when a friend challenged her to write a page a week as a means to navigate a quarter-life crisis. A page (rather slowly) turned into a novel, and she has been writing ever since. Akemi now splits her time between the Bay Area and the UK, and when she isn't writing she enjoys over-researching her travel plans, cooking without ever completely following the recipe, hiking but not too strenuously, and many other basic activities, including brunch.